I0588126

The Catalyst Coalition
From Broken to Healing Heart

Geoffrey K. Leigh

Noussentric Press

Second printing, April, 2026

Library of Congress Control Number: 2024906935

ISBN: 978-0-9985966-6-2

Book cover design: Geoffrey K. Leigh using Book Brush

Formatting: Geoffrey K. Leigh using Atticus

Acknowledgements

There are several people to whom I owe gratitude for assisting in the development of my ideas and efforts along this journey.

First, I am grateful to my children and grandchildren for providing comments and examples I could draw upon to create fiction sometimes based on life. In a few cases, our discussions that provided ideas upon which to draw for developing fictional changes that could enrich the story I was attempting to create. Finally, they are always supportive of my crazy ideas and dreams, even if they do not agree with them. For that, much appreciation and love to all of them for putting up with me and my work all these years.

Much gratitude goes out to my dear friend, Marianne Lyon, who took time to read, suggested additions and/or changes, and provided support all the way through the manuscript. She helps me find ways to expand and improve my writing that I deeply appreciate.

Another dear friend, Marianne Murray, also provided insight and helpful suggestions early in the process and improves my writing as I examine her own talented expression. While I had to keep several quirky phrases, I appreciate her feedback and ideas.

A third dear friend, Janet Tillman, helped me with key perspectives and character development that in many ways changed the arc of this story because of her input and feedback. I so appreciate her candor and authenticity, which helped me improve some of the interactions and strengths of key characters.

Some days, writing became a struggle. On many other occasions, I felt inspiration that went beyond what I oft times experience as my limited sphere. For that source, may it always become available, I express gratitude for the sense that I am not alone in this journey.

Contents

Prologue

List of Primary Characters

Audri (Dri) Giovanni: Youngest daughter of Bella and Rick. Spent time in counseling with **Doc** during high school. Age 18. (All ages as of 2018)

Tanika (Nika) Washington: Best friend to Dri and Soph in high school. Parents are Beverley and Tyrell. Younger brother is Denzel. Age 18.

Sophie (Soph): Best friend to Dri and Nika. Dri's tennis partner in high school. Age 18.

Dr. Alberto Salvador (Doc): Counselor to Dri during high school. Died in 2016.

Alexander (Alex) Giovanni: Middle child of Rick and Bella. Graduated high school in 2016. Age 20.

Sarah Giovanni: Oldest daughter of Rick and Bella. Graduated from University of Iowa, 2018. Age 22.

Isabella (Bella) Moretti Giovanni: Mother of Dri, Alex, and Sarah and married to Rick. Works in real estate. Age 50.

Rick Giovanni: Bella's husband and father to Sarah, Alex, and Dri. Owner of a local Italian restaurant in Iowa City, IA. Age 52.

Santiago (Tiago) Garcia: Younger son of Miguel and Gabriela and grandson of Dr. Alberto Salvador. Age 19.

Emma Moretti: Bella's younger sister and wife of Phil. Mother of Alisa. Age 48.

Omar Guenechia: Minor owner of Oenophilia Winery in Napa. Father of Alberto Guenechia. Age 48.

Naeem Walker: Lives in Oakland, graduate of UC Berkeley in art. Age 22.

Gabriella (Gabby) Garcia: Mother of Javier and Tiago and daughter of Alberto. Married to Miguel. Age 45.

Fadima Khalid: Born in Beirut, Lebanon, now living in New York City. Husband was Ahmad, and mother to Husayn (age 11). Age 38.

Rachel Meyer: Born in New York City, now living with her wife, Ariella, in Las Vegas. Their son is Joseph (age 13). Age 40.

Ariella Romano: Married to Rachel, lives in las Vegas. Son is Joseph (age 13). Age 37.

Kiara Wallerston: An Illinois state senator, born in India, now lives in Chicago with her husband, Sam. Their daughter is Diya (age 9). Age 41.

Sam Wallerston: A financial advisor living in Chicago and married to Kiara, father to Diya (age 9). Age 44.

Imani Jackson: Las Vega police officer. Married to Raimy. Age 24.

Carl Strunk: Boy from Kentucky. Age 14.

Silvia Stevens: Woman from Fresno, CA. Age 32.

Charlene Hoover: President of the Primordial Family Foundation (PFF). Age 55.

Chapter 1
Leaving Home
August, 2018

T rees, flowers and every imaginable weed blossom with all the energy they now possess. Grass already requires more than once a week mowing from the winter rains and moisture hanging heavily in the fresh air. People scurry about walking, running, playing, grateful for warmth and decreased rainfall, provided by longer days outdoors in the toasty ball of sky light.

Dri, Nika and Soph, the *trois Mousquetaires*, known as such the last two years of high school, finally graduate. Their mutual support and focus on high grades, excellent tennis, and good times together, pays off. Such celebrations invite additional school dances, games, and parties. The *Mousquetaires* collaborative graduation party becomes highly desired and richly attended. Even Cher-Devil, the early nemesis turned supporter after the "air clearing" conversation, arrives with a group of friends to expand the fun and diverse representation of their class. The party evolves into the Iowa's City High student event of the year.

But all attending the same college for these three beloved friends fragments in a less tidy package without a single ornamental bow.

Dri and her best friend, Nika, created two long term goals that took root during their high school years. First, they wanted to attend the same college and be roommates. These two allies had been close since 5th grade and desired to continue their cherished connection.

Their heart link expanded when Dri organized a school vigil following the physical assault on Tanika and her brother two years ago. Sophie, the third *Mousquetaires*, remained a constant participant and support of Dri and Nika.

Their triadic alliance solidified further during the emotional heart opening explorations the last year and a half of high school, based on Dri's restorative work with her therapist, Doc. Extensive exploration of their inner life and secrets combined with essential practices loosened the threads of attachments to defensive reactions.

Secondly, these three young women all exhibited a passion to play college tennis. Such desire stimulated them to expand their competitive skills. The likelihood of their dream coming true increased when all three had a great tournament during their senior year at the Iowa State Tennis finals.

Systems of higher education, however, do not always collaborate with girlhood plans. When a scholarship offer arrived, Dri was delighted that it allowed her to continue playing in college and live close to her brother and protector at UC Davis. The acceptance became a compromise for her, being at school with Alex rather than living on the same campus with her best friends.

But Nika did not exactly preserve her part of the agreement. She won the state single's championship on top of excellent grades, solidifying her scholarship to Stanford University. She cherished the opportunity and felt regret for attending alone.

Sophie decided to attend the University of Washington, also on a tennis scholarship. While she desires to be close to the other two, her connection to extended family in the Seattle area becomes a formidable allure, especially when Nika and Dri accept invitations to attend separate universities. At least she, too, will reside on the West Coast, with easy flights to the Bay Area or visits during their summers back home in Iowa City.

The positive news for Nika and Dri derives from the close proximity between their choices for higher education. Stanford and Davis remain just a couple of hours apart, DOT. Such an abbreviation typically refers to a Department of Transportation. Given the frequent standstill with vehicles, the more colloquial meaning evolved to "Depending On Traffic." Such a qualifying phrase follows any estimated driving distance in the greater Bay Area.

According to Bella, Dri's mother, who once lived in the Bay Area and loves to visit big cities, California certainly does not corner the market on onerous gridlock. All large metropolitan areas, like New York, Atlanta, Chicago, Los Angeles, or Seattle, sustain their own version of DOT. Apparently, gridlock occurs at some time or another in every large metropolitan area around the world. Love the mode of transportation. Resent when others slow the method.

For her 18th birthday, only a month after high school graduation, Dri's parents pass along an older, well utilized yet functional white Prius to take to college. A communal vehicle provides considerable utility, given that Dri and Alex, her older brother, will attend the same school. It could also come in handy if an Iowa parent visits the area. For Dri, it supplies an additional connection by sharing something practical with her loving brother. And, of course, keeping it neat and tidy will fall on her solely to complete.

Dri's excited about the car. But, now she needs to figure out how to get it from Iowa City to Davis, California. Her anxiety about driving such a long distance by herself crates a logistical challenge for which a current solution eludes her. Fortunately, Bella, who still loves the greater Bay Area, readily volunteers to help transport the car once her daughter broaches the subject. Unfortunately for her, Bella did not anticipate it would end up gorged with all the necessary college accessories.

Two drivers provide easier travel for the odyssey. Yet, Dri stresses whether such intense time together will generate a rush of reverence for her mom or deliverance when the journey is over. She worries that a three day trip may lead to the latter while hoping for the best.

During the drive across the Nebraska flat lands, Bella decides to take a risk and ask her daughter about the recent dinner with Rick, her dad, and Susan, his new wife.

"I enjoyed seeing Dad. And I'm doing alright with Susan," responds Dri. "But I feel his distance, even when we talk. He never seems totally present."

"Did working at his restaurant during this past summer help at all?"

"No, not really. He seems to focus half his attention on that other woman. Even when he and I are having a conversation. It's like he's nervous about any response she might have."

"I'm sorry, dear. Maybe it will get better the longer they're married."

"Yeah, maybe. Or he might never change. But it's nice to see him now and again. How about some different music? I'd love to hear some of your favorites."

Bella puts in a new playlist of older music familiar to Dri, having heard her mom's favorite songs so frequently. A little Red Hot Chili Peppers, Elton John, and Bon Jovi change up the pace considerably. They sing along and chat about lighter topics to pass the time.

Bella intends to help Dri settle into her dorm. Then she'll enjoy additional conversation time that includes Alex, whom she has not seen in months. Bella later plans to drive the Prius an additional hour beyond Davis for a long overdue corporeal connection with her sister, Emma, who lives and works in Napa, her favorite place to enjoy local wines. While many other areas of the state produce award winning vino, this small valley makes her feel like she returns "home."

While visiting, Bella will investigate the possibility of relocating to the vineyard valley and experiencing it from a perspective of permanently residing there. Spending days or weekends can stimulate a love of an area. But moving three decades worth of belongings 1800 miles requires careful consideration through a lens of residential relocation. Bella also wants to meet with some Napa brokers to investigate the possibility of becoming a local realtor, an extension of her work experience in Iowa City.

The day sustains a bounty of heat on the August afternoon when Dri and Bella arrive in Davis after their protracted journey. Luckily, the occasionally temperamental air conditioning performed well most of the distance, providing ambient relief on the road.

The summer sun alters the green spring vegetation into golden, dry summer hillsides. Besides dehydrating both traveler's mouths and nose, summer here bestows warm sunlight combined with cool nights to encourage lush maturation of grapes around Davis and many other parts of the California landscape. Limited drip irrigation nurtures the plants. Their greenery provides local environmental nourishment on late summer days.

Both women express relief in reaching their destination and dryer air, a pleasant relief from the sauna weather of an Iowa City August. They feel drained of reserves from extended periods when they shared songs and conversations or when one drives while the other naps, which often produced cricked necks. "Sue City Sue" or "On The Road Again" will not be sung any time soon. Sufficient amounts of mountains, sage brush, and semis elicited no further interest in traveling. Despite Dri's frequent efforts to clean, the car reeks of snack food, salty chips, and old fruit.

The weary travelers finally roll up to Alex's apartment, primed for almost any episode external to their vehicle. Yet, Dri notices gratitude for how much fun the two of them had along the way.

Only on one occasion, passing through Omaha, did Bella tear up about a memory from her marriage to Rick. In the end, it stimulated a pleasant conversation. And Dri learned more about financial struggles her parents experienced over the marital years.

After a short walk outside, a zesty lemon-mint iced tea, and a 60 second tour of his entire apartment, Alex helps Dri and Bella find the nearby dorms. As they begin to move the belongings into Dri's space, they also meet her new roomie, Jen. She arrived the day before from Benicia, a quaint little town on the Sacramento River, about 45 minutes southwest from Davis.

Alex lugs the first arm full of paraphernalia into the room. Jen's eyes light up. For Alex, such a response is so routine he remains oblivious to it. But her reaction does not go undetected by Dri and Bella. They follow close behind and laugh about it all the way back to the car.

"I can see this going to be a lot like our last year of Alex's high school," giggles Dri.

"Yeah, but I won't be around to keep an eye on you," adds Bella with her own chuckle. Her smile evaporates in the August sunshine and sadness materializes in her eyes. "I'll miss you terribly!"

Bella briefly imagines her empty nest life as a single woman with a choking sensation in her throat.

Dri notices the wetness in Bella's eyes and stops in her tracks, stimulating fluid in her own.

"Yeah, I'll miss you too, Mom. I hope you decide to move out here. It would be great to have you close."

Dri imagines being able to visit her mom on special weekends. Maybe Bella could even attend some of Dri's matches, as she usually did in high school.

Bella takes a deep breath and wipes away the optic liquid as she looks back at the 1960s style red brick dorm where Dri will reside. The grassy area in front rolls up to neatly clipped hedges hiding the building foundation. Leafy trees provide useful shade relief.

"It's very tempting, especially with your sister now in San Francisco for law school. If you all decide to stay in the area, it'll be a done deal. You'll have to put up with me here, too!"

Dri relaxes a bit as a smile burgeons onto Bella's lips and her head tilts to her right side. As Dri notices her mom's reaction, she also pays attention to a tweak in her stomach. Living closer, she would have a better idea how much to be concerned about her mom.

Somehow, their relationship has changed. Dri has not felt the need to worry up until now. Maybe the divorce transformed how she views her, a single mom on her own. Maybe it's her own increased maturity, consideration about an aging mother with no one else in the house to notice changes. Whatever it is, a shift begins for the youngest in the family.

"How's Sarah doing? She and Marsha like the city?"

"She seems to be very happy in San Francisco. Both of them apparently. I'm lucky to have you all in one area, at least," chuckles Bella. "Wish they were in town to visit. But next time."

"Yeah, I need to call her. Haven't talked with her in a while."

Dri turns her focus to the distribution of her belongings into the appropriate locations as Bella and Alex haul in the last three containers. The dawning student takes a relaxing breath as she settles into her new residence. She doesn't always appreciate her drive to make order in life, especially when chest muscles stiffen and cramp her breathing. She stops. Takes a few additional slow deep breaths, allowing more oxygen and energy into her body.

Bella invites Jen to join them for dinner. She thanks them, but she has other plans.

Alex suggests a favorite place on D Street. They all drive to the restaurant in the newly spacious vehicle.

The family members relax over dinner as they talk about life and school here, a possible move for Mom to the Bay Area, majors that interest them both. They enjoy a few laughs primarily provided by Alex, the family comedian.

Bella expresses gratitude that Alex will be around to watch over this new freshman, even if he teases Dri about it, too. After an enjoyable family gathering, she drops Dri off for the first night in her new abode, Alex at his apartment, then drives to her hotel. While parking, she notices increased excitement for her anticipated exploration of Napa Valley.

Bella spends the morning touring the campus with her two younger children, getting some idea of what classes Dri will be taking and meeting Alex's roommates. In the process, she becomes increasingly aware of her age, with all three children now having flown her nest.

Additionally, she notices a sense of relief for how well her kids are doing and apprehension for her own metamorphosing from mother to an uncharted new role. Lots of possibilities. Considerable trepidation.

Early-afternoon, she drives the Prius along I-80 towards Napa, not wanting to get caught in late day heavy commuter traffic. Once off the freeway, the route into the valley is easy, now traveling against the commuter flow. She breathes more effortlessly as she begins passing the fruit laden vineyards.

It has been years since Bella and her sister have spent much face to face time. Bella is delighted and nervous about the reconnection. She feels happy to spend time again in the house Emma and her husband, Phil, bought several years ago in Alta Heights, an older hillside section of Napa, east of downtown. Yet she and Emma have not always cherished their time together. Bella becomes aware of some apprehension about this extended visit.

Upon her arrival, Emma opens the door and welcomes her sister.

"Come in, come in. Let me take your bag," says Emma as she grabs the handle out of Bella's hands. "You'll have the downstairs all to yourself. We've remodeled the whole area. I think you'll like it. Come, let me help you get settled."

Emma leads the way into the renovated downstairs suite with its own entrance and luxurious bathroom.

"Take the time you need to settle. I'll be in the garden when you're ready with some nibbles and a chilled glass of Sauv Blanc."

Already Bella experiences a sense of vacation. She enjoys the bed and breakfast atmosphere, with an afternoon wine on the agenda.

The offer reminds her of the times she and her former husband enjoyed conversations about wine. They often would taste new ones he might feature at his restaurant or add to his wine list. Those investigations interested them both, comparing notes on the smell or nose of the wine and what they each experienced on their palates. Their exchanges primarily remained friendly and fun. Some of the most enjoyable shares in their relationship. Unfortunately, those pleasant interactions occurred less frequent than the conflicts.

Bella climbs the stairs and goes out to the garden. She spies Emma sitting at the bistro table, book in her hand, as usual.

"What are you reading?" asks Bella.

"Another book by Louise Erdrich. I love her poetic prose," she responds as she lays the book on a oak barrel near the table.

The garden is comfortable and private, with abundant jasmine, honeysuckle, clematis, and wisteria. The vines create a lush green fragrant envelope for the sitting space and clamber onto a wooden slatted shade structure.

The sisters spend time catching up on family alterations. Then Emma suggests they take a short drive downtown to have dinner at Angèle's by the river. They meet Phil there. The three of them engage in what Bella later describes as a delightful catch-up conversation over dinner, laughter, and more wine.

The next day, Bella meets with four Napa real estate brokers, appointments she set up before her journey west. The first three are larger firms that provide traditional interactions and financial structures, pretty similar to her broker in Iowa City. They are pleasant and sufficiently inviting. Nothing wrong with them. Nothing new either. Little to enliven her practice.

Her final discussion is with a broker of a smaller, regional firm that a friend of Emma's recommended. This conversation generates excitement with Bella. The firm is young, yet impactful. During the early years of its existence, some of the top local agents joined the company. They are innovative in the tools they employ, professional in their presentations, and more collaborative than most brokerages. Agents primarily work from their homes, which also coincides with Bella's transition.

Bella realizes right away that such a stimulating environment could revitalize her career and assist in remodeling her life as a single woman. Since college, Bella has focused heavily on her marriage and raising three children. Now she wants to breathe more enthusiasm and adventure into her existence. Reinventing her career could be part of that change. She will sit with her options for a few days. But her inclination after this last discussion trends toward joining this family-like firm.

With the interviews completed, Bella wants to experience diverse locales of the valley and get a better sense of whether this is a satisfying place to reposition herself. Alex talked with her about his desire to flower in Napa after he finishes college. Yet Bella knows she needs to confirm for herself any decision to move. She maintains several engaging friends in Iowa City. Life there could be easy. But that location never provided experiences as a haven for her. She remains committed to discover a place that stimulates a foundational sense of home for her new life.

On her second full day in the valley, Bella goes into the kitchen to make some coffee. She scents that Emma beat her to it.

"OK, Sis, I took the day off," Emma begins, fully dressed with her face on and dark hair in a comfortable ponytail. "Let's drive around Napa first. Then head up valley to get a feel for different towns. There are nice places for lunch in Yountville, St. Helena, or Calistoga. And we can come back along the Trail. Then you'll pretty much have a feel for most of the valley. This is only a taste, but it'll be a great start."

"That sounds perfect. I'd appreciate a guided tour. Especially when you know it so well. Just the two of us?"

"Yeah. No need to deal with the demands of others. I want to focus just on you. Besides, it will give us more time to visit and catch up without prying ears," laughs Emma.

"Speaking of prying ears, how's your daughter doing in Costa Rica? She enjoying her assignment there?"

"Oh yes. Alisa's Spanish is excellent now. She's thrilled to work as a cultural attache. It gives her a chance to connect more with the locals and understand life from their point of view."

Bella had forgotten how much she likes her sister's effervescent smiles. They seem to show up more often now than during their somewhat tumultuous adolescence. Yet, it is more than her mouth smiling. The energy emanates from her eyes and heart as well, at least it does now. Bella loves that.

The sisters spend a lively day viewing contrasting neighborhoods of the local city, at least in relation to the remainder of the valley. Fun older neighborhoods close to downtown facilitate easy access to shops and the library with extensive old trees and lush vegetation. They also visit medium age homes in surrounding areas containing established greenwood and some local shops. Even the new homes appear nice, although Bella feels more comfortable in older neighborhoods.

They then navigate north through the main street of Yountville, then back onto the main highway through Oakville, Rutherford, and on to St. Helena for a tasty lunch at the Himalayan Sherpa Kitchen. Bella adores these northern towns, sprinkled with fun stores and often intermingled with vineyards. But homes there also tend to be more expensive.

Finding a home in Napa would be more prudent, and she'd be closer to her sister and family. Still, knowing other communities in the valley could prove essential. Especially with her inclination to continue her real estate career here.

After strolling around the shops in St. Helena and Calistoga, they motor back along Silverado Trail. Without conferring, Emma decides to snatch a detour. She turns right onto Yountville Crossroad and navigates into the center of town.

Bella perceives a sense of adventure she has not previously noticed in Emma. For the older sibling, this proves both inviting and a touch compelling.

"What are we doing? Whatever it is, I'm game. This has been a lovely day with you, Sis."

"We're going to do a little wine tasting, now that our tour essentially is over. Besides, if you are going to live here, you need to start getting to know some of the 500 plus wineries in Napa Valley!" laughs Emma.

That smile appears again, aerating Bella's heart. It has been nice to reconnect with her only sibling after so many years of primarily phone or FaceTime interactions.

"OK, then. Let's do one, leaving only 499 for the future," laughs Bella, delighted with her sister's spontaneity and enthusiasm. "If I move here, we must visit them all," she says with a wink.

Emma finds a parking space along Washington Street. Bella reaches out, takes Emma's hand and gives it a squeeze. They beam at each other. Then they stroll over to the Hill Family Estate tasting room.

Emma and her husband, Phil, love these wines, both white and red. They love Doug, the father and Proprietor, who farms the grapes and helps craft the wine. They also appreciate the birthday calls from ever smiling and friendly Ryan, Doug's son, who is the Director of Sales. Emma and Phil enjoy the establishment so frequently, it becomes easy to remember staff member's names.

As they enter the cool room, Bella is enchanted by the pictures on the wall, the diverse seating spaces, and different items for sale, including a wine travel case. The scent of vanilla candles and the redolence of fermented liquid permeate the atmosphere. She walks over to inspect the wine travel case, something she never considered before today. Emma strolls towards the bar. She smiles a hello to one of her favorite hosts.

"Good afternoon, Alisha. My sister, who is going to move here, and I would like to do a tasting." Emma leans forward and whispers, "Actually, she hasn't made the final decision to move. But we are working on her. And I'd love your help."

"Always happy to assist with such collusion, Emma." An engaging smile materializes on Alisha's face that appears so big it fills her eyes.

Leaving the case behind, Bella joins them at the tasting bar.

"Alisha, this is Bella, my older sister."

"Nice to meet you, Bella. That sounds like an Italian name. Such a heritage would fit nicely into this valley," smiles the host.

"Bella, this is Alisha, one of the great hosts here at Hill Family. My sister is formerly from Iowa, on her way to relocating here, especially as she gets even more into our fine Napa wines. Could you please pour us a couple of your fabulous whites? Then maybe three less common Napa reds?"

Alisha places five Riedel glasses each in front of them, two for whites and three larger ones for reds. They begin with the Albariño, followed by Carly's Cuvée Chardonnay. To Bella, both wines taste light and crispy. The latter highlights a slight buttery conclusion.

"Delicious mouthwatering finish on these two," offers Alisha. "They are quite popular. Especially on our warm summer afternoons, like at Bottle Rock or Porch Fest in Napa."

"Oh yes, great point, Alisha," adds Emma. She winks at her collaborator.

Bella enjoys the whites. She finds the reds are even more dynamic. The Pinot has a darker color than most she has tried. The nose entices her.

"This one has a lovely mid-palate rush that is rich and juicy. It's more complex than typical Pinots."

"I appreciate your descriptions, Alisha. But could you explain what you mean by mid-palate rush?" asks Bella, raising an eyebrow as she looks at her.

"Great question. What I mean is that the flavor starts slow, about halfway back in your mouth, then actually increases as the wine lingers on your tongue. It makes you want to savor it. Does that make sense?"

"Yes, thanks," Bella responds.

Alisha pours the Zinfandel.

"I find this one bouncy, with crunchy red fruit and a spicy finish," she says.

Bella takes a taste. She does not sense anything bouncy. Yet she likes the fruit and spicy finish.

"OK, let me ask another question. What the hell do you mean by bouncy?" laughs Bella.

Alisha laughs with her.

"For me, it's almost like flavor bubbles bouncing on your tongue."

Bella takes another taste and focuses on her experience.

"If I try to imagine what that's like, I can kind of feel it."

As Bella puts down her glass, her attention goes to the front window. Couples and foursomes wander past. Alisha pours a favorite Syrah.

"I love the aromas of black cherry and toasted oak. Even some raspberry glides across the tongue. I think it has a smooth, complex finish."

Bella finds the finish elaborate, and she gets a sense of oak.

Emma suggests one more wine. At this point, Bella feels a bit overwhelmed. The many different scents and flavors inundate her nose and palate.

Alisha brings out their Origin, a Bordeaux blend and bedrock for the winery. The deep, rich color is seductive. As she takes her time, Emma picks up aromas of blackberry and raspberry.

Their host describes this as "a big mouthful of berries and cherry at mid palate that rolls into blueberry and red currant finish. You might even notice some chewy tannins hanging around the edges."

What Bella notices most is that she loves the complex palate and finish of each red. She savors the way these lovely wines last at the back of the throat. The ability to label more elements in her tasting experience exhilarates her. She also enjoys the ambience of the adventure.

Bella smiles at Alisha, then Emma, as she tastes this final wine.

"OK, OK. Enough. I'll move here!" She laughs.

Even using the cuspidor, both women consumed an abundance of bouquets and scents from each varietal, on top of the wine enjoyed at lunch. At Emma's encouragement, Bella joins the wine club and orders a case shipped to her Iowa home.

Another advantage, Bella considers in moving here, she would save on shipping costs. She laughs to herself as she begins to look at even minuscule reasons to reside in Napa.

On their way to the car, Bella feels a bit unsteady and understands why they only had one tasting stop this afternoon. After all, she can't keep up with the professional taster abilities Emma developed during her time in Napa. If Bella does relocate, she plans to emulate her sister's masterly skills.

The siblings stay up uncommonly late. They update each other on life views, circumstances, perspectives on early experiences in the East Bay, and their current families. Emma inquires how Bella is doing following her divorce. While Bella still has pain about failing in a marriage, she feels relief, given the abyss that emerged between them by the end. She notices excitement for the possibility of moving back to California, with little tethering her any longer to Iowa City.

"I want to ask a direct, personal question, Emma. It feels like there has been some reticence between us over the past 20 years that seems to have evaporated today. Am I wrong about that? Am I just imagining such a distance?"

Emma takes another sip of wine, gently sets her glass on the table in front of her. She appears to choose her words thoughtfully and carefully.

"No, I don't think it's just your imagination. I've felt it too. But I found it difficult to talk with you about it."

"What's it about? Can you share it with me now?"

"I'll try." Emma pauses for another breath, looking at the table as she reclaims her glass. "While we were growing up, I always looked up to my strong, valiant big sister. I was even jealous of you at times, which probably contributed to our conflicts. Then, after you married and moved to Iowa City, you appeared to lose yourself. You seemed to defer to your husband and become overwhelmed with children and work. It appeared you abandoned your zest for life. I missed that in you. I hated to see my spirited sister disappear. Now, it seems she's returning. That makes me happy. It's another reason I'd love to have you close. I'd love to spend more time savoring life and each other."

"Huh. OK. Thanks for your honesty. I wouldn't have put it in those words. But your description is actually quite helpful. Since the divorce, I've been looking at how easily I give up myself. Your description makes it a bit clearer. And you're right. I probably wouldn't have been very open to feedback earlier," Bella adds with a little chuckle. "And I delight in our current reconnection." Bella reaches out and gives her sister's hand a loving squeeze. "This feeling reminds me of making up after a fight when we were teenagers. It feels even more precious now."

"That could partly be because you often got your way," laughs Emma. "But that's OK. I'll get my way this time!"

The next morning, Bella and Emma enjoy one last hour of conversation. Reluctantly, Bella leaves her sister to drive back to Davis and pick up Dri. After this visit, the allure of being physically and emotionally closer to her sister adds another reason for Bella's relocation to the area.

Back in Davis, Bella shares emotional goodbyes with Alex. Then Dri painfully takes her mom to the Sacramento airport. She remains somber about her mom leaving. At the same time, she conceals her exuberance for a new adventure. She doesn't want her mom to misinterpret such excitement to be about Bella's absence.

They arrive in plenty of time for extended farewells. They enjoy a brief discussion about other occasions to visit, including Thanksgiving and Christmas. And share a few tears. Dri encourages Bella to move here and offers to spend time in Iowa City next summer helping her pack.

As Dri walks back to the parking garage, she waves at a plane just taking off, hoping it's her mom's. Bella couldn't possibly see her gesture of goodbye, even if it were her flight. It's a more symbolic than practical wave. Yet, it pleases Dri, nonetheless. It also reawakens her sadness about Mom's leaving.

As she unlocks the car door and gets in, she begins to ponder the challenges her mom faces as Dri motors towards her new living space. She wonders whether her mom actually will move here. Why she seldom mentions her hurt from the divorce. Who she will become with all the kids gone. If her mom were out here, Dri could spend more time talking with her about such matters. Then Dri's attention turns more inward.

Should I take more responsibility to help Mom? Will she be OK without my support? Do I have the spunk for all this? Am I as courageous as Alex and Mom seem to be?

As she gets onto CA-113 and drives towards her new home, she notices her inner mixture of excitement, anxiety, and sadness. She takes a deep breath and slowly exhales.

Classes start tomorrow. She's not sure how much she will see Alex as student life gets busy. So she decides to drive back to his apartment.

She finds Alex at home. He appears pleased to see her. He lounges with his roomies and invites her to chill with them.

Dri finds one of his housemates rather attractive. That helps convince her to stay. She always appreciated spending time with Alex and his beguiling friends, especially when it was Tiago, an old friend of Alex from high school. This presents a reprise of her brother's last year at home. But in this case, Dri gets invited to hang out with the good looking guys rather than sent away.

Later in the day, the two siblings drive downtown for some dinner, giving them a chance to talk privately.

"You excited to be here? This is your first real time away from Mom, isn't it?" asks Alex.

"Yeah. I'm happy, and my excitement helps balance out my regret she's not here, too. It's funny. All through high school I couldn't wait to leave home. Now I'm away, I'm missing her already!" chuckles Dri, aware of the situational irony. "Glad you're here. That helps. But I worry about Mom. And now I'm not there to keep an eye on her."

"But then you'd be living at home rather than getting an opportunity to be on your own. Besides, Iowa City's a better place to be from than to live in, if you ask me."

"Don't get me wrong. I'd much rather be here. I just want Mom closer so I have a better sense of how she's doing. She doesn't talk much about the divorce. I worry about her."

"Yeah, I agree. But when we talked, she seemed to be doing pretty well. I think there's a real positive shift. A kind of coming out. Finding more of herself rather than her focus on marriage and motherhood. I think she's in transition. In a good way."

"But I think she might be a bit depressed," responds Dri. "She just seems quiet and has low energy at times."

"Possibly. Or maybe that's how you see her because you get depressed. She does have lots on her mind these days."

Dri looks at her brother in amazement.

"Damn, Bro. I didn't think you were that analytical."

"Hey, I've had Psych 101. I know a few things," Alex says through a big smile. "Besides, I'm super excited to have you on campus. I missed home and all of you the first year. But it gets better. And having you here sure helps. Even if we don't see each other every day. And it will be great to have access to the car," laughs Alex, shifting into humor as he frequently does.

"What? You mean I don't get to be with you every day?" Dri says through a big smile. "Then, the deal's off. I'm going back to Iowa City!"

"Yeah, right!" laughs Alex. "Hey, you're getting funnier in your old age."

Dri smiles at her brother. She feels grateful for their opportunity to connect more.

"Yeah, but I'll never replace you as the family comedian!"

"No, you can't easily replace the best!" responds Alex.

Dri notices her heart opening to her brother and, at the same time, aching for her mom. Yet, she feels happy not to obliterate one feeling when focusing on another. Now, she can pay attention to more of her complete self; holding two contrasting feelings at the same time.

"Have you thought about a major yet?" asks Alex.

"I've been considering psychology. Yet, I need to focus on my tennis too. So I plan to take basic courses this first year until I feel more in the groove. Guess you've settled on one?"

Alex shares what he has been doing, already having decided on a major in enology and viticulture. He gained experience through his program's summer internship at the vineyards. During his first two years, he learned about *terroir,* root stock and clones, vineyard density, and different pruning techniques. Over his final two years, he'll study nitrogen fixation, erosion management, and organic pest control. All important aspects to cultivating succulent fruit that give rise to fine wines. None of his classes, nor this past summer's experience, covered some essential aspects of wine making: learning to drive tractors and night harvesting.

He is particularly excited about improving the sensitivity of his palate. He's learning to identify different scents and flavors of fruits, berries, flowers, herbs, and spices when he inhales the aroma. This follows by tasting the wine as it rolls around his mouth. While his parents' love of wine may have stimulated his oenophilia, moving to a university that specializes in viticulture and experiencing the vineyards, amplifies his curiosity and interest. He feels at home among the verdant vines; something he didn't realize about himself when he made the decision to attend school here.

Alex's excitement about fall semester classes and opportunities infects Dri. She hopes to explore different disciplines with the intention of discovering her own area of passion. In the meantime, Alex's exhilaration is enough for them both. And it pleases Dri to experience a strengthening of their bond.

After dinner, Dri drops her brother off at his place and drives back to her student residence. On her way, Dri lets her thoughts wander.

Whew, don't know if I feel more excitement or anxiety. I guess both. I worry about doing well, and I feel like I'm finally growing up. But how mature must I become to begin feeling more confidence?

Chapter 2
More Transitions
Summer, 2019

O ver the academic year, the two siblings see each other occasionally for lunch, at parties, going to games, or hanging out on weekends. But frequency declines as the pressure on grades increases. Dri gets into the swing of college life and enjoys the opportunity of more freedom. She savors her choice of what to do in any moment. Such independence softens her frequency of mother worrying, as do the phone calls that reassure this young woman that her mother is busy with her own attractive transition.

Dri's classes prove challenging. Yet her studious efforts pay off with solid grades. She holds her own with the tennis team, even while she conceals her pervasive intimidation. She becomes invariably anxious during practice. That shows up in spades during matches, where the competition is so much greater. She didn't realize how dramatically the skill demand increases when playing at the collegiate level. Fortunately, match play is limited for her this first year.

Dri and Tanika talk frequently, but they've only been able to see each other a few times. At the end of spring quarter, they decide to fly back to Iowa City together. Alex helps Dri out with a ride to the Antioch BART station, where she takes the metro train to meet Tanika at the San Francisco Airport. Fares to Cedar Rapids are less expensive there and the extra time together getting home is important to these dear friends. Alex gets the car for the summer, simplifying his travel for increased vineyard responsibilities and creates more opportunities to explore Napa Valley.

The childhood friends plan to connect frequently over the summer, as they did when living there. In addition, Dri looks forward to visiting with Tanika's parents again. Her friend always enjoys spending time with Bella.

Upon arriving home, Dri jumps in to help her mom with packing. She spends time in her old sanctuary as she boxes her personal items, cherishing memories of the only home and bedroom she knew before attending college. The soft green walls and indulgent mattress provided a safe haven for many years.

As she moves to stuffing items into containers through the remainder of the house, Dri has a sense of behaving like a squirreling maniac. She stashes living and dining room nicknacks into their containers, then moves to the next box. The packing gets completed carefully, yet swiftly as possible.

"How are you feeling about the move to Napa, Mom? Excited? Nervous?" asks Dri as Bella comes into the living room to assist in the process.

"I've loved this home, our home, where you kids were raised. But I'm more excited to get back to my old stomping grounds and reconnect with Emma. It will take some time to get established in real estate there. But I like the company I'll be working with. And I have put some money away to cover me during this transition. While I'm a bit nervous about such a dramatic change, mostly I'm excited. How about you? Are you sad we're selling the family home here? Will you miss it?"

"Yeah, in some ways. I'm glad to have had a year living elsewhere. I think that will make it easier to let go of this place, where many fond memories reside. Family gatherings, birthdays, parties. And I'm grateful to spend time at home this summer. I think packing will help loosen my roots here. And, like you, I'm excited about what the future will bring."

"Great, 'cause I think the house will sell pretty quickly. I've made some changes this past year to get it prepped. I've two appointments for showings already."

"Yeah, it looks great. But wasn't Dad going to buy you out?"

A lump forms in Dri's stomach as she reflects on the divorce. She never knows when such a physical reaction suddenly appears.

"He wanted to. But his new wife has a comfortable house. With the pressure and continued investments into the restaurant, he doesn't actually have the money after all. So we'll sell it and split the profits."

"What will you do if it sells right away?"

"Call the moving people, pack up the car, and be out of here with you!" chuckles Bella. "Do I sound ready?"

"Yeah, Mom," laughs Dri.

The lump dissipates with her mom's comment.

"You do sound ready. And I'll be ready to go with you, too."

"When are you going to see your dad?"

"We're going to have dinner at their place on Monday. Don't know after that."

"Good. I'm glad you're staying connected."

"Yeah. It won't be frequent. But I don't want to lose the relationship either."

The two continue to bundle up items that Bella is taking, which also makes the home look more inviting to buyers. Boxes are carefully marked as to the location they will land in Bella's new home. Then they take their neatly stacked place in the garage.

"Do we pack all of these things? Or do any more go to Dad?"

"No, he has taken all the items he wants and I wanted to get rid of. He took quite a bit. That makes moving less expensive. Then I get to purchase a few different pieces as I begin my new life in Napa. I'm excited to set up a place of my own rather than dragging lots of bad memories across country."

"Yeah, I get it, Mom. I think that's a great choice. And I'm excited to see what kind of atmosphere you create there. Maybe I could help you shop?" suggests Dri through her smiling face.

A few days later, Dri is hanging out in her room, thinking of some things she will miss with the old house sold and her life blossoming on the West Coast.

It does not take Dri long to realize that returning "home" after a year at college revitalizes old patterns. She lies on her bed reflecting back to one of her therapy sessions. She remembers a favorite quote Doc shared from Ram Dass: "If you think you're enlightened, go spend some time with your family."

Now, in her vintage bedroom, her sense of herself as an insightful, maturing young woman gives rise to that other part of her; the younger, fearful, self-hatred fragment. She did not completely dissolve the early patterns. Even with all the work she did with Doc and sharing her work with her two closest friends after he died. The early motif lingers like a bad dream, a sticky stench in her life, ferreting out the right time to reappear.

After Doc's passing, Nika suggested the three of them (Dri, Nika, and Soph) gather after school once a week at one of their homes to talk about Doc's ideas and practice some of his suggested techniques. There were a few weeks they could not meet, and the gatherings became scarce during tennis season when all three were focused on improving their court skills. But they held many meetings and explored lots of ideas during the nearly two years before all departed for college.

Dri continued a personal process, including meditation, into her first year at Davis. And yet, returning home, she notices her disappointment that all the roadmaps in her brain still exist for that energetically contracted girl, still linked to that black hole. The connections and influences may not feel as overwhelming. Yet, they remain, readily available.

Dri, wanting a temporary distraction, picks up her phone and calls Tanika.

"Hey, girl, how about a little tennis? I saw Kristina while out for a run this morning, and she would join us if Soph could too. Some doubles to keep us in shape?"

"Yeah, sure. When?"

"How about tomorrow morning at 10:00, then lunch afterwards?"

"Sounds great. At City High or City Park?"

"Let's play at the park, then go downtown. Pick you up about 9:45?"

"Great. I'll call Soph. See you then."

Finished with the distraction, Dri returns to packing up her room. As she loads her books into a box, she finds a journal, notes she made after Doc's passing to put on paper what she remembered from their discussions and practices he suggested. She stops boxing and flips through the notes she used with her friends, reminiscing on their conversations.

Her hand stops as she looks at a page with "Choice" written repeatedly down the otherwise white sheet of paper.

Yes, this was an important point Doc kept making. Choice and options.

As she comes back to her present possibilities, she begins to view her current experiences as a test or choice of which way she wants to approach life, from old patterns or new.

While the old are visible, available, their strength seems less overwhelming after her work with Doc and her continued practice over the next three years. That alone empowers the newer option, without the old dominating her life.

Choice. That's a gigantic difference, Dri says to herself. *Yeah, old patterns hang around. They let me know I have options. And I get to choose whether to go with the old or the new. Spring forward or fall back. I guess it's Lifelight Savings Time or Ancient Times, depending on which path I choose,* laughs Dri to herself. *OMG, I really am becoming my mother. Talking to myself and laughing at myself. Well, at least it's not out loud! Yet!*

She takes a deep breath, now turning her focus on finishing the last two boxes of books and a few other trinkets she wants to save for her future home she hopes to make with her own family. This idea puts a smile on her face.

With the house mostly packed, Dri takes the next morning off to play tennis with her two closest friends and one of the seniors they know from last year's team. They play three sets, trading teams, so everyone gets a chance to win with Tanika. While the recent graduate is strong, none of them match the power and accuracy of this Stanford singles player.

After the game, Kristina thanks them for some strong competition and heads out. The other three drive downtown to have lunch together, as they have done so many previous years. Today, they decide to eat at Oasis Falafel on Lynn Street.

Along the way, Soph shares her pleasure at living in Seattle and becoming a committed "Dawg." She also laughingly tells about how grateful she is to be playing doubles so she avoids having to eventually face this dominating force her dear friend has become during PAC 12 play, where Washington and Stanford compete.

Dri is gratified her inner competitor remained below the surface today, not spoiling her fun. Most of all, she feels pleasure for the three to be together again.

They order their food, find a table, and begin to catch up from the year in different cities and schools. As they talk, the young women dig in after a challenging tennis workout. Each pauses their conversation to take in bites and sips of water. They share the challenges of classes and tennis and fun they are having their first year away. Soph and Tanika both have been dating, but no guy has captivated them yet. Dri has gone out a few times, but she would rather hang with Alex and friends.

All are happy to be in new locations to experience a more urban setting. While Palo Alto and Davis remain smaller cities, their proximity to Sacramento and the Bay Area impact these towns. And Seattle? That became a burgeoning urban setting some time ago. Especially with tech and major corporations headquartered there. Quite a change for them all, even with a Big Ten university in their home town of Iowa City.

Then Dri broaches a different topic.

"I'd like to switch subjects to talk about something else, if you don't mind."

"What's that?" asks Soph.

"I'm curious if the work we shared discussing and exploring exercises based on my work with Doc has had any continuing impact on either of you? I ask because we spent quite a bit of time talking about it after my sessions ended with him. It's had an impact on me.

But maybe that's because I experienced it with him directly and then got to share it with you both. But how about it, you two? Still feel any effects?"

Dri shifts her vision back and forth, searching out any change of their expression or indication of being impacted by her question.

"You still trying to get a teaching evaluation out of us?" laughs Nika. "You wondering if you should pursue a career in education?" She laughs even harder the more she talks.

Dri laughs with her. "No. Actually, if the discussion goes well, I was going to ask you both to write a letter of recommendation for my Ph.D. in psychology!"

"Yeah, I knew you were conspiring about something," chimes in Soph, with that wide grin that makes her eyes sparkle.

As the laughing subsides, Dri chews on another bite, then continues. "No, actually, just curious if you find any use now from our conversations then."

"Yeah, I actually do," replies Soph, her smile transitioning to a more serious demeanor.

"Me too," adds Nika, her smile remaining.

"I've been thinking about the change since coming back home this summer. And I'm curious. What do you find useful now?" inquires Dri.

"It's surprising to me, actually," says Nika as she finishes chewing and appears more solemn. "But one of the suggestions I find most useful are the discussions we had about how our stuff gets aroused by others, but the hurt was already inside us. And if we are willing to look at that wound, what's getting stimulated, we can focus on healing the wound inside instead of just getting angry at others for touching on it."

Dri looks into Nika's eyes as her own heart expands from the delight this response generates in her. She feels into her heart, joy bubbling there, then spreading to other parts of her chest. To have shared this and impacted her friends feels like another way Dri stays connected to Doc.

"That's a great skill, one I'm still working on," responds Soph. "But for me, the heart opening practice is the most useful. It helps me start my day on a positive note, especially if I've been down or feel discouraged. I find I can even practice it while driving or standing in line. Not the whole meditation, of course," she says with a chuckle. "But the basics of going to my heart and encouraging it to expand, to open more."

"Wow, that's cool, both of you. Anything else?" asks Dri, feeling pleased their conversations have had such an impact.

"I've been using the meditation you suggested. It's useful, especially when life starts getting crazy," says Nika. "It often helps my brain settle down. Do you still use it, Audri?"

Dri laughs to herself. *Audri! Not only do the old patterns come back for me. But apparently former names come back to my friends too! Old habits do seem to die hard.*

Audri started using her nickname, Dri, at college. But upon returning home, her friends seem to revert back to her given name. Dri is grateful to leave out the "Aud" part of Audri. She felt "odd" enough as an adolescent.

"Yeah, I use it pretty consistently. Does meditation help you relax your body, too?"

Nika thought for a moment. "Now that you mention it, it does. I also remember you describing the first time you felt that feeling of overwhelming love, what Doc described as a reattachment. As I recall, you experienced it as a connection to something greater than yourself. I think your words were: an immense sense of cosmic love. I felt it once, I think. But I haven't been able to do it on a regular basis. Can you?"

"When I practice regularly, it seems to show up more. But when I don't meditate and ask for that connection, it's more challenging to experience," responds Dri.

"Yeah, that makes sense," says Nika. "I'll try staying with it more consistently this summer, when there's less pressure with school work and tennis."

"One other thing I especially like is the process that Doc described to you of stepping back and paying attention to more subtle sources of information, those beyond the obvious," chimes in Soph. "I even get a feel for people's energy, which is fun. Not sure how accurate I am. But I enjoy the feeling. It excites me when I start to notice more subtle aspects of our conversations. When I think about it, at least," she adds with a chuckle.

"Very cool. Thanks for sharing this. It makes me happy to hear that our time was well spent. You two agree that it was?" inquires Dri.

"Oh yeah," says Soph.

"Me too. I'm glad we did it," says Nika. "And I'm glad I suggested getting together to talk about his ideas and practices after Doc died. I think it helped you, Dri. And we got to learn more about what he encouraged in you. I'm just sorry I didn't get to know him personally. It might have been fun to have had group sessions, assuming the focus stayed off me, of course," laughs Nika. "Or maybe be a fly on the wall and watch you two. But how about you, Audri? What do you find most helpful?"

Dri stops and switches on what she envisions as an inner search light. When she first began working with her therapist, Dri wanted to bypass her feelings. Her avoidance made it challenging to describe what she was experiencing, especially to a stranger. With time and attention, Dri found her feelings became more accessible, and she was increasingly aware of internal feelings and pains. Doc kept saying it was important to shine a light on them. And especially on her belief that something was wrong with her, that she was so messed up she may even be unlovable.

When she finally felt that cosmic love connection, she experienced the truth of what he kept telling her. It was only a belief, in fact a lie she told herself. In eventually seeing that, she could begin the work of letting it go, of experiencing herself as whole and lovable. But there was considerable work between those two bookends.

She's been working with the many of the ideas and practices she learned from Doc. But what was most useful? She takes the last bite of her lunch as she scans her inner environment. She senses a glow in her heart as she identifies two gems.

"I guess I would have to say the inner reconnection is my mainstay. That's the one that helps shift everything else for me, especially when I begin to get down on myself. That practice brings me back to my center when I doubt myself or feel overwhelmed by all that's wrong in my world. Yeah, I'd say that is the most important piece."

"It's cool you continue to use that," chimes in Soph. "That would be useful for me to practice as well, especially when I get overwhelmed at school."

"Yeah, I'd recommend it to anyone. The other skill I think is most useful for me came up again yesterday. It's the process of opening to see more available options. I can get into such a negative, narrow space that I often only see one outcome. Then I get discouraged. That takes me down the same old black hole, where I feel most broken and swallowed up by darkness. If I can step back and see I have other choices, more possibilities, it helps me shift out of such a negative place," shares Dri.

"Oh, I forgot about that one," says Nika. "That would be helpful for me to do too sometimes. I don't get caught up into a black hole like you. But I certainly can see the world in a limited way. Then I get focused on only one bad option. Thanks for reminding me of that."

She pauses, looks at Dri with a big smile.

"OK, guess we'll write that recommendation you wanted".

"Thanks, but I doubt I'll go for a Ph.D. anyway." says Dri. "And thanks for taking the time to talk about this. I like reminiscing about our discussions. And I think our conversations at the time helped me with the loss of Doc," Dri adds as her eyes begin to moisten.

At the same time, she notices her heart expand in joy and gratitude for the gift of supportive friends.

Soph and Nika talk more as they finish their lunch. Dri, on the other hand, begins to reflect on her changing view of Doc. She experiences gratitude for all she learned and missed him terribly after his sudden death. Yet, to begin counseling triggered all her resistance when her mom forced her to see him.

She first saw just an old man who could not possibly know anything about adolescents. He wore the same old shoes every session, maybe not making enough money to buy another pair. He had very few people in his office, suggesting he was so bad she must be his only client.

What a change of perspective she went through over many months. What a change of heart as she slowly opened into his work. What caring when she was able to see beyond the limited view she had of him, realizing the wisdom he held inside. How she still misses the old man. Yet, grateful for his insights that influenced her life.

After lunch, Dri drops Nika and Soph off at their homes, going back to her own in order to finish filling boxes. With the items in her bedroom packed and the kitchen completed, Dri and Bella carefully place the small items from other rooms into containers and complete their work over the next couple of days.

Bella was correct that selling the house would not take long. In just over a week, their family home got in contract. The closing and recording of the transaction will take a month. Bella and Dri pack up the few items they will take in the car. At the prospect of another cross country adventure, mother and daughter recognize that they both are less nervous about sharing intense time together. In fact, both women now view more opportunity for intimate discussions as a gift.

After the movers cram the last items into the van, Dri and Bella drift through the empty house, taking some time for a final goodbye. This home has been a family sanctum sanctorum for nearly three decades and the only sanctuary Dri has known. It has been the holding structure of family events, memories, and challenges. Their stroll exudes a silent expression of gratitude and sadness for this well-loved abode, with family scents and memories.

"Sad to let it go?" asks Bella and she spots Dri looking out her bedroom window.

Dri turns and wipes the tears from her eyes. "Yes, and no. It's been a great place and challenging, too, at times. I'm glad to feel sadness for leaving, for the happy times here, and I'm still eager for the possibilities that lie ahead. How about you? You've spent more time here than I have. You sad to be leaving?"

Bella is aware of moisture in her own eyes. "It's been a wonderful chapter in my life. It's the place where I raised and launched my family. And, now, I, too, am ready for the next adventure. Ready to turn the page and let this chapter end. I'm also glad your Dad and his new wife are not moving in, taking over the place. It feels easier that strangers live here rather than have them inhabit our old home. Sorry, but it's true. And let's just keep this reaction our little secret, OK? No use hurting your dad any more than I have."

Bella flashes on a couple of recent disagreements she and Rick had about belongings and financial arrangements. The resolutions became adequate. Time and space may amplify the healing.

Dri walks over and gives her mom a hug.

"Yeah, sure. Our little secret."

The women finish their home farewells and get the last of their personal items into Bella's car for what is expected as the final Iowa to California journey. There will be return flights, but preferably no more extended drives.

Dri sets up new playlists, a collection of music for singing; some John Mayer, Queen, and the Lumineers, music both enjoy. Snacks are handy, right behind her seat, next to her tennis gear. Bella will take the first driving shift, and that makes Dri happy. She will get first pick of tunes. And with mixed emotions in their hearts, the Giovanni women head for the new Napa home.

Bella made another trip to Napa two months before Dri's return to Iowa City, finding a home there she liked in the same general neighborhood as her sister. She will close on the Napa deal shortly after the Iowa transaction is completed. The new abode provides a place to plant herself not long after her arrival. With a requested delay in van travel, her furnishings will be placed in her new abode. All this makes the transition real, experiencing both excitement and some anxiety about the transplant.

Chapter 3
New Explorations
Spring, 2020

S everal months after Bella moves into her new home, the COVID-19 pandemic hits. She is abundantly grateful to have her own place for sheltering. Her home includes four bedrooms and two and a half bathrooms, providing private space for others. The home also includes places that allow people to gather inside the house. The private back garden, lush with developed trees, flowering bushes and vines in addition to planters for growing vegetables, became a prime gathering space while the inhabitants remain sequestered.

Alex and Dri move into Bella's home when the campus and dorms close. Alex could have stayed in his apartment longer. But he reasons Napa is safer after one of the first Covid-19 cases in California ends up at the campus hospital at Davis. Nika decides to accept Bella's invitation to harbor temporarily in Napa with her second family, unsure how long her school will be closed.

Bella and Nika experience greater difficulty being confined to home, given their more extroverted personalities. As introverts, Alex and Dri find time by themselves at the computer or reading relaxes them. Still, all miss some type of physical workout. Such absence encourages them to work in or at least enjoy the garden and go for masked walks in the neighborhood. With fewer rainy days, they observe the winter brown and barren transition into spring green and an abundance of fragrant blossoms.

The viral detainees create a small Memorial Day celebration, which includes the year's first barbecue saturated in laughter. Several days later, Dri and Nika are on the couch reading in the basement family room.

Nika completes and closes James Baldwin's book assigned for a class. His ideas disturb her comfortable world view and trigger unexplored facets of her Black identity. She reflects on the fun they had with the barbecue, the same day another Black man, George Floyd, was killed by police in Minneapolis. His death sparks anger and uncertainty in her. It also stimulates inner discord as she examines her existence as a Black woman. She knew a few Black students in their high school. But her life there was about blending within a predominantly White community.

She wants to share her present inner reactions, especially with her friend. Yet this territory remains uncharted between these two young women. She gazes at Dri, who now looks up.

"How did your psych class go, Dri? Interesting?"

"Yeah. We focused on different social psychological theories about the development of judgments that stigmatize various groups of people and lead to different stereotypes in society."

"Huh. Do you stereotype me?"

Dri drops the smile and looks deeply at her best friend.

"Well . . . I haven't thought much about that. I suppose I might, somehow. I'm not sure in our society how we avoid that without serious internal explorations and dialogue. But I also know you well and love you. I believe I know you beyond some generalization."

The possibility of stereotyping her best friend sparks tension in her stomach.

She thinks to herself, *How do I separate stereotyping from differences between families and our cultural mores? We didn't talk about that in class.*

"I realize how little we've talked about the fact that I'm Black and you're White. How that creates distinctive experiences for us," says Nika. "Yet, I wonder what it means that we haven't discussed it? Is there a significant piece of me that you don't see?"

She feels a familiar desire to caretake Dri while detecting frustration over hiding her Blackness and trying to blend into a White society. She also notices fear about their relationship possibly not surviving such a challenge.

Nika's seriousness and sense of concern amplifies Dri's tension.

"I don't want to think so. But as you say, why haven't we discussed it? I see you as Black, and I don't care about the color of your skin. I care about who you are."

"But many others in our society do care. And it isn't ignored by most."

"You're right," responds Dri. "When White police continue to kill a higher proportion of Black men and people protest in support of Black Lives Matter, that changes Black lives. And I want to support you. I certainly support the reaction of Black and White people to this injustice. But I probably avoid much direct conversation and a possibility of conflict with you."

"But much of that's out there. I'm right here. Do you see all of me? That's my question."

Dri pauses for a moment, not wanting to rush into or through this pivotal inquiry. More importantly, she doesn't want to create conflicts that could harm their decade long friendship.

"Do I see you as a Black woman? Yes. Do I understand what that means to you? No, I don't think I do. We haven't talked about it. And as you ask the question, I'm also aware that I haven't asked you. I haven't raised the issue. And that embarrasses me."

"And why do you think we haven't talked about it?"

Dri again hesitates, looking inside for an honest response.

"Truthfully? I've probably avoided it. I don't even know what to ask. I guess I go back to our class conversation about White privilege. As a White woman, I don't have to deal with the same issues. In this moment, that makes me feel worse not asking. So, I don't understand all of you, no. As I become aware of that, I'm extremely uncomfortable not asking you, my best friend, about your experience."

"I don't mean to blame you for this, Dri. I haven't brought it up much either. But as I examine who I am as a Black woman, I realize I've ignored a lot of exploration in order to blend in as part of a White culture. To belong. And yes, I want to belong. With you, your family, the bigger culture. But I realize I want to be more authentic about who I am. About all of me, and quit hiding as a strong, Black woman. I'm angry that I even have to hide that part of me."

Nika takes a deep breath, feeling into her hurt, anger, and desire to be more whole in her friendship. Then she continues.

"I think my real question is, are you willing to walk this path with me? As I explore and accept who I am in the context of what I see even more clearly as a racist culture, can I share with you my fears, anxieties, and anger? Can I be honest and expect you to be the same with me?"

Nika looks hesitantly at Dri, as fear expands in her body, unsure of her friend's response.

Yet, she wonders: *What kind of friendship is this if I can't be honest about all of who I am? I need to know now, not after more years of hiding and pretending.*

Dri takes another breath and looks at her dear friend, whom she has known for so many years. Panic hits as she realizes that their comfortable girlfriend connection might not survive into womanhood.

"I can't promise to do this perfectly. But if you can't be honest with me, are we really friends?" asks Dri. "Do we really have each other's back, as we so often have said we do, if you can't speak your truth with me, from all parts of you? You know what I went through in high school and during our gatherings when we talked about what I learned from Doc. You supported me all the way. And I think we both grew from it. What kind of friend would I truly be if I didn't support and discuss this exploration with you? And I believe I'll grow from it, too. Maybe just as much, yet in a different way, from our frank discussions about this part of you."

"Thanks, Dri. I hoped that would be your response. But, like your work with Doc, I don't know where this exploration will take me. I just know I must let this part of me blossom. I need to get real about my Black identity, which, in many ways, I've stifled until now. We experience this society differently and our internal reactions are not the same because of our contrasting outer color. I want to talk about that with you, and I would love to have you walk this journey with me. That's my invitation to you."

Nika feels a lump in her throat and a relaxing stomach.

"And I accept. I want to learn more about you and your experiences, even when it's uncomfortable for me or when I don't know what to say."

Dri begins to ponder what that means; the implications of the commitment she just made.

"You don't need to know what to say. Just be honest with me and let me share what's going on in me. I don't want to avoid racial issues and injustice any longer. I'm in the process of expanding my own awareness and identity in new ways. And it's not always comfortable or pretty for me either. Shit comes up as I study issues in my African American Studies classes and talk with Black classmates, whom I would have ignored back home."

"I'm happy to talk about it. In fact, to start such conversations. I think I've been in my own fear about getting into such sensitive issues."

"But that's what I need, to say it out loud. I haven't before. And that's no longer OK. In high school, I pushed away so much, wanting to ignore it. Of course, a couple of times I couldn't. Like when Lou called me the N-word. I still hate even saying that word. Anyway, when he called me that in 5th grade and you smacked him. Or when those two racists from North Liberty attacked my brother and me at the tennis courts after 10th grade. You stuck up for us when you organized that vigil. But we never actually discussed how either of us felt about those attacks. And I never mentioned how unsafe I felt afterwards or the anger that they generated. I would joke around, play nice, just to fit in. Now, I'm sick of playing passive for White people."

Nika senses a break in her "play it nice" dam. The initial cracks allowed a slow stream to escape, where she could attach herself to a thought for sharing. Currently, the river is rushing out, much too fast at times to grab hold and express what she is thinking or feeling. They rush by in the tidal wave of objects that pass before one realizes what is in front of her, unsure what to say next. An unstoppable gush. The anxious part of Nika fears the result and wants to rebuild the barrier. Another part experiences relief in her body for the authenticity of her expression. Finally.

"It's a challenge at times to say what I feel or what things bother me," continues Nika.

"I'm very sorry I didn't ask you and that we didn't talk. I don't want you to have to hide part of yourself, especially to protect me."

"Well, I wasn't sure, at least beyond you and Soph, who would have had my back in high school. And even then, I guess I didn't totally trust you two with my truth. I guess I didn't even want to ask the question at the time."

Nika pauses as she notices her surprise at just letting her feelings out, how easy it is when she doesn't constrain them. She also notices Dri sitting quietly, speechless, and still present.

"That's why I worked so hard to excel, both at grades and tennis," continues Nika. "Yeah, Mom pushed me to work hard. But I felt like I needed to, so I fit into a group, to be safe in the school. Now, I've left that little White town for the big city. Here, people have been engaged in civil rights protests, the Black Panther movement, Black awareness, Black identity, White prejudice, White supremacy, and the resulting racial tensions for decades."

Nika looks at Dri's face, which appears to hold something between numbness and terror as her body continues to sit motionless. Nika's beginning to recognize that 'deer in the headlights look' by Whites in response to their first encounter with the raw Black experience.

"I don't know just what to say. Except, sorry, Nika. I had no idea."

"Yeah, why would you? I wasn't being myself. I didn't know if I could be honest and still have friends and fit in. I certainly didn't trust sharing my internal feelings. While there were a few other Blacks in school, I didn't connect with them. But I've gotten clearer how I've ignored the violence towards and killing of Blacks, how the focus on crime is a way to incarcerate Black men when justice is not equally practiced under the law. And the most blatant is law enforcement legally killing Black people with little or no accountability. It's like public lynchings all over again."

"And that's stimulating all the Black Lives Matter protests this summer."

"Yeah, and they're right," says Nika. "Black lives do matter. And while all lives matter, we can't honor all lives until we honor Black lives. And we won't honor Black lives until we quit sweeping racist attitudes, behaviors, and practices under the rug. Until we change policies in police departments, criminal justice systems, educational systems, and employment opportunities. As Baldwin so eloquently pointed out 55 years ago, not everyone lives with the same fear of losing their lives as Blacks do. And not everyone lives with the same likelihood of being poor, less educated, and likely to be incarcerated, all because of a rigged system."

"I agree with what you're saying. And I'd be happy to walk with you during a BLM protest sometime. I believe in this issue, and I want to support you and others," responds Dri.

"Yeah, it would be great to do that together. But there's so much more going on beyond the killings. I've been talking with some of my Black friends at school about our fears of police stopping us, our experiences of being followed by cops or detectives in stores, solely because we're Black. My artist friend, Naeem, has experienced both in the Bay Area. Even Senator Scott from South Carolina talks about his experience as a Black man, both in his home state and as a member of the US Senate. He's been stopped and followed by the police solely because of the color of his skin. And he's a Republican. Nothing but racism explains such consistent behaviors."

"And that's never happened to me. I don't even expect it. And that's my worldview as a White woman. We talked about that in our class too. Lots of my White classmates deny they experience privilege. But when we discuss the threats and fears consistently experienced by Black people, how Black parents have to warn their children about placing their hands on the dashboard and what to say when stopped by police, it becomes obvious that Whites are born with privilege. And it's all based on how Whites hold power and still treat people of color."

"And I'm uncomfortable ignoring the issue any longer. I was astounded when I watched a documentary about Baldwin. In it, he said: 'Not everything that is faced can be changed. But nothing can be changed until it is faced.' I know we need to address racism, and I'm trying to figure out my part in all this. What's my role? What am I called to do?"

"Baldwin had many great insights," responds Dri. "I appreciate your sharing his ideas. But even more, I love the whole Nika who's emerging. I trust you'll find the answers to such essential questions. And I don't know what to do either."

"But maybe you do, Dri. Maybe you just haven't made the connection yet. I've been thinking back on our lunch conversation last year, when we discussed what we got from Doc's work. What changes when we open our hearts to each other? Does that impact how we treat each other, especially in terms of racism?"

"Huh. Guess I've been too anxious in our discussion to actually think much beyond you, me, and race. But when I think of how much I love you, I would never want to do anything to hurt you. Great questions. And we must change it somehow."

"Thanks for saying that. It's an idea that's been brewing for a while. I brought Baldwin's book, *The Fire Next Time*. I thought you might want to read it. He says something in there that blew me away, an idea I've not heard from others. Let me share a paragraph with you, OK?"

"Yeah, sure. Love to hear it . . . . I think!" Dri responds with a hint of a smile.

Nika picks up the book and leafs through the pages, looking for the paragraph to share.

"Here it is. He says: 'White people in this country will have quite enough to do in learning how to accept and love themselves and each other, and when they have achieved this — which will not be tomorrow and may very well be never — the Negro problem will no longer exist, for it will no longer be needed.' As we talked about it in class," Nika continues, "my instructor suggested that Whites diminish Blacks to make themselves look and feel better than anyone else. They did that with Native Americans, Chinese, and others at times. But Blacks have been consistently used that way. Do you agree with Baldwin on this point too? Do you think Whites need Blacks to feel superior, to feel better about themselves?"

Dri's chest tightens as she considers her friend's comment, not wanting the idea to be true. But her intestinal brain says it probably is.

"Yeah, my gut and my head both say it's true. I don't think it's a conscious decision at this point. More of an addiction. Yet, it's not just about feeling superior. That attitude has been used as a justification to set up a system that maintains White privilege. When people of color can't achieve and flourish within a biased system, Whites use that as a justification for being better than others. Superior. "

"But couldn't the heart opening process assist Whites learning not only to love themselves, but also to love others?" Nika asks. "If that changes attitudes and relationships, then we could more easily change policies that would even out the system, making the playing field equal. It essentially could change everything."

"My God, Nika. You're brilliant," responds Dri, as her eyes open wider. "Those are important points I've never considered in relation to racism."

"Of course, we still need to transform many parts of our government, educational systems, and police policies. But I think the open heart would make changes easier, everything more possible."

"What I appreciate most is your focus on where to begin. That intrigues me. May I borrow Baldwin's book? I'd love to read it and get to know him better."

"Yeah, sure. And I'd enjoy talking with you more about it. I know you love me, and I love you, too. I don't feel prejudice from you or your family, like I do from some Whites. And that's what led me back to the conversations you, Soph, and I had last year over lunch in Iowa City. Sharing the effects that Doc's work had on us made me wonder how the heart opening meditation might impact people who want to change, to let go of this 'problem,' as Baldwin describes."

"Hmmm. That's a significant possibility I want to explore. I'd like to read this and talk more about it. I need help understanding your changing perspective, a point of view I've not experienced. And I want to know all of you, even the hidden parts, as you know with me."

"Of course. But let me ask you another question I've been thinking about. You created that vigil after my brother and I were attacked at the City Park tennis courts almost four years ago. Did you organize that because you thought you needed or wanted to protect me? Or did you feel like it was your responsibility to take care of me? I'm trying to understand if you, a White girl, felt like you needed to stand up for a Black girl and her brother, who couldn't do it themselves?"

"No . . . . . no, I don't think so," replies Dri hesitantly. "I certainly didn't see it that way then. But I don't think I ever considered that issue either. I was angry that you two were attacked and hurt, and I wanted to stand up for you. I didn't think you had to stand up all by yourself. But I don't think you needed me to take care of you or that you couldn't stand up for yourselves. Hell, you and a strong racket took care of yourself at the time with those two assholes. And, I thought it was important to raise the issue that attacking Black people in our city was not OK. And violence was not OK. I thought it was important for a White person to say that out loud. Just like Whites are marching with Blacks in the demonstrations to say yes, Black Lives Matter. To stand with you and say enough; enough violence, and enough perpetuating racism. It seems like Baldwin's saying the racal issue connects Blacks and Whites alike. We're in this together, in part because Whites started it and are having a difficult time letting go of it, of allowing real equality to happen."

Nika feels the liquid surround her eyes as she gets up, walks over and bends forward to give her dear friend a hug. Aware of her friend's intention, Dri stands and Nika whispers into her ear.

"Thanks, Dri. You're a great friend. Thanks for letting me talk about this with you. For your willingness to feel my pain, hear my fears and my experience, and for your desire to be in this together."

As Nika lets go, Dri pulls her tight for another hug. She clears the inner tears and drainage from her throat.

"Always! Even if I'm not clear in the moment, I promise to come back and face whatever is in my way of loving you as an equal. I don't need you to be inferior to feel good about myself. And if there is something I'm missing, I want to face it. You're the best friend a girl could have. I could ever have. And just because you were born Black and I was born White doesn't mean we can't remain close, which is essential to me. Times are changing, and I want to make sure we both are ready. You're an important part of that and a significant person in my life."

"Thanks. Well, I've got to get some writing done. We can continue this later," says Nika.

Nika returns to her bedroom to begin her paper on Baldwin's book.

Dri sits back down, a bit shell-shocked from their naked conversation. She knows this discussion about race, acceptance, and love is just beginning. She senses their heads and hearts are open to each other. Yet there is more to learn, understand, and explore.

Dri arises the next morning and heads for the kitchen to make coffee. On her way, her nose tells her someone beat her to it. As she approaches the kitchen table, Nika and Bella are sitting there with mugs in hand and a muffin on each plate, blueberry for Nika and lemon for Bella.

"There's more coffee there for you, Dri, and a muffin or scone in the fridge," says Bella.

Dri pours a cup of coffee and gets a blueberry scone and fresh fruit, then joins the other two.

"Nika and I were talking a bit about your conversation from last night," says Bella. "Sounds like an important stretch for both of you. I'd love to hear how it goes along the way. I think there's a lot I could learn from the discussion and how you work with it."

"I not only want to get clearer about myself, but also my work. I want to be involved somehow. But I don't know just what I want to do," responds Nika.

"I'd agree with that," says Dri. "This feels like an important piece of what I want to do too. And I have less clarity than Nika. Once again, she's ahead of me on this one."

"You two are young and still sorting out your lives," responds Bella. "Be patient with yourselves. I trust you both will get clearer over time."

"Easy for you to say, Mom," responds Dri. "You seem to have gotten clear pretty early in your life. You make it look easy."

"Oh no, it's not always easy," says Bella. "And sometimes it can change over time. But I'll share a quote from Rumi that has been helpful to me. He said, 'Everyone has been made for some particular work, and the desire for that work has been put in every heart.' I believe that's sage advice."

"Oh, so all I have to do is figure out what's in my heart?" asks Dri with a sarcastic laugh.

Bella looks straight into her eyes with a serious look on her face.

"Yes," she says.

Dri brushes her hair out of her face, takes another sip of coffee, still looking at her mom. "OK. I will. And you, Nika?"

Nika looks at Dri, then Bella.

I doubt it's essentially that easy, she thinks.

"It doesn't hurt to try," responds Nika verbally. "I sure want to know. Rumi makes it sound so easy. And in the end, it may be. I certainly hope so!"

After the last swig of coffee and bite of muffin, Nika cleans up her dishes and heads to her bedroom. She finishes her packing to be ready for Dri to drive her down to SFO to catch her flight back to Iowa City. With colleges requiring all classes to be online, she wants to spend more time with her parents. Nika realizes there is much to process with them in this evolution of identity.

***

Beverley and Tyrell, Nika's parents, both have big smiles as they greet their daughter at the Cedar Rapids Airport with strong hugs. Her dad tosses Nika's giant suitcase in the back, like he must have tossed running backs to the ground while he played Michigan football. Her mom watches Nika get settled in the backseat.

Nika wonders if Beverley is going to strap her seatbelt before she shuts her daughter's door. Nika loves that her parents are so thoughtful. And two years away at college doesn't seem to modify their patterns. Beverly gets in the passenger seat and straps her belt. Tyrell gets behind the wheel, buckles his belt, and the reunited family begins their 30 minute journey home.

"How's Bella enjoying Napa Valley," asks Beverley even before they depart the airport parking and drive east towards I-380 south.

"She seems to love it. Dri and Alex say they're both happy there, too. Can't believe it's almost a year since they moved. You miss her, Mom?" asks Nika.

"Yeah, I do. Miss Audri coming over to hang out, too. Wish they all still lived here," says her mom. Then she turns to look at Nika. "Miss you too, girl. I can see we're going to have to travel west more often, especially if you end up staying there. Think you might?"

"Don't know, yet. But I sure do like greater diversity out there, even if it brings up more questions and issues. Dri and I had a productive beginning conversation the other day, as you suggested," says Nika.

"It went well, did it?" asks Beverley.

"Yeah, I think it did. Still more to discuss. But a solid beginning."

"Oh, good," adds her dad. "I thought she'd be pretty open. Especially living with Bella. Not always as sure about her dad. But who knows until you say something out loud."

"So, I have a question for you two," says Nika. "Why didn't you encourage me to hang out more with other Black girls in high school? Why didn't you push me to connect with others then?"

"Because we really like Audri and her family, and it's not always about hanging out with people who look like you," responds Beverley. "Besides, Audri and Bella were strong supporters of excellent grades and tennis. We thought that could be helpful to you. And sometimes if parents push one way, adolescents push back the opposite way. We felt like you were making wise decisions. Why change something that's working? But it's another reason we thought going to Stanford when the opportunity came up would be an excellent opportunity to explore other aspects of yourself rather than going to school here. Iowa's a great school, right dear?" Beverley says as she looks at her husband, the defensive coach for the Iowa football program. Then she turns back towards Nika. "But sometimes a change of environment can be a useful thing for exploring other parts of yourself."

"Well, you were right about that, too, although you might have warned me," says Nika, with a half-hearted laugh. "I guess you didn't know how I was going to respond to challenges. I think connecting to other Black students there has helped me. It's given me the opportunity to learn from people who've had more experience with racial issues."

"I'm glad for that," says her dad. "But more importantly, any guys there who interest you?"

"I have a friend who's kind of cute and lots of fun," responds Nika. "But not sure you'd like him, Dad. He's not that into football."

"OK, then, never mind," responds Tyrell with a belly guffaw. "I'll keep looking for someone here who'll get you back home where you belong, my dear."

"Ah, about that, Dad. Not sure I want to come back here to live. Sorry, but I really like the Bay Area. It's diverse, alive, and the politics there agree with me more than here."

"Yeah, I was afraid of that," adds Beverley, noticing her disappointment appearing in her chest while her heart tells her to be supportive of her daughter's choice. "Well, then, we'll travel. I'd sure love to see some of your matches. Iowa doesn't seem to get Stanford here very often."

"Me, too," says her dad in a more serious manner. "And I'm glad you're in an environment that pushes you to explore racial issues more. It's important to ground yourself in such knowledge, no matter what career you pursue. I know something about that from my own experience here."

The three of them talk more about tennis, school, and the dorms. Upon their arrival home, Nika is happy to see Denzel, her brother. He's developed more muscle and cultivated even more spunk. Now the older sister can no longer push him around. She remains the leg wrestling champion, more from tactic than strength. She's also smart enough to decline a rematch.

She relaxes in her room, unrecognizably neat with her mother now in charge of its tidiness. But she is getting to appreciate such order in her life.

Nika treasures the conversations she and her mom have over the next few days. In particular, they discuss the development of Beverley's identity as a Black woman while at school in Ann Arbor during the early 1990s. As they relax in the family room today, Beverley hands Nika a book from her library.

"You might find this book by Dr. Romano useful in your exploration. It struck me because of its title, *Racial Reckoning*. I thought the term was very interesting in relation to what's gone on in the past and what we're dealing with now. Give it a read and let me know what you think."

Nika devours the book over the next couple of days. It gives her more information about what went on with lynchings and the climate of intimidation during the 1950s and 60s, deeds that Whites carried out with few if any consequences at the time. There is tentative relief to find some were brought to legal justice decades later. Yet she finds it informative and infuriating how people tackled racial disparities, working to put the past to rest, without fundamentally changing the status quo of privileged Whites.

The following day, she hears her mom preparing dinner after getting home from her high school job as principal. Nika enters the kitchen and sits at the island.

"Great book, Mom. Thanks. But it's also disturbing. While a few men finally came to justice, in some ways, we still are living with the terrorism their acts perpetuated on Blacks. And it hasn't essentially changed systemic racism or social justice. Wouldn't you agree?"

"Yes, in many ways, that's true. It has changed some of the formal aspects, such as segregation and voting rights. But Whites have continued to create ways to maintain the system to their advantage. The system is more subtle, but no less pervasive."

"Yeah, it's about the social justice changes that haven't happened. That's what the BLM protests are all about. Like the terrorism by police that's still happening and structural changes that need to be addressed. Greater economic opportunity, social equality, and equal opportunity for health and security."

"I agree," responds Beverley. "Change is slow, and sometimes we go backwards when enough Whites get scared they will lose their power, like what's happening now. At times such as these, Whites view themselves in conflict or struggle against people of color. But I love how engaged you are with these issues, Tanika. You surprise me how much you seem to have taken them on during the past two years."

"I'm a little surprised myself," says Nika. "But I have a lot of passion about such injustice. This feels like an essential part of the work I want to do in my life."

"More power to you, girl. But be wise about how you do it. Don't go about this the same old way. It will take some creativity and maybe a fresh approach to create more change. And I don't think we can continue pushing for change through anger. It generates too much pushback. Still, this seems like a great time to add your efforts to the cause."

Beverley wipes her hands and gives her daughter a hug, grateful for the depth of her daughter's commitment.

When Dri calls two days later, Nika talks about the book and insights she has gained. She shares her frustration, even anger at times, about the lack of social justice made so far. She relates the essence of the discussions with her mom, happy to feel solid support from her. She even talked seriously with her dad, who expressed his frustrations about racism in sports and society. Most of all, she reveals her excitement to gain a clearer picture of the work she wants to do.

"These issues do seem close to your heart," responds Dri. "And it's important work to address, for all of us. I love your excitement about it, which engages me more, too."

"I appreciate your support as well. Even when comments rush out of my mouth. You're a great friend just to listen. And I love that you want to explore these issues with me."

"I'm sorry we're not together more right now."

"Ah, we will be soon. I'll be back in August, most likely," Nika hesitantly assures her.

Over the next month, Nika continues her reading and online research. She follows the recently passed Iowa City Council resolution to bring about changes in line with the BLM movement, especially the city's move towards community policing in an attempt to reduce racial incidents. She reads about banning the Confederate flag at NASCAR and removing that portion from the Alabama state flag. Later, she comes across an old quote from Dr. Martin Luther King's 1963 speech that touches her deeply: "It may be true that the law cannot change the heart, but it can restrain the heartless."

But what if we could change the heart? Not by law, but through love and a deeper connection. What if we could open hearts and shift how we see each other, color and all? It does seem like there is a change taking place with some people, especially my age. What if we could build on that and expand it even further? The structural racism seems overwhelming. But maybe there are some cracks in the shell we could expand?

Then she reads an article about a church bell ringing *Amazing Grace* as people began disassembling a Confederate statue. The description brings tears to her eyes and some joy in her heart. That night, she decides to write a poem, using all the emotions currently stirring within.

Heritage Statues

Monuments and military bases
to warriors and generals
fighting against our union
A now united country
honors no other enemy
built many decades after
the civil war they represent
memories of rebellion
more importantly intimidation
against a freed race
who dare ask for impartiality
treatment as humans   equals
encouraging an inclusion
within an original belief
All Men are Created Equal
Women now included
emigrants from other countries
races   people   orientations   identities
asking the central question
when will all mean all
when will people of all colors
genders   orientations
be included as American
Finally coming down
statue by male statue
tower by tower
a self-serving president
defends them for political gain
ignoring the masses   majority opinions
who cheer their dethroning
the towering over people
reminders of continued subjugation

finally descending to the earth
isonomy emerging in their place
while chapel bells ring out
Amazing grace

Chapter 4
Stretching
Summer, 2020

While Dri and Tanika explore issues of racism and change, Sarah, Dri's older sister, focuses on a whole different component of the 2020 crises. After Sarah got accepted into UC Hastings College of Law in San Francisco, she convinced Marsha to move west with her. These two young lovers committed to be life partners shortly after graduation from the University of Iowa.

As they both discovered, every relationship experiences its challenges. Yet Sarah and Marsha, for the most part, believe they get along famously. They enjoy many interests, including art, running, political discussions, reading, museums, movies, and free-form dancing. The latter they discovered after moving to the Bay Area. But the splendor of their sex life may rank highest on their list. Yet, they participate in life not as duplicates of each other. They share a love of these activities and interests from contrasting views and the explorations of them all.

Sarah graduated with a sociology major. But she combines that focus with a more emotional and artistic flare with her explorations into the social impact of aesthetic environments on individuals and group interactions.

Marsha majored in nursing although her heart leans towards art. She has developed a special interest in the social symbolism of painting and sculpture. Sarah reminisces about one of Marsha's favorite paintings at SFMOMA, Georgia O'Keefe's *Black Place I*. Sarah remembers Marsha's excitement last summer to show her the painting, which

Sarah found alluringly depressing. She loves Marsha's enthusiasm for O'Keefe's works. But Sarah admires the famed artist's more optimistic and sensual pieces.

Sarah is an avid runner and convinced Marsha to participate in her first Bay to Breakers race. Marsha loves free-form dancing, dragging Sarah to Ecstatic Dance in Oakland and Sweat Your Prayers in Sausalito. Marsha lives for such creative movement, and Sarah enjoys doing these activities with her.

What forges their greatest connection is a mutual love of life and what is amassed from each other's contribution. The combination of their gifts creates an exponential rather than linear accumulation, as if love multiplies when applied generously and unselfishly. Sarah finds the aggregation addictive.

In late May, Marsha, who is now a nurse in a local hospital, calls Sarah to tell her of her mask breaking while working with a Covid-19 patient. She immediately goes into quarantine at a local motel the hospital rented for just such staff occurrences. She shows no symptoms for several days.

During that separation time, the two lovers engage in long daily conversations to maintain their loving connection. But over the next few days, Sarah notices Marsha's increased difficulty talking and breathing. Upon ending her latest discussion, she calls an ambulance to transport Marsha, who is admitted to the hospital, now a patient in her place of work. Four days later, she's moved to intensive care. Two days after her transfer, she is attached to a ventilator.

From the time Marsha left for work that fateful May morning, Sarah has been unable to visit in person, frustrating the hell out of her. By hospital orders, no visitors are allowed. These two women do not know when they will be able to touch each other again, leave a kiss on the other's cheek, or give each other tender hugs. This forced separation breaks Sarah's heart and darkens her world.

She tries to concentrate on her summer internship work with a local judge. She likes both her boss and the assignments. Yet her heart is two miles away in a hospital bed with Marsha, next to an indispensable lung machine, with hope attached that it saves another life.

Sarah communicates with her through FaceTime calls, facilitated by another nurse. Sarah's heart breaks watching her dear one suffer. Yet she's grateful to see the love in Marsha's eyes, emotions this patient cannot express verbally with a tube down her throat. The optical message helps between calls.

That is what Sarah keeps in her mind as her heart compresses under the weight of Marsha's life-saving machines. She also keeps a favorite photo of her partner's loving smile and luminous eyes next to her computer, reminding her of what this dear woman looked like before the dreadful illness. This picture contains the image she wants seared into her memory, an image that holds Sarah's love for Marsha while unable to visit her in person.

What no one can help Sarah understand is the difference in responses to the same infection. This frustrates her. She has been tracking treatments and possible remedies, constantly reading the local newspaper and following any changes she finds online. In part, no single source can help because no one yet fundamentally understands such diverse reactions. Marsha showed basic symptoms a few days earlier, and then went downhill quickly. Physicians and researchers cannot explain the difference in responses, only to say they exist. Experts work hard to understand what is happening. After all their work, the more they learn, it seems to Sarah that the less they confidently know. This diminishes her hope. The mutation of this virus is one reason for its complications, and scientists continue their work to understand its evolutionary process. What experts are finding is that the virus has a much greater impact on people of color. That does not bode well, given Marsha's partial Hispanic heritage. None of this information assuages Sarah's heart.

On Friday, June 12th, while Marsha remains in the hospital, Sarah drives up partnerless to join her family in Napa. On this day, Alex rather unceremoniously graduates with his degree in viticulture from UC Davis. As Sarah opens the door to Bella's home, she, Dri, and Alex surround Sarah's body with welcoming and sorrowful arms. They hold and love her in this time of distress. Sarah, who was crying all the way home, found yet more tears to shed for their support.

"I'm sorry Marsha is so sick," says Alex. "She's a terrific woman and seems like a wonderful partner. I hope she recovers soon." Alex leans in and gives her a hug. "I'm going to go check out this questionable Online graduation ceremony. See you a little later."

Alex goes to his bedroom to see if the web ceremony is interesting at all. Soon he gets bored. He would rather commemorate the occasion with his family in person.

Bella, Dri, and Sarah gather with Alex for a small family celebration. Tiago, a friend and member of Alex's high school baseball team, visits for the weekend. Alex is glad to have his friend join the minimal festivities. Dri, on the other hand, feels her heart skip a bit once again to see her hot friend, Tiago, and catch up a bit from the past three years.

Bella is pleased to have all three children spend time at her new abode. She has a variety of cupcakes, some ice cream, and two bottles of red wine delivered to her home. The four celebrants gather around Alex to congratulate him for his college completion. The festivity involves mild laughter, elbow bumps, and, of course, wine toasts. But in the back of Alex's mind, he is more excited about his future work endeavors

Alex relishes the completion of his classes. He now is ready to gain more experience in a commercial winery. He has tuned into the long affiliation between Napa Valley wineries and the viticulture program at UC Davis, based on close proximity and mutual interests. He follows the large number of winemakers and sommeliers who begin their study at Davis. He has seen how local wineries seek help for viticulture challenges. This interdependence of education and industry also facilitates relationships that are long and strong. Alex hopes such connections enhance his abilities to gain additional competence at a Napa winery.

Alex wants to get more practical experience in the wine industry and has been seeking a Napa winery postgraduate internship. This particular summer, intern positions have become more available, as the pandemic impacts the number of international workers coming into the country. Over two dozen wineries currently seek trained help. The change in traditional availability creates numerous opportunities for budding professionals. Yet, competition remains stiff. Luckily, Alex's advisor, who grew up on his grandfather's winery in Calistoga and maintains connections to the valley, recommends him to three prime organizations diverse in size. Alex appreciates his professor's ties and his willingness to reach out with a reference.

After three interviews, Alex decides to take an offer from a small boutique winery atop Prichard Hill, an area renowned for excellent wines. His professor showed Alex an article in Wine Spectator, a top wine magazine, which identified four wineries on the hill with the subtitle, 'The Rodeo Drive of Napa Valley?' Now, Alex is getting the chance to gain significant experience at one of them. The opportunity to expand his practical knowledge excites him. Simultaneously, his anxiety increases as he wonders whether he knows enough to do well in such professional settings.

Immediately after the family's petite July 4th celebration, Alex begins his internship at David Arthur Vineyards, an unassuming yet well known winery overlooking the Oakville and Rutherford sections of the vineyard valley. David's father began purchasing land there in the 1950s and David began clearing a hilltop area for vineyards in 1978, part of the Napa Grape Rush of the 1970s and 80s. Alex wants to gain intimate experience in the practicalities of nurturing, harvesting, and alchemizing grapes into award winning vino.

One reason Alex chose this winery for his internship has to do with the distinct opportunities he believes he will have in a more intimate setting and the diverse varietals of wines the operation produces. Like many Napa vineyards, Cabernet Sauvignon is the foundation grape of the winery. But what intrigues him is the way different settings, soils, and clones produce disparate tastes in wines of the same varietal of grape. He is hoping to learn more about such distinctions and how that impacts the Cabernet's aromas and flavors. The winery also grows varietals that are less common in this country. They nurture two traditional Italian grapes: a Nebbiolo, originally from the Northern region of Piemonte, and a Sangiovese, common in Tuscany. Alex is curious about why the owner decided to develop these wines in Napa and how he made them successful here. Finally, Alex hopes to learn more about the process of blind tastings for developing the blends David described in his interview. He has read and heard about how it is done. But experiencing the procedure would be his best educational memory.

As the green leaves begin to transform into yellow and orange, Alex increases his practical experience in vineyard management as he works closely with Roberto, the vineyard manager for over 30 years, and his staff. Alex takes copious notes of their knowledge, insights, and recommendations to help him grow and increase his competence. He learns the essentials and details of canopy management to maximize sunlight interception, minimize shading, and balance growth. He also gains insight in to the importance of driving a tractor straight down the rows or caution when backing up machinery, mostly by example but occasionally by oversight. His involvement in cultivating vineyards and winery protocol increase his confidence in a business that requires extensive and diverse knowledge to do well in a competitive international market.

Alex loved the opportunity to harvest while he was in college. He looked forward to it here, but was disappointed, as were the entire staff, when the 2020 fires produced so much smoke taint that the vintage was ruined. Fortunately, Nile was able to source chardonnay grapes from other areas for Alex to experience the processing of fruit before maturation in the vats. His sense of rivalry helped him in baseball and the classroom. He intends to apply this same spirit to his internship and career. At the same time, working as a team, as he did on the field, helps him realize the importance of collaboration in this profession, too.

After Alex's graduation celebration, Sarah drives back to her city apartment. She wants closer proximity to Marsha and more privacy for her work. Her lover continues to hold onto life as she always has, with great persistence, even though sedated with a tube down her throat. Sarah continues her FaceTime calls. She can observe Marsha. But all conversation goes through available nurses. The sight of Marsha verifies her survival when Sarah can't hear her voice.

Many at the hospital who know Marsha's work habits and jovial personality share Sarah's concern and sadness for her partner's critical state. All hope for encouraging news, any indication of improvement. Like the virus itself, Sarah tenaciously hangs on. She hopes and dreams of Marsha's full recuperation, even if it is months away.

Once back in the city, Sarah finds it easier to work without distractions, in part because limits remain on business openings. A week after returning, she finds a restaurant that delivers so she doesn't have to cook. After the meal arrives, she chooses a savory bottle of Zinfandel Bella gave her. She uncorks the wine, pours a glass, and takes a curious first sniff. The phone interrupts her focus. It's Marsha's doctor. Sarah tries to take a breath with little air coming into her lungs. Her chest muscles freeze.

"Hi. How's Marsha doing today? Any improvements?"

"Sarah, I'm so sorry," begins Dr. Sanchez, her voice cracking slightly over the phone. "But Marsha passed away about 30 minutes ago. We tried to revive her with no luck. I'm deeply sorry for your loss. I know how much she loved you, and it was obvious to us all that you reciprocated the feeling. We're all going to miss this fine nurse, a very caring person, and a great friend. If there's anything we can do to assist you in this tragedy, please don't hesitate to ask."

Sarah attempts to get a string of words out of her mouth.

"Thanks, Dr. Sanchez."

She wants to say more. She can't and hits the End button. She puts the phone on the table and sits, staring at the wall where photos of these two lovers hang. Their colorful life together, framed and set in time.

But now, Sarah's world is mutating. The shock narrows her brain's focus, as if it too is in mourning. The only important thing the brain currently contains. Her world turns into a withering gray. The wall in front of her, the table and floor, her hands, clothes, even the photographs. The only color remaining is in the picture of Marsha's smile. The photo's contrast to Sarah's gray world amplifies her loss, her lover, body, sensuous smile, gentle skin, luminous eyes. Sarah imagines a now vacant face, impacted by a virus that has just annihilated her world. She takes a drink of the gray wine and calls her mother.

"Oh Sarah! I'm so sorry!" Bella's cry is the only sound from the phone for the moment. "What can we do?" she finally asks. "Should . . . . I come get you? Do you . . . do you want to drive up here? How can I help, dear one?"

Sarah tries to take another breath. Her chest muscles still tightly cinched, allowing minuscule movements.

"I don't know." She takes another breath, hunting for words. "I guess . . . . I guess I should call her parents. But . . . Marsha hasn't talked to them since we left, when they called me . . . . the Devil. They haven't called us either." She attempts another breath. "Not sure what to do."

"I think you should give them a try. I'd want to know, even if I were angry when you left."

"OK . . . . I guess . . . . . I'll give them a call. Thanks, Mom. Talk with you later."

Sarah hangs up. Her sweetheart's phone is with her other personal items at the hospital. Given the total absence of parental communication, Sarah has no number. She remembers the name of the small Iowa town where Marsha grew up. She does have the name of Marsha's parents, and tries 411 for that city. She gets a phone number and is connected.

"Hello?" a male voice answers.

Marsha has no brothers. Sarah assumes it's Marsha's father.

"Hi. This is Sarah Giovanni, Marsha's partner."

She takes a breath, hoping strength enters with the oxygen. No encouragement comes from the other end.

"I'm sorry to tell you this. But Marsha passed away this afternoon from Covid-19. I wanted to let you know right away. I would have called earlier, but we all thought she'd get better. Very sorry to tell you such awful news with no warning."

"That girl died for us when she ran off with you, you Devil! You lesbo tramp! You ruined her. You stole our daughter. You destroyed her soul! May God strike you dead for the evil you spread. Don't ever call us again, ya hear?"

The sounds on the other end die, and so does another portion of Sarah's heart.

How can parents be so cruel? wonders Sarah. *At times, I thought Marsha was exaggerating about her parents' response. I thought maybe some day they'd come around. Not for dear Marsha, anyway.*

Sarah lowers her forehead to her bent arm resting on the gray table and sobs.

Sarah's dad offers basic understanding and support for her gay relationship, even when he lacks enthusiasm or demonstrates discomfort. But Marsha's parents come from a whole other world. One Marsha left behind. One she never wanted to revive. Now, she never will.

Sarah will honor one of Marsha' final requests. She will have Marsha's body cremated. She'll decide later what to do with the ashes. One thing she does know. Marsha's ashes will never be transported east of the Sierras.

Sarah takes another sip of her wine, pours the rest back into the bottle and reinserts the cork. She wraps up her food, tosses a few items and clothes into her suitcase, then loads her car. She turns on the engine, backs out of her parking space, and heads for I-80 and Napa. On her way, she calls Bella to let her know she's coming to stay for a while.

As she drives through the darkness, Sarah enters another world.

Did I really get a call from Dr. Sanchez? Is Marsha really gone? Is this all a dream? Or a nightmare? I can see myself driving, but I don't feel much. Maybe I'll awake from this state in the morning? Maybe I'll get to see her, feel her, touch her again? Maybe I'll get sick and go too? It's all a daze. I'm not sure where I am or even want to be. I just know I don't want to be here without her!

Bella, Alex, and Dri greet Sarah as she steps up to the door, all hugging her at once. As Bella and Dri step back, Alex takes Sarah's hand in his hand and her bag in the other, the latter more out of affection than need. The four go into the living room and sit for a moment, no one knowing how to initiate any conversation. Alex sits next to Sarah, allowing her to relax into his shoulder and extends his arm around her.

"I'm so sorry you had to go through all this. I should have been there with you," says Bella.

"No, Mom. You didn't know. No one did. We all thought she'd get better. She was young," Sarah gasps for air, "and healthy. Even the doctors thought she would recover. But you never know with this shitty disease." Sarah leans into Alex's chest as she covers her eyes. Alex's other arm caresses her head.

"Are you hungry? Can I get you something to eat?" asks Dri.

When in doubt, offer food, thinks Dri.

"No. I'm exhausted. I think I'll just go to bed. But would you put this food in the fridge? Maybe I'll eat it tomorrow."

"Yeah, sure." Dri gets up, takes the sack, gives her sister a hug, then goes to the kitchen.

Sarah looks up at Alex, gives him a hug, then a kiss on the cheek. She pushes herself up, using her brother as a stabilizer. She hugs her mom, then goes downstairs and falls into bed.

This feels better, she thinks. *Here I can be myself, whatever shows up. Here I can mourn, at least for now. If I have to lose Marsha, at least I can be around my family who know and love me too.*

Two weeks later, Alex drives Sarah to the city to get the urn from the crematorium. Alex carries it with his sister leaning on his arm. They go to the hospital where Sarah thanks Dr. Sanchez and the staff for all their support. They pick up Marsha's clothes, phone, and a few photos in a bag along with a box of items from her locker. Again, Alex carries the box and bag with Sarah holding on to his arm. Later, much later, Sarah will decide what to do with the ashes. After serious heart healing and a significant decrease in the virus, Sarah will host a tribute for their friends in the city. Until then, solitary recuperation will take precedence.

Chapter 5
Exploring the Unsaid
Fall, 2020

L ate summer surges as the pandemic continues to keep people hunkered in their homes. This provides Dri time to read and catch up on some documentaries while she remains at her mom's place. She and Alex both find the time useful for more solitary undertakings and relish the opportunity during this secluded phase of their life.

One evening, yearning to learn more, she decides to watch the historical film about Baldwin, *I Am Not Your Negro*. She asks Alex to join her. But he has some work to finish for the winery. Bella declines as she leaves to visit Emma.

Dri enjoys seeing Baldwin interact with others. Yet, his insights provoke discomfort. She continues to be amazed at his insights and quips.

After the movie ends, another title pops up: *13th*. This documentary describes shifts after passage of the 13th Amendment to the US Constitution. Instead of slavery, Whites direct their intimidation through the Jim Crow movement, then segregation, and finally on criminalization of African Americans and the U.S. prison boom. She knows little about these issues in history and decides to watch this documentary too.

The knot in her stomach enlarges and the heaviness in her chest intensifies as the film continues. She notices her familiar desire to run, do something else, put on a comedy instead of such truth telling. She fears she can't do this, stay with this dark truth. Yet, Nika can't escape discrimination. Nika's parents and brother can't just run.

What kind of friend am I in reality if I can't stay with this too?

She remains in her seat and continues to watch through her discomfort.

Dri's immersion in her books and films gives a greater sense of the struggle people of color go through in this country and have for centuries. She thinks about all the Black people who have lost their lives, the historical lynchings, previous abuse and discrimination against Blacks, Native Americans, Irish, Chinese, Hispanics, and other races. With the clashes of the current presidential election well under way, Dri sees more clearly that this country has never rectified slavery or made peace with the issue of racial discrimination.

When Bella returns, Dri tells her what she has been watching and encourages her mom to see both documentaries. Bella promises that she will over the next few days. Then they can talk about the movies.

In their next conversation, Nika recommends another book written by Eddie Glaude. The title feels encouraging: *Begin Again.*

Dri gets excited and immediately orders it, in part because it's based on Baldwin's writings. She reads about the perpetuation of what Baldwin calls "the lie" — lies about race and White supremacy we tell ourselves. She again experiences disgust with the way history has been taught in her schools and this country. More directly, her discomfort lives in the neglect and ignorance of this history. The distress in her chest intensifies once again.

Dri realizes she lives in a country that has practiced discrimination for centuries with many groups.

We have murdered thousands of Native Americans in order to confiscate the land. We have enslaved African Americans to toil in the fields or homes while also essentially enslaving the Chinese to build railroads or work in sweatshops. We fought wars and killed Mexicans to take more of this land. In the end, we claim to be a good White Christian nation that has been blessed by God to be the best in the world. Such God followers committed a lot of murders.

She feels nausea in her stomach and expanding stress in her body. While she has not participated directly, she recognizes that she also has not worked to change it either.

Doing nothing to change the situation is collusion with the status quo, she remembers.

Dri knows many challenged slavery during the 19th Century. Yet, after the civil war and into the 1900s, she gets clearer that racism and discrimination became more disguised.

We continue to lie to ourselves and our children in order to compensate for the damage we have done and continue to do. We literally "Whitewash" the truth and attempt to bury the lie. We punish people for wanting to enter and be part of the success in this country. And we do it, as many have said, for financial gain on the backs of others, calling our prosperity God's blessing on us. Ignoring and denying what we do to others in the process.

As Dri continues to read Glaude's book, her repugnance increases. It's not just what he says, but that she feels so naive, having ignored what was happening in the rest of the country while growing up with White privilege in a White community. She never even knew about James Baldwin until Nika lent her a copy of his book. She never had to face these issues or the truth of what Whites have been doing, from Jim Crow to the lynchings, the Civil Rights Movement to the justice system and mass incarcerations. And now it is the killing of blacks by people in police uniforms. It was easy to believe the lie, that there has been equal justice under the law.

She allowed herself to remain ignorant, allied with White power. This privilege Glaude describes as "the most ferocious enemy justice can have."

But what strikes Dri to her core is his reference to Baldwin's belief that subjugation of others "disfigured the soul by closing off the ability to see oneself in others, and to see them in oneself."

She notices the pain, grief, and distress that rises in her body, horrified about how such historical acts may have disfigured her own soul. Yet, Glaude's comment feels like a critical perspective she understands, something she can work on within herself first, then with others.

A promising future may help heal the ancestral adversity.

One essential feature of the promise is honoring all life, White, Black, Hispanic, every color, nationality, and orientation. This is the core of what Baldwin and Glaude are talking about with a new America.

She's deeply touched with their final conclusion. "Salvation is not separation. It is the beginning of union with all that is or has been or will ever be. Love opens up the rusted lid of the heart."

This she understands. This she has experienced. And somehow, this she wants to share with others, opening of the heart's rusty lid.

Soon after she finishes Glaude's book, Bella shows her an opinion piece by Colbert King in the Washington Post on the 9/11 Commemoration. Bella now has a subscription to the Post so she can keep up on national affairs. Dri reads his final sentence. The words seep deeply into her heart.

Referencing George Wallace and Donald Trump, he says: "Purveyors of lies and a mean-spirited 'us-against-them' virus for which, sadly, there is no vaccine. I'll work to my last breath to find one."

His comments stun Dri. Especially in relation to Glaude and Baldwin's perspectives.

But how can we create a physical vaccine against these social and emotional constructs? How do we cure deeply embedded belief structures that White people have used to accumulate financial gain on the backs of others for centuries?

She reflects back to what Nika recently suggested and her own feelings for her dear friend.

Maybe the open heart is our vaccine. Maybe that is the loosening of lies and structures that we use for the benefit of ourselves and the detriment of others. How can I truly feel love for others without opening the rusted lid of my own heart?

Nika texts one more title that she thinks might be of interest to Dri, who immediately purchases the book and devours it as well. This book by Heather McGhee raises the question of "who is an American and what are we to one another." She focuses on the deep divide in the United States between one side who emphasizes the distrust of "others" and the traditional racial hierarchy versus another where "the proximity of so much difference forces us to admit our common humanity." Rather than the demographic changes becoming the unmaking of America, Heather argues such shifts become the fulfillment of this country, our salvation. "When a nation founded on a belief in racial hierarchy truly rejects that belief, then and only then will we have discovered a New World."

The final paragraph touches Dri deeply. Heather identifies the importance of living in solidarity across color, origin, and class while challenging the economic hierarchy that tends to maintain the question of human value. Rather than problematic, diversity could be our superpower. If it were, all people would prosper. "We much emerge from this crisis in our republic with a new birth of freedom, rooted in the knowledge that we are so much more when the 'We' in 'We the People' is not some of us, but all of us. We are greater than, and greater for, the sum of us."

But for this heart freedom to happen, it must be love without judgments and separation. This change must occur from an unconditional love. Not a conditional love where our rules and judgments separate us. That unconditional state is what I feel when I am deep in my heart meditation. It is a pure, unconditional love I feel. Total open acceptance. When that happens, when I can share myself with another, I find and see myself in another way. I get back so much more through awareness, insight, and what opens up inside me. I think that's the essential focus Baldwin and others must be intending. Opening the rusty lids of our unconditional love, our unconditional hearts. I need to share this point with Nika.

For Dri and Nika, as they continue their conversations over the phone, the vision of what calls them begins to emerge. It is about opening the unconditional heart to address the racial and economic hierarchies that continue to exist and divide people rather than welcoming cooperation and collaboration. Yet, the means escapes them. So many approaches have been attempted, particularly over the past seven decades. What could these two young women endeavor to create such a change?

Ten days after the presidential election, Bella shows Dri a Ruth Marcus opinion article published in the Post that day. Marcus references a talk given to the Federalist Society by Supreme Court Justice Alito, who is complaining about changes in society. In the opinion piece, Marcus describes the speech as a distillation of conservative victimhood. She asks the question why he is complaining when the Supreme Court now has six conservative judges and is winning. Dri also does not understand. She approaches her mother for a conversation.

"What does Justice Alito have to complain about?" asks Dri.

"Because defining marriage as a commitment only between a man and a woman discriminates against gays," replies Bella. "It's essentially no different than when Whites prevented interracial marriage, told Blacks to use the back door or a separate water fountain because they are not equal. Alito may have a conservative majority on the Supreme Court, but he lost the marriage decision and, more importantly, he is losing the fight in society. More than half the people believe in equal marriage for all people, and the numbers are increasing against him. He's upset that changing the traditional religious definition of marriage because of discrimination now is being labeled as bigotry. And he supports discrimination against gays by people who one own bakeries because it is justified as religious freedom, just as Whites did with Blacks for many years in stores. Most Whites just failed to use religion as their justification."

"But he mostly is getting his way," says Dri. "Do they not see it as bigotry?"

"The truth is, it was always bigotry. It is the epitome of bigotry. Currently, we are just saying it out loud. And once the idea has caught hold, it won't go back. You can't hide the truth once it reaches the light. Essentially, he's complaining that his conservative bigotry no longer will hold power. Things are changing, and he can't stop them. Even if judicial decisions are reversed temporarily, they won't remain that way when our society is changing so quickly. That is what helped give women the right to vote, equal voting rights for Blacks, and equal marriage for non-traditional people. Now it is happening for gays and trans people."

"But it takes so long for that to happen."

"Be patient, my dear. Life is changing faster than you can see in the moment. That is the importance of taking a historical perspective and listening to those are are versed in past events."

"But it feels so slow," complains Dri, face drawn, including the corners of her mouth.

"Let me try to put it into perspective for you. Not long after I was born, Reverend King and Bobby Kennedy were both assassinated. We were deep into the Vietnam War, there was no Internet, and we only had phones attached to a landline. And James Baldwin was still alive. Now we have phones with access to entire libraries in everyone's pocket or purse. The tragic killing of those two men seem like ancient history. You feel bad about not knowing a man Whites were trying to suppress and ignore when I was a baby."

"But people still resist. They still want to hold onto the past, like Donald Trump not wanting to let go of the presidency. Look at all the people who refuse to wear masks during a pandemic because they believe it's their right not to do so."

"Change is not even or easy. And people have the right to make themselves sick. What I believe we don't have a right to do is hurt others. Even intransigent governors are beginning to recognize the fact that we don't have the right to spread a disease to other people. Like we don't have the right to drive drunk and kill people without repercussions. I don't have the right to sell homes without disclosing significant information that would harm buyers. I don't have the right to burn down people's houses because they make me angry. There are all sorts of ways we don't have the right to harm others, including the wearing of a mask. It takes patience for some people to come around. Eventually, most people agree, we limit people's right to choose when it comes to hurting others. For some, it takes longer. But, overall, we are moving faster and faster."

"OK, I see your point. I know there's always a segment of the population that is slower to change. We studied that in social psych. I just forget. Maybe someday even Justice Alito will come to that awareness. Maybe he'll be able to see himself in others who experience the result of his bigotry. Maybe he'll open the rusted lid of his heart."

Two weeks after the election, Bella hands one more article to her daughter. This time, Robin Givhan wrote an opinion piece in the Washington Post about White power. In talking about President Trump's difficulty conceding the election, Givhan points out to readers that Trump as a prime example of such power.

"White male privilege is powerful. It overrides facts. It excuses horrendous behavior. It exalts the unqualified." Then, her final comment: "The only voices that can silence that privilege come from those who also have it."

Givhan's last line electrifies Dri. While she knows this at one level within her, Givhan's affirmation fully charges her commitment to be part of the change that is important to Nika, Naeem, Tiago, their families, and millions of Americans.

Dri is clearer than ever that Nika should not take this change on by herself. Whites need to step up and take responsibility for the lack of previous change and accountability for the perpetration of White power.

Again, she thinks to herself: *Doing nothing to change the situation is collusion with the status quo.*

From her conversations with two important people in her life, Dri is becoming more convinced Nika's idea about an open heart being key to change is correct.

But how? How do you get people to open their hearts in a racist, violent society? That's the age-old question. What's the essential answer?

There's much more to discuss with Nika and Bella.

***

By December, Alex creates a productive routine that expands his experience at the winery. He gets the opportunity to help David and Tanner with tours, learning about reaching out and connecting in some personal way with each individual present, something David does with aplomb and ease while Tanner often creates it with humor. Alex so appreciates the interest and support David shows him.

Alex's favorite time with David is late in the day, when work is completed, and he will sit with his boss under the enormous Valley Oak, located across a small section of the vineyard from the winery. They sit at a table in the warm late sunlight of December. Their visits may include a sip of wine from a leftover bottle. David often shares a story or advice to help this young intern. He checks in with Alex, asking how he's doing, what he's learning, how his experience might include other opportunities to grow. With each connection, Alex encounters a genuine interest and concern from David, something he observes David doing with others as well. He savors such interactions, lapping up every particle of it.

This is something he wishes he had experienced from his own father. But such encounters occurred infrequently in his early life. His drought of caring connection intensifies the current interactions. David also provides a great model of sincere connection with others.

Alex also enjoys Tanner, the award winning Director of Hospitality. He models enthusiasm and humor in his wine tasting tours. Alex appreciates the opportunity to exercise his own joyful and humorous spirit. Between the two of them, plenty of delight passes to the visitors, especially with a little wine lubricant. Alex sees in a different way how important such connections are in this business where relationships form an essential foundation.

As work in the vineyards slows after harvest, Alex learns about organization from Laura, David's daughter, Proprietor, and General Manager. She shows him how attention to details plays a significant role in keeping track of finances and minimizing costs without reducing a commitment to quality. Laura also models grace for Alex as she suggests a change in procedure or expenses, then listens to feedback. She clearly has honed this skill working with her father, while also holding her strength when she believes a change is important. It is especially enjoyable to watch her convince her father, even though he's open to suggestions, as are all who work on this team. But it also takes a strong rationale, which Laura is quite capable of rendering.

From Candice, the Director of Consumer Relations, Alex gains an essential understanding of staying connected to valuable clients and keeping them happy. This relationship with clients has been critical during the pandemic with so few shops and tasting rooms remaining open. Such a connection also relates to the many distributors across the country that Sean, Director of National Sales, facilitates. These two key people work to enhance direct client sales. Sean also encourages restaurants and wine shops to purchase David Arthur wines. Relationships, connections, communications. These essential elements sustain a thriving wine business.

Alex seizes the opportunity to function as an apprentice with Nile, the meticulous and talented Winemaker and Viticulturist. He especially appreciates experiencing the process of blind tastings. For each Cabernet Franc sampling, Nile puts together four blends with different proportions of Cab Franc, Cab Sauvignon, Merlot, and Petit Verdot. David, Nile, Sean, and Alex taste and note the aroma and palate sense in these blends, then identify the one they like best. The tasters search for the best proportional fusion they think will develop into a prime vintage. Alex's creative juices run as he learns how different varietals merge to create the best nose and palate for the maturing wine. He gets to practice the exacting blend preparation while assisting Nile as they put together the blind tastings for the Bordeaux style of David's new Proprietary Red. This combination of two contrasting worlds, the synthesis of science and art, is what originally stimulated Alex's interest in wine making. He loves the coalescence of facts with creativity, concocting something unique in an aged tradition.

As Alex participates in this professional and fun loving team, he even enjoys caring for vegetables in the garden and getting tips about composting. He jumps at the chance whenever a new project provides another learning experience. His oenophilia proliferates, as does his confidence in how to nurture an organic vineyard, how to process the fruit, and how one goes about creating an appealing "Grand Cru" vintage. His conversations enrich his learning from the experienced and professional winery and vineyard staff. The interactions and questions also push him to improve his Spanish.

On a few occasions, he brings a favorite wine home to share with his family. Thus far, Le Boucher, the Cab Franc blend, has become his preference. While the wine's palate is exquisite, there also is a sentimental aspect. He knows this wine David dedicated to his father, from whom he inherited this prime real estate.

Alex attempts to find a full-time position at another valley winery as his internship nears closure. Fortunately, tasting rooms are open when following pandemic guidelines, and many wineries flourish compared to other service industries during the economic downturn. Wine clubs and online sales keep many of these businesses in the black when other hospitality establishments, especially restaurants, struggle or close. But challenges abound as the pandemic continues during Alex's attempt to land a new position.

Alex hopes the change in a new administration and promising vaccines will finally eradicate the pandemic and breathe new life into the economy. The expertise president elect Joe Biden and vice-president elect Kamala Harris bring to a new administration helps. But even with the Democrats holding the House and taking over the Senate, Alex knows enough about economics to understand any positive changes will take time to filter down to smaller businesses.

Early in April, Alex receives a call from Oenophilia, a well established winery in the Yountville area. Omar, one of the owners, calls around to local establishments for referrals. He knows David, who gives Alex a strong recommendation. The owners invite Alex for an interview, then offer him a position as an assistant winegrower, a concept introduced in Napa by André Tchelistcheff to suggest that making wine begins with all the efforts and care in the vineyard. After the prospective employee catches his breath, he is able to audibly say yes, both to the position and to starting next week.

Alex informs David of his acceptance of the new position, bringing to completion his 10 month internship. He congratulates Alex, then gathers the staff to celebrate his new opportunity. David opens a bottle of the 2017 Sangiovese, which all agree is tasting superbly.

"A toast to Alex in his new position. It's been great to have you here with us, and we wish you the best in your new position," says David as all hold up their stemware with a token pour. "You've learned a lot about vineyards and wine making because you take opportunities seriously. I'm sure you'll continue to do very well."

"And thanks for your support and help," adds Laura. "You've been a great contribution. I'm sure you'll have a great Napa Valley career."

Other staff express their gratitude for his contributions and friendship while there. All wish him the best as they enjoy a sip of fine wine. Yet, in Napa, Alex already knows you don't need extensive excuses to celebrate with a fine bottle of vino.

That evening, Bella breaks out another delicious bottle and Dri puts out some snacks while Emma and Phil come over for the celebration. Sarah, back living in San Francisco, drives up to join in the festivities and to hang out for a long weekend. Sarah enjoys her family's company and wants to celebrate Alex's success. Besides, for these wine lovers, this new position may be another opportunity for their favorite "friends and family discount."

For Sarah, it has been a year of great change. After the death of Marsha and spending a month with family in Napa, she completes her summer internship and her final year of law school. In May of 2021, she graduates with her law degree, a long time desire at last completed. Yet there remains a hole in her heart that Marsha used to fill. While supportive of Alex's success, Sarah's deep loss provides a stark contrast to her brother's new beginnings.

Chapter 6

Graduation

Fall, 2024

H er two older siblings continue their career development and Nika, after completing law school, begins her work for a local congresswoman. Dri remains determined to complete her training to initiate her own profession. In the moment, she questions her ability to help the clients sitting in front of her solve their disagreements. She notices her determination conflicts with her doubts.

An unusual stuck feeling arises in Dri's chest. Her muscles constrict. Her breathing becomes shallow, even stopping for moments at a time. She looks at the couple sitting on the beige couch opposite her, not sure what to ask or how to proceed. Her eyes shift to a Lilly print by Georgia O'Keefe and a paper narrative piece from the Becoming Visible collection created by her favorite local artist, Carolyn Ellis. Both pieces hang on the wall to the right of her clients. These artifacts encourage Dri to find her own narrative voice and become visible herself. Yet, in this moment, she remains unsure how to materialize her desires.

Dri recognizes the typical corner Cynthia and Dave have dug themselves into again, where both previously reported a sense of hopelessness. Dri relaxes her eyes to look at the energetic field of each. Dave's energy moves out to a dark point nearly touching Cynthia's field, which has pulled back from Dave's. Finally, after a pregnant pause, Dri decides to simply point out the obvious, hoping it will help her move matters ahead in a useful direction.

"Isn't this the same way you typically get stuck? Each in your own defensive position?"

"Yeah, that's pretty much it," responds Dave, a scowl on his face. "Stuck and angry."

His jaw muscles tighten as he says this. Dri pays close attention. She read that when these muscles tighten, it can be an indication of a rigid position and possibly judgments of others. She doesn't assume this is true, but she finds a correlation between them.

"Are you angry, too, Cynthia, or are you more inclined to run away?" asks Dri.

"I'm pissed off too. But I want to go hide, get away from it all. This is when I get more focused on my work, a distraction from the conflict, I guess."

Dri notices that Cynthia's jaw tightens as well, her muscles bulging out as she clamps her mouth shut.

Only the ficus plant in the corner looks to Dri like it may be breathing easily.

"What do you do, Dave, when she gets more focused on her work? What's your typical reaction?"

"Don't know if I have a typical one. Sometimes I want to get in her face, get her attention to stay with the discussion. Sometimes I just go about my own work."

"Are you angry because Cynthia won't continue arguing or because she won't go along with what you want?"

"No, because she won't stay with it." Dave pauses, looks intently at Dri, then continues. "Well, probably some of the other, too. It's hard for me to let go when I'm sure I'm right." His jaw muscles appear to relax slightly with his last comment, and his breathing deepens.

"Yeah, being convinced about the right solution is a tricky place to stand," responds Dri. "How about you, Cynthia? Do you get stuck in that place too?"

"Probably. But more often I just don't want to feel wrong again. I hate it when the only way to agree is to be wrong and concede." Her jaw opens faintly, with an apparent loosening of the muscle. Dri watches the two of them, then scans their fields again for any changes based on their recent comments. She notices Cynthia's energy solidifying, becoming more opaque, near Dave's field.

"Are there any other options? Does someone have to be right or wrong to come to an agreement?"

Cynthia and Dave look at each other. A softening emerges in Dave's eyes, and he takes a big breath, letting it out slowly. "It didn't use to be this way. We used to be pretty good problem solvers."

"When was that, Dave?" asks Dri.

"Before the kids got bigger."

Cynthia looks at Dave again, with a hint of a smile. "When we cared more about each other than being right."

"How long ago was that, would you guess?"

Dave continues to look at Cynthia, then turns to Dri. "Probably the last eight to ten out of our fifteen years together. When we increasingly disagreed about how to raise the children. Would you agree, Cynthia?" Dave asks as he turns again to his wife, a lightness in his face.

"Yeah, around that time, or at least when our oldest started elementary school."

"So you've been honing this pattern for some time now. Happy with it, or would you like a change?"

"Change it," the couple says in unison as they look at Dri, then turn towards each other. "This is a ridiculous situation we've created," responds Cynthia.

As Dri's chest muscles relax and her breathing deepens, she explores some alternative ways they might begin to shift. The couple agrees to express gratitude for each other before discussing a disagreement. They commit to listen carefully and hear what each other says, asking questions if there's something either doesn't understand. When both have shared their views, Cynthia and Dave commit to exploring at least three alternatives before working toward a solution. Dri guides them through an exercise to practice this new approach.

"Remember something we've talked about before. Labeling the other person as wrong is a judgment that separates you further." says Dri. "The more you separate from each other, the greater the difficulty you'll have making an agreement."

After that, Dri sets up a time to see the couple again. They then say goodbye.

Dri walks the couple out of the therapy room and wishes them well with their practice. She ducks into the observation booth to turn off the video, then goes to the student office to make notes for discussion with her supervisor.

As she completes her notes, she reflects on the session and how much her work with Doc impacts her.

When she feels stuck, she'll ask herself, *what might Doc do in this situation? How can I see it differently so I don't get stuck?*

Sometimes it even feels like he makes a suggestion if she listens carefully.

Is it Doc talking to me? Is it inspiration? I don't know. But I know I love tuning into that source of intuition. And when I do, something usually shows up. I still hear Doc telling me how judgments separate people. How true! How true!

Through her undergraduate studies at Davis, Dri became fascinated by many of the topics included in her psychology major. Her discussions and explorations with Doc covered practical aspects of human behavior and interactions. In contrast, her undergraduate courses included conceptual and theoretical views of how people develop. She loved learning about perceptions and critical environments, social interactions, patterns, and people's ability to categorize and recall these experiences. Yet, Dri finds it a challenge to integrate those theories with some of the practical questions that arise during her therapy practicums. She also tries to assimilate ideas she learned from her counseling sessions with Doc.

Dri uses Doc as a nickname for the man who was so influential in her adolescent life. He helped Dri not only with her binge/purge challenge, but he also expanded her basic sense of self. Doc identified the lie she told herself of not being lovable. Later, he challenged her to experience the love that was at her core. They worked together for less than a year. Dri resisted the first couple of sessions. With more time, she absorbed his ideas and suggestions like water nourishing a desert plant. And their intense interactions stimulated her interest in studying psychology.

After college graduation, Dri decided to pursue a master's degree in Counseling Psychology, with a focus in marriage and family therapy at John F. Kennedy University, a strong program and the nearest one to Napa. Her decision pleases her, as she likes working with clients, then discussing her progress and reviewing videos of sessions with her supervisors.

Now, after finishing her classes, she jumps into her supervised training at the clinic. Completing her hours will take about a year if she stays with her intense plan. Then she will move on to her internship, which she hopes to do closer to Napa. All her required hours will take another three years before she can sit for her state MFT license exam and work on her own.

In order to afford her graduate program, she continues to serve as a transaction coordinator for her mother's real estate work. She likes living with Bella right now. Yet she worries about how long she'll want to remain living with a parent. But she also faces the bleak alternative of lacking the finances to live on her own.

Some days, she believes it will take all three years to have the confidence she needs to do this work independent of her supervisors. On random days, her anxiety grows, like an invasive insecurity weed taking over her garden of confidence. One day, she waters the plants, the next day a sudden shower waters the weeds. Dri can control her watering, but she still cannot control the emotional rain of doubt.

Yet, an essential planting in her garden are the skills she incorporated from the work with Doc. She has increased her meditation, finding it settles the anxiety, on a few occasions even removing the roots of her uneasiness, one at a time. While some shoots keep returning, each long slow inhale breathes water on the plants of strength and conviction. When she adds the heart opening exercise, her skills feel nurtured and her courage increases. When the reconnection with her core takes place, she regains her self-trust and more presence in her being. This is the place where she desires to settle and work, when she feels most inspired and able to approach issues without much fear or ego.

If she only could remain in this loving seat in her garden, experiencing and interacting with the world from that place. This is her ongoing work. This is her heart's desire, shifting from the lie she told herself as an adolescent, that she was unlovable. Her greatest fear. Her biggest lie. It has taken years to understand Doc's vision of her, learning to trust that what she experienced then in fact was a lie she told herself. And it remains a challenge to hold onto that view as a constant companion. She keeps forgetting, and then she remembers. As Doc always said. It is not the forgetting that is critical, but coming back to remember this truth.

Feeling like her confidence garden once again has been weeded and watered, Dri checks her phone for messages. There is one from Tiago, left recently. As she listens, she notices the flutter in her chest. He is coming up to Napa on Friday to talk with Alex. He wonders if she would like to go out to dinner that evening about 6:30 pm. While her face may not show it, there is an inner smile from ear to ear. She hesitates only to catch her breath, then hits the Call Back button.

"Yeah, sure. I'd love to go to dinner on Friday. Do you have a place in mind?"

"No, not really. You want to pick? Just let me know, and I'll make some reservations."

"Reservations are a wise idea. Restaurants often get full on Friday evenings. How about the Norman Rose Tavern on 1st Street? The food is delicious, and it's casual too."

"Great. Reservations for 7:00, pick you up at 6:30?"

"Yeah, perfect. See you then. Thanks!"

With sessions finished and notes complete, Dri goes to her car and heads back to Napa. It is late enough that the 680 traffic is thinning out, and it should be an easy drive home. She'll stop at Costco in Fairfield on the way, picking up some items Bella wants as well as a case of new tennis balls and her favorite shampoo.

Given the familiarity of this route, Dri slips into reminiscing about her time spent with Tiago in high school. He still went by Santiago then. It was while he was playing baseball at UC Berkeley that he picked up his nickname, one Dri actually prefers.

In fact, with both having different names, maybe it's like two different people connecting for the first time. Yes, there is some history, some past. But they didn't go out much, given that he was a year older and left Iowa not long after Alex. And while she was disappointed at the time that Tiago was clear he did not want a romantic relationship, Dri is grateful now they made such an agreement. It allowed her to get to know him while also exploring relationships in college to gain clarity of what type of partner she wanted.

She thought about women, a choice Sarah seemed clear about from the start. She certainly adores Tanika, loves Sarah deeply, and even felt a little attraction to another senior her last year of college. But she certainly does not feel drawn to women like Sarah has been, as a primary sexual attraction. She also has not found a boy that has made her heart flutter like Tiago, even before she found out he was Doc's grandson, or Gpa.

I love his black hair, his year around sun baked skin, and those eyes! That smile. OK, his 6-pack and strong arms kind of add something delicious to the mix. But mostly, it's the feeling in my heart. That flutter. What can I say? He's totally dope! Huh, I wonder what he wants to talk to Alex about? Just catching up?

Dri realizes she suddenly is at her exit. She pulls off, gets the needed items from the store, and luckily is out of there relatively quickly. She is back in her car, pointed towards home to have something easy for dinner and maybe a glass of delectable wine with her mom.

The next three days are busy with real estate paperwork, emails, and more reading on couple's counseling. She also found a new book on energetic auras she wants to read now that she increasingly is able to see people's fields. She began with feeling what was happening, and it took some time to trust that. She is happy she now also can visualize the field and watch how it responds to her conversation with clients. Before she knows it, she needs to get ready to go to dinner with Tiago, partly to satisfy her curiosity about why he was coming up to see Alex too.

Promptly at 6:30, the doorbell rings. Dri no longer worries about when she goes to the door. That is one old habit and dating game she quit playing. She opens the door and gives her friend a hug as Tiago gives her one of those endearing smiles.

Bella comes to the door to say hello. The three chat briefly. Then Tiago and Dri get into the car and drive to the restaurant downtown. He finds a place to park not far from the tavern.

"How was your visit with Alex? I was surprised you were coming up to see him."

"It was helpful. That's part of what I wanted to talk with you about, too," responds Tiago.

"Oh yeah? What's up?"

The two arrive at the restaurant, Tiago opens the door and Dri asks at the counter about reservations for Garcia. The young hostess shows them to their table, where they get settled.

Tiago pushes the menu aside and looks at Dri with another enticing smile.

"I hear you're not seeing anyone steady these days. Is that accurate?"

Dri looks at this young man's lovely face and laughs.

"You drove up to ask Alex that? You could have just called and asked me, saving you a trip from Albany."

While Dri has a smile on her face and a laugh in her voice, there also is an increased thumping in her heart.

"Oh no. That was just a side conversation. I came up to ask Alex if he might be interested in helping me coach a baseball team at a school here in Napa. He said he would consider it and check on the possibility with his winery boss."

The smile slipped from Dri's mouth as the muscles increased their focus in her eyes, looking deeper into Tiago's.

"You're going to coach a team here in Napa from Albany?" asks Dri, rather astonished.

"Oh no. I'm not that crazy, not yet anyway. There's a counseling job opening at one of the high schools here in town that also includes a baseball coaching piece. I've had an interview for the counseling position. But I have another coming up for the coaching position. I'm trying to get things lined up for that one, hoping it all goes well. I intend to move here."

"Wow, that's a surprise. But what does that have to do with me?" asks Dri, hoping for the correct response this time around.

"Well, the last time we had a conversation about dating, I said I only wanted to be friends, my last year in high school. You remember?"

"Yeah, I vaguely remember that," responds Dri with a smirk on her face.

"Well, I'm wondering if you would consider dating me now, with no 'friendship' constraints this time?"

Tiago's face appears serious, with no hint of humor.

Dri looks at his energy field, which seems to be rather open. His heart chakra seems expansive with an even flow to it. Then she suddenly gets anxious, wondering if Tiago can see energy and doing a similar observation of her field. She relaxes and smiles, with nothing to hide in her response.

"Yeah, I'd be open to dating. In fact, I'd like that very much."

Dri's heart expands further, her breathing becomes easier, and she notices her energy has expanded to her entire body.

This feels enchanting. This feels right. Finally.

"Great," responds Tiago. "Then I hope this is the first of many."

The two talk more about what's happening in their lives, the possible counseling job, and excitement about coaching a high school baseball team. Tiago likes the possibility of sharing the experience with Alex, who he has always admired. Yet somewhere in Dri's mind, she believes that her memory of tonight's conversation probably will end at *Finally.*

Chapter 7

Ceremonies

July, 2026

Tanika and Dri again gather at Bella's home on Sunday to finalize preparations for the wedding tomorrow. Nika drops onto a chair, her left leg quivers after her drive from the city - as people in the Bay Area refer to San Francisco.

"What's going on, Nika? Your leg's jiggling. And you don't usually do that."

"We got pulled over again last night for no apparent reason," says Nika, her voice breaking. She takes a breath, letting the air out slowly. "I think the drive today re-stimulated my reaction to it." She pauses for another breath. "Even now, it's difficult to talk about."

"Damn, girl, what happened to you?" asks Dri, her eyebrows narrowing, deepening the lines on her forehead.

"You've met my boyfriend, Naeem. You know how pleasant and gentle he is. Hell, he's an artist for God's sakes. Anyway, he and I were in his car in San Jose with our friends, Beth and Sam, in the back. Some fuckin' cop pulled us over. Naeem wasn't doing anything wrong. But he rolled down his window, turned off the car, put the keys on the dashboard and his hands on the wheel, as he has every time he gets pulled over. The cop came up to the car with his hand on his gun, and I started videotaping, although I felt more like throwing up. He demanded Naeem's license and registration." Again, Nika pauses for a breath. "He gave them to the cop and asked what the problem was. The cop said he'd ask the fuckin' questions and pulled his gun, pointing it at Naeem. Then the cop shouted at him to get out of the car. He asked what was wrong and if all four of us should get out?

The cop looked in the back and saw Beth and Sam. They're White. He apparently hadn't noticed them before, or at least the color of their skin. Slowly, he put away his gun and seemed to change his mind. He said he realized we weren't the suspects they were looking for, handed him his papers and said we could go."

"My God, Nika! How many times has this happened to you in the past few years?"

"Well, only the second time for me. But this has happened five or six times at least to Naeem. Mostly years ago, before the extensive police reforms. Maybe because of his dreads and driving an expensive car. I can't fuckin' believe this still occurs in our cities!"

"Are you going to report it again?"

"Damn straight. Fortunately, Naeem got the officer's name from his badge. So, we'll file a complaint with the San Jose police department. What this cop doesn't know is who I work for," Nika says, glowering at the floor, repetitively circulating her fingers against her palm. "Jennifer, or Congresswoman Bradshaw for his sake, will be very interested in this when I get back to the office on Tuesday. We've seen improvements since the killings of Blacks and BLM protests years ago. But there are still a few creeps hanging on. Gratefully, police departments and members of congress are continuing to take this seriously."

"Great. Maybe finding a new job will be appropriate for that asshole," responds Dri emphatically. "I'm so sorry this happened again to you and Naeem."

"Thanks. I'm just exhausted as a Black woman trying to live in what for some is a White police state. It takes considerable vigilance to live in two worlds. I'm angry and fed up with our system that seems impossible to change completely. Do you have to be White to be safe in this country? To be successful?" Nika asks with disgust.

"Yeah, in many ways, still. And that's not acceptable. We've made significant changes. But I won't give up supporting your success, my friend. Or creating further modifications to our extensive racist system. We'll just keep working on ways to extend Civil Rights."

"But even as the Democrats try to initiate changes, there's still so much resistance and lethargy," responds Nika. "The Republican Party still obstructs, rules in fear, even as they flail, attempting to respond to a heavy-handed president and cabinet members."

"You're right. I don't know how to do this, but we have to keep at it. Maybe we can join forces with others, especially those approaching this from a different perspective."

"I'd like to. But I'm not sure who. I'm just sick and tired of this shit," replies Nika.

Dri watches her friend's body begin to settle, unsure whether she is completely discouraged or coming to a close with this conversation. Her leg quits quivering, and the scowl on her face begins to melt.

Dri asks, "You feel finished? Anything more?"

"No, not at the moment, I guess."

Nika takes another slow inhale and exhale as she sinks deeper into her favorite Egyptian blue chair. She looks around as she breathes, then notices Bella's favorite print, Monet's *Beach at Pourville*, across from her. Today, it looks very peaceful. Bella's living room has become the customary gathering place for this extended family, and it already provides a feeling of "home." Another breath allows her to feel into her body.

"OK to shift in the conversation?"

"Yeah, I'm exhausted with this shit."

Nika takes one more deep breath, exhaling slowly.

"So, I finished that book you loaned me," remarks Dri.

"Great. Which one?" chuckles Tanika faintly, as she takes in a breath and releases it. "I've been so busy at work and my own research, I forget what I left with you."

Dri understands such pressure, given her immersion into the extensive clinical hours in addition to her Somatic Experience training, a compliment to more traditional counseling.

"Menakem's book, *My Grandma's Hands*," replies Dri. She shares a smile. "It's fabulous. How did you know about it?"

"Oh yeah, that one. A friend at work told me about it. I decided to go through it. I liked it very much. I thought it would go nicely with your somatic training and its focus on trauma healing."

Nika now breathes regularly and slowly.

"It sure does. But I've been thinking a lot about Baldwin and Glaude's books we discussed a few years ago. James appears to be talking about the social and institutional structures of racism. Yet, at the end, he also gets into the transactional relationship between Blacks and Whites, how Whites need Blacks."

"Yeah, and Menakem identifies how that bond of trauma continues, keeping conflicting groups connected."

"It seems like Baldwin and Glaude didn't have the vocabulary or the trauma connection that Menakem describes in his book," remarks Dri.

"Yeah. It's not so much, maybe, that Whites and Blacks need each other, as Baldwin suggested. The trauma we both hold binds us together. And without healing that trauma, we'll never release the bond," suggests Nika.

"And your experience with that cop is what we Whites need to acknowledge. We need to see it for what it is and push for greater change, rather than allowing this to continue to happen in our name, a White and blue trauma response. With no mental space for alternatives or choice."

"Yeah. I like what the Minneapolis police chief suggested years ago. I can't remember his name. But he proposed we change 'police officer' to 'peace officer.' I think it's a small, yet significant change. And it seems to be taking hold in places," Nika suggests.

"But as congress and police departments continue to transform, we can heal the White, Black, and blue trauma. We can bring about greater congruence between diverse people. We can create space for alternative decisions rather than perpetuating emotional and traumatic responses."

"True," responds Nika. "But as Menakem points out, it isn't just space in our minds. It's important to create space in our bodies, where the trauma resides. Space by slowing ourselves down, settling our bodies. Space for paying attention to bodily sensations and experiences."

"Agreed," says Dri. "Love and trust are visceral responses, not just mental assessments. They have a connection to our lizard brain. To feel love and trust requires that we release our traumas and pay attention to our body responses."

"Yes. And how can we be sensitive to the feelings of others if we're disconnected from our own bodies?"

"Right. And how do we open our hearts or live from our heart's wisdom if we are not connected to our bodies. It's imperative to heal our trauma if we want to live a full and loving life. Even the mini traumas raised by fear and doubt, especially doubt about ourselves. Without knowing it at the time, I think some of my work with Doc helped me become more comfortable experiencing my body. And our work later too. When I open my heart and connect heart and body to my mind, my sensitivity to others increases dramatically. Is that true for you?"

"I hadn't thought about it just like that. But yeah, I think it is true," responds Nika.

"I love that Menakem suggests if we let go of what feels familiar in our body but may be harmful, slow down to soothe and release our pain, and choose integrity over fear, we create clean pain," remarks Dri. "When we respond from avoidance, blame, and denial, we maintain the dirty pain, which creates more wounded parts and increases the trauma. Clean pain is essential in returning to our heart. In fact, returning to and expanding my heart is essential to begin *living* from my heart."

"Oh, I think you're absolutely right. That's especially true when it comes to the issue of healing around race, which, in this country, is such a deep trauma."

"In this vein of releasing trauma through clean pain, I owe you an apology," says Dri, with a serious look on her face.

"Why in the world would you owe me an apology?" asks Nika.

"You asked me a couple of years ago whether I thought I needed to stand up for you after your attack at City Park. I said I didn't think so at the time. But the more I read about this and explore the question in my own body, the more I believe I responded from White trauma. My motives may have been caring at the time. But I also suspect that as a White girl, I felt some need to do this. At some level, I needed to take care of you. And I don't want to participate in that way any longer."

"Yeah? You think that's true?" asks Nika.

"I do. As a friend, you may need my help at times. But not just because you're a Black woman. What I see now is that I did the vigil *for* you, not *with* you. Not as equals. I want to create my own clean pain healing of trauma, speak the words that are difficult, yet need to be spoken. I want to stop perpetuating trauma and grow my capacity to stand with you, equally, lovingly."

Nika stands, pulls Dri up with one hand and wraps arms around her ally.

"I agree. I, too, want to heal trauma. I don't want it to be our bond. I want a friend and a clean heart connection. I also want to stand as an equal, neither of us diminishing ourselves for the other."

"Trauma? Stand as equals? What are my two girls talking about now?" inquires Bella as she enters and takes a seat on the couch. "Or is this a private conversation?"

"No, not at all, Mom," responds Nika.

The two young women return to their seats. Bella nurtures her own smile, big enough to reflect through her eyes.

"I love it when you call me that."

"Well, I practically live here when not at work in Oakland. And you treat me like one of your daughters."

"Glad you feel that way. Besides, knowing your mom as I do, it's a real compliment!"

"Besides, I don't think we have any secrets left," Nika says with a smile.

"I hope not," remarks Bella, laughing. "So what are you two discussing today? I thought we were going to finish wedding plans."

"Yeah, but we're waiting for Slowpoke Sarah to get here," laughs Dri. "Until then, I wanted to thank Nika for the book she left with me about trauma and racism."

"Oh, OK, another light fluffy conversation while you two wait. What's this book about?"

"It's a book written several ago now about racialized trauma and mending our hearts, says Dri. "It's a very insightful book about how we all carry racial trauma, Blacks and Whites, and how that's played out in our lives as well as carried on through generations. And the trauma sometimes gets shoved on others and amplifies their trauma when it's not healed."

"Yeah," adds Nika. "Looking back, I think that's what happened with our current president and his administration. His own family trauma, that his niece described in her book about him, increased the suffering of others he bullied and ridiculed. Or even worse, with the children and parents who were separated at the border or arrested and put into camps. He needed a scapegoat group to make himself look tough and strong. The saddest part is that I don't think he could even help himself. If you don't heal your trauma, you spew it onto others."

"It's an illustration of what Baldwin described with the transactional relationship between Blacks and Whites. A group can't feel superior unless they define another group as inferior." suggests Dri. "And we need to change it, even if some have difficulty taking responsibility."

"Yeah, I think so," adds Nika. "Defining a group as inferior perpetuates the dirty pain through avoidance, blame, and denial, as you mentioned earlier, Dri. It keeps us connected through trauma, even expanding it. Menakem cites research suggesting we pass along trauma through our DNA. But couldn't it also happen with our energetics, our own energy fields?"

"He says something about our energy, although not energy fields specifically. But yeah, I think so," adds Dri. "It extends more constricted energy to others, including children."

"OK, but is that important right now? We have to finalize some wedding decisions," suggests Bella with some hesitancy.

"But don't you see, Mom? This *is* about the wedding. It's about our children, and our own extended family too. It isn't just Blacks and Whites. It's about all people, including people of color, and how we play out such trauma. It's about how we conceive children and what we give them, both in terms of cultural beliefs as well as DNA or energetics. When trauma hasn't been healed in parents, they pass it along to children."

"Oh, wow. I didn't get that part. Who are you, my dear Audri? And what happened to my little girl that just wanted to play tennis and have fun with friends?" inquires Bella with a heartful smile in her eyes.

"That's Doc and Nika's fault, Mom! I take no responsibility. And you made me go see Doc and completely supported my friendship with Nika. So really, it's your own fault!" Dri says with a giggle.

"Alright then. I'll take all the credit!" chuckles Bella. "But seriously. It's a joy to see you two have these conversations. I'm proud of how you dig into this reading and care so much about all our healing, especially in terms of your children," adds Bella.

"Can two guys join the conversation, or is this a women's only gathering?" asks Alex as he and Tiago enter the living room. "We finished writing this side of the wedding vows and thought we'd see what you all were up to."

"Come on in, guys," responds Dri. "Happy to have you join the conversation."

"What's the conversation?" asks Alex. "What are you three lovely women discussing?"

"We're talking about how race trauma gets held in both Black and White bodies, even if we haven't experienced it directly. It gets passed on across generations and pushed onto others if we don't heal it," replies Dri. "It's based on that book I've been telling you about, Tiago."

"Do you seriously think we carry trauma, even if we haven't had negative experiences from it?" asks Alex. "I get Blacks feeling it, especially when many have gone through devastating experiences, like being attacked physically or threatened by cops. But Whites?"

"Yeah, I do, Alex," responds Dri. "It isn't just about when someone attacks us. When we threaten violence or attack others, we do something to ourselves when we perpetuate violence on other people. There's interesting research to suggest that people who impose abuse and violence also carry trauma in their bodies. Maybe like soldiers who come back from war with PTSD. Then that can get passed on to other people. And I don't want to do that. I don't want to play it out in my relationships with adults or pass it on to my children."

"OK, that makes some sense. But what if we have good relationships with others and care about them?" asks Alex.

"But you're also part of the White society, physically and energetically," chimes in Nika, her voice stronger than usual, quivering. "You've been imposing violence on different segments of your own race for centuries. Even before imposing it on other groups, like

Blacks and Native Americans. Ever felt fear when you approach a group of young Black males, even if you've never experienced any violence from them?"

"Well, yeah, sure. If I don't know them. Or I'm in an unsafe neighborhood," says Alex.

"Your reaction to them is the triggering of your trauma, even when you've never directly experienced it," says Nika. "If we don't heal it, we perpetuate the effects trauma produces."

"I think it's related to what my grandfather talked about in terms of judgment separating us and having an impact on both the person judging and the one being judged," adds Tiago.

Dri laughs. "I forget, sometimes, that your Gpa talked to someone besides me. I get so possessive of him."

"I know what you mean, Dri. I do too," responds Tiago. "But we talked extensively since I was young. And the problem with both judgment and trauma is that we distance ourselves from others. But we also constrict around it in our bodies and close off our hearts. Both then impact our relationships. That's the issue Dri and I have been discussing as she's been exploring these ideas. That's the part that worries us, possibly passing it to our children. How do we help our kids stay in their hearts if they contract from judgments and trauma?"

"OK, we can start," hollers Sarah as she opens the front door and steps into the entryway.

"Speaking of Sarah, it isn't just race where trauma takes place," says Bella, only semi acknowledging her oldest daughter's presence. "It seems like this can apply to the experience of many gays in our society, or transgender people. Don't we make up all sorts of judgments and microaggressions that impact them in a type of trauma?"

"Great point, Mom," adds Nika. "It's what Menakem refers to as the Great Othering, where we discriminate against those 'others' that we define not as good as us."

"Yet, I think race is one of the most severe and structurally institutionalized ways of discrimination," says Dri, "although gender could place a close second, especially for women of color, a double whammy."

"Sounds like I missed a great discussion. And I thought we were going to talk about cake and flowers," laughs Sarah.

"We were, 'till you ran into traffic. See what that caused?" laughs Nika.

Sarah leans in to give Bella a hug, then settles onto the couch next to her. "Well, I don't want to be a Debbie Downer. What's going on? What are you folks discussing today?"

"Actually, we were talking about how race trauma experienced by Whites and Blacks might be similar to trauma felt by women, gays, and others, both by those receiving and those perpetuating the judgments and abuse," says Bella.

"OK, I'm in. I can still feel the pain from the harsh judgments about Marsha and I being gay from her parents after she died," replies Sarah, wiping away a quickly appearing tear.

Bella caresses her arm, then allows it to remain in contact with her daughter.

"I'm sorry for your pain, Sarah," says Dri. "And for Nika and Tiago's hurts from life in a society where racial issues remain so prominent. It's as if a large segment of White straight men are so focused on maintaining their position of privilege and the standard of what humans should be like that they ignore the impact of their impositions on others. Let alone what it does to their own bodies. They disregard how physical constrictions from the perpetuation of violence and trauma impacts them, too. It closes their hearts to those excluded from the dominant group."

"I see what you mean," responds Bella. "It's like men are so competitive, wanting to keep their White advantage, they don't believe they could prosper any other way. It's as if they can't succeed if there were a level playing field for all. They've treated women like that for centuries."

"Well put, Mom," responds Dri. "Maybe Whites are too lazy to compete. Maybe we want it to come easy for us and hard for anyone else. Blacks, all people of color, really. Women, gays, transgendered. How open hearted and caring is that? How loving is that? How Christian is that?"

"Wow, Dri," remarks Nika. "I love the fire that's inside you right now. Love seeing that passion again. And as a Black woman, you get no argument from me."

"From my experience, I agree, too. I just don't talk about it much," says Tiago. "Especially outside my family. We certainly have felt it at times, although many people are very caring. But when push comes to shove, you feel the hostility, trauma probably, ooze out of some. Even when they speak nicely to you. But the question now is, what else do we do about it?"

"You all have opened my eyes further to what continues to happen in this county. It seems like this issue of supremacy impacts all our lives," adds Alex. "And you raise a key question for all of us, Tiago. How do we change it in ourselves and others? Guess I have some work to do."

"I don't want to end this discussion," interjects Bella. "I also know that we have some decisions to finalize before tomorrow. Now that Sarah's here, could we bookmark this conversation for later? It's very important. And we have some time deadlines to honor."

Nika looks around at each person in the room. She stands, holding out her hands.

"How about if we all stand in a circle for a moment."

Alex and Sarah appear unsure about her suggestion. Yet everyone gets up, taking the hand of the person on each side of them.

"Now look into the eyes of each loving person in this circle, allowing your hearts to open to that person as you see them. Send them a message of love, maybe even squeezing the hand on each side of you as you look into those beautiful eyes and the soul they reflect. We know we share concern for each other in this circle. And while we may not express ourselves perfectly all the time, underneath our words, there's love. Let's let this topic go for now, knowing we will return to it again and again, in many forms and ways, both around concern and change. But for now, know most of all, there is love and caring here. And with this, let's transition to the tasks of the wedding, which brings us all here in this moment."

The group members smile at each other, some kiss a held hand. Those present then turn their focus to tasks at hand. Dri, Nika, and Sarah go to Dri's room for some final planning of process and vows. Bella heads to the kitchen to make sure food is put away. Tiago and Alex leave for the winery, a change of clothes on their arm, to see if any help is needed to complete the arrangements.

Dri found it easy to access her attraction towards Tiago. Committing to a long term relationship turned out to be not so simple. She focused her attention on developing her private practice while Tiago stayed busy as a high school counselor and baseball coach. They would talk about their goals and desires. Dri emphasized her priority of including a mindfulness practice, wanting that to help her make conscious life choices. Yet, her parent's divorce and her father's distancing, especially focusing his attention on a new wife over a known daughter, haunts Dri in a way work won't deflect.

In a conversation with Gabriela, Alex's mother and Doc' daughter, Dri mentions her fear about commitment and emotional distance with her father. This older wise woman understood, feeling a disconnect in her own marriage at times, especially as her husband gets so focused on work or other projects. At the same time, Gabriels offers the possibility of intense inner growth, as she did with her father. Her comment becomes a gentle reminder of opportunities in contrast to devastations.

Dri's heart suggested early that Tiago cares deeply about love and creating profound connections. But her body's response to their first sexual experience vaulted her decision to create a sacred union. His tender touch, intimately tracking her responses, his presence, close attention to what she liked and wanted helped her relax. Her final orgasmic release provided an irrefutable confirmation to a long term relationship. Even with such a physical response, emotional doubts lingered.

When they later talked about that intimate experience, both described it as otherworldly. During the six months they lived together, the first experience was not always replicated. But their intimacy increased, and a consistent confirmation kept occurring. They took their time and maintained their presence when being sexual. After such intimacy, a hand caress, kisses all over the face, or simply spooning with his warm breath matching her heat soothed her heart. Finally, she decides to fall into what she experiences as the unsafe.

Now, the day arrives to publicly celebrate their nuptial rite.

Soph makes it to Napa from Seattle late Sunday to participate the next day, after plane problems created an extended delay in her flight. Tiago's older brother, Javier, arrives in town with their parents, Gabriela and Miguel, Sunday evening as well. Javier had an afternoon game with the Giants. But he received permission to miss Monday's practice for this special occasion, planned for such an inclusion.

Dri wakes grateful for a cloudless, sunshiny day. The couple invited families and an intimate group of friends to witness the afternoon ceremony at Oenophilia Winery in Yountville. The owners created an arbor of clematis, contributing a whiff between vanilla and almond. Ellie and Aubrie, winery employees who are assigned to assist, placed lace with wide white bows and tulle at the top and down each side of the structure. The vineyard rising just beyond where the ceremony takes place provides a lush backdrop. Folding chairs allow visitors to relax over the freshly cut grass. The splashes from a three tier water fountain provides some sense of tranquility. The scent of empty fermented oak barrels used at each end of the bar near the edge of the patio provides easy guest access to wine and other beverages. Barrels and the scant sound of the open wine bottles breathing compliment the setting.

Omar, part owner of the winery, a writer, and Bella's frequent companion the past three years, will perform the ceremony. Tiago and Dri enjoy his style, and all who know him approve. He can DJ for the dancing afterwards, an added benefit. Rick, Dri's father, and his wife, Susan, attend without much stress or conflict with Bella, an added gift for this occasion.

Nika adjusts Dri's dress when they hear a knock at the dressing room door. She crosses the room and opens it to see Tiago's mom smiling at her.

"Come in, Gabriela," offers Nika.

"I'm sure you have lots going on. I'll just be a minute."

Gabriela slowly opens an old, rosewood box with dark green lining inside, revealing a necklace and unleashing a sweet, fruity fragrance. She gently takes it out and extends it in Dri's direction.

"My dad's father made this Imperial Jadeite Jade pendant as a gift for his wife on their twentieth wedding anniversary. He etched the Cib, a symbol of his wife's capabilities, into this Guatemalan green stone, which also mirrored her eyes. Dad, or Doc, as you call him, asked me, just before he died, to give this to you. He said you were a Cib, like his mother; wise, intuitive, warrior strength, and sharing new ways of thinking. I tried several times. But I couldn't let it leave the family. Now, I guess it's an appropriate time for you to have it."

She blinks back a tear as she hands it to Dri.

"I. . . . . I don't know what to say," responds Dri, her voice quivering, her index finger skimming across the stone. "This is so beautiful. I'm touched Doc would want me to have this. Would you put it on me, please?"

"Oh, you don't need to wear it now. I just wanted you to have it on this special occasion."

"I want to wear it. To carry the energy of you, Doc, and your grandparents as I make my commitments today. As I say yes to your loving son. I want to feel your grandmother's strength."

Gabriela takes the necklace, unlatches the clasp, and closes it around Dri's neck. She leans in, wraps her arms around her new daughter. Her heart swells with pride and sadness. As she backs away, Dri takes both of her hands.

"Thank you!" is all Dri can say in this moment.

She and Gabriela look deeply into each other's eyes as Doc often did. Nika stands as witness to the impact Doc had on all their lives.

Finally, the special hour arrives. Omar stands under the arbor, looking over the group gathered under the shade of a grand Valley Oak. Tiago positions himself on Omar's left. He wears his father's traditional Mexican white waist length formal jacket, with gold buttons down each side. His two honor attendants, Javier and Alex, are at Tiago's left, in similar style black jackets and white shirts. Sarah, Nika, and Soph stand to the right of Omar in their sleeveless light blue knee length summer dresses, their eyes mirroring the sunlight.

All watch Dri as the music begins. She strolls down the aisle in her sleek white floor-length jeweled sleeveless dress, with lace top. She holds a bouquet of deep red roses mixed with white calla lilies, the jade necklace a stunning contrast to her dress. Rick's arm is through Dri's right, Bella holds on to her left. *Feels Like Home*, sung by Bonnie Raitt, plays in the background.

Dri approaches the group standing at the arbor. Rick and Bella release her arms and they take their seats. Tiago's parents are sitting on the other side of the aisle, beaming at their sons and Dri. The group forms a field of loving energy around this young couple. Tiago smiles with tears of joy in his eyes when he spots the jade necklace. He knew of his Gpa's request.

After the bouquet is passed to Nika, Dri and Tiago hold hands while Omar begins the ceremony. He welcomes the guests as witnesses to this magical union. He talks about love, commitment, and the shared bond that can impact their lives. How the bond impacts is up to them.

After Omar completes his remarks, he smiles at Dri. She then shares the following vows.

"I, Audri Giovanni, vow this day to always try giving you the best of me, even when I don't feel like it. To tell you my truth all the time, even when challenging for me or at times when you don't want to hear it. To tell you what I want. To show you my doubts and fears, and all those parts of me I have trouble loving. To keep my heart open and care about your heart. To honor and want what is best for you and what you want for you and for us. To welcome your tears and your anger, along with your love, and stand in my strength and love to hear it. To always laugh with you and enjoy the magic of this life. To listen to what you have to say, even if I don't agree with it. And to play with you, hoping to keep the child in me happy with the child in you. I make these commitments to you on this sacred day."

After she finishes, she looks into Tiago's eyes, sending love and excitement for the possibilities they want to create. The dark haired groom winks at Dri, then shares his vows.

"I, Santiago Garcia, vow this day to honor myself by speaking all my truth to you all of the time, even when uncomfortable for me. To honor myself and honor you while holding you as my equal companion on this journey. To love and respect you in all ways I can, spiritually, mentally, emotionally, physically. To apologize when I make a mistake, and I know I will at times, for I am not yet quite perfect," he says with another wink. "To express my own needs and insecurities without requiring you to take care of them. Tto honor who you are and what you want most in this relationship, supporting you getting that if at all possible. To express gratitude for who you are and the many lovely things you bring to this union. And to keep my heart and joy open to you in every way possible. These promises I make to you on this day of our union."

Following the vows, they place rings on each other's fingers. Omar makes a few final comments, then pronounces them married. Dri leans in and Tiago places both hands on her cheeks, followed by an extended kiss on her mouth. The audience applauds.

Tiago and Dri turn and walk down the aisle, followed by Javier and Sarah, then Nika and Alex. The final honor attendant, Soph, grabs Omar's right arm. Unexpectedly, Bella brings her arm through his left, smiling at both as they lead the audience to the patio behind the chairs.

Bella looks back at Rick, who frowns with scrunched down eyebrows. Not wanting to get caught up in his reaction, she turns again and looks straight ahead, a faint smile on her face. She feels gratitude that she now can ignore any upset from his quick temper. She has shared enough ceremonies with him already. He has Susan to walk with, so she has no sense of why he would react as he does. But then, he didn't always seem to need a strong reason. Besides, she does not want to miss walking down the aisle with this hot looking marriage officiant and DJ.

The dancing is popular, as guests respond with their bodies to the music Omar continues to play. People eat, laugh, and drink the wines. Emma and Phil join Bella on the dance floor, happy now to have easy access to Napa Valley family celebrations.

Late in the afternoon and after lots of dancing, Dri asks Tiago if it is time for them to leave. He agrees. Ceremonies and crowds exhaust him. They walk around, expressing gratitude to all for attending. Dri makes sure to thank Rick and Susan, who flew in from Iowa City.

Tiago hands Dri the keys. She wants to drive, another non-traditional option. She remains Audri Giovanni, a choice that helps her stay true to herself. She made the final decision to do so when Bella dropped Giovanni and reclaimed her family name of Morretti. Tiago happily supports her breaking unnecessary norms. He realizes benefits accrue to him as he looks at his own unquestioned rules and habits. He now encourages and participates in Dri's audacity to question mores and rethinking of rules that no longer serve their lives. Falling into the unsafe released another of those rules for Dri.

Chapter 8
Making Connections

July, 2026 (Continued)

A fter the newlywed couple leaves the celebration, Nika and Naeem relax at a table with their half-consumed piece of cake, two forks, and glasses of dessert wine. They enjoy taking a moment for a deep breath and observing others dancers or guests deep in conversation. Naeem relaxes next to his companion, grateful to live sufficiently close he could drive up this morning to participate in the festivities.

"May I join you two beautiful people," asks Soph with her hand on the back of a chair.

"Of course. Have a seat. We're just nibbling calories and watching the show," laughs Nika as she turns towards Soph while leaning back in her chair, one hand resting on Naeem's leg.

"Thanks. It's great to get to know you better, Naeem. I hear about you from Nika, but I enjoy getting a sense of people directly, too."

"I agree with you, Soph. How long are you in town?"

"I have to go back tomorrow. Happy I can relax a bit tonight. It's been an intense summer."

"What keeps you so busy?" asks Naeem.

"I'm working on a research project that I'll use for my dissertation. It's very interesting to me, but a hell of a lot of work."

"Congratulations. What's your doctorate in? Nika told me once, but I can't remember."

Soph smiles as she looks at Naeem's soft, wrinkle free skin. *Why couldn't I have such supple skin like that?* she asks herself.

"It's in global health metrics and implementation science."

"Very cool. Do you know what you want to do afterwards?" inquires Naeem.

"Still deciding. Like so many careers, it depends on what offers come in when I graduate. Since the coronavirus pandemic struck six years ago, many governments and organizations became concerned about health discrepancies among diverse populations. The interest got amplified with the disproportionate numbers of Black and Hispanic people who died from the virus in this country and others. I'd like to focus on challenges like that while also possibly getting some international experience. Maybe a position in Europe or Latin America."

"You still want to travel, eh?" asks Nika.

"Yeah, I do. It feels like the right thing for me, at least initially. And since my relationship with Trevor ended, it's a simpler decision. My parents would prefer me closer. But if I end up living overseas for a while, they'll come visit. So they win either way," laughs Soph.

"I'm sorry about Trevor. You still hurting a lot from that ending?" inquires Nika.

"I'm doing alright now. I thought we were getting along pretty well as we were. But he kept pushing to get married. I couldn't commit to more. I kept thinking the problem was my doctoral research and writing. But after the relationship ended, I realized it didn't feel like the kind of relationship where I could commit to marriage. I think all that work the three of us did after Doc's death made me pay closer attention to internal information. In the end, I couldn't ignore the subtle messages I kept getting. Trevor was fun, and the relationship was comfortable in lots of ways. But there was something about it that didn't sit right with me. It didn't feel right to make a deeper promise. It wasn't Dri and Tiago."

"I know. That damn couple sets a high bar for us all," chuckles Nika.

"It makes me anxious just listening to this," responds Naeem with an awkward chuckle.

Nika squeezes his leg as she turns to look at him directly.

"Sweetheart, we have a lot of that, too. Don't start getting into your doubting self. That will just amplify the fear and begin to separate us." She leans over and gives him a passionate kiss to focus his attention. "Stay right here with me, baby. Present. In your body. Anything less deteriorates the connection." She smiles as one hand lingers on his face.

"It feels like you two do have a similar connection. Makes me a bit jealous," responds Soph with a grin. "And I'm happy for you, today at least. That could change in a flash, of course, if that heart pain arises, and I sink into envy of you two. But on a more serious note, Dri briefly mentioned what happened to you in San Jose the other night. I'm so sorry to hear that. I understand it turned into quite a family conversation."

"Yeah, it did. I'm sorry Naeem couldn't be there for that. But, once he got here, I shared basically what we discussed."

"What's the book that got you two so excited? I don't think I know it."

"Here, I'll text you the reference so you don't have to remember it between sips of wine," laughs Nika.

She picks up her phone and sends a text of the title and author.

"You might like the book, too. It could relate to your health work. The topic's seriously up Dri's alley with her SE training, which deals with releasing trauma in general. But this would focus on healing racial issues. I think she'd be great at incorporating such work into her practice."

"Sounds interesting. Have you mentioned the idea to her?"

"In a roundabout way. And after our conversation, I'm more convinced including that aspect in her work would be powerful. But we all got focused elsewhere after ending our discussion. I'll call her later and suggest it again."

The three of them talk more about their lives, Nika's work for the congresswoman, Naeem's art, and their joy for this new couple.

As the afternoon sun begins to set, more people leave the celebration. Soph dons her white sweater as Nika wraps her royal blue shawl around her shoulders. The three of them join the remaining family members, assisting with a final cleanup of items, including Omar's sound system. Then they drive over to Bella's home. Emma and Phil agree to pick up some take-out dinner on their way.

The day comes to an end after eating a delightful dinner, enjoying additional wine, and engaging in delightful conversation at Bella's home.

Tuesday morning is focused on returning to work. It's an early start for Soph, Nika and Naeem. He agrees to drop Soph off at the Oakland airport, then Nika at her office in downtown Oakland on the way back to his nearby studio.

The next morning, Nika sits down with Congresswoman Bradshaw to recount the terror she and Naeem experienced when the San Jose policeman pulled his side arm on them the previous Saturday. Her boss takes notes, writes down the officer's name, and gets a copy of the recording. She sympathizes with their alarm and anger from the experience, reassuring Nika that she takes this seriously and supports them filing a complaint.

Nika becomes increasingly aware of the trauma's presence in her body as she chronicles the traumatic episode again. She senses some ease from the concern demonstrated by her boss. Still, she goes back to her office to explore Menakem's advice for soothing her body.

Nika sits in private, spends time breathing and relaxing, beginning a release of the trauma to allow an initial healing of her body, mind, heart, and spirit. It will take time, but she now understands how healing can happen. After some time, she turns to her work on the new legislation for her boss.

She decides to insert persuasive words at the beginning of the legislative work. She reaches for a file in her desk drawer, where she keeps inspiring speeches and words of wisdom. She pulls it out and opens it. There, on the top, is an opinion article containing the final words written by John Lewis, the congressman from Georgia and former civil rights worker. He wrote this piece shortly before his death in 2020 and asked to have it published on the day of his memorial.

Near the bottom of his article, her eyes alight on a key sentence. "When historians pick up their pens to write the story of the 21st century, let them say that it was your generation who laid down the heavy burdens of hate at last and that peace finally triumphed over violence, aggression and war."

Her eyes well up with tears. She knows from her undergraduate program what a hero he was. She remembers his memorial and the honors he received from so many, including three previous presidents, at the time of his death. He was, in many ways, one of the last civil rights leaders, another step in the closing of a movement.

His message, one she had forgotten, cuts to her heart, the depths of her spirit and soul.

I want to be a part of this solution, this generation. I want to take up the work so many like Douglas, Du Bois, King, Lewis, Parks, Baldwin, Evers, Malcolm, and many others began, changing this world, creating justice and peace for all.

Now, in this moment, her undergraduate degree in African and African American Studies, then law school, appears like a road directed at this work. Efforts not from the outside, but from the inside.

To speak and march is critical. To legislate is essential, she decides.

Nika reads the words again. Her exact steps are not yet clear, but her heart is unequivocal. This is her path. She does not know how or even why. She just knows the obvious. This is her road, her truth, too. She sits back in her chair, closes her eyes, and moves into a meditation, paying attention to what she feels in her body. Her heart rate increases, not from fear but from lucidity. She senses a burning in her abdomen, as if a light is shining the way. She experiences grounding, in her body and deeply within the earth. In this moment, she feels electrified. Her body calms and fills with energy, her mind clears, her heart opens, and her feet firmly planted in sacred transformational soil.

In this space, Nika realizes she wants to talk with Naeem about doing something different, less angry and confrontational in response to their experience.

But what? How could we shift away from a complaint and still speak our truth?

She wants to present something from strength, clarity, and caring. This can't keep happening. They came too close to another tragedy, another death of a black man and possibly a woman, too. And yet, complaints typically are confrontations, which often become a type of verbal aggression. What could they do differently? More from peace and yet clear, strong, potent?

Nika leans forward and puts her elbows on her desk, letting possibilities flash though her mind, seeking an alternative. Then, like a spark, the idea emerges from nowhere.

What if we registered a Notice of Discernment, rather than a Complaint with the department?

She remains unclear about the difference, but she has tonight, and tomorrow morning as they drive to San Jose, in which she can sort out the distinction. She clearly wants to approach this not as a confrontation with the police, but rather a clarity of judgment and prevention of potential harm to others. She will suggest further discussion, maybe even working with what Menakem calls the "Blue Trauma," that police experience. She wants to come from her heart, not her fear and anger. She intends to help create a change, not blame and condemn. At the same time, she wants to come from strength, clarity, non-violence, and peace. She wants to extend King and Lewis's work. And she wants to assist in clean healing, as Menakem advocates, creating less likelihood of passing on trauma.

Nika realizes she needs to shift her attention back to complete the legislative work, with this commitment nesting in the background, patiently awaiting further activation and development. Yet she wants her heart in the foreground as she writes.

She includes Lewis's ideas for the legislation, creating an inspiring framework that could appeal to congressional hearts as well as minds. The introduction to and the details of the bill are nearly complete. But she needs clarification of two points, and the congresswoman is at a speech the remainder of the day. She puts down her work and sits with another short meditation. She notices her body, which remains calm, her commitment clear.

Following the sitting, she begins to search online for a notice of discernment, curious if there is such a thing. She finds many different ways of constructing a public notice on fliers or billboards, to increase public awareness. But the only thing that comes up with police departments are complaints.

This may be part of the problem, the separation that creates an "us" and "them" mentality, she thinks.

She searches deeper but finds no suggestions for change other than complaints.

OK, maybe this could shift their perspective right from the beginning.

Nika begins to look through some law books for ideas of how she might approach this sharing of information in a cooperative manner for collaborative change.

After reviewing several books, Nika finds little to assist her. But there is some work, recently presented online, that was done with the Seattle, Portland and San Francisco police departments after the Black Lives Matter protests. A group of citizens in each city worked with police officers to identify important changes, training and awareness, both for the police and the public. Their focus was to raise awareness and a spirit of greater cooperation, with a focus on being community peace officers and including other professionals, such as social workers, mediators, and mental health workers becoming a key part of the total efforts.

This might be helpful. Maybe this could be part of our approach.

Nika begins to put together a list of ideas that could be central to her notice. She wants it to come across as strong and helpful, clear and caring. She then begins to translate the ideas from the list into a legal format that incorporates statements of support and change, focusing on how it can help the department and the community, coming together in a collaborative effort. Now, she feels better able to explain what she is thinking when she shares this approach to Naeem. If she can convince him to advocate for her approach and model a collaborative effort, they have a better chance of convincing the police administration to cooperate with them.

She picks up the legislative bill and reviews it once again. She feels satisfied with the direction emerging and extent of completion. There is little more she can do on it now.

Nika takes time once more for a short meditation, notices her heart still open, and takes a few slow breaths. Today, she leaves a little early and will come in as soon as she returns from San Jose tomorrow to complete this work on the new proposal. The bill is ahead of schedule, and she can focus on her other important task.

She gathers up her bag and walks toward the BART station and her next big challenge. This attorney will need to speak from her heart as much as her legally trained mind when she attempts to convince Naeem, her artistic love and community organizer, of this new approach.

The next day, Naeem and Nika drive to the San Jose police station. While Naeem is an artist, his background in working with community youth groups gave him experience in organizations. He understands the importance of getting the right person's attention. He called the department yesterday to set an appointment with a Captain Williams, who supervises officers on the street.

Nika agrees that talking to an officer in charge is better than trying to work their way up the chain of command. She understands how information gets distorted when passed along. She fears her notice would turn into a complaint no matter how they frame it. Naeem also talked with Nika about the possibility of using her connection to Congresswoman Bradshaw in securing an appointment. In the end, he said nothing. They decided to focus on the event to get the Captain's attention, not rely on Nika's relationship to power.

Upon arrival, Naeem and Nika go to the front desk, then wait a few minutes before Captain Williams comes to greet them. Nika is taken aback to see a tall, muscular, serious looking African American police officer step in front of them, extending his hand. Naeem and Nika stand and shake as they introduce themselves.

"Come into my office, please. And have a chair," says Captain Williams as the two guests follow him.

They take a seat in hard, wooden furniture, apparently selected so people don't get overly comfortable and stay too long. Nika begins.

"We appreciate you taking the time to meet with us. We want to talk through an incident that happened last Saturday. Based on our experience, Naeem and I would like to file a Notice of Discernment with you."

Nika reaches across the desk and hands him a copy of the notice describing their experience and concern with the serious potential for harm.

Captain Williams smiles as he accepts the sheet.

"I've had a lot of papers handed my way. But I must say, I've never been served with a Notice of Discernment. May I ask what the hell that is?" the Captain asks, as he clears his throat, choking down a chuckle.

The Captain's voice and smile reminds Nika of James Earl Jones, one of her favorite actors. He also carries himself like her father. Such connections induce a deep breath and release some of her stomach tension.

"We had an incident with one of your officers, which both scared and worried us. We felt the need to bring this to your attention. Not just for our sake, but out of concern for others who are stopped as well as the officers in your department who could bring about harmful consequences."

Any hint of a smile evaporates from the officer's face.

Nika and Naeem go on to tell him what happened, being clear they are here because they want to help with change, not just complain. Captain Williams appears to understand the distinction regarding a notice of discernment and seems to enter the conversation in a less defensive manner than they both anticipated. Following their description, they show him the video. They discuss their fears and those of their friends. The Captain agrees with their concerns while stating his need to hear the officer's explanation.

"Yes, of course you would want to talk with Officer McCarthy and hear his side of it," says Nika. "We just worry about how easy it is for people to be terrified in such situations. A fear response can rapidly lead to escalation, both with people who are stopped as well as with your officers. We want to increase awareness and discuss how we can de-escalate reactions. Our concern is how we can have less violence and aggression all around. And whatever we can do to support such change, we would be happy to assist."

Nika goes on to mention Menakem's work on the healing of blue trauma, which could be a valuable contribution.

"Thanks for your creativity and collaboration regarding this situation," replies Captain Williams. "Most people come in upset and angry, accusing rather than recommending another alternative. The video clearly identifies a serious issue to be addressed, and I agree with your concern. I also applaud your efforts to take a different approach. It's clear you two both care, and situations like this can't continue. I'll talk with our chief as soon as I can reach him. Please forward a copy of the video."

Captain hands Nika a card with a cell number on it.

"In the meantime, I would ask that you not share that video with anyone else until we can address the situation within the department. I assure you, we will do that."

The Captain agrees to send them a follow-up report within a month about changes they are proposing, as evidence of his commitment to continue modifying aspects of his department to prevent similar incidents in the future. He relates some of the changes they have made after the Black Lives Matter demonstrations across the country and the pressure to change police procedures and policies. He thanks Nika for the recommendation of Menakem's work, which is not familiar to him. He would like to do some reading, then possibly have another conversation about blue trauma with Nika. She agrees, and they stand to leave. As Captain Williams comes around his desk, Naeem takes the captain's hand with both of his and expresses his gratitude for his time and openness to their experience and concerns.

After they get in the car and begin their way back to Oakland, Nika turns to Naeem.

"Thanks, sweetheart, for your support in taking a different approach. I think it went better than expected, don't you?"

"Oh yes. Much better than I thought it would. And I'm glad I called for an appointment with Captain Williams, too." Naeem says, as he laughs a bit. "Still, I had no idea he was Black. Wonderful to see greater diversity continuing to happen within police departments."

"Yeah, I agree. Now we just keep encouraging it elsewhere."

Nika picks up his hand and kisses the back of it. "Love you, Babe! Glad we could do this together."

"Love you, too! And thanks for what you said yesterday about our relationship while we were with Soph. That felt reassuring!"

They chat more about their connection and gratitude for each other on the way back to their respective offices. For Nika, it is the first clear step on the path she intends to follow. Her commitment is to pay attention and recognize the next steps as they show up in her life.

A week later, Captain Williams calls Nika to talk more about Menakem's work. She gets the opportunity to talk about her own experience in healing trauma within her body. She suggests he call Menakem to talk about the possibility of him coming to do some training with their department.

Two weeks later, Nika and Naeem receive a letter from Captain Williams. He summarizes what they have done based on the evidence involved, starting with the dismissal of Officer McCarthy. This was McCarthy's third involvement in similar situations. They also found out the officer had connections to White Supremacist groups. The Captain described changes in the department that involve more racial sensitivity. He called Menakem and set up a training for the department, which he hopes will bring about not only greater awareness, but even healing in his officers. He goes on to thank Nika and Naeem for sharing their horrific experience as a way to increase awareness and suggest alternatives.

As Nika reads the letter to Naeem that evening, there is another peaceful feeling in her abdomen and heart for the path she is choosing. Naeem congratulates her for identifying and developing an alternative approach to the issue.

"Thanks to you for your contributions and support, too," adds Nika. "I feel like we did this cooperatively, as an approach from the two of us and how we addressed it with the police. This is what I meant on Monday when I told you that we have much of the same connection as Dri and Tiago. This is our way of playing out such a relationship."

Chapter 9
The Concert
Spring, 2028

The relationship between Naeem and Nika continues to develop while a major focus resides in his art and her congressional work. The deep satisfaction for both enhances their individual lives as well as their relationship. Naeem's community programs recently have expanded to increase interactions between local youth and peace officers sharing problem solving and life skills. An underlying intention involves enhanced understanding and respect for each other. With Nika's determined support, Congresswoman Bradshaw spearheaded legislation at the national level, based on work in California, to complete further police reforms. New approaches include additional interactions between police review and community boards that would allow for Notices of Discernment for any problematic interactions.

As Nika and Dri anticipate their own family development, environmental concerns also grow. Nika begins making connections with other congressional representatives from California. The group introduces legislation to finally eliminate single use plastic bags, replacing them with increasingly strong compostable materials. During this time, the Republican Party's influence increasingly declines from the MAGA and Christian Nationalists. Such changes allow the proposal to gain Senate approval and gets signed by the President. These changes enhance Nika's experience and confidence in the congressional process.

While Dri and Nika focus on family and social issues, Alex concentrates on his new winery position. Any attempt to describe the new Oenophilia red blend looked straightforward two days ago. After last night's argument with Erica, nothing comes easily. Alex's stomach continues to churn, his throat burns from the erupting words he threw at her. And she returned the favor. Back and forth, one hurt after another. The continued faint scent of a near-by vanilla candle at his home computer, similar to the one in Erica's apartment, reminds him even now of their harsh messages. Alex remains insure he could still call her his girlfriend after that heated interaction.

An ad pops up on the new touch screen computer, interrupting his feeble attempt on the wine description.

"The Concert of the Decade," it reads at the top. "Downtown Las Vegas Events Center, July 1st, 2028."

Typically, Alex finds such ads annoying. But today, this stupid banner intrigues him.

Maybe attending such an event together would bring the waring couple closer. Add some fun to balance their struggles. Besides, he's never been to Las Vegas. A phenomenal concert provides a great reason to visit.

Alex manages to get tickets for Erica and himself. The prospects of healing the wounded connection brighten.

But anticipatory plans don't always provide a promising omen for relationships. Two weeks after the purchase of tickets, this forever couple experience a demolishing struggle.

Following a series of 'apologies,' the two combatants manage an amicable resolution to the conflict. In the process, however, the relationship dissolves completely.

Alex's mood plummets even further after the separation. The connection apparently meant more than he realized. For someone who typically expresses upbeat and jovial behavior, this dampening of spirits takes him into unfamiliar and unnerving territory.

With the opening for a travel companion, Alex asks Dri to accompany him instead. She steps up with glee.

For a small surcharge, Alex changes names on his companion ticket, and Dri reimburses him for half the stay at the Golden Nugget, strolling distance to the event location. Alex's mood brightens somewhat, now attending with someone whose company he enjoys.

Dri discovers double joy. She could not endure the way Erica increasingly denigrated and ridiculed her brother. With her gone, Dri now gets to join Alex on another adventure. This change in relationship status becomes a win-win for her. The behavior of Erica also amplifies Dri's gratitude for her husband, Tiago, and the respectful relationship they've developed.

When the day arrives, their travel goes smoothly. They experience a taste of the sweltering atmosphere walking through the jetway as they depart their plane. The weight of their
carry-ons contributes perspiration to the mix. Past Security, Dri spies the shuttle desk for
the electric train transport to the Nugget.

Dri scours the landscape as they ride the train towards their hotel. The immensity of
solar panels and other collection devices amaze her, a sensible yet unknown aspect of this
desert landscape. She guesses the dramatic improvement of recyclable water and sodium
batteries she read about may have something to do with the large number of electric cars
she also notices along her way. The fact that they last much longer also helps her feel batter
about the change.

Luckily, they find a lull in the front desk crowd when they arrive at the hotel. Dri
suggests they leave bags in the room and the AC running while they cruise the Strip. Both
intend to make this maiden Vegas voyage a momentous weekend. Given the heat, they'll
spend most of their time inside vehicles or buildings. Neither are beguiled by gambling.
Still, they share excitement to explore some of the hotels and casinos, maybe even take a
gondola ride at the Venetian. Alex's suppressed emotions dull his typical responsiveness.
So Dri hails a cab, and they cruise south.

Distracted and somber behavior leaves a vacuum in the protective role Alex usually
plays for his younger sister. Dri will never forget his response to one of her sophomore
dates. A guy dared honk for her upon his arrival at their home. The threatening anger in
Alex's face as he walked out and expressed his outrage at the sophomore for disrespecting
his sister by such behavior told the essence of the story.

To Dri, he always felt like her guardian, partly due to her father's decreasing family
involvement. Given her years of college and continued maturation, Dri finds it easy this
time and sweet reciprocation to take on the mantle of watchful tenderness in Alex's current state. Neither discussed such a protective transfer. But that's often the way informal
arrangements become altered.

They heard of the buccaneer fight at Treasure Island and wish it still existed. But the
indoor gondola ride gives the appearance of visiting Venice. The volcano at the Mirage
proves less impressive than the descriptions. Wandering around shops at the Paris hotel
gives them a taste of the famed city. But the abundance of American tourist uniforms
of white shorts and black socked tennis shoes easily overwhelms any sign of authentic
Parisian ambiance. After two additional hotels, the glitter, facade, and opulence of the

lobbies, pathways, and upscale stores mires them in weariness and stifles any remaining pleasure.

The flashing lights, throbbing music, and seductive smells all demand attention while at the same time taxing their ears, eyes, and by now overly sensitized skin, especially for a young woman more intrigued with solitude and spacious conversation. This bombardment of the senses feels overwhelming to Dri.

Maybe if I were an advertiser or a narcissist, thinks Dri, *I'd be more comfortable with this kind of barrage. Like the husband of the last couple I saw in therapy.*

She grabs Alex's arm and turns him toward her.

"How would you feel about heading back to our cool, peaceful room for a *siesta?*"

"Oh, I'm with you, Sis. Let's go. Think I'm inundated already."

She finds another cab, and they return to their hotel. An afternoon snooze after getting up early to catch the recently developed electric shuttle to the Sacramento Airport seems like a great reboot before the concert. Besides, Dri doesn't experience her usual energy. But does experience some nausea.

Following a rest in the welcome air conditioning of their room, both slip into their colorful concert attire. Accustomed to evenings that cool off in Northern California, they take jackets and ride the elevator downstairs in search of a light dinner. Given the sweltering air that continues outside, they realize it is early for jackets. Besides the lovely scents coming from the nearby restaurant facilitates a decision to satisfy their hunger at a hotel eatery.

The establishment is crowded, given its proximity to the event. But they are able to get a table under what Dri describes as a delightful caricature of an Italian *ristorante* on the wall. The painting provides her a pleasurable sense of a restaurant within a restaurant. They chat, laugh, and enjoy their food, as Alex begins to resemble his joyful self.

With relaxation and sustenance, Alex and Dri delight at finding a cool mist being pumped onto the canopy covered plaza where a street used to exist and the event will be held. They walk for a bit, then show their tickets to enter the barricaded area. They both desire a comfortable place to stand before it overflows with people.

A swarm of humanity soon populates the entire quarter. They observe the diverse audience; young and old, crazy hats, colorful jackets and shirts, tight dresses and full skirts, which entertain them until the concert begins. A whiff of beer stimulates Alex's desire for a brew. With the band in the wings, he decides to wait for additional digestion before quenching his thirst.

The first band plays a set of blues and early hot jazz. As they sway to the music, Alex leans close to Dri's ear and asks if she remembers the time the family drove from Iowa City to attend the Bix Beiderbecke Festival in Davenport. She turns and nods with a smile. It was their introduction to New Orleans jazz, and they developed an appreciation of its style.

The second band plays a tribute to Woodstock, with a guitar player who could have been Jimi Hendrix reincarnated. Bella, their mother, is too young to have been conceived when her parents attended Woodstock. But Alex often teases her about loving the music of that era based on her conception at the festival.

This group pumps up the crowd, getting everyone moving to the vibrant beats. The dense audience makes dancing a challenge. But Alex points to a few off on the side who are able to move their whole bodies to the music.

As Dri claps and sways, she suddenly hears repeated *pzoot, pzoot, pzoot, pzoot, pzoot.* She looks around, then feels Alex, who stands behind her, slink to the ground. She turns to see if he has slipped on something and notices blood oozing from the side of his head as he lies motionless.

She immediately drops to check on him, hearing screams and noticing people now ducking for cover, as several more *pzoot, pzoot, pzoot, pzoot* ring out.

Dri pulls Alex's head and upper body into her arms, but feels no animation on his part. She realizes now what's happening, but she can't move.

Again, *pzoot, pzoot, pzoot.* Her adrenalin drives her to run, while her heart tells her not to leave her brother there alone. She hears loud *blam, blam, blam, blams,* deafening echoes across the plaza and the smell of gun powder filling the air. Two more *pzoot, pzoot,* followed by several *blam*s, and the firing ends.

The mob of people continue to scream and scatter, rushing for any shelter or safety they can find. Dri can only press her jacket against Alex's wound and caress his head in her lap. She notices a faint scent of lavender mixed with coconut from his morning shower. Tears flood down her face. She whispers his name. Her body instinctually rocks back and forth.

As the chaos begins to subside, an arm reaches down. Dri looks up into the face of a man wearing a dark blue uniform. With a bright light from the walkway shining behind the man's head, in the moment he appears angelic. The man puts his hand on Alex's neck, then he waves into the crowd and two other personnel begin to rush over, bringing a gurney with them.

"Hi, ma'am. I'm Luke." Then he turns to his partners. "He has a weak pulse. Let's get him out of here." He turns back to Dri. "Ma'am, do you know him?"

"Yes . . ." stuttered breaths and sobs intermingle. She swallows, and tries again. "He's . . . ," quick gasp, "my brother."

Dri continues to cradle Alex's bloody head as the two others kneel, putting gloved hands under his body to lift him onto the newly arrived gurney. The subtle stench of chlorine from the latex gloves makes her stomach churn.

The First Man asks for her brother's full name. Dri believes she tells him correctly. In her present state, nothing feels certain and names do not register. The First Man shares her brother's name with the other two, who begin to steal Alex's motionless body away from her. They lift him steadily and cautiously onto the waiting gurney.

Dri knows in her head that gloved protection is wise, yet in this moment it appears these hands eliminate any direct human contact. Seeing this brings on another wave of intense grief and anguish.

First Man continues with the inquiry.

"Ma'am, do you live here or are you visiting?"

Dri holds on to Alex's hand until his body is too far to reach. She slowly stands with First Man's assistance. He places his arms around her shoulders with enough strength to let her know Alex is better off going with the other two medics. As he is wheeled away, First Man continues to hold Dri's shoulders reassuringly.

"They will rush him to Sunrise Hospital. It's the closest emergency service. He'll be there quickly. Do you have local transportation?"

"No," is all Dri can manage. She feels cotton spreading in her mouth. Little else.

"We'll get you there, ma'am. They'll do everything they can. But time is of the essence. I'm sure you can understand that."

First Man is wrong. Dri cannot understand anything, especially how this could happen at some joyous event. Her head is too full of fog for any thought to penetrate her discombobulated brain. She can see Alex being rolled away. She can hear noise around her. And she can stand upright with First Man's help. That is the extent of her capabilities.

"Excuse me, ma'am. What is your name?" First Man asks.

Another breath to slow the tears.

"Audri. Audri, are you hurt at all?"

Dri turns her palms towards her face and now can see they are covered with blood. Her clothes have globs of blood where she had been holding her brother's head. She mentally scans her body, conducting a superficial internal check.

"No . . . . . I don't think so. . . . I think all this . . . . . is from my brother."

"OK, Audri, let's clean off your hands. We'll get you to the hospital to check on Alex."

Tears again begin flowing freely down her cheeks, just hearing this medical professional say Alex's name and thinking of him being rushed away from her.

First Man continues to steady her shoulders.

"Can you walk with my support, Audri?"

She takes several steps, relying on First Man's strength.

"Yes, I guess so. Thanks . . . for your help," says Dri between sobs.

She looks around now at the crowd, noticing other bodies being carried away and people crying, holding on to each other. She remembers the two of them were not alone here, as the stillness in her ears morphs into deafening sirens, some people shouting, others sobbing.

They approach an emergency vehicle and First Man grabs some wipes to clean Dri's hands and arms. Then he introduces her to a woman in a police uniform. All Dri hears is Officer. Names all seem foreign, disconnected from what is happening in the moment. Apparently Officer is taking Dri to the hospital.

The two women walk to the police car, drive, and park in the emergency zone. Officer gets out, opens the door, and supports Dri as they go into the emergency entrance.

"Audri, why don't you sit here, and I will see what I can find out about your brother. What is his full name?"

"Alex . . Giovanni,"

Officer goes over and talks with the nurse behind the desk for a few minutes, then goes inside the double doors. After a while, she emerges from the entryway with a woman in a white coat. Officer walks over and sits next to Dri while White Coat Woman kneels in front of her.

"Hi, Audri. I'm Dr. Gonzalez. Alex is your brother, correct?" White Coat Woman asks.

Dri attempts to move her head, believing it is going up and down.

"We began working on your brother as soon as he arrived. There's no easy way to tell you this. I am very sorry, Audri, but your brother didn't make it."

White Coat Woman puts her hand on Dri's knee.

"He took a single shot to his head. The medics did the best they could under the circumstances. But he died on the way over in the ambulance, and we couldn't revive him."

White Coat Woman goes on talking, giving her more information. But all Dri hears are random sounds. Words have no meaning to her. Nothing is registering in her brain. It feels fuzzy and crammed. No room for anything else. She notices physical sensations. Sadness and grief inundate her body.

"Audri . . . Audri," White Coat Woman says again.

Dri raises her head to look at the figure still squatting in front of her. "What? . . . Yes?"

"Are there other people we should notify? Your parents, maybe?"

Dri looks into the woman's eyes. Strangely, in that moment, she notices.

She has ocean blue eyes. Like Dad's. But less cold.

Then nothing. She tries to think of what to say.

"Um . . . I don't know . . . Ah . . . I guess . . . my mom?";

Dri finally can articulate enough words to inform White Coat Woman of her mother's name and telephone number. Then the fog rolls in again from her ocean of sorrow. White Coat Woman pats her knee, gets up, and walks away. Dri leans back, allowing her uncomfortable chair to provide some semblance of support. Standing and walking seem completely out of the question. She does manage to move her arm up to rest her head.

Currently, there appears to be little distinction in her brain between overwhelm and vacant. Then, slowly, waves of thought forms emerge within the fog.

How does a numb body move? she wonders. *How do I leave, go anywhere? What do I do? Should I call Mom? Dad? How do I tell them their only son is gone? How do I tell them Alex is dead? Is it my fault? If I hadn't agreed to come with him, would he still be alive? Why not me instead of him? How will Mom live without her favorite?*

Dri feels Officer's hand touch her arm and the waves subside.

"Audri, can I get you anything? Are you hungry or thirsty?" Officer looks at her for a moment, then continues. "At some point, I'm afraid, we'll need you to identify your brother's body. Will you be up to that?"

Oh God! I didn't think of that! I want to see him again. I can't see him like this!

Dri takes a deep breath.

"I don't think I can."

Tears roll again, and Officer hands her a tissue.

"I know it's very difficult. I'm happy to go with you, if you want. But as the only relative in town, it would be easier if you could do that. And it would be a quicker release of the body. Do you have a place to stay tonight? You could do it tomorrow."

"Yeah. We hav . . . . I have a room at the Nugget downtown. All our . . . . my stuff's there."

"OK, let me check with the doctor. Would you like a ride back to your hotel? You OK to stay there tonight?"

Officer looks at Dri, who again falls into an expanse of fog, unable to find words to express herself.

"Would you like anything to help you sleep tonight? I'm sure the doctor would give you something if you feel like you might need it. You've been through hell tonight! I can only imagine the horror of your experience," she says, tears now running down her own face, not quite clear how to attempt comfort with such tragedy.

Dri draws in a lung full of air as she separates herself from the gentle woman.

"Yes," she says, as she looks at Officer's face. Her eyes well up, stimulating wetness again in Dri's. "I would appreciate a ride back to the hotel and something for sleep. I'll try getting it together to identify his body . . . . . tomorrow."

She continues to look at Officer, words dissolving into alphabet soup, floating along without sense or meaning.

Officer stands, then walks through the double doors again. She returns in a few minutes, or instantaneously, Dri's not sure which, with White Coat Woman.

"I got a hold of your mother. She wants to talk with you when you have a chance, no matter what time tonight." She hands a prescription to Dri. "This should help you sleep. Here's my card too. It has my answering service number on it. They can reach me any time. So call if you feel unwell or have any problems."

White Coat Woman pauses for a moment, then continues.

"Audri, I'm so very sorry we couldn't save your brother." Again a pause for a deep breath. "Is there anything else I can do to help you this evening?"

"No, thank you, doctor." whispers Dri. She looks at White Coat Woman's eyes, so like her father's. But now they fill with moisture, something she seldom witnessed in her dad.

The woman squeezes Dri's hand, gets up and disappears once again behind the magical doors, beyond which people may or may not exist. Or maybe they move into another universe.

Dri takes her time to stand and Officer guides her towards the pharmacy, then back to the police car. When they arrive at the hotel, she parks in the emergency section, then walks Dri into the reception area. Officer walks up to the desk and whispers with the clerk for a few minutes, then comes back with another key.

"They comped you an extra room for tonight so you don't have to sleep in the original one. You can take care of your belongings when you've had a good rest."

"Thank you," is again all Dri can utter. Officer accompanies her up the elevator and helps her retrieve a few items out of her old room, then get into the new one.

Officer gives Dri a squeeze on both shoulders, then steps back. "I'll see you in the morning, downstairs. About ten o'clock? We'll figure out transportation to the coroner's office and the airport. Here is my card. Call me if you need anything, OK?"

"Thank you."

Dri shuts the door, pulls out her phone, wilts onto the floor with her back to the wall. She sits. Finally, she pulls up her Favorites and presses her mother's number.

Dri has no clue where to begin this dreadful conversation. She cannot begin to think about dealing with identifying the lifeless body that once was her brother and protector.

Today had been her first opportunity to repay some of the safeguarding she experienced from Alex when they were growing up. In the end, though, she failed to keep him from harm, to take on the mantle as a protector of a loved one. Here was her first chance. It feels to Dri like she botched the job.

The next morning, Dri awakens to several knocks. She stumbles out of bed and flounders towards the entry, slowly opening the door. Bella stands on the other side, tears running down her cheeks. She throws her arms around her daughter. They hold each other.

Dri rests her tearful face on her mother's shoulder. Bella feels her weight slowly collapsing. She moves them both to the bed so Dri can lie back down. Bella draws back her hair, cupping her daughter's wet cheek with her other hand. A whiff of unsullied citrus from the sheets faintly calms her breathing

What can I do to make this situation bearable, thinks Dri?

They share sadness and support through loving touch. Her mom whispers a few affectionate words of concern and love. Yet none of it alters the loss that crushes hearts.

Bella slides her arm under her daughter's head. She caresses her body. Kisses full of her own despair get placed on her daughter's cheek while Dri crushes her mother's form against hers, sobbing into her neck.

After a while, both experience exhaustion. They fall back to rest on the bed, their bodies bankrupt. Their voices remain silent.

Dri cherishes the comforting contact. She appreciates the first time to relax since her brother's body was removed from her lap.

Dri images her hands covered with Alex's blood. She revisits the wet stickiness.

"I couldn't protect him! I couldn't stop it!" and begins to sob again.

"I doubt anyone could have, Audri. I'm sure everything happened too quickly. You can't blame yourself, darling. I'm sure no one could have saved him under the circumstances," whispers Bella, feeling the boulder in her own throat, slipping down to crush her broken heart.

As the waves of sorrow gradually recede, Bella haltingly sits up, brushes her hand across Dri's face and hair, and gazes into her eyes. She then looks around the room and notices the absence of suitcases. Her fatigued body feels some energy rising to deal with tasks still at hand.

"I guess we'd better get a few things done. If you give me the other key and room number, I'll gather up your clothes and get them packed to leave."

"Thanks . . . . . It's by the TV . . . . . The room is four doors further down the hall . . . . on the same side," Dri mutters.

"OK, I'll be back in a few minutes. You able to get dressed?"

"Yeah. I'll take a shower . . . . . and get ready," mumbles Dri.

Bella slowly rises, extends her arm to help Dri get up, then gives her one more hug.

"Be back shortly."

Bella packs both suitcases while Dri showers and puts on the clothes her mom brings upon her return. Then they take the elevator to check-out.

"Thanks so much for the extra room. It was helpful," whispers Dri to the receptionist. As she turns back around, she spots Officer from last night.

"Were you able to get some sleep?"

"Yeah, ... thanks. The pill helped."

Dri glances at the badge on Officer's uniform, finally remembering her name.

"Thanks for all your support, Officer Jackson. You were extremely thoughtful last night. I was kind of out of it. Oh, and this is my mom, Bella."

"You're welcome, Audri. And I'm so sorry for your loss, ma'am," Officer Jackson says as she turns towards Bella.

"Thank you. And thanks for all your assistance with Audri . . . . . Still can't fathom it," responds Bella, wiping away fresh tears. "Doubt if I ever will!" she says, shaking her head in disbelief.

"Totally understandable. This is a horrible situation. I'm just glad we got the shooter when we did, before more people were hit."

"Yeah, me too," responds Bella. "Guess you had no clue?"

"No, unfortunately we didn't. Still digging into it. Probably take some time to understand why, but at least we know who did it."

"So glad Audri is OK. Very grateful for that!"

"I believe her kneeling to check on her brother saved her life. I'm really glad for her quick response," says Office Jackson.

"Oh God! I can't even imagine the horror of that possibility," responds Bella.

Tears flood Dri's eyes at Bella's comment, matching her mother's response. Her heart expands as she absorbs her mother's concern.

Officer Jackson, not knowing what else to say, tells them about identifying Alex's body, then gives them directions to the Coroner's office.

Dri and Bella thank Officer Jackson once again.

They go to the valet stand to pick up the rental car and drive to the nearby office.

One final awful task to complete here before catching their flight back to Sacramento. Dread for the funeral tasks still ahead of them.

Dri feels grateful to leave this place. She simply wants to throw off this living nightmare, wishing it would remain in the desert to decompose.

Chapter 10
Spring Blessing
March, 2029

A fter the shock of Alex's assassination, Dri and Bella found decisions difficult to make. His death seemed so brutally random. They continued to question why him, while being grateful Dri also was not killed.

Even through their anger and pain, they faced several key choices not discussed much given Alex's young age. In his first 30 years, Bella's son didn't talk much with either parent about options regarding funerals or other death related details. Fortunately, after the funeral of his maternal grandfather, he mentioned his desire to be cremated. Taking up precious earth space for his "body to rot," as he would say, never made sense to him. Both Bella and Rick knew this and agreed to honor his preference. Instead of a formal funeral in a valley where relatively few people knew Alex, his parents agreed to invite family and friends to gather together in honor of their son and his impact on people's lives.

Phil and Emma volunteered to have the gathering in their lush private garden, a supportive atmosphere for such an event. Most of those attending shared their favorite moments and memories of Alex, some touching, others funny, representative of the different ways this young man impacted people. Bella was surprisingly grateful for the loving share by Susan, Rick's new wife. Bella realizes that no matter how briefly or intensely people had interacted with Alex, they were significantly touched by him. Such an impact intensified the joy for his life and the grief of his loss.

In the months following Alex's memorial gathering, Dri and Bella spent considerable time together. Their interactions were sprinkled with moments cherishing their own connection and sharing gratitude for life.

Their conversations also included fierce heartache and intense loss, at times rage for the emotional debris delivered by the gunman. His life apparently gathered intense heartache and anger. Instead of dealing with it directly, he imposed his pain on the 11 families of the people he killed and the 22 other people he wounded. In the end, Dri believed that all in attendance at the concert were traumatized by the event, in one way or another.

Dri postponed her clients for a month or referred them to other therapists, even though it produced mixed feelings for her. It had been only a year since she became a licensed counselor, and her practice was starting to blossom. But she needed time and space to get herself together before she could be emotionally present with other people's struggles.

She also found a local therapist who specializes in grief work, and their sessions aided Dri in the process. Long, empathetic, and loving conversations with Tiago added another essential ingredient in Dri's healing. She felt lucky to have created sources of support in what felt like her handcrafted environs.

Bella usually would throw herself into distracting activity, such as increased work, when she felt pain. To stay focused on her grief, with Dri's encouragement, she took some time off, asking a colleague to collaborate or temporarily cover for her. Without using work as a distraction, Bella faces her grief more directly, in part through sessions with the same therapist Dri found. Bella also avoids her previous habit of drinking more heavily to dull the pain. Rather, she made the clear commitment, like Dri, to face the heartache now instead of postponing her grief for later. The pain would not end by doing this, but neither woman wanted to bury it, either. Bella found the benevolent conversations with Omar to be another source of comfort.

Sarah, on the other hand, was in a newer relationship and overwhelmed at work. It was more challenging to take the time off to process her grief directly. Fortunately, she and her partner, May, were able to get to Napa on weekends, where she would surround herself with loving family solace.

But Rick was right back at the restaurant, focused on any activity that would keep him busy. One particularly useful task was to increase the tasting of new wines for his specials or the wine list, often needing to consume the bottle to verify his decision.

On this sunny Sunday, Dri reflects on her healing over the eight months since Alex's death. She sits at the second hand dining room table, looks at the waning posy of red roses, and finishes her afternoon tea. Her thoughts wander towards her tardy daughter. Caterina was expected seven days ago and still is a no show. Audri feels like she could arrive any time, but why put off life waiting for something you can't control? She's grateful to be developing such an outlook. She relaxes her need to manage every detail in her life, which provides more space for living, breathing.

Not wanting to postpone life on this beautiful spring weekend, Dri decides to make a family dinner, in the tradition of her mother. Given the uncertainty of how much more time she and Tiago will have to themselves, she wants to relish a delicious meal together before their lives are transformed by the arrival of Caterina, their new baby. She has experienced small contractions over the last two days. This afternoon Dri is feeling extra energy. She would like to make good use of it, partly to diffuse her anxiety of this maternal transition.

Caterina's determination to take her time is not a big surprise to her mom. Dri has, at times during the past couple of weeks, tapped her impatience on her extended abdomen, as if to say "OK, I'm ready." Whenever she has done so, Cate has tapped back, mirroring the number of times her mom lightly taps her belly, as if to respond, "I hear you, but I'm not ready. And you're not in charge of this."

Dri's hunch is that tenacity is going to be a significant characteristic of her daughter, one to be negotiated between the two of them the rest of their lives. That may not be true; it's just a hunch. But these extra days of wait and communication provide initial evidence.

Dri rises and strolls around the sparsely furnished two bedroom apartment. Her sense is they are mostly ready. The baby's room has light green walls, highlighting a picture of swimming dolphins and one of Alex's vineyard photographs. His print revives momentary heartache tears, once again subsiding with a few slow deep breaths and several tissues.

As she finishes her orange spice tea, Dri takes her favorite purple mug to the kitchen. She glances out the window over the sink to the luscious trees and developing vineyards beyond their apartment complex, as she regains her sense of ease. She puts the mug in the dishwasher and opens the refrigerator to get the wild mushrooms she carefully picked out at the local farmers' market on Thursday, anticipating the possibility of making her infamous risotto. She retrieves the saucepan and skillet, along with the other ingredients. She pours some oil into the saucepan and sautés the mushrooms, generating a favorite scent. In the skillet, the oil crackles as she fries the scallions, adds the rice, additional oil, and cooks the fusion briefly until the rice turns pale and golden. She pours in some dry, inexpensive sauv blanc, which is absorbed by the rice as it cooks. She then pours in portions of broth, and will stir the risotto occasionally until finished.

This risotto recipe became Dri's specialty while working in her father's restaurant the summer after high school, a year after her parents divorced. Supervised carefully, she spent her time in his kitchen, wanting to gain more cooking experience. It also provided a way to keep a connection with her dad, despite her animosity towards his new girlfriend, Susan, the restaurant hostess. Dri's hostility provided determination to successfully master recipes in what felt like a competition with the "other woman," for her father's love. She hadn't intended her feelings to show up that way, but she did appreciate the drive they provided. A summer's experience was sufficient to gain some culinary confidence. And their relationship improved somewhat after Dri left for college. Infrequent short visits with Dad and Susan work better for everyone.

"OK, how can I help?" inquires Tiago, as he appears from the bedroom, where he's been reviewing notes at his desk his of meetings with students. He walks over to Dri, wraps his arms around her, and places a kiss on the side of her neck. "You look stunning, chef!"

"I thought your offer to help was sincere. After that comment, I know you're lying!" laughs Dri, feeling enormous and sensitive about her body size.

"I get your discomfort carrying this baby. But the beauty radiating from your face and eyes doesn't change, my dear."

Tiago softly removes the spatula from her hand, turns her towards him, one hand around her waist and the other moving up behind her head, pressing her lips passionately into his.

When he pulls away slightly, she looks into his eyes and feels into his energy. Dri knows he's speaking his truth. She smiles.

"Thanks, sweetheart." Dri looks at Tiago a little longer, then turns in his arms to pick up the spatula and stir the risotto. "Would you put together a salad for us? And open a bottle of wine? I would like to make a toast, and I'm sure you'd enjoy some wine with dinner."

"Yeah, happy to do that."

Tiago reluctantly lets go of Dri and goes over to the small wine refrigerator, a standard appliance in their valley. He looks at a couple of bottles, then chooses his favorite, a David Arthur "La Boucher," from the winery where Alex did his internship. Tiago opens it and places it on the table to breathe. He gives a moment of silent gratitude for his lost brother-in-law, then turns back to collect the dark wooden bowl and ingredients for the salad.

With the risotto finished, Dri scrapes it into a bowl and places it on the table. She sets the table, steps back to look, then inches their place mats closer together.

I can't believe how much I enjoy working together in the kitchen, thinks Dri. *While I love my dad and my brother, neither were particularly involved with cooking. Does he help just because I'm pregnant? No, he's always been helpful. Love his mother,* laughs Dri to herself. *I must thank her next time we talk.*

After Tiago puts the salad on the table, he places a wine glass at each setting, then gets water for both. He enjoys helping, yet he feels the knot in his stomach. He pays attention to his nervousness about the arrival of this new family member, excited and anxious too.

Am I ready for this? thinks Tiago. *I have a lot going on at school, and baseball season is starting to heat up. Am I seriously ready to be a father? I love Dri tremendously, and I'm nervous. I'm unsure how to balance work and family. I want to be supportive, and I also want to be honest. Would my hesitancy make her more anxious? Should I say something? Maybe.... but now?*

With everything ready, Dri moves over to the table. Tiago pulls out the chair for her to sit first. She kisses him on the cheek as she slides into her seat, then helps him scoot the chair towards the table as far as possible in her present state. He sits and pours her a tiny sip of wine, followed by a small serving for himself, wanting to be supportive of her choice not to imbibe.

Dri looks at Tiago as she raises her glass. He smiles at her as he raises his.

"To love, connection, gratitude, family, and parental wisdom. May we be conscious parents," she says. "And to you, a loving husband and soon to be father."

"*Acuerdo,*" responds Tiago, and they both take a sip.

As he lowers his glass, he reflects on this woman he adores and has known ever since they became friends in high school maybe 14 years ago. He is grateful he spoke his truth then, deciding to be friends rather than pursuing a romantic relationship. It was tempting, as she is physically, intellectually, and authentically attractive. Yet so much changed for him after graduation. It was easier to be at college, focusing on his studies and baseball, without trying to maintain a relationship.

Besides, his grandfather made an insightful suggestion. "If you still are attracted to Audri after college and she to you, when you both may feel clearer about who you are and what you want, that would be a great time to explore a deeper bond with more maturity."

Tiago is happy he followed the suggestion and feels lucky Dri was interested in him when they reconnected after college.

Tiago passes the risotto. Dri raises the bowl close to her face, breathing in the tantalizing aromas of morels and chanterelles. The creamy flavors have coalesced into her favorite combination of chewy rice with wild mushrooms.

Tiago and Dri chat about the delicious food and their appreciation for her experience cooking at her father's restaurant. Tiago lets the smile slip away as desire for honesty regarding his anxiety rises within. He takes a sip of wine for fortification, inhales a deep breath, then begins.

"Dri, I want to share what's going on with me. I'm nervous about having this baby and the changes it's going to make in our lives. I just need to say it out loud so you know directly."

Dri takes a breath while staring silently at him for a moment.

"Ah . . . don't you think it's a little late to change your mind? This baby's coming, whether you're ready or not," she says, trying to contain her sudden resentment beyond how it probably appears on her face.

"I know, I know. . . I'm not changing my mind . . . I'm just not sure I'm ready for this or know what I'm doing."

Tiago takes another sip of wine, fearful whether he should have said anything at this point. He continues his explanation, hoping for the best.

"There's a lot going on at school, especially my coaching responsibilities with the baseball team just starting their season. I'll try to be with you in every way I can. But I want to tell you, so you know what's going on inside my head these days too. I know you can sense it at times."

"Yeah, I get not feeling secure. I'm not either. Maybe no new parents feel confident. But giving power to your doubts won't help either of us."

Dri surprises herself at the words coming out of her mouth. She reflects momentarily on her discussions with Doc. The most ironic thing is that she's spouting teachings to Tiago that she learned from his grandfather. She's not sure presently whether she wants to laugh or cry. Maybe both.

"I agree with you," responds Tiago. "I don't want to give them any more power than they have in the moment. But I also want to be honest about what's going on in me. I don't want to hide anything that could come between us. I feel like if I don't say anything, you may get a sense of something going on and have to wonder what it's about, then worry unnecessarily."

"You think your hesitation about being a parent makes me worry unnecessarily?" responds Dri, her voice raising along with her concern as her cheeks refashion to crimson.

Tiago takes a breath and reaches out to touch Dri's hand resting on the table.

"No, that's not what I meant. I know I want to be a parent. I just have some anxiety about doing it well. If I'll be good enough. Yet, I'm committed. Ever since you shared your dream about this baby, I knew this was right. I just want to express my anxiety and doubts about how to be as strong a parent as I can. It's my shit. Not doubts about having a child. I promise to work through this, and I'd love your support."

Dri inhales Tiago's words and feelings, paying attention with her heart along with her head. She inhales deeply, blows out slowly, and removes her hand out from under Tiago's, followed by interlacing her fingers through his, pulling them toward her so their arms rest on the table.

"OK, I think I can hear what you're sharing without my anxiety pushing back so much. I don't know exactly how we'll do this either. I, too, am nervous. Both our moms have talked about their lack of sleep the first few months, and how cranky they could get at times. We're going to need to be careful, I think, with each other and with Cate."

"Yes, I agree. I just want to be clear. And I'm glad your mom wants to help us."

"Me, too. I know she's excited about holding her first grandchild. I just hope her enthusiasm lasts!" she says with a single chuckle. Then her face grows serious again. "We're in it now, so all we can do is our best. Sorry I got a little reactive. I'm committed. And nervous, too."

Tiago smiles at Dri, unlaces his hand, then brings her fingers up to his mouth for a kiss. He picks up his wine glass with his other hand in a toasting gesture.

"To love and patience as new parents!" he says with a grin.

Dri reciprocates the gesture with her glass, and they both take a sip.

"I'll certainly try my best, I promise you," says Tiago, resting his glass back on the table. "OK, now I think I can digest more of this delicious meal."

He releases her hand and takes a bite.

"Thanks for talking about your anxiety. I knew something was bothering you, and I don't like to guess or wonder. Glad to hear you haven't changed your mind about this either," she responds with a faint laugh.

Dri removes her hand from his and takes a taste of salad.

"You know, you are sounding more and more like Gpa." Tiago grins at her.

Dri responds after swallowing.

"Yes, it surprises me sometimes how your grandfather's words just flow forth without me even thinking about it. Some days he even feels near."

"Yeah, to me, too. I wish Gpa were here to greet Cate. I think he'd be happy to welcome her arrival, even, or especially, with my anxiety."

Tiago shares a subtle grin.

Dri starts to eat more risotto, then suddenly drops her fork, spits her food back onto the plate, and doubles over, to the extent possible. She wraps both arms around her extended belly. Her attention focuses solely on her pain.

"A contraction?" asks Tiago, his eyebrows furrow as he lowers his fork to the plate. He reaches out his hand, touching her arm in comfort. Any other form of support seems impractical.

"Shit... Yeah... And a strong one. But it's still early, I'm guessing, not being an expert at this."

Dri rocks slowly forward and backward as the pain begins to subside. After it passes, she sits up to consider having more dinner, hesitant to eat anything further.

"Do we need to do anything?" asks Tiago, in a soft, quivering voice.

"I don't think there's much we can do until the contractions get closer. I had a few mild ones yesterday and some today, but this one's much stronger. Keep eating, and let's see how they go. And grateful for you being here."

Dri sits back to relax in her chair, waiting to see when the next stab will strike. She feels into her joy and gratitude for their relationship and the support Tiago provides while being aware of her increasing anxiety for the upcoming process. Dri is excited to release Caterina from her womb and embrace her with physical arms. But she's in no rush to go through the anticipated transitional torture.

Dri would like another taste of her risotto, but she fears she may not keep it down through this painful process. And she doesn't want to compare tastes in opposing directions.

Tiago takes a few more bites of dinner as he keeps a close eye on his wife's physical response. To assist with his anxiety, he takes another sip of wine. He tries to enjoy the nuances of taste as it moves across his palate, wanting to savor its finish. His attention scurries about, between the wine and his wife's pain in front of him.

"Love this wine," he says. "It's a great day to celebrate with it, in all our anxiety. And to Alex, who introduced it to us!"

Even the reference to wine and her brother can't distract Dri, no matter how hard Tiago tries.

The expectant mother agrees with his reference to the wine and Alex. But she decides a trip to the bathroom may be timely. As she gets up, Tiago begins to rise.

"I'm OK, dear. I think I can do this part by myself," she says with a chuckle.

Dri goes in to expel the fluids from her bladder. As she finishes and moves to wash her hands, she bends over, caressing her baby, as if that would relieve the pain coming on again.

"Tiago," she shouts. "Time this one, please."

Tiago rushes into the bathroom and extends his arm around Dri.

"OK, got it. Any other way I can help?"

"Not much yet."

The pains continue, stronger and more consistently, yet all this is novel to Dri. She feels little confidence in knowing what else to do. She's grateful for her pre-natal classes and happy her classmate is standing next to her. She focuses on her slow inhales and exhales, keeping her attention and one arm on her daughter.

After the fourth exhalation, she feels a sudden wetness running down her legs. At first, panic takes over. Maybe she lost control of her bladder? But she just emptied that. A recognition arises of a progressing process. Again a pain, again doubling over, again her belly embrace.

"Eight minutes apart, roughly."

Dri remains bent over, breathing to the best of her ability in her position. Eventually, she uprights herself and looks at her co-conspirator.

"OK. Grab your keys, wallet and phone. I'll get my phone and bag. I think we need to go. My water just broke!"

Tiago goes to the dresser and pockets his wallet and keys. Dri picks up a towel, wipes her legs, then totters to the kitchen to get her phone as she passes the table. She moves towards the door, grabbing her bag from the front closet, as she prepares herself for the next stage.

Fortunately, they live less than a mile from the hospital. They haltingly walk to the car. Tiago opens the door for her as usual. Dri cautiously gravitates into the front seat as quickly as a mother about to give birth can move, and her husband fastens her seat belt.

The strap feels imprisoning in her condition, but she won't take any chances at this point in the process. Tiago runs around, flops into his seat, and starts the engine.

"Hang in there. We'll be there shortly." Tiago says cautiously.

"Yeah, I'm fi...."

Dri's voice trails off as she attempts to bend over in pain, agitated that her seatbelt stops her desired movement. His right hand moves briefly across her back.

Tiago rushes as safely as possible, not wanting to add to their complications. After three frustrating red lights, he pulls into the hospital lot and stops at the emergency door. He jumps out as an attendant, on watch at the entrance, comes out of the automatic doors with a wheelchair.

"My wife's water broke and the contractions are less than seven minutes apart."

Tiago notices a tinge of pride at the clarity of his words rolling off his tongue. Right now, his practice from class seems wise rather than ridiculous.

"You get her door. I'll position the chair," replies the attendant.

Tiago begins to feel a speck of expertise as the attendant responds to his announcement. He pulls open the door as Dri unfastens her seatbelt. The young attendant, whose dark curly hair falls over the back of his green uniform, grasps the underside of Dri's forearm to help her out. She uses the armrests to position herself into the wheelchair as the attendant holds it steadily for her. Then the young man begins to whisk her towards the double doors while Tiago returns to the driver's side.

"Let Mom know, too, will you?" calls Dri as she gets pushed away.

"You got it," shouts Tiago as he climbs into the driver's seat to find a nearby parking space.

Chapter 11
The Memorial
June, 2029

"Knock, knock," calls out Bella while swinging open the front door. "I'm here to pick up the Spring Street home fliers and have another turn with that beautiful baby."

"Yes, of course. Come in, Bella," responds Tiago in a loud whisper.

Bella smiles at Tiago, sitting on the far end of the couch with Dri nursing her baby in the rocking chair nearby. Bella walks around and leans over, kissing Dri on her unwashed brown hair and smiling at her three-month old dark haired grandchild. Here she is, little Cate, wrapped in a lavender blanket, lovingly cuddled in her mother's arms. Three generations of women together again. Bella views this cozy scene with a relaxed face and broad smile on this warm Saturday morning.

"How you doing today, Kiddo? Get some sleep last night?" asks Bella as she sits at the other end of the tan couch.

"Yeah, I'm doing well. This one's starting to sleep a little better at night, for which I'm eternally grateful," says Dri with a hint of a smile. "Well, I think she's finished eating. I'll try to put her in the crib. She may sleep again for a while."

"Wait. Before you go, let me get another picture of you two beautiful girls," pleads Bella.

"OK. I have plenty of bad photos to blackmail you with, too," Dri says with a big grin. She straightens her purple robe, then slides a hand through her disheveled hair.

"I'll bring out those early Christmas morning photos of you, before you showered and looked presentable" she adds with a chuckle.

Ignoring the threat, Bella takes several shots and extends an arm to help Dri rise with her adorable granddaughter. Cate already has transformed this family upon her entrance. Bella believes she will impact all their lives in much greater ways. The new grandma softly places a kiss on Cate's head before Dri leaves to put her down for a morning nap.

While Dri is busy with Cate, Bella meanders in time, reminiscing how Dri impacted her life in unexpected ways. She never thought her daughter would be such an emotional pillar on which Bella can lean when experiencing difficulties. It's not like the roles are reversed. That may come later, as Bella gets older and possibly needs support. This is more like viewing Dri eye to eye, a position of equals, a direction quite different from the downward looks she gave her daughters when younger and pretended she had all the answers. Bella's curiosity shifts, as she wonders how Cate might impact her mother.

Upon her return, Dri shares her news.

"A woman from the mayor's office in Las Vegas called yesterday. She's inviting us to come there next month. They've created a memorial for those who lost their lives in the shooting last year. She says the mayor would like us to attend the dedication ceremony."

Expressing the words out loud, Dri's eyes redden.

"What?" exclaims Bella. "Oh no! I couldn't possibly go back there. Ever."

"Yeah, that was my reaction too. I didn't think I could be present again in that space where Alex last stood. I didn't want to. I thought, what good would it do except bring up more pain?"

"Yes, glad we agree," responds Bella.

"Well . . . . except Tiago and I have been talking. They've constructed a memorial, which I'd like to see. Others will be there to honor those killed. As I thought more about it, my decision never to return became less rigid."

"Seriously? Why?" asks Bella.

"Apparently, Alex's name is going to be on a small plaque, along with the other 10 people who lost their lives. We missed the vigil they held the day after the tragedy. And I began to think about Alex's name being there without any of us physically present. The more I considered it, I realized I wanted to see the plaque and honor him one last time there in a very personal way, even with the intense grief it will generate. I'd rather experience such sorrow than not be there to acknowledge him at the ceremony."

Dri's eyes shift from Bella to Tiago.

"I suggest you consider going, Bella," adds Tiago. "I'm happy to be there with you both, despite the sadness it will trigger in all of us. I know I wasn't there those two dreadful days when Alex was killed. But I'd be there this time. I'd be surprised if Sarah didn't want to come too."

Bella looks at Dri, then Tiago. Both appear serious, even determined in their professed resolution. She pays attention to the anxiety in her stomach just considering a return trip to Las Vegas. Her own no-return commitment begins to crumble as she peers into the faces of these two young people. She hates it. Her decision to avoid that city felt clear and solid, comfortable, even easing some of her grief. Now, she's faced with a modification that makes her protective wall more porous to her remaining pain. Already she begins to encounter her grief, oozing through the breaches.

"I get it, Mom. I feel grief rising in me too, just thinking about it. I can see your energetic struggle, and I feel similarly. Yet, it seems important to honor Alex by being there. And they've offered me an opportunity to say a few words, reflecting on his life."

"Well, that would be sweet. Whew! This is a shock to my system." Bella pauses for a moment, looking again at their determined expressions. "But I guess if you can face it, I can."

Bella hesitates to check internally once more.

"OK. I'll go with you, my dear. How could I not if you're going?"

The decision feels right in Bella, yet it revives the pain that increasingly propagates through her body. She pulls out a tissue from her pocket to wipe her now runny nose.

Dri watches as her mom's energy shifts between contraction and expansion, with streaks of steely grey, piercing the otherwise colorful field. Dri guesses the metallic band is a barrier to separate additional pain

"Thanks, Mom! I'm so glad you'll go too. I feel like I need to be there in honor of Alex and all he did for me."

In the end, Sarah and her partner, May, Tanika and Naeem, Soph, Emma and Phil all make plane and hotel reservations to attend the memorial as part of the family support. Susan agrees to take charge of the restaurant so Dri's father can attend. Javier can't join them, but Miguel and Gabriela make reservations to be with the rest of the family for this gathering. Omar also desires to support Bella with his presence during a challenging experience, which she appreciates. This time, all fly out of the Oakland Airport in order to accompany Nika and Naeem, an important part of the extended family.

All arrive on June 30th for the ceremony the next morning, then plan to return to their homes later that day. The travel is smooth and easy. The plane is only half full, leaving plenty of room for their inner tension to expand. Both Dri and Bella thought their grief would not strike until they approached the old downtown area. Surprisingly, their sorrow intensifies as the flight nears the city itself.

They take the newly remodeled solar powered tram to downtown, near the Fremont Hotel, where they hold reservations. Bella had suggested to everyone they not lodge at the Golden Nugget, where Alex and Dri stayed last year. It would only bring back additional miserable memories. After checking into the hotel, family members go out to the covered section of the Fremont Street mall to look at the memorial. A lectern and a dozen chairs are placed on a small platform in front of the new monument.

The City of Las Vegas constructed the memorial, which lies in the middle of Fremont Street, the location of last year's concert. The structure includes a circle of red desert sandstone blocks that encompasses a fountain. In the center is a large 11-foot tall grey granite rock, with water bubbling out the top and sliding into the pool below. At the west end of the fountain is a large plaque, which contains the words: In commemoration of those who died here and to remind us all of life's value and sustenance. July 1st, 2028.

The fountain includes 11 ornamental water spouts evenly spaced around the ring, commemorating the individuals killed by the gunman. At the base of each spout is a stone plate with the name, city and age of one of the 11 victims.

The group walks around the circle slowly reading each name and where the attendee formerly resided: Las Vegas, Reno, Los Angeles, Chicago, New York City, Atlanta, and London. The last name they see, just to the left of the lectern, is the plaque which reads: Alexander Luigi Giovanni, Napa, CA. Age 30.

Gabriela passes out a tissue to Rick, then a few others. She came prepared for those who forgot or thought they might get through this with dry eyes. The family members stand there, motionless and wordless, no one apparently wanting to break the silence. They glance at each other, then to others strolling along Fremont Street, momentarily distracting their pain. Some hold hands, others stand by themselves, peering into the water or at the rock, time suspended.

Bella, standing slightly behind Dri, places a soft hand on her daughter's shoulder. She feels Dri's weight starts to sink and quickly puts an arm through hers while Tanika grabs the other side. Dri catches herself with their support, grateful Tiago is holding the sleeping Cate. At that moment, their baby begins to cry and squirm. Having steadied herself, Dri reaches out and takes her from Tiago. Cate settles onto her mother's chest. Dri rocks and kisses her with Tiago's hand reaching over to softly rub the baby's back. With such reassurance, Cate begins to settle again. Slowly, the group turns away from the monument, full and exhausted.

"Do you know what you want to say tomorrow?" Bella asks Dri.

"I've written a draft of my remarks. But I want to go over it again tonight," says Dri.

"I know you'll do great," offers Soph. "I remember your talk at the Iowa City vigil for Nika and her brother after they were attacked at the tennis courts by those two racist *connards*. Excuse my French. But you were inspiring then, Dri, and you'll be great tomorrow, too."

"I agree," adds Nika. "Anything we can do to help?"

"I'd like to talk with you two for a few minutes before the ceremony tomorrow."

"Yeah, sure. Any time," says Nika.

The group moves back towards the hotel, searching for a dinner location on their way. After eating, they find a seating area in the hotel bar. They drop into somber, connective conversations, with a subtle laugh now and again as someone tells a favorite Alex story. Bella looks towards the people sitting at the bar, unable to verbally participate. Her uncontrollable grief spills onto the soft cushions and floor, continuing to ooze from the plentiful supply in her body, saturating everything around her. Dri reaches out and takes her mom's hand in both of hers, their heads turning towards each other, watering eyes mirroring each other. They both take a deep breath, knowing they can escape tomorrow afternoon.

Slowly, individually or in small groups, people wish others a restful night's sleep as they depart for their rooms. Rick remains in his seat, as Bella and Omar say their goodnights. She feels moderately anxious leaving him alone, an old caretaking habit. Yet, Rick seems more engrossed with his drink than his ex-wife leaving. His lack of response reassures Bella and provides another opportunity to extend the independence shift in what remains of their relationship.

At breakfast the next morning, Tanika and Soph join Omar and Bella, who already are seated at a large table with Sarah and May. Those sitting act sedated, consistent with the mood of the two joining them. Later, others expand the group. There is minimal conversation, as all seem more focused on the upcoming event than the food that ends up in front of them.

As the extended family members finish and leave generous unconsumed portions along with their tips, they make their way towards the monument for the 10:00 a.m. ceremony. People continue to gather, and the crowd re-stimulates Dri's trauma from a year ago. She suspires several times.

Nika recognizes Dri's reaction. She moves over behind her and places both arms around her waist, giving her a loving and supportive hug. The two stop for a moment so Dri can soothe her body. Then they join the others in the middle of the audience.

Mayor Garner walks up and stands behind the lectern, then invites the speakers to come up front and take a seat. She welcomes everyone to this solemn occasion, thanking especially those who traveled many miles to be here in honor of the victims.

She expresses gratitude for the people of Las Vegas who were at the vigil the day after the senseless shootings. The mayor also thanks the downtown merchants who began the financial drive for this memorial. Then she calls on three mothers, two fathers, and one other sibling to share something about the family members they lost that day. There is reverent applause for each set of comments, several touching stories and historical anecdotes about the victims. The speakers talk with choked and quivering voices, pauses to calm their shaky hands, and silent moments to dissolve a throat lump. Audience members are patient and understanding, feeling their own reactions and grief.

Tears become pervasive, both from speakers and the audience. After the others have spoken, the mayor introduces Audri, "who is here from Napa, CA, to honor her brother, Alex, also from Napa, who was attending with Dri that dreadful day."

Dri steps up to the lectern. She takes a moment to peer out at the several hundred faces and tear streaked cheeks gathered, now all eyes on her. One more deep breath, as she looks out at her family for support, then begins, hoping to clearly express what's in her heart.

"What do you say to a large group of people who have been traumatized by the sudden loss of a dear one? How do you help with a few simple words? How do I empathetically say I am sorry for your loss when my heart is still deeply grieving and missing my own brother."

Dri wipes away moisture escaping down her cheeks.

"I do know what to say to the professional personnel who acted so quickly to this tragic event; to the peace officers who stopped the shooting, the EMT, fire professionals, and other emergency personnel; to the nurses, doctors, and staff members at the hospitals; to those professionals at the coroner's office; to the hotel managers and staff who were generous with their facilities and services. Thank you. To the City of Las Vegas public officials who were supportive then and again now for this memorial and ceremony; to all the people of this city, who have been so benevolent and caring, and who did not deserve another shooting like this. Thank you. From the entirety of my being, I am grateful for your graciousness. My heart goes out to every one of you for your own healing, no matter how you were connected to the tragic event that day.

"Alex was a caring, funny man. He loved baseball, his family, the art of winemaking, friends, and people in general, probably in that order. He also loved life, maybe more than any of us. He was a happy person, who infected others with his joy for living. It's ironic that the shooter got the happy one and not me."

Dri pauses momentarily, suspiring to inhale her tears.

"And yet, maybe there's a lesson in that for me and others. Maybe it's my responsibility to carry on that love of life in honor of Alex. Maybe my responsibility includes cherishing and savoring life over tragedy, joy over violence, and love over hate.

"My family and four month old child came here with me. One thing that has become clear to me after Alex's assassination is that my husband and I have brought another child into this world of hate, violence, greed, and injustice; where we collectively seem to care more about politics than people. We care more about guns than justice. We care more about the almighty dollar, Euro, yen, and peso than we care about peace and love.

"Today, I make two personal promises in honor of Alex. First, I commit my time and energy to work towards greater justice. For as wise people have said before me, there is no peace without justice. Without justice and peace, there is no true love. And how can I honor Alex without sharing that love of others and love of life based on justice. But rather than justice creating peace, and peace allowing love, I think we need to turn it around. It is *being* love that brings peace, and it is sharing that inner love and peace that brings about true justice. Such outcomes start with ourselves, especially those of us with privilege and power. For the real change begins with a transformation of the heart.

"Secondly, with the support of my husband, I commit today not to bring another child into this world until we as a nation have established a fundamental commitment for change in how we all live with each other. Until we care more about peace and justice than we care about what we have and what we can buy, especially guns. Until we care more about heartful connections with ourselves and others than we care about ego, power and politics. Until we care more about this earth than the objects we hold so dear. I will not bring another baby into being when we allow life to be so easily taken. That will mean additional gun reform in this country. But that also means we make a solemn commitment to solve problems and differences through peaceful negotiations rather than war and killing. We emphasize caring about people and life more than being right, or turning to guns and violence as our solution, as individuals and a nation.

"We have come a long way in the past seven decades, and it is not far enough. We have more to do, more to accomplish, to fulfill Dr. King's Dream for all of us and for this world. The Black Lives Matter movement has led to important changes with our peace officers and with black, white, and blue trauma. We have continued to work towards peace in the Middle East and greater cooperation between nations. And there is still more to do.

"We have not opened our hearts to each other or even ourselves in many cases. We have not eliminated shootings in this nation. We have not eliminated our soldiers' killing in other nations and the wars between nations. Until we accomplish these changes, there will be no lasting justice or peace. There will still be hate and judgment. There will still be separateness and violence. There will still be grief and trauma. There will still be a caste system in this and other nations where, as James Baldwin said, we look down on one group of people to feel better about ourselves. Until we eliminate this at an individual and local level, we cannot eliminate it at a national level. Until we eliminate it at a national level, we cannot eliminate it at an international level.

"In homage to Alex, these are the commitments I make this day to honor his life and mine. His life and yours. To any of you who have lost loved ones here or who are simply tired of senseless killings, I ask: what commitments will you make today to ensure this kind of tragedy does not happen again here, or anywhere else? How will you encourage change?

"Thank you for your presence here and your time. And may we all find true peace."

Dri gathers up her papers and turns from the lectern towards the chair where she was sitting. The audience, who had been silent, other than some sniffles during her speech, begin to cry and clap out loud. Some turn towards their own family members, some mumbling, others hugging, heads on shoulders, arms around children, pulling them lovingly close. A few smile through their tears as they applaud. The response continues until the mayor walks up the lectern.

"Thank you, Dri, and all of the speakers for their thoughtful remarks and reminders of those lost here. And I wish you the best, Dri, with your courageous pledges and inspiration for change. May we all find a way to make this world a better place. Thanks for attending today."

As the crowd begins to dissipate, Dri's family comes up to congratulate her for the speech and express surprise for her commitments, especially the second one. They continue their congratulations as four women and one man slowly emerge from different parts of the crowd and move towards them. Dri spots the small cluster, patiently hovering just outside her family gathering, and excuses herself.

"I'm sorry to bother you. But I just wanted to thank you so much for your comments. My name is Rachel, and this is my wife, Ariella. We're from Atlanta, and we lost our son, Joseph, here last year."

Dri is struck by the tall, dark haired woman in a green summer dress, shoulders slightly stooped, seemingly from sorrow, who looks at Dri through tearful eyes. She clutches her wife's arm.

"Your words were very inspiring, and we loved your resolutions. Do you have specific plans about how you want to proceed with your first commitment?" Rachel inquires.

A slight smile appears on Dri's face.

"No, not exactly." She turns and pulls on Nika's hand, who drags Soph up with her. "These are my two dear friends, Tanika and Sophie. The three of us have talked, and I have their commitment to help me. But we have not yet made plans as to how we'll proceed."

"Excuse me, but I want to help too if you are going to form some group to address the issues you so beautifully identified today."

A brown skinned woman, probably in her 40s, steps up beside Rachel.

"My name is Kiara, and this is my husband, Sam. We lost our daughter, Diya, who was here from Chicago with friends."

Tears slowly roll down her cheeks. She wipes them away with a handkerchief, then pushes back her thick black hair, her dark eyes a stark contrast to her tan summer dress.

"We want to support your efforts as well, if you'll have us."

Dri smiles at Kiara and Sam, not sure what to say.

"Yes, of course," she finally adds.

Then she notices another woman still hanging back a bit from the others, waiting patiently. Dri looks directly at the woman whose white embroidered kaftan sways as she walks up towards the group, the end of her beige hijab hanging loosely down from one shoulder. Her mouth is not covered, and Dri notices a slight, yet serious smile. She moves next to Kiera as Dri focuses on her.

"Yes, please excuse me as well. My name is Fadima. I lost my son, Husayn. He and his friends were here from New York City. He was killed and a friend injured. I also lost my husband just two years ago during a robbery at our local market. I, too, am sick of killing. Not only here, but also in Lebanon, my homeland. I would love to be part of your efforts to create change."

"I don't know what to say," responds Dri. "I'm stunned. I talked my two friends into joining me. But we haven't worked out any details beyond their agreement. I'm so touched by your generous offers. I wasn't expecting anyone to respond to my commitments so immediately."

"Well, instead of all of us working individually, maybe a collective effort would be more effective," suggests Rachel. "We could exchange contact information and begin a conversation about ideas and ways we might collaborate."

"I like that idea. How about entering your names, phone numbers, and emails into my contacts," says Nika as she holds out her phone. "Then on the line that says Company, why don't you just write Coalition. That way, I can still find you when I can't remember everybody's names," she adds with a self-deprecating chuckle. "Today has been rather full and emotional. My memory doesn't always serve me well under such circumstances."

"Wonderful idea," says Kiara, who is closest to Nika's phone and takes it to enter her contact information. "At least, we can stay in touch and see if we can't come up with something together."

She hands the phone to Fadima, who enters her information, then passes it to Rachel.

"Great," responds Nika as she gets her phone back. "I'll be in touch in the next couple of days with a list of everyone's names and contact info. That way we can easily connect with each other whenever we have some idea to share. Dri's in Napa. I'm now in Oakland, and Soph is in Seattle. It will be great to have more people in different locations. And I have a corporate account for the new Share app, which makes it easy to have any number of us participate in video conversations, even with our phones. If you just download the app, I can set up connections for all of us. I'll forward the link when I send out the contact info."

"That sounds great," says Rachel. "We'll do that when we get your email."

"Thanks again," adds Dri, "for connecting with us. I'm sorry it took such a tragic event to bring us together," Dri says, as she lays her right hand over her heart and extends her left hand, palm up, towards the new associates. "But maybe something good will grow out of this group. Maybe we can prevent others from having to go through this."

Dri's eyes water as she completes her comment, with memories of Alex particularly present again, her heart heavy.

"Yes, hopefully. And thanks for sharing your ideas, for taking this initiative," responds Kiara, now standing across from Dri, bringing her right hand up to her heart and placing her left palm under Dri's. "I feel some hope from your words and our connections,".

"I agree," says Ariella. She places her right hand over her heart and left palm under Kiara's.

"Whatever I can do to help, I'm in too," adds Sam as he follows the others with his hands.

"Yes, me too," says Fadima and follows Kiara's lead. "Thanks to you, Audri, for initiating this effort."

"I'm in," comments Soph with her one hand already over her heart and left under Fadima's.

"I'm in, too," responds Rachel with a smile and extends her hands to her heart and the developing circle.

"I, too, commit to this group and the intentions we develop," adds Nika, right hand over her heart and left hand sandwiching the group with Dri and forming a committed hand circle.

The eight of them look into each other's eyes, complete strangers no longer, hearts full of sorrow, yet now sprinkled with hope.

"Thank you all!" whispers Dri in a choked up voice. "We will be in touch and not let this initiative fade away, for Alex, for Joseph, for Diya, for Husayn, and all the others who died here, to remind us of the importance and value of life."

Disentangling their hands, several give hugs or namastes in reverence to the others, then the members disperse. As they step away, Dri notices one other person standing off beyond the group. She recognizes her for all the help she offered last year.

"Officer Jackson! How great to see you. Nika and Soph, this is the officer I was telling you about. She was so helpful to me when the medics took Alex away, trying to save his life. Officer Jackson, these are the two best friends a woman can have, Tanika and Sophie."

"Glad to meet you both," replies Officer Jackson as she shakes Nika and Soph's hands. "You two have quite a friend. A tough cookie with an amazing heart."

"How are you? You look great," responds Dri.

Officer Jackson turns back towards Dri.

"Yeah. I made Lieutenant last month, which keeps me even busier. And life is going well. But I was wondering. Could you use a peace officer as a part of your group? I would love to contribute to it, too."

"Of course! We'd love to have your perspective," adds Dri.

"Absolutely," responds Nika, handing over her phone. "It would be great to have a sister involved, from my point of view."

Officer Jackson adds her contact information and returns Nika's phone.

"That's wonderful to hear. I, too, want to see more change. We've done some solid work, incorporating the '8 Can't Wait' platform here in the department. But there's more to be done, that's for sure."

"I agree with Nika. I think it would be important to have the perspective of a peace officer and the experience of another person of color when we talk about change. Thanks so much for your interest," says Dri.

"It's great to see you again, Dri. I'm excited about the potential of this developing group. And I look forward to connecting more often. Well, I'd better get going. I have a few more things to do around here," says Officer Jackson.

"Thanks for coming by. It's great to see you, and thanks again for all your support last year. I'm so happy we'll stay in touch," adds Dri.

Officer Jackson shakes hands again with the three women, then leaves the group as Dri's extended family gathers near her. Dri notices her fatigue, drained from the emotional waves pouring through her body during and after the event, her eyes parched, no fluid remaining.

The family begins to walk back towards their hotel in small, hushed tone groups, some with an arm around another, others holding hands. As they near the hotel, a shroud of silence comes over the group, accompanying them into the lobby and on to their rooms as they collect their bags. Each group leaves their key at check-out, then they gather once more for some lunch.

Following a meager eating, the extended family members take the tram back to the airport for flights home.

As she says her goodbyes at the Oakland Airport, she shares with Dri how her words touched Nika's heart, without knowing how they might impact her long term. Nika pays attention to her lingering sadness that remains from the ceremony and the way it blends with appreciation for Dri's comments and meeting the strangers after the ceremony.

Dri and Nika share the same perspective, knowing it will take time to see the effects of their efforts. But they trust there may be more hope than sorrow arising from these final interactions and the hand circle commitment that developed from this grief laden event.

Chapter 12

The Foundation

June, 2029 (Continued)

A s they exit the Oakland Airport, Dri holds her daughter, whose head rests on her mom's shoulder with one hand on the back of Cate's heart. Dri holds her tight while sorrow for Alex also resides in her heart. The two follow Tiago and Bella, as Omar leads them to his dark blue Tesla in short-term parking.

Once they reach the 880 freeway, Bella suggests they stop to pick up some food and drive to her place for dinner. Emma and Phil, driving back in their own car, will join the others there. Bella, longs for heartful sustenance. She expresses her desire for a quiet evening that focuses on remembrance of Alex, whom she is missing intensely.

Bella lays out plates and silverware under the new garden pagoda. Family members pick at the food. They feel the need for physical nourishment, but lack much appetite. Dri feeds Cate and puts her down in the crib Bella keeps for her granddaughter. Omar opens a bottle of wine he brought over before leaving for Las Vegas. Dri desires to talk about loving and missing Alex, yet her body is spent from the intensity of the day.

Finally, Bella breaks the silence.

"I don't know if this hole from Alex's death will ever be filled."

She turns to look at Dri.

"That doesn't mean I love you and Sarah any less, dear Dri." She reaches out, grasps her daughter's hand and gives it a squeeze. "But there is a vacant spot, that place where I love my son. It's like an arm is gone, and I'm so grateful to have two legs. And the legs can't replace the arm. It's just different."

"I get it, Mom," Dri says, feeling her chest contract around her grief, bringing her hand up over her heart. "I have a hole inside me, too. I love you, Tiago, Cate, and Sarah. Emma and Phil. Tanika and Soph. I get that it's just different."

"I'm glad we went to see the memorial and participated in the ceremony for all who died there, including Alex," adds Bella. "Maybe it's even useful to say goodbye again and honor how much I love and miss him. Even with all the pain and pressure, I'm glad we were there. And I'm really happy to have heard your remarks, Dri. But I'm a little surprised about your commitment not to have another child. You can't prevent killing by not having a second baby."

"Excuse me for jumping in, Bella. But the issue is slightly different than that," responds Tiago. "It's about not bringing more children into a world where we so easily rely on violence, where we don't seriously value life. It's not a forever commitment, but rather creating fundamental social changes before we add another life that the world doesn't cherish."

"It's like we can get another arm, and we don't want it so easily taken away," Dri adds. "Before we bring another child into this world, I want to work towards a radical shift in the overall merit of human life and avoid moving so easily towards violent responses to others. I want to transform behaviors that separate us as human beings."

"I applaud your desire for change, Dri. I really do. But another child could help with that effort, especially the way you and Tiago will raise it. With my help, of course," responds Bella with a scant smile. The first of the day.

"But we need to say 'enough,' not continue to participate in the same old way." Dri leans forward towards Bella as she continues. "We've made some important reforms around policing, increased efforts to support the development and success of more minority businesses, and challenged our dramatic pay discrepancy. We continue to do more and more to try saving this earth. But like I said at the memorial this morning, this society has the view that justice creates peace, and peace allows more love. I think we need to turn that around. It's inner, core love that creates greater peace, and inner peace from an open heart can't help but lead to more equality and connection between us. We keep arguing about what is and isn't justice before we open our hearts. Until we make a fundamental alteration and feel the love at our core, we will continue to rely on power and violence to create justice rather than creating a foundation of love that brings about greater peace and equality. If we don't begin to make such a shift, I won't be ready to bring another child into a fundamentally violent, racist, and power focused world."

Bella looks at Dri as the words and thoughts infiltrate her body and touch her core. She detects uneasiness by the issues her daughter raises. Bella thought she knew this young woman intimately. But Dri shares ideas that begin to crack her view of the world and the foundation of her life.

"I'm touched and disturbed by what you're saying right now, Dri. I thought I knew you so well. And then you rattle the ground on which I've been standing all my life. I don't disagree with you. I guess I just feel overwhelmed by the vastness of change you are suggesting. I don't think I'm ready for it. And in a world slow to evolve, it feels unrealistic."

"Then my ideas have come across clearly," says Dri, the corners of her mouth turned up slightly. "If I were not suggesting a fundamental transformation, it would be much easier, but also less effective. It's why I'm so pleased that a few people already are volunteering to join our efforts the first time I speak out loud about it. Even Officer Jackson wants to participate. We will need millions, even billions more. But it's a start, and it has to begin somewhere. I invite all of you to join us. We certainly could use your support. And only when you're ready."

"I don't feel ready for political activism to create social change. I'm still deep in mourning for Alex," responds Bella, her eyes watering when she believed her reservoir dry.

Dri looks at her mom while she checks in with her own heart.

"Mom, we will mourn Alex's death the rest of our lives. What has gotten clear to me since the invitation to speak is that I choose not to wait. I don't want more people die while I focus on my grief. If I want to honor Alex in his death, I need to begin now to honor those who still are alive by creating a peaceful love revolution, a shift in people's hearts that prevents more people from dying from violence. I get that you may not be ready to participate. I respect that in you," she says, checking in again to make sure she remains centered in her core and heart. She wants to be clear, yet not come across as blaming her mom for making a different choice. "It was your son who died, and I know you need to follow the grieving process in your own way. For me, the course will take on a path, hopefully, of transformation and prevention. That's the way I am choosing to honor my grief process. And I love you for the way you pay attention and trust your decision and path," Dri adds with all the sincerity she can muster.

"And I choose to participate with Dri in this peaceful revolution," adds Tiago. "We've talked about it. I agree with her desires, and I want to be a partner in that movement. I, too, dearly miss my friend and support. Even while I'm young, hopefully with much life ahead of me, I want to begin now. We never know how long we have."

"Wow. I don't know what to say," responds Bella. "I guess I need some time to take this in, to sit with it a while before making a commitment in any particular direction."

"I have to agree with my sister on this one," says Emma. "I'm intrigued with your ideas for a fundamental shift. But so many people have tried different approaches that end up going nowhere. I worry this, too, will not impact enough people to make a change. Yet, I also want to support your efforts, Dri. Believe me, I want to."

"I invite you to take your time, Aunt Emma and Mom. Of course, everyone needs to make their own personal decision. I won't pressure anyone to join our work. And I won't wait for anyone either. I'll do what I can, starting now. I'll try to build on the commitment of Nika, Soph and Tiago, as well as the six people who stepped up this morning. Ten people is a good beginning."

Dri turns to her mother.

"This feels like my life's work, Mom. It feels like my particular work, secretly placed in my heart, as you mentioned from that lovely Rumi quote. And I can't ignore it any longer."

"But what about your therapy clients, and your assistance with my real estate transactions? Will you quit working? Quit earning money? What about Cate?" asks Bella, her voice louder and sharper than she intended.

"No, I won't quit working, and I won't quit my family."

Dri turns and looks at Tiago, searching to feel the solidness he provides. Then she turns back to her mom.

"Tiago and I have talked extensively about this in the past month, and he agrees with me. He wants to be an active part of this. We don't know exactly how. We just know we want to begin now and figure out how to proceed along the way."

"But it will take you forever to impact enough people to create such a fundamental shift in world views and behaviors. Even in a lifetime, visionaries haven't brought about such change. I'm sorry, dear. I want to be supportive of what you're doing. But it just seems impossible."

Bella's eyebrows narrow towards the bridge of her nose as she looks deeply into Dri's calm face.

"Mom, you remember what you told me about change some time ago? That everything seems to move faster and faster? Tiago wondered about that too. But then he began to play around with an idea that became prominent during the Covid-19 pandemic, the exponential curve. Tiago, you're better at explaining this than me. Would you describe what you found?"

"Sure. If each one in our small group of 10 people persuaded one other person each day to join us, we would reach the entire world population of 8.4 billion people in 30 days. Now that undoubtedly is too idealistic. Let's say each one of us touches the life of one person a month, encouraging them to live from an open heart, love from the core. Just one person a month to change and join us. We could reach the world's population in about 30 months, or two and a half years. In less than three years, using social connections, social media, the Internet, and video conferences, we could impact the population of our entire world. Now, not everyone is going to change, especially that quickly. But say it takes five years, or 10 or 20. It's still a possibility. Dri and I believe we have to try."

"Apparently, that's the way a virus or bacteria tends to grow. And what if we could develop," Dri puts her fingers in the air to demonstrate quotation marks, "a love virus, an infectious idea that gets spread at the rate of bacteria growth or like the wildfires we keep having in California, which, when big enough, perpetuate themselves. What if we could do that? Would that seem a little less impossible?"

"I'll tell you what feels impossible. Winning an argument with you two these days," responds Bella with love in her eyes and joy on her mouth. "I'm touched by the energy and commitment that emerges in our discussions. I still need to sit with this. Like my move here, I need to be clear within myself, not just convinced by your logic and heart filled words. But I have to say, it also will take some effort to tell you no, if that's the answer that shows up in me."

"I can't ask for a better answer than that, Mom. Thanks."

Dri places her plate, with food mostly consumed, on the table along with her empty wine glass. She stands, bends forward to hold both sides of her mom's head in her hands and kisses the top of it.

"But I think we had better go. It will be easier to move Cate now than later, and I'm exhausted. You OK with that, Tiago?"

"Yeah, it's been a long, intense day. I think it's important to get to bed early this evening. Thanks for the food and hosting tonight, Bella, and for more delicious wine, Omar."

Dri gathers up her plate and glass, taking them into the kitchen. Tiago helps get dishes and glasses into the dishwasher as Dri collects their belongings and gets Cate secured in her car seat. They give hugs all around, thanking each family member for showing up and their support, including dinner. Then the family of three leaves for home.

The next day, Dri sets up a time on Share to talk that evening with Nika about developing imminent steps. She meets with two couples for counseling at her office during the morning, then works at home on some transaction paperwork for her mom. She has time during Cate's nap to put together ideas for her discussion with Nika while Tiago takes his turn to fix dinner.

Later that evening, Nika and Dri discuss completion of the email list and distributing it to everyone. Dri commits to begin work on a manual that could assist people in the kind of ideas and skills Doc divulged to her, and that she later shared with Nika and Soph. She tells Nika that Tiago has volunteered to help, both with writing and editing, even contributing additional information his grandfather taught him over the years.

Nika turns to the possibility of forming a nonprofit, which they had previously mentioned, and suggests they create it now. Such an organization would be important for soliciting funds and volunteer time, even charitable professional contributions, to support their efforts. Nika will get the email distributed, including a request that at least three of the new volunteers be members of the nonprofit board of directors. There remains much to be done, but both women are happy with the direction the group is taking and hopeful the efforts will continue.

"I'll put you down as Executive Director for our nonprofit organization?" asks Nika.

"I've been thinking about that. I need to work on the manual, which you and Soph could provide feedback to as you go through it. But it's going to take quite a bit of time to draft, even with Tiago's contributions. Would you have the interest and time to take on the ED role? I think you have a clear vision for our group, and you have been instrumental all along the way in making this happen. Besides, I think you're better at leadership matters and would be a sensational first director. I'd love to be Program Director. What do ya think?"

There is a long pause in the conversation, and Dri watches Nika's face through the video as she processes this possibility.

"I'm taken back by your recommendation. I knew I wanted to be involved. But I don't know about such a leadership position. Seriously?"

"Yeah. Seriously. You get what we want to do. And you're a great manager. We'd be lucky to have you in that position, and better off than what I think I could contribute in that role. Of course, you'd have all my support."

Dri witnesses the silence that appears again as Nika's shoulders relax.

Nika feels excitement growing for this opportunity. She pauses and looks at Dri.

"Does this have anything to do with my questioning your lead in the vigil and whether you felt like you needed to do that for a black woman?" asks Nika, with some hesitation.

"Huh . . . No, I don't think so. It first has to do with your qualifications and competence. Am I happy to have a super sharp and strong Black woman take the lead in this? Yes! Is color the primary reason? No. Is it an added benefit to have a woman of color as director? Yes," Dri says with confidence. "We already have some diversity, and I want to include more, as I'm sure you do, too. It doesn't hurt for us to model that in our initial organization. But, from my point of view, this decision has much more to do with your heart and head than your skin."

"OK, with your support, I'd be honored to take this on. Then we'll see where it goes and who may want to take it on next. You know I want to run for Congress in two years. And that will take considerable work. But I'd love to take this on for now. I may just not be able to do it long term, that's all."

"I remember. We'll cross that bridge when we get to it. Until then, you'll be fabulous!"

Over the next few days, Dri is thrilled that the original volunteers, including spouses, are excited to be a part of the group. Fadima, Ariella, Kiara, and Imani volunteer to be board members. It is only through these emails that Dri finds out Imani is Officer Jackson's first name. Rachel is happy to volunteer for a secretary position on the board, and Sam would be willing to contribute as treasurer. With apparent ease, the group has a full board to begin their work.

Emails begin going back and forth as the initial volunteers mention others in their communities they think may have some interest in joining the group — friends, extended family members, and neighbors after individual experiences were shared upon their return home. Dri emails plans to develop a manual that includes ideas and experiential exercises that could serve as foundational information for new members, assisting them to learn a perspective shift, develop new skills, explore their own defenses, and expand options for ways of interacting with others, solving differences and conflicts, all leading to greater expansion of the heart.

Nika sends out another email suggesting the possibility of getting together to discuss the approach of the group and include others who show interest in their work. She proposes a retreat, two or three days to work on the mission, the non-profit organization, and ways different people could contribute. Everyone agrees to the gathering. Fortunately, most of the people live in major urban areas where travel tends to be less complicated and expensive.

The next day, Nika responds by sending out a shared spreadsheet where people can fill in weekend dates in the fall they are available to get together. She also suggests a hotel near the San Francisco airport where people could stay at a reasonable rate and use a meeting room for their gathering. Group members agree to share the spreadsheet with friends who have an interest in participating to identify times they also would be available. Then Nika will pull all the information together, pick the best dates for the greatest number of people, and set up arrangements. In the meantime, Dri and Tiago will work on some ideas and experiences to present to all who attend so everyone gains a sense of direction and can assist with the group's mission and manual.

What was particularly touching were three personal responses.

Rachel wrote: 'While I'm still grieving Joseph's loss, it feels like my involvement with this group will also help give me focus on creating change, believing he didn't just die in vain.'

In her response, Kiara said, 'Thank you for taking the lead in this work. My heart still feels broken, and I hope that the healing I am doing and the focus on living from the heart will help me heal in ways I otherwise might not consider. It gives me hope for a lighter heart.'

Finally, Fadima shared a favorite quote from Rumi she keeps on her bathroom mirror since she lost Husayn: "The wound is the place where the light enters you."

These are the kind of messages that encourage Dri, Nika, and Tiago to continue with their efforts and make them all worthwhile. Sparked by the last response, Dri lays a white rose under Alex's photograph of the vineyards in Cate's room.

Near the end of October, a small group of 29 people meet near the San Francisco Airport for two and a half days. The room is bright with neutral tan walls, and it reeks of institutionalism. Bella and Emma bring four vases of white Daisies, yellow Sunflowers, orange, and red flowers, highlighting summer's transition to fall, and giving more life to the room's atmosphere and distracting from the spot eluding carpet.

Besides the original 10 interested members, 13 family members and friends come to investigate the direction and fit with those assembled. Bella, Sarah, May, and Emma attend to help host and get a better sense of where the organization is bound besides helping with Cate while Dri and Tiago are involved with the gathering. Tiago's parents, Gabriela and Miguel, also participate to get a better sense of what their son and his new family are undertaking.

The first day, Nika welcomes them all and expresses her gratitude for their interest and commitment of time and funds to attend. Dri follows with a moment of silence for those who died in the shooting, and, as an outgrowth, connected the initial group.

She then leads the participants in a discussion of ideas and exercises to experience the beginning of a shift towards living all of life from an open heart. Nika, Soph, and Tiago share responsibilities for facilitating other discussions and exercises. At the end of the day, Dri spends time talking and guiding those assembled in a heart expanding meditation that she learned from Doc and has been practicing nearly daily for 13 years now. As the exercise comes to a close, the participant's shoulders appear relaxed, necks seem more flexible, and faces look serene. Yet the most appealing aspects remain the smiles on each mouth and coruscating eyes.

The focus for Saturday is the development of a vision and mission statement to further organize the nonprofit. They spend over three hours discussing violence, racial, and financial inequities to come up with a general statement regarding a vision and the mission statements that would accomplish their overall objective. The final hour is spent wordsmithing their statements and creating priorities that are comfortable and appealing to all.

Imani raises her hand, and Nika calls on her.

"Before we go on, I want to ask a question. In all these mission statements, there is no mention of your commitment, Dri, not to have another child until there is a fundamental shift in our nation. Why not include that one, too?"

Deadly silence drops onto the group as everyone's eyes turn towards Dri.

"I haven't brought it up or suggested it as part of our mission because I think it is such a personal commitment that Tiago and I have made. I am fine talking about it. But I think people need to make such a commitment on their own, not part of our organizational statement."

"I get that. But I also think it's important to put it out as a possibility. Some of you probably are through having children and may have less struggle around it. My husband, Raimy, couldn't make it here this weekend because of a previous commitment. But he and I have been talking about this. Our oldest child was killed by a stray bullet from gang violence three years ago. After hearing your remarks at the memorial, Dri, I raised this issue with him. We were thinking about having another child. But we were inspired by your commitment and agree with you. While it should never be a requirement, I think we also ought to mention it. What if #10 says, something like, consider not bringing children into the world until we truly honor life."

"Wow, that's a big one. What do people think?" asks Nika.

Side conversations begin as people discuss this issue. Finally, Fadima stands up.

"I am a strong supporter of having children. Yet all of us are here because life is so easily taken away, and governments around the world seem cavalier about human life in many ways. I am shocked at myself, but I also find that I agree with Imani. We just ask people to consider it."

Nika takes a deep breath. "Anyone disagree?" She pauses and gives time for people to respond. "OK, here is what we have.

"The Coalition Vision Statement:

Learn to live from an open heart, caring about ourselves, others, and our environments.

The Coalition Mission Statement:

1. Develop and share heart opening information and opportunities
2. Support individual emotional growth and openness
3. Emphasize authentic, honest communication responsibility
4. Prioritize peaceful approaches to conflicts, avoiding harm to others and violence
5. Prioritize race equality and remove any barriers that maintain race inequality
6. Create greater financial equality, with a maximum 5:1 pay differential
7. Emphasize inclusion and equality of all (Gender, Race, LGBTQ+, Religions, etc.)
8. Encourage greater community service, constitutionalism, and respect for elections
9. Increase awareness of our connection to the earth and caring for our environment
10. Consider not bringing children into the world until we truly honor life

"Any questions or concerns before we vote? Seeing no hands, all those in favor of adopting these statements, including the new #10, say aye."

There was an unanimous response.

"All those against, say nay."

Silence captured the group.

"The statements are adopted. In the near future, we'll work on strategic ways of using the mission statements to achieve our vision."

"Thanks, Nika. This feels appropriate to me," says Rachel. "And I think it will help balance the pain I still feel about my son's death. And thanks, Imani, for raising the last issue."

"I hope it does help you and all impacted so radically by that violence," responds Nika.

"Yeah, I agree," adds Fadima. "I appreciate the opportunity to use my pain to create some important changes for our world. Who knows how long it will take. But working at it feels good."

"I also found it useful," adds Rachel. "Maybe helping others will assist in my own healing in the loss of Joseph. As the saying goes, 'pain is the opportunity to wonder.'"

"I certainly hope it helps all of us," responds Dri. "I know I want to heal my own pain through this work, and I certainly am happy to support anyone else. Please, let me know, as we continue our work, if there is any way I can support your healing, too."

After lunch, Soph shares with the group her intention to take a job in Paris with an international health organization. Participants are surprised and express hope she will stay involved. Gabriela suggests she might do some work for the group while there, which could be encouraging. Soph states her intention to continue participating, but she suggests it would be difficult to remain a member of the board of directors, especially with new job responsibilities. She also commits to continue assistance with program development pieces.

Further organization of board service and rotation is worked out for people eventually to serve three year terms, with a third of the board members up for reappointment or rotation off at the end of their term. In addition, committees are formed for program development, fund raising, and membership expansion.

"I don't think I've ever experienced such collaboration and ease in the development of an organization with people who do not know each other well. I think the activities we did yesterday have helped this process. They certainly did for me," says Sam.

"I agree," says Kiara. "I loved the heart opening exercise and did it again this morning."

"And as someone who doesn't do these kind of exercises often, I have found it useful and touching. I appreciate being a part of this group," adds Imani.

"I'm very glad this has been helpful," adds Tiago. "These practices sure have helped me in my life, and I think they will be important in making this a different kind of group. Thanks for sharing your reactions."

Nika looks around the room and asks, "Is there anyone else who has a comment to make?"

No one indicates the desire to respond.

"Ariella, you look like you may want to say something? No pressure, but I want to make sure everyone has a chance to do so."

"Yeah, I want to, and nervous about it. But I'd like to volunteer for the program committee. And my friend, Joan, also would like to assist. We both have experience developing workshops and exercises for clients and groups. But I wasn't sure you wanted any more input."

"Oh, Ariella, I would love your help!" responds Dri. "You too, Joan. While we have some basic ideas of what we want to include in the manual and initial trainings, we don't have much experience in developing exercises. And besides, beyond our initial ideas, you may have others that would complement and expand what we want to do. This is about how we create a change in a large population, and we're going to need all the help we can get. Thanks, we'd love to have you participate and enrich this work"

"Great. We'd love to be a part of it."

On Sunday, Sam, as the new treasurer and chair of the fund raising committee, asks whether there should be a membership fee. It would be a productive way to raise funds. Yet, to a person, group members realize they do not want to eliminate participation because of lacking funds. Sam agrees and says he and the committee will work on other ways to raise funds.

Having taken care of business matters, Tiago requests that group members spend some time talking with at least five people they don't know, learning two new pieces of information about each one. This turns into more light-hearted dyadic conversations and enlivened energy.

While participating, Sarah is surprised as gentle laughter arises at times while people focus their attention on other's eyes. Kiara initiates a Namaste bow after her interaction with Sarah, who responds similarly, bending while maintaining contact with Kiara's eyes. This begins to feel like an expansion of Sarah's own heart as she considers its meaning. She knows the literal meaning of "I bow to you." But what touches her is the more spiritual meaning, recently learned from her yoga class, of "the divine in me respectfully recognizes the divine in you."

What a lovely way to recognize each person in the group, she thinks.

After her interaction with Kiara, Sarah completes each new conversation with a bow. She notices other participants share the same connective ending. Yet, the intensity triggers a chuckle at times with Sarah, too.

Finally, Dri leads a closing circle where each person, with a hand over their own heart, says "welcome" to each of the other members. As two people connect, Dri asks that all members describe a daily heart opening practice each intends to do after returning home. Once again, people frequently include a Namaste bow.

Nika expresses a final thank you and promises to keep in touch with each group member. Afterwards, people say their farewells and begin their departures.

Soph walks around to share a goodbye hug, as she has a plane to catch.

The remaining original volunteers from the memorial gather with Dri, Nika, Tiago, and Bella to disclose their appreciation for the gathering and amplify their commitment to the group. It is a small beginning, yet already the 'love virus' seems to be spreading.

After everyone else leaves, the extended family members go into the hotel restaurant to relax and debrief experiences of their first formal gathering. Green plants surround the eatery, and the fountain at the far end of the greenery provides fluid ambience. The sudden smell of food stimulates their appetites. They all order something to eat and a glass of wine. A meal allows space to relax and enjoy conversations. Dri uses the occasion to feed Cate, who starts her own fussing for food.

"Before we begin to discuss the last three days, I want to thank you for your help and support getting everything ready and making sure it all ran smoothly," says Dri. "Mom, Aunt Emma, Sarah, Gabriela, Miguel, and May, I especially appreciate your assistance in hosting and taking care of little things so our guests felt welcome and enjoyed themselves, not to mention your essential assistance with Cate. I appreciate you being here."

"You're welcome, Dri. Wouldn't have missed it," responds Bella.

"Yeah, me too. I was pleased to be here and assist you," says Sarah. "I'm impressed with your vision and mission statements as well. They are lofty goals. But they need to be, in my opinion. And very appropriate."

"It was very interesting. We're glad to have been here too," adds Gabriela.

"Well, your presence and assistance are much appreciated. Now, how do you think it went?" asks Dri.

"I'm pleased with the whole thing," responds Nika. "I think people enjoyed it. I like the new people who are interested, and they seemed to get what we are trying to develop."

"I was impressed," adds Sarah. "I haven't been as involved, but I love where this is going, what you're wanting to do. I'm in! I want to stay involved in some way or another. Like all of you, it doesn't bring Alex back. And I too miss him so. Yet, I think it is a great way to honor his memory, as well as the others killed at the same time."

"I'm so glad this appeals to you, Sarah," says Tiago. "I know that means a lot to Dri, too. I also thought everyone began to see what we want to do. The discussions and exercises on Friday seemed to go well and set up a great process for developing our mission on Saturday. I think that sequence was effective."

"As someone around the edges but not involved in the development of this, I agree that the activities you did on Friday gave people a sense of scope for the nonprofit. Then they got to practice some of that with the interactions on Sunday. I think that was a useful idea," added Emma. "I enjoyed going through this as well as helping with some hosting and baby support."

"I don't think I get it all, and I'm still not convinced about not bringing any more children into this world. It would be the end of humanity," says Miguel, looking sad. "I try to understand what Tiago keeps explaining. But otherwise, I like what you are trying to do with the efforts of this group, and that part I think Gabriela and I both support."

"Thanks for sharing that, Miguel. I'm sure Tiago and Dri will keep trying to explain why that's so important. But were there problems any of you experienced this weekend?" inquires Nika. She looks around at the faces of her extended family.

"It might have been useful to get to know the new people earlier," suggested Tiago. "I didn't think about it beforehand. But we might keep that in mind next time."

"Great point, Tiago. Thanks. Anything else?" People look at each other in silence. "Well, if you think of anything, please let me know. I will work on getting a summary out to the group. And thanks to you, May, for keeping notes of our work and decisions along the way."

"Happy to help. And thanks for including me in the group this weekend," replies May.

The conversation evolves into other topics about the wine, food, and getting back to their homes. Soon after dinner and hugs, the group members disperse towards their cars and drive home. With Tiago driving, Dri, Bella, and Emma can relax and chat.

"After this weekend, Mom, what do you think of our chances now?" asks Dri.

"I still have high hopes as well as my concerns and doubts. And I think you just need to proceed as if you will be highly successful."

"I agree with all of that," says Dri. "As Helen Keller said, 'Life is either daring or nothing.' So let's be daring. And that's what we'll do. Right, Tiago?"

"Absolutely! That's what we'll do. Work our hardest. Try our best," responds her husband, Dri's ever increasing "Rock of Gibraltar" partner.

Chapter 13

Connections

March, 2030

O n this early spring Sunday, plants respond to the warm rays. Mustard continues to flower in the vineyards after winter's rains. Fragrant blossoms suffuse the garden and waft into Bella's living room as Dri and Bella play with Cate on the floor. The one-year-old tears up paper, tosses ribbons left over from presents, as her grandmother relishes the sight.

Although it's three days beyond Cate's birthday, she doesn't seem to mind late presents, as long as there is food and play time. She, of course, ate little of the delectable lunch, which produced a lingering savory scent of pesto. Omar provided a new Oenophilia red blend, one people continue to enjoy. Bella and Dri keep their glasses out of Cate's easy reach while Tiago and Omar finish the dishes and put away leftovers. Then these two men head for the pagoda to relax and enjoy rare dyadic conversation.

Tiago lets a sip of the wine roll around his palate, then waits to experience the finish at the back of his mouth.

"I love this one. What varietals are in this luscious blend?"

"It's our new blend of Italian and French grapes: 65% Sangiovese, 15% Cab, 15% Merlot, and 5% Nebbiolo. I'm happy with it too. I think this vintage coalesced well," responds Omar.

"How is everything going at the winery?"

"It's been another productive year. We're pleased with the aging of our 2028 vintages, although we won't bottle for several months. The reds are coming along nicely. We'll introduce a new one during our 50th year celebration this fall. With strong wine scores last year and loyal consumers, we continue in solid shape.

"Are you involved with any of it these days, besides being a part owner," asks Tiago.

"My brother manages the winery intently, and my sister revels in making the wine. They have a great salesman and an excellent vineyard manager, and she has strong people to assist her. I mostly just consume their efforts. I participate with tastings and blending. My sister appreciates my palate input. Sometimes I help with harvest or bottling when they need an extra hand."

"Well, I still appreciate you arranging for our marriage to take place there. As I've told you before, I loved your comments."

"Thanks. It was fun and a real honor. I'm grateful for your confidence in me."

"It was Bella's suggestion. And Dri and I both trusted our sense about you."

"I talked with Dri a while ago about how she gets a sense for people, what she feels they are like, even whether to trust them. It almost seems like an intuitive reading of a person. Much of it apparently developed from her work with her counselor in Iowa City. But tell me, how did you learn to get a sense of what people are like? Did you see the same guy?" asks Omar.

Tiago gives out a small laugh. "Yeah, I did, but not as a counselor. I grew up with him. He was my grandfather."

He takes another sip of wine, savoring it on his palate before swallowing as he watches Omar's eyes widen and head shift backwards.

"Oh, that surprises me. I didn't know that. I understand you and Dri were acquainted in high school. Did you date then, too?"

Omar peers at the deep purple in his glass, then savors his own sip. The berry flavor and hint of leather in the finish briefly capture his attention. He looks back at Tiago.

"No. I was a year older than Dri and a year younger than Alex. I hung out with him because we played baseball together, and I used to see her when I was over at their house occasionally. But we didn't connect until my last year of school. By then, I was busy with studies, baseball, and prepping for college. She and I became friends, went to a couple of games, a few movies and dinners together. We both enjoyed spending time with each other. But I didn't want to get romantically involved with anyone. I was attracted to her. Yet, I felt I should wait, and my grandfather agreed. Not that there was anything wrong with Dri. I thought she was amazing, and he did too."

"But not enticed enough to date?" chuckles Omar.

"Not at the time, primarily because my focus was elsewhere. We ended up going to different colleges, and it wasn't easy to get together. We saw each other a few times while at school, partially again because of Alex. But I wasn't ready to get serious. I dated some in college. But, no one compared to what I thought of her. I loved her smile, her insights, her open heart, and humor. And it seems she had the same reaction, although she apparently didn't see me as that funny when we talked about it later. We can't all be perfect," Tiago says with a laugh.

"Sounds pretty much like a match made in heaven," suggests Omar. "My first marriage was kind of that way, while she was around."

Bella opens the door and steps out onto the patio. "You two doing OK?"

"Yeah, great," responds Omar. "Should I open another bottle of wine?"

"In a while. Dri's putting Cate down, then we're going to go for a walk. I'll leave the baby monitor on the table here in case Cate wakes early. We should be back in an hour or so. You two alright with that?"

"Yeah, great by me," responds Omar.

"Me too," adds Tiago.

"OK, fabulous. Maybe I'll open another bottle when we get back, then check in about joining you," says Bella

"Perfect. Thanks, *mi amor*. Have a fabulous walk," replies Omar.

"We will. See you in a while."

Bella turns and steps back into the house.

"So, how long were you married?" asks Tiago as he looks back towards Omar.

"Almost 13 years. We have one son, Alberto, who works at a winery in Chile, getting some great experience. Given that he grew up with Spanish, it's helped his adjustment there."

A smile comes over Tiago's face as he lets out a laugh. "Alberto was my grandfather's name! Even on this vast globe, it's a small world. So, if I may ask, did you and your wife divorce?"

"No. She died of breast cancer about 18 years ago, when Alberto was only 10. He and I lived by ourselves for many years until he went to college. Then he spent time in Italy before moving to Chile. He's fascinated by different approaches to making wines and wants to gain more experience before returning to Napa."

"I'm sorry about your wife. Bella didn't mention that part, at least to me."

"Thanks. Guess we all go through loss at some point. It's part of living and important to carry on the best we can. As I recall, Dri's therapist, your grandfather, died a while ago. Is that right? I thought Bella or Dri mentioned that."

"Yeah, rather suddenly during surgery almost 13.... no, 14 years ago. Dri was still his client. It was a shock to us all. She and I were grateful for our friendship. It allowed us to share our grieving experience. Maybe it was a prescient event for sharing the grief of Alex's death."

Tiago raises his glass.

"A toast to your wife, to my Gpa, and to Alex."

"Absolutely. *Salud*."

Omar raises his glass in the air, and both take another sip. Then Omar's eyes glance down to the concrete stamped patio.

"Yeah, another sudden death. I was glad to be in Bella's life when it happened, trying to provide what support I could. I think her awareness of my wife's passing helped us."

He pauses for a moment, turning his glance back towards Tiago.

"So what do you think happens when we die?"

"That's an interesting question that my Gpa and I . . . . sorry, my grandfather and I talked quite a bit about."

"Is that what you called him, Gpa?"

"Yeah. It was a name I came up with when young and couldn't pronounce grandpa. It started with Grpa, but later simplified to Gpa. That sounded better than a partial dog growl." laughs Tiago. "My whole family ended up adopting the name. It didn't sound as old as 'Grandpa,' especially for a man who was very aware and full of life. I think he enjoyed it too, because he signed all our cards that way."

"I kind of like it. May I use it when my son hopefully gets married and has children?"

"Yeah, of course. We'd be honored. Well, anyway, my Gpa was fascinated by all the near-death research. He consumed almost every book he could find on the subject and was amazed at the impact it had on people's lives. He read about other subjects, but that was one that interested him the most. Anyway, he and I would end up in long conversations about what people would experience, the common view that there was some part of us that existed after death, an energetic consciousness."

Tiago looks at Omar's eyes, seemingly exhibiting a slight glaze.

"Are you familiar with the topic, Omar?"

Omar shifts in his chair, alertness reappearing on his face.

"Yeah, a bit."

He paused, as if to take it all in. Then he continued.

"But aren't there some critics who suggest that these people just hear others talking or imagine such occurrences, like a drug induced experience or something?"

Tiago smiles at his reaction.

"Yeah, I've read some of that too. I suspect people are trying to dismiss what they don't want to believe. Gpa and I talked about their critiques. You can't prove the experience. But their critiques don't begin to explain the fairly consistent and dramatic changes that occur in these people's lives after such experiences. I guess that can happen with drug trips, but not as consistently. And that's as important to me as the out-of-body experiences they describe."

"OK, good point."

"Anyway, the reports frequently focus on love. Not just the emotion, but as our essence. How that transforms their view of life afterwards. Many relate insights about reincarnation, the importance of learning from our lives, a life review many experienced, and how that review was about healing and growing, not about punishment. I remember one story Gpa frequently told others about a fundamentalist preacher who primarily talked about fear, punishment, sins, and hell. After the man's near-death experience, all he wanted to talk about was love. But is wasn't just talking. He acted from love and shared his life from a loving heart."

"That's pretty amazing. I hear Dri got interested in the topic, too. I guess from her work with your Gpa. Seems she influenced Bella to read more about the topic. So what other ways did your Gpa impact your life? Did you do any counseling like Dri did?"

"No, not in a formal way. But with Gpa, any conversation could end up as an informal session. Like when I would ask about problems with friends, with my parents, my own discouragement, or even how to improve my baseball skills. For example, I had trouble staying focused when up to bat. He would ask what was going on with me beforehand and going through my head when at the plate. I would tell him about my self doubts, how anxious I would feel in my stomach, even my hands shaking a little when batting. We also talked about what he called my 'monkey mind,' as my thoughts were all over the place. Like a monkey jumping around in a tree. So he also taught me to meditate, which helped my concentration tremendously. In some ways, it's like what would happen with the pitcher, played by Kevin Costner in the movie, *For the Love of the Game*, where everything else fades away. Only Gpa taught me well before that movie came out. Still, it was fun to watch someone do that, having experienced something like that already."

"Wow, that's cool. It must have helped you quite a bit."

"Yeah, my brother and me both. I think it's one reason we both made it to Berkeley, and he still uses it now that he's playing with the Giants. But it helps well beyond baseball. It's something to help you keep a focus in life, in presentations, or when you start to feel down internally. But that is just part of it. It's changing the lie you tell yourself and learning to trust your instincts. All these work together to create a happier life and not get so reactive to others."

"Would you talk more about the lie we tell ourselves?" asks Omar. "I'd like to under-stand what you mean by that."

"I would say the most important thing he taught me was how we typically create a lie that can evolve into a whole web of false ideas about ourselves and our abilities. We ended up exploring the issue until I got clear about it. Then he helped me see it as a lie, a distortion about who I was."

"Seriously! And did finding it help you?"

"Well, not just finding it. What helped the most was shifting it."

"Do you mind me asking what the lie was you told yourself? Maybe it would help me see if I do something like that."

"In Gpa's experience, we all do some form of it. After talking a long while, what I realized is that I basically felt incompetent and empty inside. So then I would compensate by researching lots of information or secretly practicing in order to look competent. Then we put that together with the way I had to practice being competent in private so it would look like to everyone else that I was a natural. Before I could ride a bike, for example, I would practice in the basement all by myself when others didn't know. When my dad took me outside and said it was time to learn how to ride, I pretended I didn't. He put me on a new bike and, magically, I could do it well. He and Mom thought I was amazing. So did my older brother, who took a while to learn how to ride. All the private practice, reading or research would make me look great to the world, which helped compensate for the way I felt inside, a feeling no one else knew until Gpa and I talked about it. When I finally told him, he just smiled and patted my knee. 'Yes,' he said, 'that's how some people twist their lesson.' What he suggested is the same heart opening meditation and reconnection process he later shared with Dri. It made a big difference for both of us, although neither of us know the other practiced it until many years later.

"That's interesting. And what difference did it end up making for you?"

"For me, once I felt the connection to something greater than myself, as many people from the near-death experience describe, I knew there was not just emptiness inside of me. While the empty feeling did not just magically go away, I knew that was not all there was to me. That the feeling I was completely empty and incompetent was a lie. I still experienced emptiness at times. But the more I practiced what Gpa called the reconnection, the more I could see and feel I was linked to everything, like energetically to my family. I began to especially feel connected to others who had gone through such experiences, like the near-death episodes. The change was a slow and fundamental transformation in the way I felt about and viewed myself."

"OK, when can we set up an appointment?" chuckles Omar. "I could use some help with exploring a possible lie. Your Gpa must have been a great support to you and your family."

"Yeah, he was. But it wasn't just him. He worked with my mother since she was a little girl, and she's helped me, too. I was just getting to know about the Enneagram when Gpa died. So there was a lot I didn't understand yet and wanted to know. Fortunately, my mother learned it from him, and she could help me understand more after Gpa was gone. And she and I still talk about it. Sometimes I have more questions, or at other times we share an insight that comes up. And it's always fun to watch a movie and guess what Enneatype a character might be or even someone in public life."

"I've heard of the Enneagram, but I don't know much about it. And I'm not very interested in putting people in another category. I think we do enough of that already."

"Yeah, I agree with that. But the most important part of identifying an Enneatype is to understand the tool better, not just judge people or categorize them. For me, the most significant aspect of this approach is to realize how each type distorts an essential lesson for us to learn. When we expand our understanding of what we often feel, see, or do based on that distortion or lie, then we can free ourselves from it. In that freedom are all sorts of possibilities, including pure awareness from the body, silence of the mind, and the consciousness of love."

"Oh, OK. Is that all?" chuckles Omar. "Sounds like a lifetime of learning. I think I'm too old to start such a journey."

Tiago laughs at his reaction. "I don't think we're ever too old to start. And Gpa didn't either. The important thing is not to wait any longer. Once you begin to understand the basic lie and the way we color everything from that view, you can begin to see yourself and the world around you with less and less distortion. In the end, it allows us to more clearly be aware of our true nature, love. It's just another tool to get to our essence, like those people who have gone through near-death experiences."

Tiago looks down at the monitor, just to make sure Cate appears settled and remains asleep.

"Oh, wow. I had no idea. And has it been useful for you, to get to your essence?"

"Yes, one of the most useful tools I've found. For me, the greatest value is in the essential lessons and letting go of the lie. For example, my lesson is to expand my view to see both the whole of our existence as well as the parts and pieces. It is seeing the whole rug, while also recognizing all the threads and weaving that creates the pattern. In that wholeness, I am a piece, and the piece contributes to the whole. And as that piece, I also connect to love. When I stay clear of that understanding, I am neither incompetent nor empty."

"That sounds healing," Omar softly responds.

"Yes, it is. And the connection to cosmic love is what Dri experienced about the time Gpa passed. It wasn't through the Enneagram, but the heart meditation that she learned. The process is not as important as the outcome, no matter what means you use."

"And what is Dri's lesson?"

"I think it best if you ask Dri that question. I'm sure she'd be happy to explain it. But I'll leave that for her to share."

"OK, that makes sense. But is connecting to one's essence your intention with this new coalition you're wanting to develop? The manual you two are working on?"

"Yes, that's one of our hopes. It's not about getting everyone to think like us, but rather to help people explore different processes that get them in touch and connect to their own essence, core, true nature, or higher self. It's essentially the same thing. It doesn't matter what you call it. What matters is that you own, use, and respect it. What matters is that you feel the love that composes your own essence and let it spread from there. What I've experienced and seen or read about others in that place is greater concern and kindness for yourself and and other people. That's what changes you and the world. When we're in that place, I think we're better people."

"Is that the only way to be better people? To access this place?"

"Oh no, of course not. There are lots of people now who are kind and care tremendously about others. But such caring permeates more of your life when we can live daily from the core of love and an open heart. It's like what happens from a near-death experience. But not all of us go through such encounters. So we want to find other ways to help people access their essence. This in turn tends to lead to more sharing, less taking, less harm to others, and experiencing the love of the universe. That is why enlightened people sit on the top of a mountain, totally blissed out. They are in the ecstasy of our being and the universe."

"That doesn't sound so bad," chuckles Omar.

"Oh, it's not. There's nothing wrong with that at all. But sitting there doesn't change our world. It only changes your perspective, your personal experience, or those who learn from you. But most of us spend our lives in the distortions, focused solely on the physical world, material things, without incorporating the essential lesson at the same time. If you want to make the world a better place, Omar, would you go sit in a cave or on top of the mountain and do nothing? Or would you get involved with change?"

"OK, I see your point. But lots of people are trying to change the world from their point of view, from what they see as the right way. Are you any different?"

"We're not that different in wanting a change, only in where we focus the foundation of the transformation we want to see. Our focus is learning to live with each other from our essence, through an open heart in this physical world. What we seem to do currently is more about living out our lies, our distortions and wounds. Blaming others for our hurts, and finding ways to ignore our own pain while separating ourselves from others to make us feel better. We think racism, gender discrimination, financial inequities, and violence would all improve if we lived from more open hearts. That's why we are not just trying to end these injustices, but rather encourage people to live from their own essence, which then creates more fundamental peace and justice."

"It sounds like you and Dri have shared considerable discussion about these ideas. You've also had time working this out with your Gpa. I would need time to mull this over, to think more about what you're suggesting."

"Of course. I think this attraction to something deeper in our lives was one of the attractions for both Dri and me when we knew each other in high school. But it took some years for us to gain more clarity ourselves. Then we could envision it in terms of a relationship. Now, we also want to pass it on to Cate and others, if it is appealing to them."

"And will you raise Cate with these ideas?"

"That's our desire. Of course, the day by day actions will not come out perfectly. But that's also why we both want to have a partner who agrees with a shared approach, a useful collaboration for any couple co-parenting."

"And what if Cate doesn't want to learn to do this, Tiago? What if she rebells?"

Tiago looks at him and smiles. "Sounds like you've raised a child yourself, Omar. And, as you already know, we don't get to control their choices ultimately. But we can lovingly give Cate the option and encourage her along the way. Gpa believed it wasn't about teaching a child young and then leaving them on their own. He thought we had different choice points in our life as we get older. And each point provides an opportunity of whether to walk the path of consciousness or focus primarily on the physical world. There isn't just a single choice."

"What do you mean, there's not a single choice?"

"Gpa talked about his own experience choosing a focus on consciousness, and then getting caught up with shiny objects and a more worldly life. After a while of living that way, he found he was not as happy. So he shifted his focus towards greater love and consciousness. As he did so, his joy increased. While his mother tried to encourage that from the beginning, we are free to choose in this life. So it's more about paying attention along the way, trying different options, sometimes shifting our priorities over time. Cate, I think, will have lots of opportunities to choose, and we can simply provide love and support for her, no matter what road she walks."

Again Tiago scans the monitor, and Cate appears settled.

"Yeah, I get that. I wasn't too keen on Alberto going to Italy at first. I thought he ought to stay here, where I could help make connections for him. But then he wouldn't have experienced learning how to make them himself. In the end, I think his intuition about going was right. And I'm forever grateful for simply supporting him and encouraging hard work and doing well, in whatever he did."

"I agree. And that's what we'll try to do with Cate. We'll give her as many resources as we can to live from her heart and intuition, to focus on a conscious life. And she'll decide what she'll learn, take with her and leave behind. But I don't think we ever leave it so far we can't recover it. And most importantly, we'll model such a life as parents. That certainly was important with Gpa's mother. Not just the words she said. It was how she lived her life. And my mother, too."

"Yeah, that's important. I think that's had an impact on my Alberto."

"Still, kids make their own priorities. My Gpa spent time with my brother, Javier, as well, sharing the some information. But the suggestions Gpa made didn't feel as essential to him as I think they do to me. At least at the time. I love my brother, and we are different in our choices, even with the same Gpa, Mom, and Dad. My mom focused on it more than my dad did, too. Just like Gpa's mother did more than his dad. It hits us all differently. But Cate will be at least a 5th generation for some of these ideas, starting with my great-grandmother. Who knows how long before her. And Gpa came back to it after other explorations."

"Well, do you ever use these ideas in your counseling work at the high school or as coach of the school baseball team? Is it useful at all there?"

"Great question. I'm still figuring out how best to incorporate some basic skills that also do not feel like I'm imposing something too odd on students without a parent's knowledge or permission. In many ways, I incorporate these concepts within the general approach of an accepted counseling practice, because so many of them fit. Then I feel comfortable explaining or justifying my work. And, as with all children, the way I live my life at school, in counseling, and on the field can impact others without saying many words."

"And is it possible to incorporate these ideas into an accepted counseling practice?"

"Yeah, it is. I'm just taking my time to do it. Slowly at first and based on where the student wants to go. For example, I can help kids learn a focusing meditation, a useful skill for many parts of their life, as part of coaching. Or I can help kids see other possibilities when they get focused on only one outcome that they want to avoid. Essentially, my Gpa did the same thing within his own counseling practice. Only if a client wanted to pursue a particular direction and found it helpful would he follow that course."

"So, how do you do that?"

"Let me give you an example. There's lots of talk these days about core strength or core values. But no one has a single definition of core. So I use the idea to take it a little deeper, helping students go further with that idea. I include a core feeling or intuitive sense, if they seem interested. If not, I leave it at that or even back off some. And if a student has a hard time focusing, I might suggest they watch that movie, *For the Love of the Game*. I get them to follow what Kevin Costner learned to do, letting other thoughts go, essentially wiping out the crowd noise, to focus on his pitching. The brain actually is gathering more information that we can process. We have to dismiss some sources just to focus on others. When we learn a type of meditation, we actually can retrain our brain on whether to go with the thoughts or let them pass through without attaching to them. When kids get stressed, it's when they attach primarily to the information that generates and amplifies their anxiety. It's not an easy habit to change, especially after years of attachment. But we can talk about how they can learn to do that, to focus so directly they let everything else go. When they are in that space, it's a type of meditation, letting thoughts fade or move out of your head. But I may not label it that, unless they seem interested."

"And is this how you spread your personal gospel?"

"No. This isn't about getting people to think or see the world just like me. It's about helping people shift into greater awareness, consciousness, and a larger perspective if they want to go there. There are many ways to do that. Tibetan Buddhists learn to meditate with their eyes slightly open, while Vajrayana and Zen Buddhists do it with eyes closed, although all sit. Sufi's move for meditation. Others walk, run, or dance. I breathe and bat. Which is the correct form? It doesn't matter. What matters is they all want people to see or connect to something deeper, at times even their true nature. That's what interests me. And if someone is not interested, I honor that, too."

"But how does that change something like racism? As a young Latino man, you must have experienced prejudice at times in your life. Yet so many people who perpetuate racist ideology and behaviors call themselves good Christians. The Spanish Conquistadors called themselves faithful Catholics. Yet they murdered and enslaved people. The Southern plantation owners who used slaves to make them rich called themselves devout Christians. The evangelicals who supported Trump and his incarceration of children at the border and his white racists focus, called themselves ardent followers of Christ's teachings. If Christianity can't end racism, what chance do you and your small group have?"

"A great question, Omar, and the essence of our quest. Let me tell you a story. My Gpa had a dear friend from his graduate program who was an evangelical Christian and extremely conservative. He also was racist, especially towards blacks. They lived in Los Angeles, where he fit right in with others sharing his attitudes. Years later, he came to visit my Gpa, who noticed that his friend had changed. He talked about blacks with respect, and he apologized to my grandfather for talking about people that way. My Gpa asked what had made the difference, what made him change his attitude. The man said, 'I realized I couldn't live the teachings of Christ and treat others this way.' Some Christians don't get that, and some do. What my grandfather sensed is that he had a more open heart. He believed that was the key. Open hearts simply reinforced his emphasis on connection to our essence, which seems to help hearts remain open or even open fuller."

"Well, OK. That might work with Christianity. But what about other religions?"

"It doesn't matter your religious beliefs. What matters is how willing you are to open your heart and live that way. That's basically what people say from the near-death research.

We may not impact many people. Yet, I think open hearts are contagious. And if we can help people open up theirs more and more, I think we can amplify the message of Christ, Buddha, and other great teachers. In many ways, the Sufi's believe the same thing about Mohammad's teachings, and even some of the old prophets in Judaism. Traditionally, Jewish teachings focus more on people truly sharing and giving than some Christian churches."

"OK, I think I have a better sense of what you are saying and wanting to do. I just have one more question. How old are you again?" asks Omar with a chuckle.

Tiago smiles back at him. "As my Gpa would say, wisdom isn't just in the body or brain. Sometimes the greatest wisdom of the ages is in your heart and true nature."

"It reminds me of that George Bernard Shaw quote, 'Life isn't about finding yourself; life is about creating yourself.'"

"Oh, I haven't heard that one. But, with all due respect to Mr. Shaw, I would modify it slightly. I think life is about reconnecting to your core or higher self. If that is true, life is about finding and creating yourself. It's important, I think, not to get trapped in false dichotomies."

"What do you mean by false dichotomies?" asks Omar.

"People present what appears to be two opposites, like it's either light or dark, agree or disagree. We know that as the light begins to increase in the morning or the sun goes down in the evening, there are gradations at both times. We also can both agree and disagree with a statement. If I asked whether you were were happy or sad, what would you say? Are you one or the other?"

"Well, I'm often very happy. But sometimes I get sad, especially when I experience the loss of a loved one."

"Understandable and natural. And in some moments, do you ever feel both at the same time? Are you sad about something while also noticing happiness about something else, and holding both in your body simultaneously?"

"Not sure. Maybe. I probably shift from one to the other, even if they both are present. I don't know if I've ever attempted to hold both at the same time. Could be interesting to try."

"More importantly, from my view, is that we simply get away from the assumption that we live in a purely dichotomous world. For example, if someone asks whether I want to travel or not, I sometimes say, 'Yes.' I'm not just trying to be cute, but rather to identify mixed feelings I may have about something. Part of me wants to travel. Another part wants to stay home. And I like to practice acknowledging the presence of two, what appear to be, opposites, like with the quote from Shaw."

"That's interesting. I'll have to play around with that. Could be insightful with what goes on inside me that I don't notice."

Bella slides open the patio door, and the the two women step out. "Is Cate still sleeping?" asks Dri.

"We haven't heard a sound from her. I've been checking the monitor, and she still seems settled. Think she may be sleeping too long? Maybe she won't go to sleep so easily tonight?" asks Tiago.

"Yeah. Let's wait a little longer, then I may go wake her up," responds Dri. "Meanwhile, are you two at a place in your conversation we could join you?"

"Of course," responds Omar. "But let's gather inside. I'm starting to feel chilly."

Tiago and Omar take their empty wine glasses, moving them and the monitor inside. The four gather in the living room for more social conversation and, except for Dri, some additional imbibing. They laugh, talk about the coming spring, favorite flowers and their sequence in blooming.

Tiago appreciates the light, social conversation. Yet, it isn't the type that feeds his soul. Fortunately, the nearly two hours of interaction on the patio will nourish him until he and Dri can share about the patio talk.

The babbling from the bedroom informs the adults Cate is awake and ready to meet the world again. Tiago goes to get her, his own babbles mirroring her sounds. Her screech gets louder at his talking, and he responds with a comforting laugh. The father and daughter reappear after a quick change, preventing the others from sharing in the odious gift she left for her dad.

"OK, here's the birthday girl, ready for more fun. And you're all welcome. I changed her," says Tiago, smiling at Dri, who responds in kind.

Cate is placed on the floor for more paper and ribbon fun, one of her favorites. The adults talk about what's going on in their lives during the spring and coming summer. As the shares begin to fade, Dri shares her need to leave. She and Tiago have more work on the manual before the first ShareShops are offered.

"OK, I'll bite," says Omar. "What are ShareShops?"

"We've tried to set up some workshops to let people know what we are doing and to learn about the information and skills we want to share with others," responds Dri. "But trying to do this in person is challenging for people to attend at a certain place and time.

It also is more expensive for us and for them. So we are starting to try using the Share app through computers and mobile devices to spread the information farther and faster. Then we tape the presenters and make that available through our website so people who missed it can access the information that way. It's not as great as in person. But it certainly reaches more people and those who can't attend a live gathering."

"That sounds useful and an important alternative for people who can't travel," says Bella.

"Yeah, it seems to be. And people appear to appreciate both, especially if they can participate when the session is initially offered rather than just from the recording," says Tiago. "We also developed follow-up Share sessions where people can ask questions and discuss how the changes are going."

"That sounds very useful," says Bella. "Well, thanks for coming over. It was great to be part of the birthday celebration for my adorable granddaughter."

"Oh, Mom, thanks for hosting this, for the great food, and lovely conversation on our walk," responds Dri.

The young family gather up their personal items, and Tiago gets Cate into her car seat. As he gets her settled, Omar approaches him.

"Thanks for the conversation, Tiago. It was lovely getting to know you better and what you two desire to do with this coalition. It gives me a lot to mull over. But I also was wondering. Have you and Dri ever done barrel tasting? It would be fun to have you come to the winery and sample different vintages as they mature in the barrels, picking up more oak, then sampling some from a new bottle and an older one too," says Omar.

"No, I've never done that. I don't think Dri has either. It sounds interesting and fun to see the difference."

"Yeah, I think you'd enjoy it. The newest wine can taste pretty green. But that's part of what's informative about it and how it changes over time. Let's set up a time after we bottle this summer to do that. It would be fun to host you both."

"Sounds great. Now that we talked about how human lives coalesce, we can experience the same process with vintages," laughs Tiago. "Sounds like a great time. Thanks!"

"Yes, it'll be fun."

Omar extends his arms, and the two men embrace. Tiago moves towards Omar's right side instead of his left, placing their hearts closer together. After hugs and smiles all around, the young family takes their leave.

Chapter 14

Expansions

July, 2030

L ate Monday morning, Nika calls Dri, who doesn't answer. A message will have to do.

"Hi, my friend. I have great news. I just received the financial report from Sam, who's been doing a yeoman's job as treasurer. He received a second large anonymous donation. He knows the names of the two contributors for reporting purposes, but we agreed he wouldn't tell anyone else. Still, I think we now are ready to hire an executive director. Ariella thinks it's an excellent idea and is willing to chair a search committee. Naeem and I will meet you at Oenophilia on Wednesday afternoon. But I don't think we'll be in any shape to talk business afterwards. I was wondering if you and Tiago would have some time Friday morning to go over some organizational items. Text me if that works. Love you!"

She hangs up and looks over the report once again.

This is great. Everything's coming together. And I can let go of some responsibility!

It's another warm sunny Wednesday as Naeem and Nika drive through Napa Valley, enjoying the vineyard views as they approach Yountville. They take a right at the light onto Madison, then on up Yountville Cross Road as they make their way to Oenophilia winery. They park next to Emma and Phil's car, then walk inside to meet Omar.

"Hey Emma, Phil, how are you both?" says Nika as she passes through the door Naeem is holding open. "I see you brought Bella with you, too. Great to see you all."

She continues to chat while sharing hugs.

"Hold the door, please," calls out Dri, smiling at the doorman dressed in tan pants and a long sleeve white shirt with a sparkle showing through his big smile. "Great you guys could make it," she says as she leans in for a one armed hug from her favorite artist.

"Oh, we wouldn't miss it," responds Naeem. "Great to see you too, Tiago."

The two men share hugs before going inside to greet their host.

One more car pulls into the lot and parks next to Naeem.

"OK, we're here too," shouts Sarah as she climbs out of the passenger's seat and closes her door.

May locks the car and joins her as they hustle towards the inviting door Tiago now holds open for these additional guests.

"Welcome to Oenophilia," says Omar as the guests make their way towards the tasting bar.

His dark wavy hair contrasts with his sun kissed skin in a long sleeve blue shirt, light blue pants, and sockless blue shoes. The women are in plain or patterned sundresses with shawls or sweaters over their shoulders.

"I'm so glad you all could make it here today. I know Bella's excited about this, and thanks, Tiago, for helping to organize it."

Omar points to two young women standing behind the tray of glassware.

"This is Ellie and Aubrie, hosts here at the winery who will be helping us today. If you have questions, they can answer them too. Glad you got the message about long sleeves or sweaters. The barrel room can be chilly, even in July. Help yourselves to a glass here on the tray and let's go into where we age the wine. But don't worry. You won't get much older," Omar says with an adolescent laugh.

Aubrie and Ellie wear big smiles, along with the tan pants and black winery golf shirts, as they greet people and make sure each guest has stemware. The group enters into the tall, semi-darkened and chilly room, gazing around at the copious barrels in rows stacked three or four high. There is a scent of wet oak and yeast. The first thing Naeem notices is the purple hue around the middle section of each container.

"Why are all the barrels purple in the middle?" Naeem asks.

"Great question, Naeem," responds Omar. "First, it tells us the barrel contains red wine. And, more importantly, it hides all the drips I make from stealing wine with my pipette," he adds with a laugh.

Omar pulls out the stopper at the top of one barrel and dips in his "wine thief" pipette to remove some vino, allowing a small amount of Sangiovese to fall into each glass. The guests begin to put their noses deep in their glasses, following Omar's example, to get a strong sniff of the wine. This first one is young, and the guests learn what a "green" wine in its first year smells and tastes like.

"Don't get too caught up in what might even seem like a bitter taste. This will mellow out in time. Try to imagine what two more years on this wine would be like," suggests Omar. "Our next vintages will assist you with that vision."

The guests, new to this experience, sniff and taste again. There is talk between them as they compare this educational experience to their traditional tastings.

"OK, not the best wine I've ever tasted," laughs Emma. "But I enjoy learning and experiencing this process. It's fun and interesting, especially with this crowd."

They move on to taste a Cab from the same vintage. This is followed by the scent and taste of both wines from a vintage a year older. Tiago finds these two later samples give a clearer indication of what the wines will smell and taste like when more mature. And they are more appealing.

Finally, Omar leads the group back up to the tasting bar, where Ellie and Aubrie have opened a bottle of each wine from a vintage another year older that more closely resembles the consumption palate. They also opened the same two wines from the 2023 vintage, which some anticipate may be the vintage of the century for Napa Valley. The last two bottled wines taste much closer to the ones they are used to drinking.

"I love these two, especially the Sangiovese. Something a little different for Napa," says Bella. "And thanks for the barrel tasting. It's interesting to get a sense of the maturation process and see what a difference a year makes."

"Yes, a year, or seven, makes a big difference," adds Naeem. "And this winery was such a lovely setting for Tiago and Dri's wedding. I find this place very romantic."

He then reaches into his pocket and pulls out a small, velvet box. He drops to one knee in front of Nika, then opens the lid.

"Will you marry me, Nika? Would you do me the great honor?"

Nika exhibits a mixture of shock and pleasure on her face, which does not distract from the smile on her mouth and her stunning dark eyes against her yellow dress.

"Yes! Yes, I would be honored," Nika replies.

She reaches for Naeem's hands and pulls him to standing as he removes the princess cut black diamond band from the box and places it on her left ring finger.

"I want you to know, this is not just the wine talking," says Naeem. "I have been planning this for some time. It just seems like the perfect day and place to ask such a question, surrounded by others who love you, too."

He wraps his arms around Nika, who wilts into his kissing embrace. The others clap, then wait their turn for a congratulatory hug from the future bride and groom.

"Thanks for letting us be part of this special event," says Dri. "So glad this day has come."

"Me too," says Naeem. "I've been a little nervous about her response. She has so many plans and things going on in her life. I was worried she would want to wait longer."

"We haven't set a date yet," laughs Nika.

"Do you have a place in mind for the marriage?" inquires Omar.

"No, we haven't gotten that far," responds Naeem. "This is the extent of my current plans, waiting to make sure I get the right answer."

His eyes glisten as he smiles.

"Well, if you want to use our winery, I'm offering it as one possibility. Just keep it in mind," Omar adds. "I'm sure my siblings will agree."

"Thanks. That's extremely generous of you," says Nika. "But what if we want to get married in the winter?"

"Then we can hold it inside. We have a large meeting room I can show you sometime and maybe serve a dinner in the barrel room. There are several possibilities."

"Very sweet of you. Thanks," Nika replies.

"Thank you so much, Omar, for the barrel tasting. This was fun and generous of you," says Tiago. "I appreciate your invitation from our springtime conversation and glad we could do it when others are in town."

"It was my pleasure to have you all here," responds Omar as he turns towards Bella and shares a smile. "I thought you would enjoy it, and I have a great time hosting. The family sees it as sharing with the community and more people having an enjoyable experience at our winery. So, they're happy to have me do it."

As Bella walks towards him he reaches out to take her hand.

The group members chat for a while, some enjoy a little more wine. Slowly, all begin to share their thanks and goodbyes, especially with Omar, Ellie, and Aubrie, three fabulous hosts.

Bella stays behind to ride back with Omar, who first does a little more cleanup with Bella's help. The others slowly walk to their cars, with more conversation and laughter. Finally, they all drive over to Bella's where the entire group will have dinner.

The newly engaged couple drive over, as they will be staying with Bella for a couple of nights. May and Sarah follow them home, with plans to spend the weekend.

The following afternoon, July 4th, the entire group gathers again at Bella's place for a barbecue and celebration of Alex's life. It has only been two years, and Bella invited them all so she wouldn't be alone today. All responded with pleasure to her invitation. And Dri is happy to be in their company. Besides, it doesn't take much of an excuse for this group to gather together. They all enjoy delicious food, great conversation, and wonderful wine.

Phil volunteers to barbecue the chicken and fish with Nika assisting, mostly with conversation. Omar is happy to be behind the bar, with Dri in charge of drink orders and delivery. It's generally an easy time, mostly deciding whether to drink white, rosé, or red. Bella takes charge of the salad and side dishes in the kitchen, with Emma as sous chef and Tiago on cleanup. Sarah, Naeem and May set the table while Cate sleeps for a while.

Following another delicious meal and quick cleanup, the extended family gathers in the inviting lush garden to share memories and stories. Even Cate is awake by now and part of the share.

Dri talks about Alex's humor, wishing she could have gained more of his gift with quick responses and funny stories. Tiago shares stories from their baseball world, which was more fun because of Alex's commitment to excellence as a player and as a comic. Family members are smiling in response, although Dri is aware of the underlying melancholy she experiences and believes is shared by the group. As she notices this, she pulls Cate closer, as if caressing a connection to her brother. Having recently awakened, Cate surrenders to the embrace.

Emma and Phil talk about the fun times when Alex came out with the whole family for Alisa's wedding many years ago. They still laugh at a couple of pranks he played on their daughter and new husband. Phil then talks about Alex's insight regarding the groom, telling his uncle he didn't seem like a great guy. As it turns out, he was right. The marriage only lasted a couple of years, about 18 months too long. It was the first time Bella heard this about Alex and was grateful to hear about his insight.

"I'm sorry Alisa's marriage didn't last, but it seems like she's better off without him," responds Bella. "How is she feeling about it these days?"

"She would agree with you," says Emma with a smile. "She's happy to be working in Costa Rica. She'd never have taken the leap with the US State Department if she had settled down so early."

Phil nods his head in apparent agreement.

The stories continue, as each pair of eyes focus on the person speaking. Even the rose bush next to Nika seems to be attending intently as she laughs. She shares how Dri liked to do laundry downstairs, close to Alex's bedroom. Then she would try nonchalantly to hang out with him when his attractive friends were there, especially Tiago. Dri chuckles and admits she tried, but it wasn't until college that Alex actually let her stay.

"Still, the attempt was a fun challenge," adds Dri. "Alex was a good sport about it. He knew what I was up to, he admitted later at college. It was a contest for him, seeing who would be the most persistent. I think he won again." Dri laughs hesitantly as sadness manifests in her chest again for her dear brother.

"He was always someone I could talk to when I was down, and especially as I began to own being gay," says Sarah. "He always supported me, even when friends began teasing me in high school. He was vigilant with my defense."

Sarah's eyes water, finally breaking over the edge and rolling down her cheeks as she concludes. Omar and Emma pass around tissue boxes.

"I will always miss him," says Bella, as she looks down at her hands wringing her tissue. "I still don't think this interminable hole will ever go away. And I appreciate all of you sharing stories and some of his humor, which he always spread, even when I would get angry with him. It was difficult to stay mad as he made such humorous comments, hard as I tried."

A slight smile mixed with tears show up on Bella's face with her final comment.

"We will always miss him, Mom, responds Sarah. "He was a great brother, with a hearty laugh and a loving heart."

"I agree," adds Dri. "And I miss Alex bringing great wine home when he was an intern at David Arthur Vineyards," she says with a chuckle. "I'm thankful that Omar took over that role, as you are very generous with your wines, too. Thank you."

"I know David pretty well. A great guy," says Omar. "Maybe we could talk him into a barrel tasting sometime, as a contrast to our wines. He also has an Italian series, including a lovely white blend. And I love his Cab Franc."

"Yeah, that was Alex's favorite too, although David's Elevation is fabulous and famous," adds Dri.

"My brother was telling me about a quote from Rich Aurilia about David's Elevation wine that was in the Chronicle years ago. Are you familiar with it?" asks Tiago.

"Yes, I am," responds Omar. "David told me about it when I was up at his winery several years ago. An interviewer asked Rich: 'If you were on death row and the warden let you have one glass of wine, what would it be?' Rich said, 'I'm going to take the David Arthur Elevation. That's one of the best wines I've ever had.' What a compliment to David. But it's no surprise. He's made some great wines."

"Your family does too, Omar. I love them," says Emma.

Bella notices a relaxation in her stomach.

"Alex mentioned something about a quote from a famous Giants player, but he couldn't remember what it was," shares Bella. "Glad to finally hear it."

She feels some relief as the topic expands to other aspects, still related to Alex but less directly about him. As the conversation continues, it evolves even further, although never completely away from her son. Today, Bella is grateful to remember some of the humor and delightful times while never completely evading the emptiness permanently left by his death. Still, it's an easier balance this year over last. It helps her heart inflate a bit, a little more open, as she reminisces about him,.

Later in the evening, the group goes to the front porch in an attempt to see fireworks in the valley. They get a glimpse of a few through the trees and some directly west. It's a joyful ending to the day that still is tinged with an aroma of sadness. Yet, there is some joy in gathering, relishing in each other's company. Delectable food and wine add another sensuous layer.

On Friday, Tiago, Cate and Dri arrive at Bella's just as she, Nika, and Naeem are finishing breakfast. Tiago fills two mugs with coffee and heads for the living room where Nika joins them.

Bella walks into the living room.

"I'll take this adorable one. Then you three can talk more easily. Besides, I haven't seen her since yesterday. How are you, adorable Cate?"

The two return to the kitchen to hang out with Naeem and more coffee.

"OK, no more suspense, please. Tell us the good news," requests Dri.

"With this second donation, we have over $2 million in our account! It's amazing. The number of members is slower than the donations, but we're still growing. I think it's time to hire an executive director to begin doing more organizational matters. And probably a half-time accountant too. I hate to push Sam too much as treasurer. I think we should get him and the new director some help."

"That's fabulous news," responds Dri. "But don't we even get to know where the donations are coming from?"

"I talked it over with Sam," says Nika. "The contributions are legitimate. But they wouldn't be anonymous if we all knew. And both contributors were clear about not disclosing their names. I think we need to honor that."

"Yeah, I agree," comments Tiago. "Could Sam send them a Thank You card? It would be thoughtful to share our gratitude, anyway."

"He already has done that," says Nika, as Tiago gives Nika a big thumbs up. "We're in agreement with that too. Right now, we have 213 members, which is great for 10 months, and the numbers are increasing steadily. We also have received about $45,000 in other donations. I asked Sam what he thought about hiring two staff members. We would need to keep fundraising, but he's supportive of it. Just from interest and current donations, we pretty much could cover those two salaries. We still need the board's approval. But what do you two think? Should we take the risk now or wait?"

"I'm inclined to take the risk," responds Tiago. "We are having solid success with the ShareShops, and they seem to be attracting more people who are excited about what we're doing. I think an ED would help keep enthusiasm high, which could be important all around."

"Yes, I agree," says Dri, as she shifts her focus from Tiago to Nika. "Let's take it to the board and see what they think. You said Ariella's willing to chair a search committee?"

"Yes," responds Nika. "She will ask at least two other board members to work with her. I think she would make a great chair. Then we may need to talk with Sam to see if he would at least serve on a committee to find the half-time accountant. I think that would be important."

"Oh yes, I agree with that too," adds Tiago. "He knows so much about finance. I think he would be a critical member. Could we also use someone not on the board to assist in the search, with board approval?"

"Who are you thinking of?" asks Nika, as her eyebrows narrow towards the bridge of her nose and her eyes intensify her gaze at Tiago.

"Well, Sarah was the first to come to mind," says Tiago. "Or maybe Omar? Either might be willing, and Omar knows at least something of the area from his business dealings."

"Excellent ideas," adds Dri. "I second that. I think we should ask board members, both about the hires and member support for the committees. We could use some extra help."

"OK, I'll put it on our agenda and present it at our video conference meeting next week," says Nika, now looking back at Dri. "One other thing that I thought might interest you, Dri. Out of our 213 members, we have had 51 women follow your lead and commit to no more children until we make more changes with gun control, violence and killing. And others are considering it, so I hear. I'm actually a little surprised by that, but the idea makes sense to them. I find that interesting."

"Wow, I'm surprised," responds Dri, her eyes opening wider and eyebrows extended upward. "And pleased, too. While it was important to us, I wasn't sure other women and couples would make such a commitment. It touches me."

"I think people are being touched by what we are trying to do, and this just brings another element of commitment to the change," comments Nika. "I've also been talking to Congresswoman Bradshaw about introducing another round of gun legislation to address some of the violence and killing still occurring, especially in our cities. She wants to talk to Kiara about anything happening with the Illinois Senate, now that she's a member. She's also talking to other members of congress, especially within the growing progressive segment of the Democratic Party."

"That sounds great. I'd be happy to help with that any way I can," adds Tiago. "I've been doing some research online since the CDC has been able to research gun violence again. It continues to be a concern among high schools, even though there have not been as many shootings. But there were so many in the previous three decades that administrators still talk about it, and I need to keep up on it as a school counselor."

"Fabulous. If you could start gathering some ideas and send them to me, I'll collect them from other sources too," responds Nika. "Well, we'd better get home. Naeem wants to get some work done this afternoon, and I need to do some myself."

"Thanks for all you do in heading up our board, Nika," says Dri. "I know you have lots of other things going on with work and all. But I really appreciate your constant efforts with this."

"Well, it does feel like my work. When your mom mentioned that quote from Rumi, I thought it was a little simplistic. Doesn't feel that way any longer," says Nika, with one of those sparkling smiles.

Naeem and Nika pack up their items, share hugs all around, then get in his car to drive back to Albany.

Bella sits on the couch, holding a happy Cate. Dri smiles at the mental picture of these two, grandmother and granddaughter, quite satisfied to be with each other. Dri watches Cate's eyes move to a squint and the ends of her mouth begin to turn down. She knows where this is going. She moves to the couch, sitting next to her mom as Cate begins to whimper.

"I'll take her, Mom. And thanks for taking such excellent care of her while we talked about coalition stuff."

Dri takes Cate into her arms, pulls up her top, unclasps one side of her bra and begins to breast feed her daughter.

"Always happy to hold my adorable granddaughter," says Bella. "That reminds me. I had an amazingly lucid dream last night that I wanted to share with you."

"Sure. What was it?" asks Dri.

"I was walking along this path in a park, holding this little boy's hand. He pointed to a swing off to the side. So we walked over and I lifted him into one with a strap in front. Then I pushed him for quite a while. He was happy as can be, just swinging back and forth. He eventually held up his arms like he wanted to get out. Then we were at the sand box with the buckets and shovels. We sat in the sand and played for a while. Finally, he looked up at me with a big smile on his face. Then he said, 'Thanks Grandma. I'm ready to go home now.' I don't know exactly how old he was. Maybe three? But he talked plainly and knew what he wanted. He reminded me a little of Alex, when he was a baby. But this boy had dark black hair, not the light brown Alex had. And he didn't look like Alex. But he had a similar feeling about him. It was so touching, and he was so loving. I didn't want to wake up when I did. I wanted to remain in that dream for a long time."

"What a beautiful dream," says Tiago, his voice soft and tender.

"It reminded me of the dream you had before Cate was born, Dri. Didn't that little girl talk to you in your dream, too?" asks Bella.

"Yeah, she did. She looked at me with a big smile and said, 'OK, Mommy, I'm ready.' That's all she said. I didn't know what to think. But I guess I wasn't surprised that our baby was a girl."

"I admire your commitment to change the world, Dri. But I think you should consider another baby. This one felt like yours, too."

"I appreciate your concern, Mom. But I'm committed to this, and Tiago is too."

"OK, I'm just sayin'," replies Bella. "Like a few other dreams I had, this one felt so alive, as if I was totally present in the moment with this boy in the park. The park was incredibly green, the sun was shining but not overly hot, and I could even smell flowers near there. It was more like a memory than a dream."

"How amazing," says Tiago. "I love it when my dreams are in color. So few of them are."

There was a knock at the door.

"Come in, Omar. It's open," says Bella in a loud whisper, not to disturb Cate, who just closed her eyes, moving to that settled sleep state without removing her mouth from Dri's breast.

"Hi, all. Glad you three are here," says Omar, also in a loud whisper. "Well, you, too, Bella, given that we're going to go to lunch. But I wanted to catch Tiago and Dri. I have a little gift for Cate that I thought you might enjoy."

Omar is carrying a small package wrapped in brown paper with a yellow curled ribbon in the middle. He hands it to Tiago, as Dri's hands are full.

Tiago unwraps the package to find a poem printed in forest green ink with purple matting surrounding it and framed in dark green with a slight gold around the edge. He inspects the beautiful work, then holds it up for Dri and Bella to see.

"Read it to us, would you, please?" inquires Dri.

Tiago reads the following poem:

To My Unborn Child

What I want to tell you
is that you are enough
you do not have to
do anything to be loved
you do not have to perform
or achieve
or earn a merit badge
this needs to be repeated
over and over
be who you are
and love what is before you
What I want to tell you
is be courageous

be your own hero

embrace friendships

release fear   unworthiness

continue to laugh

even when you can't

remember why

What I want to tell you

is be a doggie   hell raiser

wiggling   sniffing

inquisitive   wordless

passionate for a rub

a treat   a ball-catch

not worried

about next spring

What I want to tell you

is be awake   a trailblazer

scoff illusions

that keep us believing

that what we see

in the world is gospel

that keep us from recognizing

the truth that lies

underneath

Marianne Lyon, September, 2020

"Where did this come from, and who is Marianne?" asks Tiago.

"She's a local writer that I know from our Napa Valley Writers group," responds Omar. "I love her work, and I think she's a remarkably talented poet. She's had lots published and later became the Napa Valley Poet Laureate for two years. She wrote this poem several years ago and read it at one of our recent gatherings. I asked if I could share it with all of you. I thought it would fit nicely with what you two are wanting to do, Dri and Tiago, including the way you want to raise Cate. It might be inspiring in her room, or somewhere that would remind her of this message all her life."

"That's a lovely thought, Omar," says Dri. "How thoughtful of you to have it framed, too."

"Well, OK. I have to give Bella the credit for that," says Omar. "She suggested the idea and picked out the colors. And I enjoyed doing it for you all."

"Thanks," says Tiago. "We'll put it in her room today. Maybe read it at night before she goes to sleep. I love having it, and what a beautiful poem. I agree. It is the essence of what we want her to know. Actually, as I think about it, it's the essence of what we want everyone to know."

Chapter 15
Lies and Covers
June, 2031

Tiago experiences both nervousness and excitement. Or at least he distinguishes some difference between them, even if subtle. He knew they were similar, having encountered hefty anxiety before batting. As his baseball skills improved, he noticed excitement going to the plate. It was similar, but more pleasant. He wasn't always a great hitter, but his percentage improved considerably when he learned to focus his attention. This decreased his anxiety and replaced it with excitement. On the other hand, today is different. He has never hit a workshop out of the park, especially on his first at-bat.

Dri, Tiago and Gabriela, his mother, collaborated on a workshop to teach people about self-deception and defenses. The ideas are based on the Enneagram. Tiago began studying this perspective as an adolescent with his grandfather, then continued with his mom. But learning about something and teaching it are not the same, as he has experienced. Even after playing baseball many years, Tiago had to develop effective ways to coach and mentor student players. Dri has been working with this approach to change for several years now. His mother has taught individuals to work with the Enneagram, but she has not taught it with assistance from others.

With enough lead time, Tiago was able to find a common date to accommodate family members who wanted to attend and the rest of the board of directors. Now, after several months of planning and writing, the day has arrived. Soph was able to come in from Paris, and Alisa, Emma and Phil's daughter, flew in from Costa Rica for a family visit at the same time.

For such an intense workshop, Gabriela suggested a warm, nurturing setting. Omar generously offered the meeting room at the winery, which can comfortably accommodate 19 participants plus herself as the workshop leader. The windows overlooking the vineyards create a bucolic ambiance. There are paths for strolling around the winery, garden, and vineyards during break and lunch for a reflective and relaxing time.

Rather than rent hotel rooms, Omar hired a shuttle to pick up and deliver the nine people who would be flying into the Bay Area. Bella, Emma, and Omar volunteered their comfortable guest bedrooms and baths to host the out-of-towners. Fadima, the new executive director of the non-profit, allocated funds to hire a videographer in order to produce a high quality recording to share the information with others through the website.

No, no pressure today, thinks Tiago. *And why did I volunteer to help organize and teach this workshop?*

The participants begin to arrive, and Aubrie, one of the Oenophilia Winery hosts that family members had met at the barrel tasting, shows them to the meeting room. Along the way, she points out the restrooms and then the refreshments available as they reach their destination. Ellie, another winery host, is checking on the food, coffee, hot water for tea, and cold water, making sure enough of everything is available. Both young women are proficient at making guests feel welcome and comfortable at the winery, especially with convivial chit chat.

Tiago and Dri make sure each participant gets a name tag, then introduces them to others in the room they may not know. After brief conversations, guests help themselves to breakfast foods and coffee or tea, then find a place to settle at the table. When all are settled, Tiago welcomes them to the gathering.

Dri then gives them a task to find out from each other person in the room: 1) a favorite place the person has visited, 2) if the person were an animal, which would s/he be, and 3) a color they don't like to wear. Guests smile as they get up, wander about the room, gather the information from others, then sit back into their chairs, knowing a little more about each other.

After the introductory interaction, Tiago introduces Gabriela. He tells the group how she developed an interest in this tool from her father, desiring a greater understanding of herself.

"To begin the conversation, I want to ask you a question to consider over the next three days. The question is this: What is the worst thing you say to yourself about you? What is the secret negative view you hold about yourself? This is what we call the lie. This is what I want to help you see in yourselves this weekend, which holds you back from being your loving self, learning the undistorted lessons of life."

The faces in the group look somewhere between curious and shocked. For most, they also appear to be asking themselves this question.

Gabriela begins with some history of the Enneagram, an overall description of the approach, then provides an overview of the physical, mental, and emotional triads.

"What I think is most important to understand about each type is the way a person distorts a primary lesson of that type. This alters how she or he views the world. Once the distortion is understood, the other helpful piece is knowing the lesson each of us can learn. These are two sides of a double edged sword. When we can cut through the alteration or distortion, we can more easily see the lesson. In order for that to happen, however, people need to get exceptionally honest with themselves. Otherwise, the distortion, or self-lie as I like to call it, never gets recognized. It never comes into the light. If we can't see it, it's tough to change."

Gabriela looks into the eyes of people watching her while others take notes in the provided workbook. She turns her focus to Tiago.

"I've asked a couple of people who have been working on their distortions to share them with the group so you get the idea of how this works. Tiago, you willing to share your lie with the group now?"

Tiago takes a deep breath, silently blowing out the exhale.

"It took some time to clearly see my lie. With help, I was able to see how I feel empty inside, even incompetent. It's not something anyone ever told me. It's like I picked up cues and interpretations of events along the way to build this view. As a result of this inner belief, I spend considerable time gathering information that people might want to know. I even collect esoteric details, so I look competent when I talk. Or I'll practice a skill or talent in private, then look amazing when I can perform so easily. But it doesn't change the way I see myself or the lie. In fact, it perpetuates it. It's exhausting."

"Thanks, Tiago. It's not easy to talk about such a lie. But saying it out loud also takes some of the power out of it." Gabriela shifts her attention to Dri. "Dri, would you mind sharing your lie with the group?" asks Gabriela.

"Yeah . . . . . Never done this in a group before," says Dri. "When I first realized it, I shocked myself as I said it out loud. But I believed for a long time that I was unlovable. It was nothing I had ever heard from anyone. My family cares about me. Yet, somehow, I began to believe this. More importantly, it felt like I had to be perfect in order for someone to care about me. To be OK. To love me. Such a belief also made it easier to hurt myself, both physically and mentally. As Tiago said, it's exhausting. And a change takes time and patience. But it can happen. And it opens so many other possibilities in the process."

"Thanks, Dri," says Gabriela. "My father talked to me when I was a young adult about the Enneagram as a tool. It didn't appeal to me at first. I wasn't interested in labeling and categorizing people. And you certainly can use it that way. But when I began exploring my particular distortion, the information began to eat away at my defenses and challenges. It's like shining a light on a knot. You may be able to untie a complicated knot in a string in the dark. But a light usually helps. I'm hoping this tool assists each of you to unravel some defenses. I hope it shines a light on a possible distortion or lie you may make and desperately grasp within yourself.

"We don't know if everyone does this," Gabriela continues. "But neither my father nor I have found anyone who didn't create such a deceptive fabrication. Like Tiago and Dri, it took me some time to discover my self-deception. When I was young, I believed there was nothing wrong with me. I thought I was just fine, seeking out truth and defending justice. As I looked deeper, I realized that truth and justice were localized, meaning they existed in some places and not others. If I were not on the side of where truth and justice existed, then I was wrong and bad, feeling guilty for not doing something right. Eventually, I realized I had avoided those feelings at all costs. I had to make sure I was on the right side of truth. I must be correct and appropriate at all costs. Not an easy task, but essential for my deception. To avoid self-blaming, I had to be the perpetrator of truth. I had to be strong, right, and effectuate justice, no matter what it takes. From this view, I'm good only when I'm strong and in control of the situation. As Tiago and Dri pointed out with their lies, this too is exhausting."

Nika raises her hand, and Gabriela acknowledges her. "That does sound exhausting, like the others. What did you do to realize and change it? That's what interests me the most, especially since I relate to this issue. Injustice triggers me often."

"Great question, Nika, and one at the core of all these distortions," responds Gabriela. "First, Dad shared with me the lesson, the other side of this sword. For me, I expand my awareness to know reality and nature exist, and my task is to experience them in an undistorted way. My truth and a contrasting truth both describe a part of reality. Rather than maintaining a dualistic view of truth, I can work to understand the contrasting perspectives. Instead of trying to figure out who is right and why I am," she says with a smile, "I look at what's underneath it all. This gets us away from an unquestionable truth from people or groups, such as a religion, for example. I began to look at how we all are a part of a whole. We all are part of a pure, translucent, self-existing boundless presence of nature and the world around us. Instead of holding on to the anger and rage that drives and protects this distortion, we focus on something that allows us to get beyond the dualistic world we have come to know. We see beyond localized truth to a greater whole. And what would you guess helps us look beyond a single perspective? What would help us see beyond the limits we have put into place in a dualistic world, which supports these lies?"

There is silence in the room as people look at their notebooks, each other, or the table as they ponder the question. Finally, Nika speaks in an unassuming tone.

"Love . . . . . from an open heart?" she says.

"Exactly. Love, the essential or core lesson for everyone. A challenge for all of us. This was the second aspect of change for me. I needed to experience that expansive love that comes when I open up my heart and allow myself to experience the world from that space. Finally, I also needed to know that I was not disconnected from this boundless presence. When I began to experience a greater connection beyond me, that made a big difference too. But we'll talk more about these two pieces on Sunday."

Gabriela begins to focus on the physical triad, which include Enneatypes Eight, Nine, and One. She describes Type Nine, with a focus on the belief that love is localized, existing some places and not others. For this type, if love is not everywhere, it may not be available or present in that person. And that is the lie they hold, that love is not inside them. So they focus outside for the love they want to experience. They seek love from others. After going through other aspects in more detail, she asks if this issue resonates with anyone. Slowly, Omar raises his hand.

"Yes, that resonates with me," responds Omar. "It's easy for me to be nice to others because I want people to love me. But the truth is, I feel like there's nothing to love inside of me. So I avoid conflict, try to always keep the peace, or will be funny to reduce any tension."

"Well done, Omar," says Gabriela. "That's what a Nine tends to do, wanting to gain love from the outside, for they believe there is little to none on the inside. I'm a bit surprised you saw this so quickly. But I applaud your self honesty."

"I had a little help along the way," responds Omar. "Tiago and I had a conversation over a year ago about his lie, and I've been thinking about it ever since, wondering about mine. He later suggested a book about the Enneagram, which I began to study. I've been trying to pay attention to my distortion, but your description hit it on the head."

"You had the conversation and did some reading. But the focus on our subtle defenses, which we typically hide, can still be challenging. Don't dismiss my complement so easily, please, as Nines tend to do." Gabriela looks deep into his eyes with a warm smile on her face.

Omar looks at her silently. He takes a slow, deep breath, then feels himself open up his typical guard to allow the kind words inside his protective shell.

"Thank you. Not only for your words, but also for pointing out how I so easily divert or dismiss positive responses. It is a pattern. One not easily broken. But I'll keep a light on it and see what I can change."

Omar turns up the corners of his mouth as he returns her caring gesture. Gabriela moves her gaze to look at others and continue the discussion. Omar looks out over the vineyard to reduce the immediate tension and sit with a possible change in this view of himself.

"OK," says Gabriela. "Let's take a break for lunch. There is food at the back, and you're welcome to eat here. You also might spend a few minutes strolling in the garden or vineyard and let our discussion digest with your food. Let's begin again in an hour."

Dri walks into the garden to spend a few minutes after lunch. She spots Fadima coming towards her. "How's the workshop going for you, Fadima?"

"It's intriguing. Never talked about his before. But I haven't figured out my lie."

"There's several more we haven't discussed at all yet," responds Dri. "By the way, I want to thank you for taking over the Coalition's Executive Director position. It's taking a heavy load off Nika, and it seems like you're a great fit for director. If there's anything I can do to support you, please let me know."

"Oh, I will, I promise," says Fadima with a grin, as the two walk back to the room.

After lunch, Gabriela goes on to describe the Eight Enneatype.

"The primary distortion here is what I described as my own lie. Anyone else get a strong call to actions when they observe injustice?" she asks.

Nika slowly raises her hand, not eager to admit her trigger and distortion.

"Thanks, Nika," says Gabriela. "I know it's not easy. And it will be a benefit to you knowing both your distortion or lie and a primary lesson to be learned."

A moment later, Rachel's hand also goes up.

"I think this one may be mine too," she says. "When Dri talked at the memorial, I could not get over to her fast enough to say I wanted to help with the changes she wanted to address. Lies and injustice have also been motivators for change with me. But I never thought about the lie being on the inside, about something I held within myself. This feels extremely uncomfortable, yet useful to me too. I even notice some relaxation in my chest as I admit this to the group. It's like removing a weight from my body I didn't even know I was holding."

"Thanks, Rachel. And that's an appropriate description of the relief people sometimes feel when they recognize a burden they have been carrying without even realizing it. I particularly encourage you all to focus on the lesson, on where you want to go, rather than primarily on the distortion. As you give more energy to the former, the latter will more easily dissipate."

Next, Gabriela begins describing the distortion of the One Enneatype, with a focus on perfection.

"Like the Nine and Eight Enneatypes, the distortion is that perfection is localized, meaning it exists in some places and not in others. With this belief, the people who fall in this type believe that rightness falls outside themselves, accompanied by a comparative judgment. If the person is not right, they are wrong or flawed. The reaction is to make themselves better, constantly improving, striving for perfection, which is impossible with the constant critical voice. That inner critic telling them what's wrong is loud, clear, and constant. There is always something wrong, an improvement to make. This critical view leads to constant and insufficient improvement to remove the flawed or wrong parts of one's self. But the one thing they never attempt to remove is the distortion and judgment itself. Anyone feel a connection to this approach to life?"

Dri raises her hand. "While my lie began with believing I'm unlovable, the foundation of it was that I was flawed and needed to change. I needed to be better at grades, tennis, my body. It all needed improvement, which caused me to develop an eating disorder, hurting my body rather than improving it. But I couldn't see it that way with the distortion. It was just another attempt to be perfect. In the end, I think it was also a way to punish myself for not being better, for being flawed. And as hard as I tried, I was not better at tennis than Soph, who often saved me in games, or Nika, who had unmatched power in her strokes. So then I would beat myself up for the imperfections, the many ways I wasn't perfect. In the end, it was such a relief to relax into being myself, wanting to make some aspects of my life better without beating myself up for not being perfect. Allowing love in that was all around me and that I ignored. I knew better in ways. But I thought others couldn't see that I was bad, imperfect, and therefore unlovable."

Dri grabs a tissue to wipe away tears flowing down her face, tears of exhaustion in living the lie so long and tears of joy from a change.

"Beautifully described, Dri. Thanks for sharing," adds Gabriela. "Any others feel the strain of needing to be perfect or striving for perfection to overcome the judgment of flaws?"

Sam slowly moves his arm above his head. "I couldn't have described this as such before today. But I've been living with this all my life. It's been useful for my career, because people count on me for catching mistakes other people don't. And I get rewarded for that, which simply seems to perpetuate the judgments. But it is exhausting, always striving for perfection in myself and all I do. And it's never enough."

There is a clear sadness in his face.

"It may become evident to many of you that these constant efforts to improve bring little joy to his life," says Gabriela. "In fact, there is little joy in any type when we live behind the distortion. That's the relief Rachel described and experienced by many when we no longer have to carry this lie that turns love and joy into struggle and despair. It is exhausting to live that way, and usually a relief to let go of it. Yet, we're so attached to the way we see the world that it's sometimes a difficult task to stare it in the face. It's an immense challenge to see and admit what we've been doing. It's a bad habit that's difficult to break. In ways, some describe it as a type of addiction. Yet, like any strong habit or addiction, it can change. The process is not always easy. It may be simple, but that does not mean it's easy. The neural pathways are deep in our brains."

Gabriela looks around the room to people getting restless. "Let's take a 20 minute break," she suggests. "There are snacks at the back. You can get something sweet to eat or take some time to stroll and relax. This can be intense information, and it's important to unwind a bit as we go through this material and internal inspections."

As the group breaks, Rachel and Phil come up to thank Gabriela for the information and support in looking at a new possibility for themselves. Then Ivy, the videographer, approaches.

"You're presenting truly interesting information," she says to Gabriela. "I'm excited I got an opportunity to be here today to record this. Do you have any suggestions of books that might be helpful to me after the workshop to learn more?"

"Oh yes. I'll pass out a suggested list of books with a little information about each one at the end of the workshop. I think many people, if they get something out of it today, will want to do more reading and study. I certainly did after my dad and I first talked about it. I'll make sure you get a copy of that too. And thanks for doing the recording. It'll be great to have."

"Oh, you're welcome. This is one time I should probably have paid to record this for the group," responds Ivy with a chuckle.

The participants settle back into their seats and the conversation dies. Tiago takes over as facilitator and begins to describe the emotional triad, which includes Types Three, Two, and Four. In this triad, each finds a different way to gain acceptance and approval, even love from others. He begins with Enneatype Three, which focuses on others seeing the person as doing well and achievement through hard work. Here, the lie these people tell themselves is that without work and impressing others, they would not be loved. They would feel worthless and have no value in life. This is the Three Type distortion, which he talks about in more detail.

After describing this type, both Emma and Fadima admit they relate to this description. Emma shares her increasing awareness of the emotional distress she feels when not achieving. Fadima talks about how she typically has unrealistic expectations and jealousy of other people's success. There are more questions and discussion of how these points differ and what is similar. After their shares, Tiago thanks everyone for their attention and contributions, then adds one comment before he ends today's session.

"We have talked today about the difficulties and weight of the distortion or lie. But this evening and during the day tomorrow, I would like you to ask yourself two questions. First, how has this distortion limited you? Secondly, how has the distortion been useful or helpful to you, too? We'll talk about these questions more on Sunday. Have a relaxing evening."

The participants chat with each other as they gather up their belongings, then leave for their cars. Omar expresses his exhaustion to Bella, then gives her a hug. He gets into his car to help guests get settled on this first evening at his place. He later joins Bella, "sacrificing" his master bedroom to two of the out-of-towners while he stays with her. Some people go out to eat while others arrange to pick up food eaten where they are staying, preferring a casual atmosphere.

On Saturday, Tiago welcomes the group back, answers a few questions, then begins the description of the Two Enneatype.

"In this case the delusion is that will and choice are localized, with intention and will existing in some and not in others. Individuals with this type stay more aware and pay closer attention to needs and desires better than recipients know of themselves. Thus, people help others because they understand needs and intentions better than some do who are less aware and driven to know. In this way, they attempt to become appreciated and loved by how much they care for and help others."

After more discussion and a few questions, Sarah and Ariella both thought they might fit into this type. Ariella expresses some sadness that she would ignore what others sometimes said they needed because she felt like she knew better what they wanted. Sarah shared her fear of being unwanted for herself alone. This made her work hard to know her father's intentions and where she could facilitate his aspirations to make sure they were achieved.

Dri looks at her sister with shock on her face.

"I had no idea that was going on with you. I just thought Dad loved you more, in part because of your achievements and just seemed to understand him better than anyone else."

Sarah chuckles at Dri's comment.

"I did understand him more than anyone, except Mom. But I had to work hard to achieve that. I had to make sure I was needed and loved by him. I falsely believed he wouldn't love me if I did anything less than that."

"And this is the way it works," adds Tiago. "We develop a belief, a distortion, which then drives us to behaviors that we don't need to do. But in doing those, we reinforce the lie."

Tiago goes on to explain the Four Enneatype. As he describes it, rather than feeling a connection to our origin, people develop the distortion that the origin of everything is separate and unique. This leads people to feel separate from an original source, leading to a sense of estrangement and abandonment. These feelings create the sense of jealousy for others whom they believe must feel connected to source even if these people do not. This also elicits pain because they don't feel such a bond. The lie they live with is that they have no inherent identity, significance, or worth. They believe they are valued only if they find their significance and are true to it, which leads to strong creativity. But because they are unique and no one essentially understands them, they only feel normal when they feel pain from this secret longing and dismiss other alternatives.

When Tiago asks if anyone relates to this, Soph and Naeem raise their hands. Soph realizes this lead her to finding purpose in her health related field in a unique way from many others. Naeem shares his search for meaning through workshops, lectures, non-traditional explorations, finally leading to his desire to express his pain and creative ideas through painting. In this way, he addresses issues in a unique manifestation that others just don't see. Tiago compliments them on their insights and authenticity.

Raimy speaks out to say he has a question, and Tiago encourages him to ask it.

"What if you don't feel enough trust in a group to speak about your lie? What if I'm uncomfortable saying my secrets out loud?"

"Great question, Raimy," responds Tiago. "You raise a common concern expressed in many settings when we talk about such intimate aspects. People can be afraid when they don't know others in a group, not sure they want to be vulnerable with sensitive, personal information. But I'll share with you something my grandfather told me when I asked a similar question. He said, 'in the vulnerability lies the self-trust.' It is challenging to trust others. But when they respond negatively, with ridicule, laughter, or disparagement, they trigger the pain we already are holding inside. So you get to see it, work with it, and heal it. Without that inner pain already inside us, we would not feel hurt by another person's response. We might even laugh it off. But also in the vulnerability is the clarity of the lie. And the lie often is connected to extensive hurt. Only when we get clear about the lie, speak it out loud, without concern for other's responses, we get to see it more clearly. If someone responds negatively, we also get to see the pain we are holding around that, too. We try to minimize the negative reactions in here, creating a safe space, so we can deal with one issue at a time. But to trust one's self in how we will deal with whatever comes up allows us to see more clearly what we have been hiding from ourselves. Does that help?"

"Yes, it does," says Raimy. "I think I'm a Two Enneatype. I work hard to figure out my wife's needs or anyone I get through my EMT work in order to be appreciated. And I agree with all of you. It, too, is exhausting."

"Well done, Raimy," says Tiago. "Now that you see it, you can begin to transform it."

Gabriela stands and expresses her gratitude for Tiago's lead with this triad, his first time leading such a discussion. After she says that, the group applauds his efforts and effectiveness. Then the group breaks for lunch, with more time to wander around the grounds.

Gabriela sits at a picnic table in the garden eating her lunch. Bella approaches her and asks if she can join her.

"Of course. Please, make yourself at home."

"Thanks. And may I ask you a question?" says Bella, placing her lunch down, then sitting.

"Sure. Ask away," responds Gabriela. "Not sure I'll know the answer, but happy to talk."

"How do you know these distortions are a lie? Is there any proof of that?"

"Excellent question. I asked my dad the same question when he told me about my lie. At first, he just asked me to trust him. Later, when we began to play with the open heart meditation, I had increasingly longer glimpses of an undistorted view, which began to strengthen my belief that I had been holding on to a distortion of myself. As we continued our discussions, I began to see that what I assumed to be true may not be. Then, much later, I had an amazing experience that convinced me it was a lie. But I wasn't clearly convinced until I experienced the opposite, a clearer undistorted perspective. Then it was increasingly difficult to hold the distortion as true. The experience convinced me through my open heart, mind, and body that he was right. And I'm going to talk about that more and Dri's doing an exercise tomorrow that may help you experience the same thing. You may not know tomorrow. But as you continue to practice, I hope it will help you, too."

"That's some reassurance. I hope it's a lie. But I'm not convinced yet."

"Understandable. And don't take my word or Dri's either. It's essential you know it's a lie. You feel the truth of that. Give yourself some time to explore and find out for yourself."

"Great. Thanks." The two finished their lunch with more social conversations, then go inside.

In the afternoon, Gabriela takes the lead again. She begins by talking about the mental triad of Six, Five, and Seven. She begins with the Six Enneatype.

In this case, the distortion is an insecurity in life because they believe there is no solid foundation internally, no true nature in themselves. If there is no inner security, they tend to look outward for it, seeking something external to hang on for a sense of safety and reduce the fear that such a belief produces. This can often be a large organization, such as the military, religion, or a corporation. At the same time, there can be lots of doubts about the organization, which can lead to criticism or finding fault. It may be a push/pull, a desire to belong while also able to find faults with the institution. Because the primary energy focuses on mental acuity, they are excellent at finding both positives and problems. Like the other Enneatypes, they are not particularly adept at seeing the distortion they have created.

"Does anyone identify with this approach to life? An issue of fear and doubt while also defending the establishment to which they belong?" asks Gabriela.

Imani raises her hand. "Yeah, I kinda think this might be my distortion or lie. I often wondered why I was so committed to being a police officer while struggling with the force at the same time. I thought it might be because of my gender or race, both of which can be challenges within our organization and city. But I have this uncomfortable feeling in my gut that it runs deeper than that. This feels like it might be true for me."

"It's not always easy to tell. But if there is an emotional reaction, it typically is another telltale sign of accuracy. At times, we react to what feels like an automatic response. It's very quick. Yet, when we look deeper, we can see that we are having a contractive emotional response to an idea. That can give us a clue something inside us is acting as a protection. What is it we are defending? Why such a reaction? This can be an important technique to looking at something our defenses say we don't want to see clearly. That often is an important time to investigate."

"How do we do that?" asks Rachel. "How do you suggest we investigate when we don't know where to look?"

"Start with the reaction," responds Gabriela. "Begin to ask questions, sometimes just sitting with the inquiry of the hurt until you begin to gain some clarity. For example, I began to ask why injustice got me so upset, especially when the issue was not as important to me. I could have a similar reaction to racial injustice and someone not being treated fairly in a grocery store, unrelated to race. Were both equally important? From my reaction, one would think they are. But when I asked myself that question, they didn't carry the same weight. So why did I experience them in the same way?"

"You're suggesting we have a conversation with the pain inside?" asked Rachel.

"Yes, in a way, you could do just that. Or you can simply sit in the silence. Clear your mind. Wait for feelings or information to come up. To appear. Open your heart and ask questions. Just keep an open mind in what might come up for you. Pay attention to physical sensations too. That began to help me see what was getting stimulated in me, helping me distinguish something about the way I hold justice that was about me, not justice itself. In the silence, sometimes an epiphany can occur. Tiago, maybe you could share an example from your work too?"

"Sure," Tiago responds.

He takes a moment to consider what he might say, then begins.

"I began to look at why I needed to practice skills in secret? Why was that important to me? What was I hiding? It wasn't that Mom or Dad required me to be proficient. And that's when I began to see and feel the sense of incompetence I was hiding. If I looked competent at something, I didn't have to face the issue driving my behavior. Does that help?"

"Yeah, it does," replies Rachel. "Sometimes I don't like to look at what stimulates my response. And that's the fertile soil for discovery, it seems."

"Exactly," says Gabriela. "There are all sorts of treasures hiding below the surface when we shine the light and explore them. There is all sorts of richness in the inquiry."

Tiago begins to describe the Five Enneatype from his own experience. "For this distortion, I held the fear that I was helpless, useless, and incompetent. The only thing that helped me feel OK was if I mastered something. I spent quite a bit of time alone, trying to gather information or develop skills that would demonstrate my capability. It was my focus on baseball that took much of my time. But when I would get anxious, it was difficult for me to concentrate in order to be a strong hitter. I went to my grandfather for some help, and he taught me to meditate and focus my mind. It was only after that he asked why that was so important. That's when I began to see what was driving my desire for competence and information."

"I heard that organizing or putting collections in a particular order is another characteristic of this type," asks Alisa. "Is that true?"

"Yeah," responds Tiago, "frequently people organize information and items, again as a way to feel capable or accomplished, being able to cite information available to you, 'just in case.' You could use my baseball tickets as an example. I have every ticket to a professional or college baseball game organized by team and date. On the back of each one is the final score and who attended the game with me. Or my CDs. They are by genre, then alphabetical by group or lead player."

The group shares a light laugh for the effort and detail to organize such collections.

"It sounds like you know something about this Enneatype, Alisa. Have you been studying this approach before today?" asks Gabriela.

"Yeah. A friend and I began studying the Enneagram in order to understand some of the people in our office," says Alisa. "We heard it was a good way to understand different types of personality. But I've never heard about distortions, lies, or lessons. And that's the reason I came home for a visit to see my family now. They told me about this workshop, and I wanted to expand my experience with this approach."

"Well, that's an accurate response from this type. Do you relate to it at all?" asks Gabriela.

Alisa laughs. "Oh yes. I don't have baseball tickets, but my CDs are in a similar order and my books the same way. And even as I gather more details about this tool, I realize it's an example of a way for me to feel more accomplished with others. I had a little doubt. But it's gone after today." She laughs harder.

"Well done, Alisa," says Gabriela. "It's useful when we can laugh at some of the things we do and think it's perfectly normal. We sometimes even think people who don't do that are abnormal. Nothing wrong with me. Except, of course, the response of some types, when everything is wrong with me."

"And now I want to describe the final type," continues Gabriela, "the Seven. This one often looks like there are no real problems, especially from the person experiencing it. In this case, the distortion sees development and change as localized and possibly separate from themselves, which can result in a sense of being disoriented or lost. This brings on a fear of being deprived and trapped in pain. Then such people believe they are valued if they get what they need, which helps them to avoid the pain. Thus, they focus on planning, having fun, and finding all sorts of ways to feel happy and satisfied. These are happy people on the outside, constantly moving to the next fun activity, project, or job. It is difficult to stay with one thing, as it often eventually brings up the pain. So they keep planning and moving, making light of life along the way. By planning, they live in the future, avoiding the pain of the past or present."

"OK, OK. I admit it," says Bella, laughing. "This one obviously is mine. But what's the problem with this one? If I avoid pain, then life is good. I don't see the downside to this."

"No, many don't with this type," responds Gabriela, lacking a smile as she looks at Bella. "But let me ask a few questions. How many projects go unfinished? How often do you move on to something else because it's no longer fun? And what do you do when you can't move on? What do you do when you can't distract yourself from the pain?"

"I plan something else that's fun. I keep active doing something," she says, continuing to chuckle.

The smile slowly slides off Bella's face as she looks deeper.

"I run," she remarks, the smile no longer remaining.

"Yes, in your mind, your emotions, or in your body, you find some way to avoid through activity. And that can limit your options or lose something close to you because you can't stay, either emotionally or physically. And how's that working for you?" Gabriela asks gently.

Bella sits quietly, looking now at the table. Then she turns her gaze back towards Gabriela.

"It seriously minimizes my options, sometimes. And while I don't feel lost inside, I lose in the process, when I get honest with myself."

"Yes, and that's the downside," continues Gabriela. "You cut off options, people, achievements, and even a sense of place sometimes. But what's important is that loss is common to all the types when we can't see opportunities for growth. When we keep our focus narrow by not challenging the distortion or lie."

"Yeah, I'm beginning to see that too," adds Kiara. "Sometimes it drives me to do wonderful things. And sometimes I don't even see options because I'm so busy planning the next exciting thing, the new way to make me happy. I'm so busy planning and pursuing happiness I forget to live in the present. Much of my life is in the future. It's increasingly clear this is my approach."

"Great awareness, Kiara," says Gabriela. "Knowing that will help you make a choice to be more in the present, giving you more options. Being aware and present in your body will help you. Your body can only be in the present."

"I have a question," says Fadima. "How do we know that these distortions are a lie? How do we know this isn't the way we are naturally, just part of our personality that can't change?"

"Thanks for asking that, Fadima," says Gabriela. "It's something we wanted to address at some point, and now seems like a great time. Dri, would you like to lead your exercise now?"

Dri suggests that each person find a relaxing position in their chair or sitting on the floor using pillows that are available in the corner. Participants move around, exploring a sitting posture that is fresh and comfortable. Or they pick up a pillow and find a way to be at ease on the floor.

Then Dri asks them to close their eyes and take several slow deep breaths. She suggests they focus on their hearts and the energy both inside and surrounding this organ in their chest. Since board members did a similar meditation at the first retreat, this is not new to them. Nika and Soph have practiced this at least periodically for the past several years. But for a few, Dri knows it may be novel and make them anxious.

Dri pays attention to telltale facial gestures. She suggests people not work at this, but relax, breathe, and pay attention to the heart. After focusing one's attention there, she encourages people to allow the heart to expand and open more. Even little bits at a time are helpful. As people begin to feel comfortable there, Dri directs them to ask the question of themselves as to whether they trust the lie or the lesson more for their Enneatype.

"Just hold both in your mind, the distortion and the lesson of your type. Which feels more authentic to you? Which one resonates with your open heart more? Which one encourages to open your heart more? Which one does your heart open up to more? For a few minutes, I suggest you explore these questions and notice how your heart and body respond to each one."

After allowing the group several minutes to explore these questions in the heart, Dri requests that they take a deep breath and open their eyes. She recommends that they continue to utilize this exercise to find out more about their responses to these questions. Then the group ends for the day.

On Sunday, Gabriela welcomes the group and begins a discussion of how they are doing and answering questions they have. Then she begins to review the lesson of each Enneatype, clarifying how the learning is the other side of that double-edged sword from the distortion. She again answers questions and clarifies differences between types.

Following the review of the nine lessons, Tiago raises the questions he asked Friday evening just before ending the day. They discuss how the distortion has been useful or helpful, which is why we invent them.

Bella suggests that if we have a smaller sense of ourselves, we don't have to push so hard to grow. Fadima, with a hint of sarcasm, offers that it was easier to fit into our society. Omar refers to the ease and simplicity of having a limited view of who we are and what we can do. Alisa proposes such a view can provide a place to focus our energy and efforts, ignoring more expansive views and talents, which can be difficult to develop.

Tiago suggests they talk about how each distortion limits their lives and constricts their options. The problem people discover is that while the lie has helped them not to notice what they are doing, it also prevents them from expanding options that could help them grow and limits their focus to understand and live from their lesson.

Nika suggests it also shifts us away from our hearts and makes them less likely to be open to others. She shares some of what she and Dri have been discovering about racial injustice and the challenge to recognize others in ourselves when our hearts are impenetrable.

In the end, Tiago suggests, living from our lesson encourages us to explore or try something we otherwise might not do. It nudges us to examine a different view of life.

The discussion takes up much of the morning, and the group breaks for lunch, individual conversation, and contemplation time.

Participants gather together again an hour later. Dri asks them to take a comfortable position in their chair or on the floor. This time, more sit on pillows, often with their backs against the walls. Dri suggests that they take a deep breath and close their eyes. After a brief pause, she directs them to focus their attention on their abdomen or gut. She asks them to explore the center of that area to see if they can find an energy center. Such a location would contain stronger energy, possibly with an energetic connection to their heart and up to the center of their brain. A connection also might extend down into the earth. Again, Dri pauses to give people time to be with their exploration. Then she continues.

If someone doesn't feel confident about an energetic center, Dri suggests they focus on the area most like that or imagine one right in the center of their intestines. Once a location is identified, allow the energy to expand outward in all directions. If that seems too challenging, they can concentrate on one direction at a time, then move to another. Dri pauses, allowing people to explore for a time.

As the energy expands for participants, Dri, noticing the expansion, continues.

"Imagine your attention is right in the middle of that center. While there, ask this question: Is there anything greater than me to which or whom I connect? At first, family members and friends may come up. But stay with it. See if there is anything more. Listen for that soft, subtle response."

Dri pauses again for a moment.

"If you get nothing, increase the energetic connection between your gut center and your heart. Let that grow, then ask the questions again, and wait. Just see what shows up."

Again there is a pause, letting people focus on anything that comes to them.

"It may not be today, or tomorrow. It wasn't for me and others. But in staying with this process, people often become aware of information or connections they did not know existed previously."

Another short pause.

"Before ending this, ask the same question you asked yesterday. Which feels more authentic to you, more the essence of you, the distortion or the lesson? The lie or the learning?"

Dri quits offering questions and lets the people sit with possible answers. Then she asks them to take another deep breath and open their eyes.

People gather back at the table to share their experiences.

Bella mentions how relaxed she feels. Naeem, Rachel, and Omar feel like they experienced a confirmation that the lesson was more central to them than the lie. Bella, Nika, and Sarah agree. Kiara and Phil said they didn't feel much, although they too are aware of being more at ease and soft. Fadima mentions she still feels some connection and appreciates the experience.

Gabriela looks at the group and asks another question.

"What is one way you can honor yourself once you are aware of your lie or distortion?"

After some consideration, Imani suggests being easy on yourself. Emma says she wants to relax into the lesson rather than pushing herself further.

"That is critical if your type is Three. Driving yourself to learn the lesson is to perpetuate the lie. That's lovely, Emma."

There is more conversation about the experience and gratitude for the workshop as they near the end. Before they dismiss, Gabriela has one more suggestion for them to take home.

"Remember, you have two powerful inner voices. One is from the distortion, because we all have asked for its help to protect us when we know of no better defense. But once you hear the subtle inner voice of the lesson, the essence, the higher self, you are accessing the most useful voice you have. It is not as loud as the voice of the lie. The distortion is a denser energy, and it strengthens as you listen to it more frequently. But if you practice the exercises we did yesterday and today, there is not a more insightful and clear voice than your own inner wisdom, your own inner strength. You just have to learn how to hear it clearly and pay attention to what it has to say."

"What does the inner voice of the lesson sound like?" asks Kiara.

"Well," responds Dri, searching for the best descriptors for a somatic experience. "Let me try to share what I experience. The voice informs in different ways at different times. Sometimes, it shows up as words, even the image of a word or a soft, subtle response. I experience or see images more as soap bubbles than loud noises, soft and delicate. Or an experience will appear in your life, and the voice is a sense of confirmation of a message or truth. It's not like your ears hear my voice and your brain processes the information, as you do now. Responses are heard through the gut or the heart instead of the ears. It can be an experience of inner joy, expansion, or a confirmation rather than informing. The key is to be open and pay attention, to listen with our whole body and being."

Gabriela leads further discussion about the two voices, then adds one ending comment.

"We have tried to provide a foundation from which to explore both distortions and lessons. Please feel free to connect with me, Tiago or Dri if you want to ask questions or just talk through something. It also may be useful to keep discussing this with each other. There is much to explore and discover in this process. And thanks so much for being here this weekend."

There is somber chatting and hugging as the workshop ends. People slowly gather up their belongings and the handouts distributed at the end. Finally, people begin to say farewell and move towards their transportation home.

Chapter 16
Sacrament and Service

February, 2032

N aeem sits and takes a deep breath for the first time since breakfast yesterday. He pays attention to the weariness of his body, his drained emotions. Yet, his dream relaxes in front of him. Following several years learning to navigate a relationship with a tenacious and passionate woman, the magical wedding is completed. He and Nika committed to a legal union. Now, they celebrate with family and friends on this Valentine's Day.

He looks over, watching Kyrone, his father, and Alyssa, his mother, kick it up on the dance floor. His two brothers also are swinging out there, DeWayne with his wife and Rashon with his husband. Omar has put a special set together that includes requests from the newlyweds, including many oldies from the early 2000s that are cherished by this crowd.

Naeem notices his feet tapping the floor, an indication that exhaustion will not stop his body movement for long. He looks at Nika's fingers tapping the back of the chair next to her, a sign she too will not let a little weariness stop her feet from stepping to the music being played. It's an old tune. But Ronson's *Uptown Funk* won't allow this gathering to sit still. After about 30 seconds of that, Nika grabs Naeem's hand. The happy couple shake their bodies as they move to the dance area.

This music transforms the whole atmosphere from the songs when the couple entered the nuptial scene in the meeting room of Oenophilia. Naeem strolled to Al Green's *Let's Stay Together* as he made his way to his position in front. Nika and Tyrell walked down the aisle to *At Last* by Etta James. These were the songs to each other, with contrasting tempos to the current dance music. But slow, sexy dancing is their preferred style. Later in the set, Nika asked Omar to play one of her favorites: Aretha singing *Natural Woman*. Moving to such music, Nika melts into her husband's arms, thrilled this day finally has arrived.

They sway on the barrel room floor. Nika whispers into Naeem's ear.

"I'm so glad I included this title in my vows. You make me feel this way, always have. Hope you always do!"

Naeem pulls his head back to look into his lover's face. "That's my plan," he replies, a broad smile on his mouth, her heart in her eyes.

As he continues loving Nika's eyes and body, his request follows hers: Sledge's rendition of *When A Man Loves A Woman*. After that comes Naeem's other request, *Feels Like Home* by Hannah Grace. Not the same genre as most of their music, but the tune carries an important message.

"At home is what I feel when I'm with you, my love," whispers Naeem into Nika's ear. "I love you so!"

Tears of joy fill their eyes as they look at each other again, their bodies continuing their sway to the music. As it ends, Naeem gives his love a passionate kiss while pressing her body against his. When they break, an applause arises from those gathered to bolster this union.

With Omar at the DJ station, Bella leaves the area where she has been dancing solo to join Gabriela and Miguel at their table.

"Why aren't you two out there dancing?" she asks.

"I don't like to dance to this music," responds Miguel. "Actually, I don't like to dance much at all, unfortunately for my wife. But she might like to join you. She loves to dance, and apparently you do too." He chuckles like Tiago as he says that.

"Want to, Gabby?" asks Bella, now close enough to use her family name. "I'm up for it."

"Yeah, sure. I'd love to dance. But I don't do much solo like you."

"OK, well, let's go have some fun."

Bella holds out her hand as an invitation, and Gabriela holds the finger tips as they both prance onward. When they start to swing, Bella looks over and smiles at Alberto, Omar's son, who finally moved back from Australia to work at Oenophilia with his dad.

After several fast dances, the two women leave the floor semi-breathless and happy. They return to the table where Tiago's older brother, Javier, is sitting with another young man.

"Hey, Javier," says Bella as she sits across from them. "Nice to see you again. How's your winter break going? And how will the Giants do next year?"

"A break is good, thanks. And I think we'll have a solid year. Let me introduce you to my friend, Owen. He's our starting second baseman and part of the reason for our success. He came up to Napa for the weekend. Owen, this is Bella, Dri's mom. I drug him along, just in case there are some beautiful single women at this event." Javier's cheeks turn a light red. "For him . . . . . of, of course. My wife's over visiting with Tiago," he says with a tentative smile.

"You're first visit to Napa, Owen?" asks Bella, smiling at Javier's befuddled explanation.

"No, I've been here a few times," responds Owen. "I'm usually at home with my family. But they're traveling on a cruise right now. So I decided to hang out with Javier. I have to get back to the South Bay on Monday to finish my new contract negotiations. First time at this lovely winery, though. It's very relaxing."

"Oh great," says Gabby. "Hope the negotiations go well. Where do your parents live?"

"I grew up in Phoenix," responds Owen.

"How did you like growing up there," asks Miguel.

"It was a great place to live, especially with spring training going on there. I was able to watch lots of great players and get their autographs. Pretty hot in the summer. But you adjust."

"Where did you play college ball?" asks Bella.

"I played at Arizona State. I was lucky to stay in my home town. Would have played against this guy, if he weren't so old," snickers Owen as he slaps Javier on the arm.

"OK, kid. Enough teasing me about my age. But I can keep up with you," he responds and thumps Owen's arm to continue the hormonal exchange.

"By the way, Tiago has been telling us some of what you've been doing with the Coalition," says Owen. "I think my family would be interested. Tiago told us about your website. I'll share it with them."

"Thanks, Owen. That would be great," responds Bella.

Javier looks across the room at his younger brother.

"Well, I think we need to go. Tiago is waving us over. He may know someone for Owen to meet. I asked him to see if he could find a beautiful woman for this great guy. Great to see you all. And we'll be around tomorrow. Maybe we'll see you again."

The two young men rise and push in their chairs.

"It was nice to meet you all," says Owen. "Hope to see you again soon. I could get you a couple of tickets to a game, if you like, once we start again in April. I'll keep in touch through Javier."

"That would be sweet, Owen," says Bella. "We would love to see you play again. Tiago says you're a great second baseman. I've only seen you once, and you looked terrific. I'm not as good a judge as Javy's brother. But from what I saw, I'd agree. Best of luck next season."

"Thanks. I think we'll have another solid year. Have an enjoyable evening."

With that, the two leave to talk with Tiago and Dri.

"He seems pleasant," says Bella as she turns towards Gabriela.

"Yeah, Javy says nice things about him."

"By the way, Gabriela, I haven't had a chance to talk with you much since the workshop several months ago," says Bella in a lowered tone.

The music continues just soft enough for conversation.

"I wanted to thank you for the insights about the Seven Enneatype. I've been doing more reading from one of the books you recommended, which has been useful. But your comments about the downside of my type were very helpful."

"Oh, thanks," replies Gabriela. "But how have they been helpful? I'd love to know."

"I'm going to go get a little more wine," says Miguel, more focused on the empty glasses than the new topic of conversation. "Can I get you two more first?"

"I'd have a little more Syrah, please," says Gabriela.

"I would love more Sangiovese, if you don't mind," responds Bella.

Miguel picks up their glasses with his carefully balanced in between them. He quickly returns with a generous pour for each of them. Then he disappears.

"Does he not like to talk about these ideas?" asks Bella.

"He had an interest for a while," replies Gabriela. "But he doesn't show much anymore. I think that may have something to do with Javier showing less interest also. But Javy's wife and I have talked quite a bit. So who knows. Javy may get curious again when their two kids get older. Struggles there can sometimes recreate a curiosity. Anyway, back to you."

"I found your points about the downside of my type extremely useful," says Bella. "As I examine my choices and where I focus my attention, I see aspects I hadn't noticed before. For example, I stayed in the marriage a long time, until the kids got older. Then I was ready for a change. I also saw something similar with where I lived and even how I did my work as an agent. I like new experiences and attempting something different, challenging. Guess that's one reason I do well with this type of work. Each buyer, seller, and listing is a new adventure. And it's difficult to stay with something when I get bored."

"But what's the worst thing that happens? What's the real downside?" asks Gabriela.

"I realize I'm just avoiding any pain, even looking closely at what's going on inside," replies Bella. "The pain in my marriage, pain in my life. I try to stay with surface issues just to avoid looking at what's going on underneath. Yet, when I look, it's not as bad as I assume at some level. I also don't reveal as much of my authentic self. And in that way, I miss that in connection with others, if I'm not careful. Those are the kinds of interactions that mean the most to me. So I undermine what I most desire."

"Great insight. Seeing that will help you make different choices for yourself."

"But how do I let go of planning, especially for others. I think that's what's bothering me about Dri being so involved in this Coalition. It feels like a type of control on my part. How do I let that go? How do I allow her to make her own choices without me pushing her?"

"I applaud your question," says Gabriela. "What's important in your case is to stay present with yourself and allow the world to unfold in its own way. You get to decide for yourself, but you don't get to decide for others. If people ask, share your wisdom. Otherwise, allow others to make their own plans and decisions. It's not easy. But the other important thing is not to run or distance from yourself in the process. That's often how sevens let go of control."

"What do you mean, distancing from myself?"

"I mean to energetically leave your body," responds Gabby. "Don't take all your energy to your head, your mind. That's a natural place of escape for a Seven. Or you may simply shut down your feelings altogether. In more extreme cases, people absent themselves from their body, experiencing no feelings at all. For example, if I begin to feel bad or guilty about what I have done, I can numb out that part of my body not to experience it. On other occasions, I become angry. I have to be careful not to take my wrath out on others.

If I'm not paying attention to what is going on inside, I can project or deflect my rage on other people rather than pay attention to it inside myself. This is numbing, cutting off, or leaving parts of myself where I don't want to see."

"What do you suggest I do instead?" Bella asks.

"In this case, stay in your body and your heart. It can hurt to see others make what seem like mistakes to you. But each of us has our own lessons to learn. Paying attention to my physical reactions became a significant lesson for me. Now that your girls are older, let them ask for your insight and perspective. Let them unfold as you allowed yourself to do."

"Oh, wow. Easier said than done," replies Bella.

"Yes, I agree," says Gabriela. "And that's your practice. With Omar too. When he wants your advice, tell him the truth. When he doesn't, be careful to not get into planning for him. That would be your shit, not his."

Bella takes a slow deep breath, aware this will not be an easy practice.

"Yes, deep breathing at such times is important. Breathe your energy and awareness back into yourself. Don't let it get too spread out and diluted by focusing elsewhere."

"Thanks, Gabriela. That's not easy, but it seems helpful."

"If other questions arise or you just want to talk more, let me know. I'd be happy to discuss this further. Learning is best when it's an ongoing process, not just one discussion. Besides, I enjoy talking about this with you and would love to continue our discussions."

"Oh, yes, I would too," replies Bella. "It's great to develop a closer connection to you. And I'd love to talk about this more. I think I'll need more help and insight."

"The discussions help me too," adds Gabriela. "Even as I make suggestions or talk through your questions, I gain from the interactions. And it's fun to have someone to talk about this more, especially with Tiago not around so much. I could use another person's reflections and insights as well. We all have our work, my dear. No matter what our type."

"Do you think it gets easier if we raise children with this perspective? Does it help them have fewer challenges along the way?" asks Bella.

"I do. But it's still based more on a hunch than evidence. My dad got into the Enneagram as I was getting older. It was part of what got him back in touch with his roots and expand what he included in his therapy. So I only experienced the insights later in life and didn't use it as a tool when the boys were young. But I think Tiago's early interest made a difference in his life compared to his brother's. I'm hoping that Tiago and Dri, both knowing this while Cate is young, will help them stay more conscious with her development. I think it will. It was a reason I was glad when the two of them started dating and eventually married. We'll see, I guess."

"That's very interesting. I hadn't thought too much about that part of their parenting until now. But I hope it helps too."

"It doesn't hurt that you and I can support them incorporating these insights along the way, either. Young parents can get so involved with daily tasks that they can ignore the larger perspective, as I'm sure you experienced at times. I sure did. But we can support them to remember what's most important when they get caught up with all the minutiae."

"I'm glad you moved out to the Bay Area finally. It will be great to have you nearby."

"Oh, I am too. With Mom and Dad both gone and the boys living out here, there was little keeping us in Iowa City. Once we figured out jobs, it was a pretty easy decision. Of course, we have a much smaller place. But we have an extra bedroom for kids to stay. And drive time isn't that bad when you can do a little planning."

Omar appears at the table, holding out his hand to Bella. "Last two songs. Will you dance with me, please?" he asks Bella.

She stands, reaches out for his hand and moves to the dance area. They put arms around each other and begin a slow sway to Nat King Cole's *When I Fall In Love*, which is followed by Nat and Natalie's *Unforgettable*. Bella balances between moving her body and singing the words in her head. She knows Omar played these two favorite songs for her.

Even Miguel takes Gabriela's hand to dance her to these loving songs, showing that part of himself he frequently has a hard time exhibiting in public. As the music slowly fades, Omar walks over to turn it off while most couples are embracing. Then an applause erupts for the music and wonderful times.

People gather their personal items, begin to share hugs and farewells, especially with the celebrated couple. Naeem and Nika move to use Omar's microphone. Naeem holds it so both can be heard.

"Thank you all for coming to celebrate with us," says Nika. "It means a lot to have you join us here, participating in our our joy for this union."

"And a special thanks to Omar," adds Naeem, "and his family for allowing us to hold this sacred event here at their enchanting winery. Once again, you are so generous, Omar. Thank you so much."

"Please drive carefully. I don't want to be defending any of you in court," laughs Nika. "More importantly, we would not want any harm to spoil this wonderful event. And thanks for your well wishes and sharing your love. Both of us appreciate it. Oh, and thanks for not bringing any rice to throw," says Nika with a big smile.

"And thanks to Omar for the fabulous dance music," says Naeem as he pulls the mike toward him. "And Nika doesn't always get the last word," Naeem says with a boisterous laugh.

"Yes, I do," laughs Nika, who kisses her man to prevent any more words being expressed. She takes the microphone in her other hand, extending it out to anybody who will remove it from Naeem's reach.

Those still in the barrel room where the reception was held laugh and applaud at Nika's playful response. Knowing her private expression of respect and admiration for Naeem makes it easy for him to participate in her fun and humor. The couple moves towards the exit to extend hugs to the others on their way to their transportation home.

As Gabby nears the door, Bella gives her a hug and thanks her again for her suggestions. "Happy to talk more," responds Gabby, as she gives Bella's hand a final squeeze.

Nika and Naeem are among the last to leave, giving Omar and Bella an extended hug. They will drive to the city and spend a couple of days there. Nika's upcoming work in Washington and her election postpones any honeymoon plans. Such a trip can occur in the near future, hopefully with more to celebrate. For now, Nika and Naeem feel pleased to have the legal union complete.

For this event, Omar hired a clean-up crew so all could exit without sanitation duties. Bella gives him an extra hug that they both can leave now and celebrate their own connection.

Cate wakes early the next morning. Dri decides to take her to the park while Tiago completes his recommendations for the gun legislation that Nika's boss is introducing to Congress. He has reviewed what has been passed during the previous decade and what seems to be the current needs. Excitement and anxiety fill his body. There is pleasure to participate in another attempt to limit access for people who would kill others, as happened to Alex and witnessed by Dri. The pain still permeates the family, just below the surface some days. His work to prevent more of that feels important. Yet, he's not certain he has identified all the critical elements.

Tiago summarizes previous work completed during the 2020s. President Biden and the next Democratic president lead efforts to pass gun legislation reform. Tiago ties it back to the time Democrats took over the House and the Senate. Following the death of a conservative Supreme Court Justice, a shift in the court's perspective took place when the seat became filled by a judge who diid not believe in the originalist legal view.

He documents what they were able to pass: requiring universal background checks, banning the purchase and possession of firearms for people with history of mental illness on a federal list, banning the purchase of weapons for people on the NSA No Fly list, and banning sales from gun shows without background checks and a three day wait period, which people can apply for prior to a show.

Tiago outlines another round of legislation passed four years later. These regulations required people to be 21 to purchase a gun, renewed the bump stock ban, eliminated immunity for gun manufacturers who knowingly put weapons of war on our streets, and funded gun violence research by the Center for Disease Control and the National Institute of Mental Health.

Tiago then reviews the research findings that have emerged since the last legislation. Such results point to other factors that could increase health and safety in the country. This becomes the focus of Tiago's proposal. Essentially, the new legislation would:

1.   Eliminate Stand-Your-Ground laws;

2.   Ban gun purchases and possession by people under domestic violence restraining orders;

3.   Requires renewable license for gun ownership, which includes:

a.   Gun safety training (every 5 years);

b.   Owners must store guns in locked safe without child access;

c.   Gun insurance by owners, similar to car insurance;

4.   Right-to-carry in public requires an additional license related to job or special circumstances;

5.   Voluntary buy-back program for assault rifles, except at shooting ranges, where people can pay to use them under controlled circumstances;

6.   A maximum of 15 round magazines;

7.   Internal serial numbers to track each weapon (similar to cars), reviewed with each renewable license, and guns will be impounded if the number has been removed; and

8.   Financial support for mental health curriculum to develop healthier resolutions of conflict and mediation of differences training in family preparation classes and schools, decreasing the tendency to use guns for solving conflicts.

In each case, Tiago cites the research that supports it to assist Congresswoman Bradshaw's presentation to her colleagues in Congress. She has been putting together her arguments with Nika's help. Tiago will email this to Nika shortly, having it available for her when she returns to the office on Tuesday. This not only will assist the congresswoman's presentation. It also will facilitate Nika's goals. She will go to Washington to assist in the discussions, the House committee's review of the legislation, and interviews with experts in the field.

Tiago's excitement stems from the possible fulfillment of his dream to reduce violence in schools and society. Changes in previous legislation decreased school shootings, yet they still occur. In addition, he hopes that as violence decreases, opening of hearts increase. One point he emphasizes in his proposal is the basic question asked by many: What good does it do to make kids smarter at math, science, history, or writing if we don't know how to deal with each other emotionally? This question addresses the final issue in his recommendations.

His emphasis begins locally by assisting others and reaching out to help in the community with his high school baseball players and students he counsels. His fantasy aspires for more. If this legislation can get passed, he will shift efforts to increase concern for others through educational programs, conflict resolution programs, and greater community service. Helping others often opens hearts.

The Coalition's continued success nurtures this dream. Now with over 12,000 members nationally and growing numbers internationally, the foundation for change strengthens the possibility. Fadima, as the executive director, energizes the group, particularly after the Enneagram Workshop last year elevated the enthusiasm of the board. Once Ivy put together a professional video of the gathering, several thousand members gained from the information, able to access the training through their website. In addition, Sienna, the new Coalition fundraiser, is doing well increasing corporate and individual donations. Now the organization can pay Dri and Ariella part-time for their educational contributions and have funds for Sienna's base salary. At the same time, their financial foundation continues to solidify.

Tiago taps into his satisfaction as he emails his proposal. His hope brightens as these ideas begin to take concrete form.

After Dri and Cate return from the park, the family spends time at home playing and relaxing, fatigued from the wedding efforts like others in attendance last night.

Late the following morning, Tiago calls Nika during a break between appointments at school. He wants to answer any questions she might have about his work.

"Hey, how was the brief honeymoon in the city where you two basically live?" asks Tiago with a touch of laughter.

"It was lovely to just relax for two days, see a few sites we don't usually visit, and talk about our desires for the future?"

"Terrific," responds Tiago. "I hope you could relax and get some restful sleep too."

"Yeah," laughs Nika in response. "In between a little physical exercise. Funny how you can get in touch with bodily desires once you let go of some stressors."

"Well, a little exercise is useful, especially when it's so rainy outside. So, did you get my proposal? Any questions?"

"Yes, I got it, and it looks great. Thanks for the references regarding the mental health curriculum. That was the place my work was weakest, and they'll help considerably. I haven't shown it to my boss yet. I want to finish getting it into a legislative format. But I think it will be strong. I believe we have a solid shot as the President finishes her term. If not before the election, then maybe during the lame duck session."

"That's great. Have you met the President yet?"

"No. We will when I get to Washington next week. I'm so excited to meet her. The first female President. But for me, a great source of inspiration, given that she is the first Democratic president from California and grew up in what would be my district of Oakland and Berkeley. I'm hoping to get her endorsement for my election. I hear she will. But I'll feel better hearing it from her lips."

"Oh, I totally understand that. I would too. And how are you feeling about the election?"

"I'm nervous. The primary will be my biggest challenge, given the heavy Democratic district I'm running in. So far, it's looking pretty strong. But I'm anxious. This feels like such an important step for what I want to do with my life. I'm not sure quite what I'll do if I lose. I'm hoping I don't have to face that issue."

"We'll do what we can to support you. How's the financial part of the campaign going?"

"We're getting lots of small donations and a few big ones. After I return from Washington, I'll do more local fundraising. Sienna is giving me helpful advice, as well as my boss's development officer. She's helping me too. We have a strong start. I just need to dig in once I have done my work on the East Coast."

"Any problems you're encountering?"

"Well, Charlene is raising more Hell."

"Again? What's she doing now?" asks Tiago.

"As the face of the conservative Evangelical fundamentalists, she created another flailing attempt from a dying Republican party. As you know, she's been running lies in the conservative press and on television about our Coalition's efforts. But now she's rallying around a conservative Democratic candidate in the primary. I don't think he has much of a chance in my district. But the lies can hurt me and our group beyond the election. They put together ads saying we won't let women have babies. And others that claim we will force CEOs to cut salaries, just because we want more equitable pay rates. Their lies are pissing me off. I can rebut them. But still, she's a weasel and another puppet for conservative men. They now go after anyone who represents change. And that I do, I hope!" she says with a chuckle."

"Yes, you do, Nika. What can we do to help?"

"Just keep talking and helping with calls. I rely on you and Dri's support. I just need to connect when I get down. Bella and your mom too. Nothing else to do right now. Knowing you're there for me and Naeem, who can get the brunt of my frustration, sometimes, helps us both. Our connection is critical for me right now."

"That we can do. You've always got that. I'll inform the others too. I know they'll all help you get through this. I'll keep in touch with Naeem. That may be easier with all you have going on. He's a great guy. I really like him. So connecting with him will be easy."

"Thanks, Tiago. And for all your help with this too."

"Well, keep breathing, my friend. We'll stay at it and do all we can. And maintain your exercise regime. It will help keep you calm. I know Naeem will be happy to encourage that part of your life. He told me so."

Nika laughs again. "Thanks, Tiago. You and Dri are great friends and supporters. I hope I don't let you down."

"You couldn't do that, my dear. You are who you are, and we love you for that. Who you are is much more important to us than what you are. You know that!"

"Yeah, I know that. When I'm in my heart, I know that anyway."

"Well, I guess that's your own answer, isn't it," responds Tiago. "And know that we all love and admire you too, my friend."

"Yeah, I guess you're right about my heart. Thanks! And thanks for all your efforts with this legislation. I'll talk to you when I get back from Washington."

"OK. Over a bottle of wine to celebrate."

"You got it. Talk to you soon."

"Yes, and the best of luck in DC."

"Thanks. See ya."

Tiago hangs up, excited about his work and the increased flow of this project that accelerates with combined efforts. He experiences the pleasure for his contributions as part of the strong group that coalesces around the revolution of opening heart's rusted lid.

Now, Dri and I just need to help Nika feel and spread the love. The lubricant for the rusty lid.

Chapter 17
A Wonderment
September, 2032

"How about this long sleeve shirt today, Cate?" says Dri, holding up a bright yellow pullover with white ruffles at the cuff. "It's going to be rather cool with the rain."

"No, I want this shirt," says Cate. "I like the cute kitties on this one."

"And what does a kitty say?" asks Dri.

"Oh, mommy. Kitties say meow. Don't you know by now?" says Cate, her mouth straight and her eyebrows pulled downward at the top of the nose as she looks at her mom.

"Yes, dear," says Dri with a chuckle. "I was just checking."

Cate puts her hand through both arms and helps her mom straighten the shirt down to her waist. She pulls on her pants, then slides her feet into the slippers her mom is holding. Cate turns and goes over to get her soft, furry black dog, her favorite stuffed animal. Then she turns and looks at her mom.

"Mommy, do you remember when I came to you before I was in your body?"

Dri narrows her eyebrows and stares at her daughter. She hears the words, but her head balks at digesting them. She must not have heard her daughter's question correctly.

"What did you say, my dear?"

"Do you remember when I came to you before I was in your body?"

Dri thinks back, wondering if she had talked about her dream to others while Cate was around. She doesn't recall doing so.

How else could she know about my dream? And was it Cate? It was a little girl. She looked like Cate, at least kind of, but I don't recall her face exactly. I think I was too surprised by it all to remember details.

"Did Daddy and I talk about my dream with you?"

"No, mommy. I remember. I came to you and said I was ready. Don't you remember that?" asks Cate.

"Of course I remember that. But how do you remember?"

"'Cause I was there, too, Mommy. I said that."

"Um, well, that just surprises me. That you would remember. Most kids don't remember anything before they were born."

"Well, I do, Mommy. And I'm glad you and Daddy decided to have me. It's the only way I could come live with you."

Cate's straight face stares back at Dri, who feels the uneasiness in her stomach. Yet her heart feels at rest, expansive and serene.

"I'm so glad we decided to have you, too. I'm excited you remember as well. Let's tell Daddy when he gets home, OK?"

"Yeah. I'll tell him, too," Cate responds. She walks over to her mom and sits in her lap.

Dri wraps her arms around her, pulling Cate in against her chest. She extends her energy to touch Cate's heart directly from her heart. Her head leans into the space between her neck and shoulders, giving her a kiss. This practice of energetically connecting with Cate's heart started while she was in utero. Dri has continued the practice ever since, especially when Cate is upset with something.

I'm grateful Tiago started creating such connections later, too. I love that we both have such energetic contacts. Guess that was another attraction to such a loving man.

"I sure do love you, my sweet Cate. So glad to have you here."

Tiago gets home while Cate naps, or "having her quiet time" as they now describe it.

Dri shares what Cate said to her earlier in the afternoon. Tiago's head moves back, his eyes open wide, staring into Dri's. He isn't sure whether to gasp or laugh.

"She said what?" asks Tiago.

"She asked if I remembered when she came to me before she was in my body."

"She said that? She wasn't asking if that happened? She was asking if you remembered?" asks Tiago, his eyebrows still extended upward, not moving anything except his mouth.

"Yes, exactly. Asking if I remembered," replies Dri.

"Did she say anything else?

"She said she was glad we decided to have her. That it was the only way she could come live with us."

"Wow. I can't believe she said that. I mean, it's just a challenge to believe. I'm not doubting you. But I'm shocked at the question she asked. I've never heard children say that."

"I looked up the issue online. I guess there are a few people who have been investigating such reports. And they've found some support for what kids have told them. In some cases, kids have talked about a place they describe before coming to earth. Even sometimes they have talked about knowing events or interactions from this life, such as my dream and conversation with the little girl. I was so surprised by the dream. I don't remember exactly what the little girl looked like. But she was similar in ways."

A smile finally emerges on Tiago's face.

"That's fascinating. I can't wait to talk with her when she wakes up."

"But let her tell you about it. I just wanted to give you a head's up."

"Oh, yes, I will."

Tiago gets up to get a glass of water, then hears Cate giggling in her bedroom. He goes in to get her out of her bed and bring her into the living room.

"Daddy, did you know that I came to Mommy and told her I was ready?" Cate says.

"Yes, I did, Baby Girl. But tell me what you remember," adds Tiago.

"I came to Mommy and told her. I said, 'I'm ready, Mommy.'"

"And what did Mommy say?" asks Tiago.

"She didn't say anything. She just looked at me. I think I surprised her. But she did smile."

"I'm not surprised. And Mommy and Daddy are still smiling and loving you," says Tiago.

He looks over to see an immense grin on Dri's face as she watches and listens to this conversation, her hands resting in her lap.

"And where were you when you saw Mommy?" asks Tiago.

"I was with Mommy, silly," responds Cate.

"Where were you before and after you saw Mommy?" tries Tiago again.

"I was in this special place, watching you."

"And what did that special place look like?"

"It was warm and light. There were lots of pretty colors. And there were other kids there. They were mostly watching people here. Others were playing with each other. They were waiting for their time."

"Do you ever talk to them since coming here?" asks Tiago.

"Not like we talk. But I hear them sometimes. When I wake in the mornings. And they hear me. But not like you do," replies Cate.

"And what do they say to you?" asks Tiago.

"They're just happy for me. And I'm happy for them. Someday, they'll come too," says Cate.

"Do they know when?" says Tiago.

"Oh no. Their mommy's and daddy's have to decide too. And some aren't ready."

"Do you remember anything else?" asks Tiago.

"I was happy there. And I'm happy here, too. Like I was there," responds Cate.

"Well, I'm certainly glad of that," responds Tiago. "I would hate to have you be sad here."

"I am, sometimes. But mostly I'm happy."

"Can Daddy have a big hug, Baby Girl?"

Cate walks over and puts her arms around Tiago's neck, then gives him a peck on his mouth. "I love you, Daddy."

"I love you too, Cate."

Tiago holds her as if she were his precious gift. On days like today, he knows she is.

Dri gets up to begin dinner as Cate starts to play with her table and tea set. She gives her dad a cup of tea, as they both imagine drinking it. They play more until dinner is ready, then sit at the table and have a more typical conversation.

Tiago looks over at his daughter, still amazed at their earlier conversation. His heart feels full, and there is an ease in his body. He perceives the magic in their precious conversation. Suddenly, his grandfather seems near to him, as if coaching the three during these interactions. His Gpa's nearness feels exhilarating and sad simultaneously. In this moment, he chooses a greater focus on the exhilaration.

Later that evening, Tiago works from his bedroom desk while Dri works from the dining room table. Now that Nika is running for Congress, both are committed to help her. They make calls to people in her Oakland, Berkeley, San Leandro district, explaining how effective Nika will be as their new congresswoman. Both find it relatively easy to talk with people about her. She spent the last two years as the current congresswoman's legislative director and frequent local spokesperson. This helped for many to know of her already. Given Tiago's time living in Berkeley, he can talk from that perspective as well.

Nika viewed the opportunity to jump in when the current congresswoman decided to retire, and her chief of staff decided she did not want to run in her place. While Nika is still young, her law degree and the last seven years working in the local office as well as spending extensive time in Washington helped her decide to take this opportunity to serve. Being the chief architect for the gun legislation passed in congress also helped her connections with other state and national congressional members to endorse her candidacy. With success in the primary, her win has a good possibility in this heavily democratic district. Still, the other strong democratic candidate will provide stiff competition in the fall election. And no one wants to take chances with such a prospect.

There is a knock at the door as it swings open. Bella notices Dri on her phone and stops just as she is about to speak. Dri says goodby and puts her phone on the table. She gets up to greet her mom.

"Hey, Mom. How are you?" says Dri on the rise.

"I'm well, thanks. The showing was excellent, and I think we will get a solid offer on this one. Did the fliers for the new listing arrive today?" asks Bella

"Yeah. They're here on the counter." Dri grabs the package and hands it to her mom. "Do you have a minute? I'd love to share something that happened today with Cate."

"Sure," responds Bella as she heads for the couch. "What did my darling granddaughter do today?" says Bella.

A big grin emerges on her face and a sparkle in her eyes as she mentions Cate's name.

Dri informs her mom about the initial conversation she had with Cate this morning. Then she shared the interaction Tiago and Cate had this afternoon.

"Are you kidding me?" responds Bella. "I've heard of kids making such statements from some reading I did years ago. But I never thought it would happen in my family. I knew she was amazing, but this proves it!"

"I guess it's not unheard of. But I had to learn about it from the Internet. It's not clear if it's becoming more common or just more people willing to talk about it. The great thing is that parents don't hush kids up so much. They appear comfortable sharing the information, more now than in the past. Still, it's pretty shocking when it happens to me."

"Yeah, I'd agree with that," adds Bella. "I assume you'll support her reporting of this."

"Of course," says Dri. "And I'm certain Tiago and I haven't talked about my dream in front of her. I've hardly talked to anyone about it since her birth. Given that, I can't explain it any other way than accurate. I don't see another explanation."

These two mothers talk more about what an amazing child she is, along with their biases. They move on to some upcoming real estate transaction deadlines and a couple of showings that Dri may need to do, as Bella has conflicts. Finally, they say goodbye and Bells leaves for home.

Dri sits back down at the table to do another half hour of calls for Nika's enterprise. She has never been so involved in a political campaign. But she has never had anyone she believes in so completely as her dear friend from high school. And people generally are responding positively to the calls. They commit to voting and frequently agree to encourage a friend to vote for Nika or even take someone to go vote in person.

Chapter 18

A
Transformational
Effort

Fall, 2033

F or the autumn meeting of the Coalition's Board of Directors, Nika carves out time
on the agenda to discuss a new initiative. With Nika's election to the U.S. House of
Representative last November, she puts herself in a position to submit legislative pieces
directly.

The passage of the gun legislation last year occurred with advocacy by Coalition
members throughout the country along with other groups who championed the cause.
This new law included essential funding for conflict resolution programs to be taught in
schools and family preparation programs. The work Nika hopes the Coalition Board will
approve in today's meeting would propel the resolution of disputes further, even with her
uneasiness in accomplishing this enormous task.

Fadima and Dri dropped off the Coalition Board when they began to get paid for their
administrative and educational efforts, reducing the potential for a conflict of interest.
Omar was elected in Fadima's place, and Bella was elected in Dri's place. Sarah was elected
when Soph moved to France. Sarah's membership provides the group an additional legal

perspective. The election also gives Sarah a greater opportunity to impact social change, an increasing interest of her legal efforts. Rather than spend money on travel, the group continues with digital meetings, a common practice carried over from the mandatory method during the 2020 pandemic.

As ongoing chair, Nika calls the meeting to order from her apartment in Washington, DC. All members are present, and the minutes from the previous meeting are approved. They move to the Executive Director's report of the group's continued increase in size, now 163,837 members. But Fadima reports a slowing of new participants, apparently due to increased false advertising by the Primordial Family Foundation initiative (or PFF), headed by Charlene Hoover. This conservative fundamentalist group has increased efforts to fight many progressive proposals in Congress, and the Coalition currently seems to be high on their enemy hit-list. They are left over from the Christian Nationalist conservatives in the declining Republican Party. But their methods of perpetuating anger and falsehoods remain the same.

Taylor, the Coalition's accountant, reports on fundraising efforts, donations, and expenditures. The financial status continues to be strong. Taylor summarizes the highlights in each category.

"We have had an especially strong period for member donations," says Taylor. "The Primordial Family Foundation, an oxymoron from their actions in my opinion, has increased efforts in their advertising campaign against us. But the ads also seem to have stimulated larger donations by our members. I'm not sure the best way to counter those ads, but I set aside some funds to work with. I would say we have at least $520,000 for that. It's not a large amount for advertising. But maybe we can solicit more funds through the ads, too. That could help."

"Great idea, Taylor," responds Nika. "Thanks for your report, analysis, and suggestion. Fadima, are you comfortable continuing to provide verbal responses to reporters on TV and radio? I think those have been going well."

"Yes, I'm happy to keep doing that. My previous work at the UN doesn't hurt with a few credentials, and Sarah's written responses have been invaluable."

"That's great. Sarah, you willing to continue helping with written pieces?" asks Nika. "I worry about anything formal coming from my congressional office. But I am comfortable giving you any feedback or ideas if you wish to discuss them first."

"Yeah," says Sarah. "I'm happy to assist with that. And I appreciate your perspective, Nika, when I want to run something by another member or get another legal point of view."

"Excellent. Then let's talk about how we should proceed with the PFF ads. I think a couple of you have suggested we simply ignore them and go about our work. But I know a few of you suggested we run some of our own ads in response. The discussion is open on this piece."

"I would recommend we begin running some ads in the locations they run theirs," offers Sam. "I don't think we should attack the ads or the group. That would be contradictory to our mission. I think we just promote what we are trying to accomplish as community education pieces. Let's clarify the truth about us in the process. We also could solicit funds to support our efforts, whether or not we apply those to additional advertising."

"I'm not opposed to those kind of ads," responds Imani. "I just don't want to get into a fight with the group. I think we take the higher road in this case."

"Yes, I'd agree with that," responds Sam. "I just think now is an opportunity to accurately inform communities what we're about. Let people know what we're trying to accomplish. It's an information campaign, not a reaction to the other group."

"I like that idea too," adds Kiara. "If we have some money to inform others about us, that could be a plus all the way around."

"I agree," says Rachel. "Informing people and sharing our website may stimulate more interest and members. That could be a great opportunity for some positive publicity."

After several more responses and additional comments, the board votes to commit $500,000 to begin an advertising campaign for the Coalition, focusing on accurate information about the group's mission and encouraging interest in participation. The motion passes with unanimous consent.

Nika, with some trepidation, next brings up her desired topic on the agenda.

"I propose we develop an alliance of leaders and groups who would support a national priority on peaceful approaches to conflict and avoidance of harm to others. Such lack of harm would include a priority of race equality within this country as well as internationally. It also would commit to honor human life, providing support for families of young children and pregnancy prevention, while preserving a woman's right to choose. Primarily, it also would place top priority on peaceful resolution of differences and avoiding any further armed conflicts, with family, friends, and foes."

"This is a huge undertaking, Nika," responds Rachel. "While I love and commit to the idea, do you think we're ready to take a lead in this?"

"I do, Rachel," says Nika. "I think we could get former presidents, military personnel, congressional members, and other leaders to be part of the alliance. After seeing the support for the gun legislation we passed last year, I think people are ready for this."

"But are there other things we should get in place first?" asks Kiara.

"With the extensive police reforms and funding for mental health professionals passed as well as single payer health care insurance, we have been laying the foundation for such a commitment," responds Nika. "I also think the sliding scale assistance program for college tuition and trade schools bill passed in 2028 is making a significant difference in narrowing the economic and educational gaps. I think we now need to bring all these efforts together to transform our previous reliance on violence to peaceful resolution of differences. The focus would be within families, communities, our country, and our relationships with other countries."

"What about our ad campaign?" asks Sarah. "Would it take a back seat to this?"

"No, I don't think so," says Nika. "I think we can do both. We can do the ads while some of us lay the foundation for this larger issue. I believe it's time for an alternative strategy and focus. Bullies perpetuate bullies; violence perpetuates violence. It's time to let peace perpetuate peace and love perpetuate love."

"I love the idea," says Ariella. "And have since we organized our Coalition. But how do you recommend we go about this? Where do we begin?"

"I suggest we begin by passing a proclamation by our group that is shared with all our members, asking them to sign on to the declaration," responds Nika. "Then we begin sharing it with others we know or where we have some connection. We can begin approaching other people and groups we think might be interested, both nationally and internationally. Once we have sizable support, I will introduce the proclamation and commitment into Congress. Of course, I'll try to get others, middle-of-the-road and progressive Democrats, and attempt to get even the few moderate Republicans left to become co-signers or support it at least. I think once we have a significant group of leaders from different industries and walks of life, Congressional members will have to pay attention to it. Hopefully, we'll already have key leaders in the House and Senate behind it."

"You think we can do all that?" asks Sam.

"Not overnight, obviously," says Nika. "It will take time to garner support from different segments of society. That's why I think we start now. It may not pass the first time it's introduced. But that's been true of many significant pieces of legislation that eventually won enough support for approval. Like gun reform laws. Or changes in health care. They all took time to gain enough support to pass."

"We're going to need someone to head up these efforts," suggests Tiago. "We all can work on it, but I think we need someone to keep up with the organization of it all."

"I'll certainly help with the organizing and paperwork," offers Fadima.

"That would be great," adds Nika. "And I think it would be useful to have a board member, maybe as a co-chair. Someone who could speak for our board, too."

"I would be willing to step into that responsibility," responds Sarah. "I don't feel like I've done enough to end the kind of violence that killed my brother. I want to do more."

"Oh Sarah, I think that would be awesome," says Sam. "And a law degree behind your voice doesn't hurt either." Sam quietly applauds as he makes his last comment.

"I think to have a spokesperson who also is lesbian would be an important symbol for the LGBTQ community," contributes Rachel. "There has been way too much harm to them, and might help energize their support for the commitment, even among conservative members."

"I know there probably are some concerns about taking on this kind of leadership commitment by our group right now," adds Nika. "But are there any objections to this? Let's talk about those."

"I guess I'm a little concerned about the financial commitment at the same time we are committing to an ad campaign," suggests Sam, often the voice of reason or caution regarding financial expenditures. "At the same time, I agree with Sarah's comment. I'm not sure I've done enough to address Diya's death. So there's another part of me that wants to proceed with this now, too."

"I appreciate you raising the financial issue," says Nika. "We certainly don't want to ignore that or put the Coalition in jeopardy. Are there any funds available for this venture?"

"Well, we committed $500,000 for the ad campaign. There is another $20,000 from that pot we could use," adds Taylor.

"We also could do a fundraising effort for this," adds Sienna. "I know a few people who might be willing to contribute, maybe even right away. We could start with the $20,000, then expand as funds become available for this project."

"That would be great, Sienna. Fadima, does it work for you and your plans of fundraising for Sienna to focus on this right now?"

"Yes," responds Fadima. "She has another small project going. But she's very competent. I'm sure she can take on both. Right Sienna?"

"I'm sure I can," says Sienna. "I had our other project in mind when I suggested this. It'll be fine."

"Great. Are there any other concerns or objections to this initiative?" asks Nika. "I'm excited to begin moving on this. But I also don't want to push it over people's objections."

"As the newest member of the board, I wasn't sure about taking on such a huge endeavor," offers Bella. "But as I have gotten clearer about the mission, it seems to me that this is a prime initiative for this organization to tackle. It took me some time to get comfortable with where this group was moving and what it would take on. But now, I like where this project takes us. I don't think we could do anything more important at this time. I'm all in favor of it."

"I move that we adopt Nika's proposal and commit to helping bring this to fruition," says Rachel. "I will help connect to people I know, both for support and some fundraising."

"I second the motion," adds Omar, the next newest member of the board. "I, too, commit to encouraging people to support this initiative and will also help to raise some funds."

One by one, each of the other board members vote in favor of the Proclamation, agreeing to work on sharing it with others and assist Sienna in raising funds for the project.

Nika looks at the faces of Fadima, Sienna and Taylor as competent staff, and each board member on the video call.

"I'm so touched and gratified by your support," she says. "And I'm excited about moving ahead. This is a project I feel comfortable with my office being a part of the alliance. And I'll start to make a list of people I will begin contacting now that we have a formal adoption by our organization. I'm thrilled about this. And I know Dri will be too. Tiago, will you take on the pleasurable assignment of informing her?"

"I would be delighted to do so," responds Tiago. "But maybe, as chair and her best friend, it would be your appropriate role to do so, if you would prefer."

"You know what?" asks Nika. "I would be excited about doing that. But another option would be to include her in the last few minutes of this call. That way we can all see her face and hear her response. After all, it is the whole group who has made this happen.

Not just today, but over the past almost four years. Fadima, would you see if you can get an invitation to join us while we take care of a couple of other items?"

"I'd be happy to do so, if you don't need me for a few minutes," says Fadima.

"No, I think we'll survive a couple of minutes without your attention. Now, as you all know, we need to set up an official rotation for board members. You all have served admirably for the past four years. And, as we discussed at our last meeting, we would love to have you serve one more year. Then, starting next July, two of the ten remaining members will be up for reappointment or rotate off each year, with a limit of three terms starting in 2034. The only exception would be board chair, who could serve one additional term. Those rotating off will be replaced by new members, with the entire board up for election or reappointment over a five year period rather than the three years suggested originally. Taylor has agreed to help us pull numbers one through five from a hat as we focus on each member. We also have a provision that a member can serve a second term if desired and approved by the board. Any questions about the process?"

There was silence from the group as members looked at each other on their screens.

"OK, then let's begin with me," says Nika. "Taylor, what's the first number?"

Taylor reaches in her big brimmed purple hat with a red feather sticking out the back. "The first number is 2," she says.

"OK, I'll serve two more years before rotation. Let's proceed with Sam, who is next on my screen."

Taylor pulls out a 5, and a sigh of relief escapes out of several mouths for the financial stability he has provided and will continue to do so for at least another six years. Then they move around until all terms have been identified. This will give an orderly rotation of board members while providing some consistency for the board itself. As they finish, Dri shows up, having joined the video meeting from her Napa apartment.

"Welcome back to our board meetings, Dri. Thought you were through with these, didn't you?" laughs Nika. "We won't keep you long. But we wanted to inform you as a group that the proposal to proceed with the proclamation has passed unanimously. We are excited, with a hint of caution from all of us, to initiate this immense and essential task. We wanted to pass along this information from all of us."

Dri's mouth and eyes transform into a huge grin, with sparkling tears of joy escaping from her left eye.

"I'm so glad! And it's fun to see you all and hear it from the whole group. Thanks for your confidence and encouragement to get this moving. This is even larger than the goal

I envisioned when we met at the memorial in Las Vegas. And now it's getting established in earnest with all our support. I'm so grateful for your efforts and advocacy all along the way. We will do this together, with the support of lots more!"

All present break out into applause. Dri knows their clapping goes beyond her comments. Rather, it is for the group, the satisfaction of the way they all have come together creating a different vision and way of living. It has taken years of work, and it will take many more. As Dri and Nika look at each other, with Bella, Sarah, and all the others present, there are smiles all around at the initiation of a huge and pivotal endeavor.

"Thanks for starting this, Dri, and for joining us today to share this announcement," says Nika. "And I think that ends our meeting. Is there anything else that needs to be said?"

"Yes," responds Rachel. "I would like to recognize the four young people we lost five years ago that brought us all together. Ariella and my son, Joseph. Kiara & Sam's daughter, Diya. Fadima's son, Husayn. And Bella's son, Dri and Sarah's brother, Alex. And thanks to Dri for her commitment to make a change in this world. It was an inspiration to us all. And out of our sorrow arises an endeavor to create change. May it all work out well."

"Thank you, Rachel, for speaking this out loud and reminding us," says Nika. "Let's take a moment of silence to remember those we've lost."

There is silence among the group. Finally, Nika speaks again.

"Let's also notice the gift of creating a change so our loss was not in vain."

Again, Nika quits speaking for the group to feel into her words.

"Now, thank you to all current and former board members for making this fantasy the beginning of a reality. We will see most of you at our next meeting in March."

Attendees share their farewells as they leave the meeting.

Nika tunes into her expanded heart, a confirmation she has made the right choice. She feels into her excitement to be launching a piece that feels like "her work." She walks her road, now curious to where else it leads.

***

After the blissful news from the board meeting, Dri finishes Cate's lunch and puts it down in front of her at the table.

"I don't want that!" screams Cate, as her arm sweeps across the table in front of her and sends the bowl of soup splashing to the kitchen floor.

Dri walks over to Cate and picks her up in her arms.

"OK, let's go talk in your bedroom," she says to her four-year-old with as much calm as she can muster in the moment. She carries Cate, who now is screaming and trying to hit Dri, into her bedroom and shuts the door behind them. She puts Cate on the floor, who begins slapping the carpet and kicking her feet. Dri sits on the floor in front of the door and watches her daughter in her second tantrum this week.

Dri takes a deep breath, slowly exhaling, blowing the air out of a circle formed with her lips. She takes in another breath, then exhales again as she watches Cate slow her slapping and kicking.

"You ready to talk?" asks Dri.

Cate says nothing. She lies still on the floor, tears now forming in her eyes.

"Come sit in Mommy's lap for a minute, would you please? Let's talk."

Cate remains lying on the floor, then slowly turns onto her side, away from Dri. She stays there for several minutes, then sluggishly sits up, turns, and crawls over towards Dri, who holds out her arms. Cate crawls onto her lap, her head resting on Dri's left shoulder. Dri rubs her back with her palm, then holds it on the back of Cate's heart as she brings her head down to rest on the top of her daughter's sweaty head.

"Sorry life has been so hard the last couple of days," whispers Dri. She lifts her head and kisses Cate on the top of hers and gives her a squeeze. "I know you get angry and frustrated. We all do at some time. And there are other ways of handling your upset besides throwing things, hitting, or kicking the floor. I just want to help you learn another way that will be more useful to you and for others around you."

Dri feels a tear drop onto her arm. She gives Cate another squeeze and a kiss on her neck.

"I love you, dear. And it's not OK to just throw objects or hurt people because you're angry. We need to use our words too."

Dri sits quietly just holding Cate in her arms, allowing her to continue settling into her embrace.

"You remember last year when you asked me if I remembered when you came to see me before you were born?" asks Dri.

"Yeah," whispers Cate.

"How did your heart feel then?"

Cate is silent for a few moments, as if thinking about Dri's question.

"It felt warm and soft."

"And how does it feel now?" asks Dri.

Cate is silent again for a moment, then responds.

"It hurts."

"Yes, it hurts when we are full of anger, kick, throw, and scream. Do you like your heart better when it hurts or when it's warm and soft?"

"Warm and soft," whimpers Cate.

"Yeah, me too. May I rub your heart gently?"

"OK," whimpers Cate again.

Dri places her right hand over Cate's heart as her daughter turns in her arms, then steadily and gently she makes small circles on Cate's chest.

"Just feel into my hand. Let's see if we can warm and soften your heart."

Dri continues to rub Cate's chest with her hand as she places small kisses on several places on her head. After a while, she asks again.

"Is it feeling any better?"

"Yeah, Mommy."

"Excellent. Just notice that. Let yourself enjoy that feeling. This is when I feel best. You might learn to do that, too. Feeling your heart, warm and soft. Taking slow deep breaths. Letting that feeling spread."

As Dri sits in a moment of silence, she pays attention to her gratitude for noticing her own anger before letting it come out in her words and actions. That she could shift to Cate's hurt and focus her efforts there.

She doesn't know exactly how to teach alternatives to children. So she just keeps exploring and talking through possibilities with her mom. She has done lots of reading about child rearing, and her training in family therapy adds another perspective. Dri feels grateful for her mom too, and the important ways they seem to influence each other. Three generations of women, still learning, exploring new alternatives, with increasing desire to live from their hearts.

Cate gets up and begins to play in her room. Dri looks at Alex's photograph hanging on Cate's wall of local vineyards. She reflects back to his excitement about blind tastings and blending, a process he learned during his internship at David Arthur and later practiced at Oenophilia Winery. He loved the synthesis of science and art, a fusion that animated him. She also reads through Marianne's poem once again, hanging near the vineyard photograph.

It seems to Dri in this moment, supporting children in their growth is a parallel process. Here too, she takes what she knows from theories and research and apply it artfully with a parent's intuition and all the grace she can muster.

Yes, this too seems to be what Doc was talking about when he suggested she trust her intuitive knowledge.

The manner in which we coalesce these two contrasting views of the world requires all the inner wisdom we can access. A little of this combined with some of that. And now we'll try to practice such an approach at a national and international level, seeing if we can't learn to solve our adult problems without violence. Attempting to create a new blend of human interactions through peaceful solutions.

Chapter 19
All About Relationships

February, 2034

Naeem and Nika celebrate their second anniversary in Washington, DC. During her initial term, Nika tried to pass or be involved with several pieces of legislation that would improve life for those in her district. These included the transformation of nuclear to cold fusion power plants, well before the expected transition dates. Another legislative accomplishment provided increased funding for transforming plastic products into a greater number of clothing, bags, and other uses to eliminate the further waste, now that plastic product production has been eliminated. She cares little about the limelight. She simply wants to represent the concerns of people she represents in Congress.

On this Tuesday evening, Nika takes the night off. Naeem makes reservations and takes Nika out to a little Italian restaurant near their apartment for a celebratory meal. Nika orders baked ziti and Naeem the *cacio e pepe* lasagne. The waiter recommends an enchanting bottle of Chianti, and the two celebrants exchange simple gifts. Nika receives a heart shaped locket with a photo of the two of them from their wedding. Naeem receives a silver band with "N & N" etched within a rose quartz stone attached atop the ring. They grasp each other's hand on one side of the table while lifting their wine glasses for a toast with their free hands. "To many more years of joy and happiness with the most amazing and beautiful woman in the world," says Naeem.

"Yes, yes," responds Nika. "To the most loving husband and greatest artist I know."

As Nika takes a sip, she hears a familiar voice on the television. She pulls her hand out of Naeem's grasp and taps his as she lowers her stemware.

"Look, love. Our ad is running!" Nika's eyes widen and the ends of her lips curl upward as she sees clips of the work the Coalition undertakes.

Naeem turns to see rotating photos on the screen, Omar's deep, compassionate voice in the background. The ad presents Coalition efforts to employ more peaceful conflict resolutions, continue to increase justice, actualize more equitable pay, and engage in community service.

"What do you think? Do you like the new ad?" asks Nika.

"It looks great. And I love Omar's radio voice. He could be an announcer any day" responds Naeem. "Are these running everywhere now?"

"No," says Nika. "Just where the Primordial Family Foundation ads are running lies about us."

"Well, I like it. Simply stating what you are doing. Attacking no one in the process."

"Yeah, that's our approach. Stay positive, passionate about what we want to accomplish."

They continue their meal, sip more wine, and later water to balance their liquid intake. The waiter comes back to clear their plates.

"Would you like to see our desert menu this evening?"

"What chocolate desserts do you have?" asks Naeem. "I know that's all my wife wants," he says with a big smile on his face.

"We have a dark chocolate cream cake and a creamy double chocolate pie with fresh berries and mint on top."

"We'll take one of each on this special occasion," responds Nika with oodles of energy.

The waiter returns with two plates filled with delight.

"Happy Valentine's Day," she says.

"Thanks. And our first wedding anniversary too," adds Naeem.

"Oh, well then, Happy Anniversary, too," she adds, a pleasant smile filling her eyes.

After the waiter walks away, Nika smiles at Naeem.

"Happy Anniversary, darling. And I think she's attracted to you, sweetie." Nika chuckles as she watches Naeem's response.

"Or you. One can't assume any longer, my dear. You should know that." Naeem laughs.

"OK, right again," laughs Nika. "Anyway, she seems pleasant and does a great job. I like this place. Thanks for thinking of this one for our celebration."

The two savor each bite as they share desserts, both lovers of dark chocolate. They sip the last of their wine as Naeem reaches out with his other hand to take Nika's.

"Glad we could be together for this and enjoy the evening," says Naeem. I know you have lots of work tomorrow. And I want to go to Georgetown to talk with the Gallery owner about a possible exhibit. It would be great to convince him to do at least a small show here in DC."

"That would be exciting. Seriously, hope it works out, love."

Naeem pays the bill, they stand, put on their coats, and stroll to the front. They step out into the chilly DC breeze, snow on the ground and crispy air. They pull their coats tighter and adjust their scarves closer. Nika slips on a piece of ice, grabbing Naeem's coat to save her fall.

Simultaneously, she hears a loud 'daaaht' and feels a sharp pain in her left neck and shoulder. She grabs it, intensifying the pain, then goes onto one knee as a liquid warms Nika's upper body. Naeem moves downward, holding Nika's arm. Another 'daaaht' rings out, then a 'tzeeet' with a thud on the building behind them. They now both fall flat to the ground, looking around and sighting a man standing behind a car. The man, in a dark cap aims again, but he notices people now gathering. He puts his pistol into his pocket, turns and begins to run.

Naeem pulls out his phone and dials 9-1-1. The operator comes onto the line. He informs her of shots fired, hitting his wife at the restaurant's address. He hangs up, then moves Nika's coat to see blood seeping through her light blue dress.

"You OK, Nika? Other than this wound? You hit any other place?" Naeem frantically looks over her body for any more signs of wounding.

"Nothing . . . . but this one, I think," she responds softly, her voice shaky.

"The ambulance will be here soon, I hope." Naeem catches his breath, his gaze steady.

Naeem hears the sound of two different sirens rapidly approaching, bright lights flashing. Two police cars roll up, one after the other, to the car where the man was standing. Two officers jump out of each car, one set moving towards them, the other apparently assessing the scene.

"What happened here?" asks the first officer as she approaches.

Naeem speaks, as he hears his wife softly moaning.

"My wife and I came out of the restaurant. Two shots were fired by somebody, looked like a man with a baseball cap, shooting from behind that dark car right in front of yours. The first one hit my wife. The second, luckily, missed us both."

A third siren approaches, this time an ambulance. Two people rush out, pull out a stretcher they roll up next to Nika. The two attendants begin to carefully hoist Nika onto the gurney.

"This woman's been shot. You alright, mister?" asks the nearest police officer.

"Yes," responds Naeem. "I'm fine. But please, get her to the hospital quickly."

Naeem's eyes remain on Nika, his heart pounding from fear and the deep love he has for her.

The attendants move her to the back of the ambulance and push it into the transport. Naeem, who follows closely behind, steps into the ambulance before anyone could say no. The attendants get in and begin their race to the hospital.

Once at the Emergency entrance, attendants quickly transfer Nika inside with Naeem rushing behind them. They call out for help, then push her through double doors.

Another attendant stops Naeem, suggesting he complete the informational data at the front desk so they can proceed as soon as they know what's required next. Naeem, in a liminal space, attempts to look through the windows or doors as they open. But Nika now is out of view. He goes over to the front desk, requesting the pile of paperwork required for his injured wife.

With the final signature on the last section, Naeem returns the electronic tablet where he entered all their information. He finds a seat and pulls out his phone and looks at it.

Should I call her parents? Make them worry without knowing what's going to happen? They'll want to come out, but it may not be necessary. Should I wait until I know? Where are the instructions about phone calls that should accompany the emergency handbook?

He decides to call for his mom's advice.

"Yes, I would give them a heads up," his mother says to Naeem's question after his response to the obvious first question as to whether Nika is OK. "I would want to know right away. Then you can call with an update later."

"OK, Mom. Thanks for the advice. I'll let you know as soon as I learn anything more."

"Wait. Are you OK?"

"Yeah, Mom. I'm fine. He missed me, thank God."

Naeem calls Nika's folks. Her mom answers. He tells Beverley what happened, making sure he immediately tells her she's alive and seems to be doing well. It was only a flesh wound, they believe. He'll call with an update as soon as he knows more. Her mom can hardly speak and thanks him in a shaky whisper, then hangs up.

As Naeem looks up, he sees a man in a white coat approach him. He sits in the chair next to Naeem and smiles.

"Hi, I'm Dr. Laghari. I'm the one who took care of your wife. We just completed closing up the wounds to her trapezius. Fortunately, the bullet passed directly through the muscle without doing any damage to the clavicle. She'll be sore for a while. And I don't want her to move her left shoulder right away. She'll need to take it easy and let it heal. But she'll be fine."

"Thanks, Dr. Laghari. I appreciate your help and knowing she's OK. Can I see her now?"

"Sure. Come with me. I'll give her a prescription for some pain pills for the next few days. Do you have any questions?"

"No, I don't think so," responds Naeem, as they approach Nika resting in her bed.

She looks over at him and smiles as he gazes into her eyes, making sure she's OK.

"Dr. Laghari, the police are here and would like to ask your patient a few questions. That OK?" a nurse asks.

"Yeah, have them come in. We're pretty much through here."

Dr. Laghari turns back to Nika.

"Let us know if there are any complications. Otherwise, make an appointment with your physician in two weeks for a follow-up check."

A man and a woman dressed in dark brown and black overcoats come through the doors and over to Nika's bed.

"Hi, I'm Lieutenant Adams and this is Sergeant Milbank," said a woman in a deep, firm voice, bearing badges. "You the victim who was shot in front of Alphonso's earlier this evening?"

"Yes, that's me," says Nika.

The woman proceeds to ask Nika her name and address, her occupation. The officers stand up a little straighter when she tells them her office is at the Rayburn House Office Building.

The lieutenant asks her to describe what she remembers from the incident. Then she asks Naeem to add any other pertinent information. Both provide similar accounts of what happened, each adding small bits of information as they proceed. Neither can provide more than sketchy information about the shooter. Naeem adds that he thought there was a white 'NY' on the man's cap.

"Well, we think we have the man who shot you," adds the lieutenant. "He matches the limited description you provided, and two other people witnessed the incident, giving us more details. He tried to hide in a nearby subway station. Fortunately, one person saw him go down the steps to the Red Line. There wasn't a train right away. We'll hold him while we gather more evidence."

"You're lucky you moved, Nika. Otherwise he may have hit your heart. He didn't seem to know much about guns or ammunition," says Sergeant Milbank. "He still had his Glock 19. Fortunately for him, he didn't try to use it when we surrounded him. Fortunately for you, he used a full metal shell. Guess he was cheap rather than determined to do damage. Anyway, that's all for now. But we'll need to talk more later."

"Thank you both," replies Nika. "I appreciate letting us know you have him. Think I'll rest easier with that information."

The police officers leave and Nika begins to breathe more easily. Naeem takes her hand, caressing it with both of his. A nurse comes in and holds out another tablet displaying a release form.

"If you sign this form, you'll be ready to go. I'll get a wheelchair to take you out front. Do you have a car here?"

"No," responds Naeem. "We'll take a cab home."

Nika rests for a couple of days at home with her caregiver husband, but soon returns to work. Naeem stays another week to make sure she is doing well, then returns to their place in Oakland, allowing him to get back to work.

Naeem arranged his flight in order to drive Nika's car to the airport to meet Tyrell. He gives his father-in-law the keys upon arrival and informs him of the car's location. Tyrell gives him a hug, thanks him for this exchange, both avoiding cab fares.

"And thanks so much for your care of Nika," says Tyrell. "Yet again, we get to see how much you care about her beyond your words."

"Of course," responds Naeem. "I will always try to protect the woman I love."

Tyrell gives him another hug, then both move in the direction of their transportation. This father is anxious to see with his own eyes his daughter remains safe.

Four days after her father arrives, the same two officers show up at Nika's office, asking to see her. Nika, hearing them in the reception area, opens the door and invites them to enter.

"We've done more investigation of this guy, reviewing everything on his computer," begins the lieutenant. "While he has some loose connections to subversive groups, including marginal association with a White nationalist group, this isn't shaping up like a hate crime. It's looking more like a hit because of your leadership with The Coalition. He's active in the Primordial Family Foundation group. Not a leader, but seems to have been focused on some of the lies about you killing babies and undermining our constitution. Do you know anything about this group?"

"Yes, we're familiar with them. We know they've been spreading disinformation about what we do, apparently in an attempt to undermine our mission. They've said some nasty and inaccurate information. But I've not heard anything going this far," says Nika with an exhale, shaking her head.

"As far as we can tell, he was acting alone," the lieutenant continues. "Just another fanatic who got pissed with what you were doing and took change into his own hands. He's been charged with first degree attempted murder and assault with a deadly weapon. So far he's denying the charges and seems angry. I'm pretty sure we'll have enough evidence, especially with the witnesses and your husband's testimony, to convict him. He's using a public defender. Doesn't seem to have many resources. But we'll let you know. Anything else come to mind that might help us?"

"No, I don't think so. But thanks for the update. Any idea when he'll come to trial?"

"No date is set yet. But he has to come before the court within 70 days. There may be delays, but that's an estimate for the initial hearing."

"Would you let me know please? I'd like to attend."

"Sure. But if you or your husband testify, you can't sit in until after your testimony."

"Yes, we're aware of that. Thanks."

The officers thank Nika for her time, then leave.

She sits at her desk, feeling into her anger that this man tried to kill her because he believes the lies that are circulating and decides to take the law in his own hands, as has happened so many times in this country in the past.

At least now, it seems like the police aren't treating us differently because we're Black. Maybe some things really have changed. Still, I want to see how the actual trial goes. I won't be able to sit in until after I've testified. But maybe Naeem can attend after his testimony when I can't be there.

Nika's cell phone interrupts her thoughts. She sees the call is from Fadima. Nika answers.

"Hey, Nika. How are you doin'?" Fadima asks.

"I'm feeling better, thanks. Still pretty sore. But each day the wound gets better. And my dad's here to help me. Naeem had to get back to teach his class in Oakland and to paint. Looks like he's going to have a show next year in a DC gallery."

"That's great news. I understand they caught the guy who tried..." Fadima hesitates. She was about to say the word kill, but then realized she did not want to put that word out there. "... the guy who shot you?"

"Yeah, they think they've got him," answers Nika. "And they have a couple of witnesses. Guess the guy was enraged by the lies about us, but apparently not that sharp. Lucky for me. How are you? How's everything going with The Coalition?"

"That's the other reason I called," says Fadima. "Bella and Omar have suggested we connect with a Native American tribe in Northern California about what they've been doing, their approach to climate change issues, and their work in restoration. Would you be able to get away? Or is there someone from the board you would want to represent you?"

"No, I can't leave right now. I'm swamped with legislative issues. But Bella and Omar would represent us well. And if Dri could make it, she might be interested from the educational standpoint. That would be a strong representation of our group."

"I agree. I don't think I'll go to this initial meeting. But if we decide to continue with some connection to them, I might join in, too."

"I think that's a great idea, Fadima. I would support that if the first meeting looks promising. How about if they write a brief report about their initial meeting along with any recommendations they might have?"

"I'll suggest that," responds Fadima. "I'll ask them to send the report to me, then I can get it out to board members."

"That sounds perfect," adds Nika. "And you doing OK? Everything else going well?"

"Yes, thanks. I'm doing well. With my son out of college, life is easier. He is working here in New York. So it's easy to see each other. And Coalition memberships seem to be picking up again. I think our advertising is helping, as well as our increasing presence on social media. Taylor's doing a great job of that too. And Sienna is doing well with her accounting work and seems happy. So now, you just need to completely recover. Then we'll all feel better."

Nika chuckles. "I'm healing as fast as I can. I'm tired of this slowing me down. I don't have my usual energy. But it's coming back. Just a little impatient. As usual."

The two share their goodbyes, then hang up. Nika sits back in her chair, now noticing both hope and anger. She typically experiences hope when everything goes well with The Coalition. And this new potential connection to work with what a Native American tribe is doing with the Earth creates an additional sense of encouragement. At the same time, her anger towards this stranger and his attempt to stop them infuriates her.

As she explores the outrage, she senses her response is not just about the shooting. There is something more to it. She picks up the phone and calls Dri.

"Hey there, do you have a few minutes to talk," asks Nika when Dri answers.

"Yeah, sure. This is a great time. Cate is in quiet time right now, and there's no emergency getting these forms to Mom's clients. How are you doing? Continuing to feel better?"

"I am, thanks. And Dad's here helping. I could do OK by myself, yet it's great to spend some time just with him. But I have some issues about the shooting I'd love to process with you."

"Of course. Happy to talk about anything with you," responds Dri.

"I'm aware of the anger I feel at this guy shooting me," says Nika. "But it feels like there's something more. And I'm having difficulty putting my finger on it. I'm not sure what it's about."

"OK. Tell me this. When you feel into the anger, what comes up for you? What images or thoughts appear?"

Nika closes her eyes and sits for a few minutes, paying attention to what arises when she focuses on her emotion. She sits a bit longer.

"It's more than anger. It feels like pure rage."

"OK, well done," responds Dri. "What images or thoughts come to mind with that rage?"

Finally, a thought flashes in Nika's mind.

"I'm angry at the Primordial Family Foundation, that they keep attacking us with their lies."

"Excellent. Anything else come up as you sit with this?" asks Dri. "Just freely associate. Notice whatever shows up."

Nika sits longer, just watching what appears.

"Yeah, the injustice that Whites impose on Blacks, like this guy imposed his anger on me. In fact, the injustice that goes on all over, including us being stopped for our color. Others shot and killed." Nika stops talking to notice again if there is anything else.

"There's rage for the imposing of beliefs and limitations on Blacks for centuries. I'm angry about it all."

"Great awareness and connection," says Dri. "Just stay with it." Dri goes silent.

Nika quits talking, feeling the emotions currently circulating around her body, spreading all around. Rage fills every part of her body, as if it's going to blow it apart. And yet, it doesn't. She realizes it's her fear saying that. But the rage sets her body on fire, circulating flames all over. Nika sits and watches the flames.

"What's going on now?" Dri asks.

"The rage feels like a fire in my body, burning without actually destroying anything, except maybe a few loose bits of garbage here and there."

"Are you able to just stay with it? Not running? Not avoiding? Not distracting?" asks Dri.

Nika pays attention to the fire. It now seems to be slowing. Flames continue, but are smaller, like the fuel that keeps it burning is decreasing.

"Yes, and it seems to be lowering."

"So, it has your attention. It's given you important information, and now it's decreasing. Is that right?"

"Yes," says Nika. "The rage is still there, but it feels less forceful, destructive."

"The question now is, what do you want to do with that rage? A useful thing about anger and rage is that they are motivating emotions. Unlike depression, they often move you to action. At the same time, you may not want to just act out with the rage, as the guy who tried to shoot you probably did. You're clear about the anger for people taking their view of justice into their own hands. The rage of one race enslaving, killing, and degrading another race. But your response doesn't have to come to the same emotional reaction from the rage. It can include your ideas of what you want to do in response, how you choose to act rather than some autonomic response. That's the difference between you and him."

"And it's important in terms of other principles I believe, like working for justice and living from my heart."

"Yes, exactly. As you feel the rage and open your heart, what do you want to do? What would you do from an open hearted place, while using the motivation of anger and rage to create a change? How could you do it differently than using the rage to simply seek revenge?"

"I don't know in this moment," responds Nika. "Nothing clearly comes to mind."

"That's alright," chuckles Dri. "You don't have to make a decision right now. But those are the questions to be asking. Pay attention to your rage and your heart. Don't separate them as you seek an answer. You don't want to bury the rage. That keeps it in your body as trauma, as we talked about years ago. You want to do something to let it go, mend, create a change that can heal that part of you. At the same time, include your heart. That will keep you connected to your ideals and prevent more trauma from coming in by doing something destructive to yourself or others. As you know, I'm just a reminder of insights you've helped me to learn. And sometimes, when we get emotional, we may not see as clearly. I'm just your external memory."

"Well, thanks for the reminder and your help. I just needed to talk it through. I'll stay with your great questions," says Nika, still deep in thought.

"Happy to assist and remind you. As you have done with me so often, my dear friend."

"I'd better get back to work. Thanks again, Dri," says Nika, then ends the call.

Over the next several days, Nika continues to ask the same questions, often just before she goes to sleep or when she first wakes in the morning. Several possibilities arise, but nothing gets clear or feels like it's the answer. She consistently keeps it in the back of her mind as she goes about other work and decisions.

Two weeks later, Lieutenant Adams calls her phone. Nika notices her hand shake slightly as she answers.

"I wanted to let you know that you and your husband won't need to testify. Our case weakened when one of the original witnesses turned out to be a bit unreliable. Still, we had a solid case. But the DA and the defendant's attorney agreed he could plead guilty to second-degree attempted murder and avoid a trial and possibly harsher sentence. So he did. The guy pleaded guilty. He'll be sentenced next Tuesday at 9:00 am in the Moultrie Courthouse, if you want to be there."

"Thanks, Lieutenant. Yes, I do want to attend. I appreciate you letting me know." When Nika puts down her phone, the anger comes up again. This time it feels like pure revenge.

The following Tuesday, Nika skips the debate in the House over a new bill. She's not sponsoring it, and she's pretty clear how she'll vote. Besides, it looks like it's going to pass anyway. She takes a cab to the court house and finds the correct room. Half the seats remain empty. She decides to sit near the back.

Soon after Nika arrives, the bailiff asks the audience to rise, the judge enters and sits, then everyone can be seated again. Nika sits directly behind Carl, the man who is about to be sentenced. She doesn't want to get his attention. She wants to notice what she experiences as the judge hands down the amount of time he'll serve. Of course, most defendants do not actually serve their full term. But usually at least half. And the total sentence will determine the minimum he will be behind bars. Nika is curious to know if she'll agree with it or not.

The judge begins by reviewing key facts in the case. Then she asks how Carl pleads. His attorney says, "guilty, you honor." The judge then asks Carl if he understands the implications of this plea. He says he does. After a little more discussion, the judge sentences Carl to 10 years at the Federal Correctional Institution in Cumberland, MD.

Nika is a bit surprised. She expected a lower sentence. Yet she also doesn't rejoice at the amount of time.

I wonder how taken in Carl was by the Primordial Family Foundation group? What made him get so angry he would try to kill me? What was his motivation? Was it personal to me, or just as the head of our board?

Nika becomes aware that instead of getting answers she was seeking, all she got were more questions. Instead of the issue being resolved and finished, more unknowns arise that disturb her.

The judge adjourns the court. Nika immediately rises to leave. Just as she reaches for the door, she feels a tug on her coat. She turns to see Lieutenant Adams, who walks out with her and nudges her to the side as if wanting to speak.

"Well, the guy got what he deserved, even with the lesser charge."

"Yeah, he'll be away for a while," says Nika. "Thanks for all your help with this and keeping me up to date. I appreciate it."

"Sure. You doing OK?"

"Yes. I'm healing well and getting on with my work, thanks."

What Nika failed to mention was the uneasy feeling after the verdict. Given she doesn't know what that's about, she avoids saying anything.

"Well, good luck with your work. Glad you're doing well."

The officer shakes Nika's hand, turns and leaves.

Nika stands still for a few moments, still processing her questions.

What's going on with me? I just don't get it. I thought I'd be much happier at his sentencing. Instead, I feel confused.

Finally, Nika leaves and takes a cab back to join the congressional discussion. Yet, her mind meanders. She brings it back to the topic being debated on the floor, then her thoughts roam again. She continues to focus on the back of Carl's head, his relationship with the Primordial Family Foundation, his drive to shoot her. She ought to feel the rage. Curiosity shows up more often instead.

The Lieutenant told me he was young, I think. Maybe 21, 22? How does anyone decide to shoot me without any direct contact with me? How does he get so angry with so little life experience? I know it can happen. But I need to know more about him.

Nika attends the floor discussion without actually hearing any major points. As it ends, she picks up her papers and walks back to her office. There are a couple of calls for her. She escapes into her office for uninterrupted meandering.

The internal dialogue dominates Nika's thoughts over the next two weeks. She talks with Naeem about it. But he doesn't understand her focus on this man. He suggests she just let it go and concentrate on her work.

She tries. She can't give it up. Her father returns to Iowa. She now is alone and obsessing.

The following Saturday, she has nothing scheduled. She gets up, dresses, and makes some breakfast. There is lots to read, and work on new legislation awaits her attention. But today, she gets in the car and drives just over two hours to get to Cumberland Prison.

She parks and goes in to tell the guard who she wants to visit. He checks the visitor list and fails to find her name. She hands him her congressional ID, telling him she's here on an official investigation. He looks over the card, looks at her, looks at the card again, then puts it down. He picks up his phone and calls the warden. He talks for a few minutes, then hangs up. He hands her back the card.

"OK. You can visit this time. But if you want to come again, you need to complete this form and return it at least a week before your next visit. You also need to complete this Notification form today."

He hands her both and a pen, then directs her where to sit.

Nika returns with the one completed form, putting the other in her coat pocket. The guard stamps her hand with "invisible ink." He tells her hands are checked with a black light going in and returning from the visitor's room. Nika thanks him, passes through the metal detector, then waits for two others so the five can be escorted together into a seating area within the visiting room. She takes her place and waits for Carl.

About 15 minutes later, Carl enters wearing khaki pants and shirt with a brown t-shirt underneath. His eyebrows narrow as he looks at her, then sits.

"What the hell are ya'll doing here?" Carl asks.

"You know who I am?" asks Nika.

"Yeah, I know. Why are ya'll here?"

Nika says she just wants to talk, to understand him. She relates some of the less personal questions that have been roaming in her head.

"Would you tell me a bit about yourself? I want to understand who you are," says Nika.

"Why should I? Ya'll recording this? Ya tryin' to use this against me?" asks Carl.

"No, not at all. There is no recording. There are no notes. I just want to know."

Carl scowls at her, apparently trying to figure out how this could be a trap.

"No, I don't think I want to talk to ya. I don't trust ya. Ya'll are stranger than I am, lady."

"Well, then, what's the harm in telling your story to a woman stranger than you?"

"The harm? You might use it against me somehow," responds Carl.

Nika studies his face for a minute while also checking in with her heart, currently thumping faster. Suddenly, a piece of her answer comes clear.

"Do you have any prior arrests?"

"Yeah, one when I was younger for jackin' a car."

"But no priors for attempting to kill someone or shoot anyone?" asks Nika, focused on his eyes and face.

"No. Only for car jackin'. I've done thought about it at times. But never done it."

"Look, you tell me your story honestly. I will need to verify a few facts to feel comfortable. I'm an attorney and don't easily believe people. But if you tell me the truth about you and why you ended up shooting me, I'll write a letter supporting your application for commutation of your sentence. You can't apply right away. But I'll write one as soon as we're finished, which will be in your file when you do apply," says Nika in a calm, determined voice.

Carl sits quietly, as if studying Nika's face. "What if y'all are lyin'? What if ya're just sayin' that but won't do it in the end?"

"You might make a strong attorney, too," says Nika with a smile. "You also know better than to trust everyone." Nika thinks for a minute, then continues. "OK. Here's my offer. I'll write a generic letter in support of your application and give it to the Warden with this form I have to submit in order to visit you again. He'll keep it in your file. If you tell me the truth about your story, and I often know when people are lying, I'll write a more detailed and convincing letter at the end of our conversations. Either way, you get a letter. But if you tell me the truth about why you did what you did, I'll write a much better one that will be more helpful to you than some generic format. Deal?" asks Nika, staring into Carl's eyes.

"What if you don't like what ya hear? What if I say somepun ya all don't like?" asks Carl

"You're a young man with only one prior," says Nika. "I suspect one reason you got a longer sentence is that you shot a member of Congress. I don't know that for sure. But judges tend to frown on such acts. I'm sure I can find one solid reason to write a stronger letter, even if I don't like all that I hear. And I promise to do that, no matter what you say. So if you tell me your true story, you get a stronger letter from the member of Congress you shot. I just want the truth. As I'm telling you the truth right now."

"Yeah, I read people pretty good, too," responds Carl, looking directly into her eyes. "I kinda believe ya. OK, it's a deal,".

The two begin their conversation. Carl tells her about his family and home in rural Kentucky. He grew up in McCreary County, a ways outside the small town of Pine Knot. It was a beautiful place to grow up, living in the Daniel Boone National Forest. But it also was the poorest county in the state. His dad was a grill cook in a little cafe, and his mom worked as a personal care aide in a local retirement home. He is the youngest of five children, and they were doing alright until the pandemic hit, when Carl was eight-years-old. First, his mom got Covid-19 from her work. She survived, but she was out of work for three months during her recovery. The first relief bill helped them get by, and it helped his dad's cafe stay open. But when the Senate refused to pass another relief bill and his mother remained out of work for so long, they were never able to get caught up on their house payments.

They managed as long as the moratorium on foreclosures was in place. But they lost their house the next year. They found a smaller place to rent, but by then his father was drinking heavily. He eventually showed up at work drunk and was fired. His mother went back to using pain pills, stealing them from her work. She finally got caught and lost her job, putting more stress on the family. The two oldest siblings went to work to help the family, but it was difficult to compensate for the lack of income and literal helplessness from their parents.

Carl was always interested in cars. His curiosity helped him eventually get a job in a repair shop, where he learned how to fix and supe up cars. Unfortunately, that also led to racing as a teenager, for which he got three tickets and his license revoked. Unable to get to work, he lost his job. He decided to steal a car so he could get to Lexington to find a new life at seventeen. But the cops found him first just outside McCreary County. That gave him three years in a detention facility.

As Carl reaches this point in his story, a guard informs him that he has to return to his cell.

"Thanks for a great start. I really appreciate it. I'd like to come back, but it probably won't be for a couple of weeks. I have lots going on at work. I'll complete this form to get approved as a visitor and send your basic letter to the Warden early next week. You should be able to ask about it by the time I come back. How's two weeks from today?"

"Let me check my busy schedule," says Carl with a chuckle. "Yeah, that day's good."

"OK, I'll see you then. And thanks, Carl. I appreciate you making this deal," says Nika.

"Ya'll are nice to talk to, I guess. But I want to know something about you too, OK?

"Yes, that seems fair. I'll start sharing during our next visit."

Nika and Carl both rise, moving in opposite directions. Nika gets the "invisible writing" check on her way out. She goes to her car, feeling alright about the partial answer of how she wants to respond.

Chapter 20
National Commitment
April, 2034

B y Monday, the conversation with Carl provides ease in Nika's body and slow relaxation in her mind. Many questions remain unanswered. But the initial information at least allows her to begin understanding this man. She doesn't comprehend yet how the PFF aroused his rage or why he shot her. Even the beginning details reassure her curiosity that answers eventually will emerge. Having begun the process allows her to focus on her congressional work.

Nika arrives at her office bright and early this Monday morning. Autumn, her primary assistant, hands her messages as she walks by, then she settles into her inner office. As she goes through the phone notes, one jumps out at her. Speaker Sanchez would like her to call about the proposed resolution Nika sent to her just over a week ago. Nika returns to the outer office.

"Autumn, would you please call Speaker Sanchez's office and set up an appointment at her earliest convenience to discuss the legislative piece we went over last week?" requests Nika.

"I'll do it right now, with pleasure," responds Autumn, a smile accenting her rosy cheeks.

Nika goes back to her desk. She wants to highlight points that will be critical when she meets with the Speaker. She thought about some on her way to work. She'll make a list, to assure she covers them all systematically. It will remain a working list, with other items added as she talks with additional congress members, encouraging their support.

This first attempt at a concurrent resolution will lay out the sentiments of both the House and Senate. While it will not have the force of law, it identifies the priority of Congress to find and incorporate non-violent means in resolving conflicts, domestically and internationally. The recent bill providing funding for conflict resolution programs and centers broadens the foundation for such a priority. Nika realizes this is an important next step in the continued metamorphosis of this country's historical addiction to violence as a means to control others and determine specific outcomes. She also knows it will take more than an expression of sentiment to build a lasting transformation. And progress typically develops one or two steps at a time, often including one going backwards. But she wants to focus on forward.

On Wednesday, a smile by the receptionist greets Nika as she opens the door to the Speaker's office. "Go on in. Speaker Sanchez is expecting you, Nika. She's just finishing a phone call. Have a seat, and she'll be with you in a minute. Thanks for being so prompt."

"Of course, Cheryl. I don't need a tardy notice to start such an important meeting. And thanks for your constant smile to greet people. It's very calming."

"Thanks," Cheryl says with an extended smile.

Nika walks into the Speaker's office and waves hello, as she sees the Speaker on the phone. She sits in the usual chair and waits for her to finish.

"Yes, that sounds great. I'll see you next Tuesday."

Speaker Sanchez hangs up her phone and gets up from behind her desk.

"Thanks for coming, Nika. But let's sit over her on the couch. It's more comfortable."

Nika stands and joins her in her relaxed sitting area.

"Thanks for seeing me, Speaker Sanchez. I'm happy to talk about this resolution."

"Call me Luciana, please. First, how are you doing physically and mentally? I'm sure it was a rather traumatic event. And I hope you're taking time to continue your healing."

"Yes, thanks. I'm doing fine physically and pretty well emotionally. It was a real shock. As you said, traumatic. But I'm doing better on both fronts, thanks," says Nika.

"Great. I'm glad for that. Now, I've read the resolution and have talked with a few of the co-sponsors. You seem to have gotten them pretty motivated to support this."

"I hope so. Or at least that's what they tell me," replies Nika, as she continues to look directly at Luciana.

"Well, I think you being the fourth member of the House to be wounded and the fifth to be shot since 2010 has increased members sensitive to this issue. Especially with two of you being wounded in the last five years. Changes in gun legislation have decreased shootings in the population. But House members feel like we should do something more basic to address the issue of killings and violence in this country. Your resolution has brought this to the forefront."

"I'm pleased with that. There certainly has been lots of conversation about how to word this resolution."

"And the group has done a great job," responds Luciana. "I kept reading the quotes from Gandhi over and over. They touched me deeply. 'Nothing enduring can be built on violence.' And, 'Nonviolence of the strong is infinitely braver than their violence.' While some question the inclusion of these, I think they ought to stay. It's going to put more pressure on the Democratic Party fissure. But that's happening anyway. And the progressive segment of the party seriously wants this to pass."

"I'm glad you feel that way about the quotes. I like them too. What about the quote by Martin Luther King, Jr.? Are you alright with that one too?" Nika asks.

"I think so. Let me read it again, just to make sure." Luciana opens the papers and reads the following quote from King's 1967 speech at the annual SCLC convention.

"I am concerned about a better world. I'm concerned about justice. I'm concerned about brotherhood. I'm concerned about truth. And when one is concerned about these, he can never advocate violence. For through violence you may murder a murderer but you can't murder murder. Through violence you may murder a liar but you can't establish truth. Through violence you may murder a hater, but you can't murder hate. Darkness cannot put out darkness. Only light can do that."

"Yes, let's leave that in, too. I think it's important to build on the issue of justice in our own country as well. I think it also will solidify support from different groups, making it more likely to succeed."

"Great. That one is important to me for personal reasons," says Nika. "I read that when I spent some time at the MLK Institute at Stanford. I don't mean to put more pressure on the party. But I think the issue is critical for the future of our country. Do you have any other suggestions or essential changes you still want to see?".

"Yes, I do," says Luciana, as she looks down at the papers she's holding. "For one thing, the Senate has some wording changes they are recommending," pointing to the papers. Luciana turns back to look at Nika. "If we made those now, they could pass it without changes, avoiding negotiations between the two chambers. I've marked up several modifications that I'm hoping the co-sponsoring group will not object too strongly about. Senators are particularly concerned about the phrasing of the section on international conflicts, which could have significant implications. And they want to make sure it's worded so our allies and enemies know we'll try to do all we can to resolve differences. But we are not yet ruling out military interventions, at least as they see it. We don't want the Russians and Chinese to think we are pushovers immediately, even with Putin's apparent failing health."

"Understood. We just want to place greater emphasis on all peaceful alternatives first. I'm happy to look over any suggested changes," responds Nika.

Luciana hands Nika the papers she's been holding.

"If you would get that group together and work out the details, then we can take a final look at it. Call me if you or anyone in your group has any questions."

Nika grasps the papers.

"Will do. And thanks so much for your support, Luciana."

"Well, your Coalition and that National Alliance you put together made it difficult to ignore. And you made the actual process easy. You've been open to negotiating the basic concepts while holding on to your most important elements. And I think members are impressed with the way you've gone about this. It doesn't seem to be based in anger, but in a desire to help make our lives and country better. Stronger, really, by developing more resources. So that has facilitated people seeing this resolution with less initial resistance."

"That pleases me. I'll work on a meeting with the co-sponsors as soon as I get back to my office," says Nika.

"By the way. Will this resolution encourage a change in your Coalition mission statement? Will women reconsider bringing children into a more peaceful world? The increasing numbers making such a voluntary commitment has brought considerable pressure on the party. Some are concerned about that spreading, and others are tired of the disinformation being spread about it."

"The board is going to discuss it at our next meeting. Then a vote will be taken by our membership. But I think this might lead to such a change."

"Excellent. Great working with you on this, Nika," adds Luciana. "And it shouldn't hurt your reelection efforts this fall. Everything looking good there?"

"Yes, so far. I have a minor challenger in the primaries. But my Oakland staff tells me he isn't that strong. He's part of the more conservative segment of the party, which is less popular in my district. We'll see how it goes."

"Well, if you do run into any trouble, let me know. We don't want to lose you here."

"I appreciate that. I want to stay as well," adds Nika as they both stand.

Nika shakes Luciana's hand, then turns to the door.

"I'll be back in touch as soon as we have another draft."

"Great. Talk to you then," responds Luciana with a smile and a wave.

Nika returns to her office and asks Autumn to set up a meeting with the co-sponsors as soon as possible. Then she goes in to get some work done at her desk. As she puts her hands on the keyboard, her cell phone rings. Nika is surprised by the caller.

"Hey, Soph. Great to hear from you again. I haven't talked with you in months. Sorry I haven't called. Been pretty swamped. But how are you doing?"

"Fabulous, actually," says Soph. "I just agreed to take a different job."

"Yeah? Where?"

"Want to guess?" asks Soph, a half laugh in her response.

Nika guesses Des Moines, Seattle, and finally San Francisco. Soph says no to all of them.

"OK, I give. Where?"

"DC!"

"Oh my God, seriously? When will you be here? What are you going to be doing?"

"I just accepted a job with the World Health Organization in their DC office on 23rd Street in Foggy Bottom. It's just over three miles from your office. I'll be there in about two weeks."

"I can't believe it!" shouts Nika. "Does Dri know yet?"

"No, she's my next call," exclaims Soph. "I'm excited to move back to the states. I've loved it here in Paris, and my French is much better. But I'm excited to be back. And I get to experience DC for a while. Can't wait to see you!"

"It will be great to have you here, too. Naeem gets back here from time to time. It will be fun for the three of us to get together."

"Yes, that will be fun. And I'm excited to show you my new surprise," suggests Soph.

"What surprise?"

"You'll see when we get together. I'd like to get more involved with the Coalition again, too. While I shared our work with a few people in France, I'm missing you guys and your new initiatives. Do you think there is something I could do again to help?"

"We'll find a place for you. Lot's of new developments going on, and we could always use more support. I'll start looking around. Then we can talk about it when we get together here in DC. Do you know where you're going to live yet?" asks Nika.

"No, not yet. They have a person who's helping me. I've been talking with her about a small apartment somewhere for now. But I'll let you know as soon as I find something."

"Great. Oh Soph, it will be so great to see you again. Glad you're going to be close. Not quite like high school, but still pretty damn good."

"Yeah. I'd better go. I have a few more calls to make. But we'll talk soon."

"Great. Hope it's an easy transition here," responds Nika and ends the call.

Nika sits back in her chair, thinking about all the changes the three high school friends have been through over the last sixteen years. She doubts any of them could have predicted where they have ended up today.

How did we all get here? Was it completely accidental? Was there some master plan? Wish I knew. What I see are all the little decisions that accumulated into this path, this trail from City High to Stanford to law school to the House of Representatives. This was not my initial goal, I don't think. Yet all the steps lead to this. My intuition? I wish I understood how this happens. What I know is I'm grateful that it has.

Nika shakes her head and brings her chair upright. There remains much work to do. She pulls out the marked draft Luciana gave her and begins to read through it. There are lots of minor changes, a different word or a few words, additions or replacements. But nothing major, so it appears.

This shouldn't be too difficult for us to make the desired changes and get moving on this resolution.

Autumn gets the co-sponsor meeting set up for Friday morning, 9:00 am, in a conference room just down the hall.

Nika is the first one to arrive and gets the room set up for the other eight in the group. The members enter, chatting about this bill or that. A couple talk about what they are planning for Memorial Day in a few weeks.

Nika calls the meeting to order and shares her discussion with the Speaker. Most are encouraged by the support she and other leaders are showing for the five page resolution. Two members share their discouragement that others keep insisting on tamping down their direct statements. But as the group walks through the suggested modifications, they are less substantial and focus more on softening the language without significantly modifying their main points.

Most changes are made rather easily. Still, as Nika is learning with committees, they end up taking an hour to make a final decision on three words. Nika continues to respire, calling on all her patience. She knows it's important to let the group struggle for a little while rather than impose some easy solution, at least easy in Nika's mind. And they do struggle. Yet, the changes get made and the resolution seems to be shaping up in a form increasing numbers can support.

Following the meeting, Nika asks Autumn to make the final changes and put the file in the same shared computer folder. With changes made, Nika sends it back over to the Speaker. It doesn't take long for Nika to draft her email to Luciana. The resolution gets resubmitted.

Luciana later emails back that she will introduce it on the floor next Tuesday, with a vote on Thursday. That was quicker than Nika imagined. But she is happy with the timeline. This will be completed before she flies back to Oakland, spending time with Naeem and daily campaign events for the next two weeks.

More emails wait for a reply. But Nika decides to call Sarah about the ads. They have not talked since the shooting, except for a message from Sarah to get better as Nika was healing. She picks up her phone and finds Sarah's number, then calls.

"Hey, Nika. How are you feeling these days?"

"I'm well, Sarah, thanks. I got your message. Sorry I didn't get back to you. It's been a bit crazy around here since the shooting. But the Speaker is going to introduce our resolution next Tuesday on the floor, then call for a vote on Thursday. And Sarah? Thanks for all your efforts with the Alliance. I know it took considerable effort to pull people together, and you worked long and hard on this. And now, it looks like we have the votes to make this real. Great contribution!"

"Thanks, Nika, for the opportunity and support. I got to meet some great people I otherwise wouldn't have met, and I'm proud of what we pulled off. We all did it. Thanks to you, too."

"Oh, so glad our joint efforts made this happen. In the meantime, the wound is healing well and I can finally breathe a little easier. And how are you and May doing?"

"We're doing well. She's keeping busy at work, and so am I. The relationship is going well too. She's a joy in my life. I'm lucky to have her."

"That's fabulous. Say, I wanted to follow up with you about the ads. I love what you've all done with them. I think they're great and effective. Omar's voice is a nice touch, and it's fun to have someone from our group be the voice behind the ads too. Great idea."

"Thanks, Nika. I'd heard you were happy with them. But I didn't want to bother you with another call. I know you have lots going on there, too."

"Well, I just wanted to catch up and let you know how much I appreciate your hard work in getting these out. I think you've done a terrific job. Just what we needed."

"Wonderful. Thanks. But I wondered about making another one, trading off with this first ad so people don't just see this one thing. I was thinking about making one in relation to the resolution, assuming it passes on Thursday. We could talk about what a great thing this is and how people could work together to make the peaceful resolutions a reality, locally, nationally, and internationally. We don't have to focus on the Coalition in the ad, but simply say we support the resolution as a Coalition. Then call for others to join in with their support."

"I love the idea! That would get more word out about the resolution as well as the Coalition. Have you talked with Fadima? Do we have funds to run more ads?"

"No. I wanted to talk with you first. I didn't want to get ahead of myself or you."

"I appreciate that. Why don't you talk with her about the basic idea? Let her know that you and I have talked and that I support it. I'll call her once you've had the conversation. That way you can be clear about what you're suggesting directly. Then I'll call to talk through the finances with her and share my support for the idea."

"That sounds great. I'll call her now. And thanks for your encouragement," says Sarah.

"Of course. I'm happy to embolden creative ideas. Thanks for all your work."

Nika ends the call and pulls up the latest financial report. The funds don't look great for another ad campaign. But maybe Fadima has an update of contributions since this statement.

Late in the day, having completed her work, Nika calls Fadima.

"How are you doing, Fadima? Thing's going well?"

"Hi Nika. Yes, work seems to be going pretty well. The PFF has put out another ad, saying we force women to abort babies and how we are ruining our country. I think in the end it makes them look worse than us. But I'm still not inclined to sue them or send a cease and desist letter. I prefer Sarah's suggestion of putting out a positive ad about the resolution and calling on others to support these efforts."

"Yes, I agree. But when I look at the last financials, I'm not sure we can afford another campaign. Has anything changed since that report?"

"Yes, actually, it has. Sienna was able to get several large donations in addition to many small ones just for such a campaign. Some newer members are upset with the PFF ads and want to respond with another one. We have collected a little over $800,000 in donations over the last month from a variety of places to do something else. Want to focus on Sarah's idea?"

"I think that would be great. It would help identify what else the Coalition is doing, inform people about more of the resolution intentions, and it would emphasize the implementation of peaceful solutions in a variety of ways. I think this is great timing all around."

"I agree. I'll put it on the agenda for our June meeting," responds Fadima. She takes a breath, then changes the subject. "And how are you doing, Nika? Still healing well?"

"Thanks, Fadima. Yes, I am, both physically and emotionally. I had a long talk with Dri a while ago, and I'm sorting out some emotions that came up from the shooting. As I continue to get clearer, I'll share more with you. Maybe we could talk at our annual meeting in September, when we are together in person. It feels like more of a face-to-face kind of conversation."

"That would be great. I look forward to it. And glad you're healing well."

"Thanks, Fadima. I appreciate you checking in about it. I'll talk to you soon."

"Yes, thanks. Talk soon."

Nika again sits back in her chair. It has been an intense few weeks, some downs and more ups. She takes a deep breath and sinks into her gratitude for where she is and what she's doing. She has supportive people in her life, on several different fronts. And now it's time to make some reservations for dinner with Naeem when she's home the Friday of Memorial Day weekend. It's not always up to him to make them. And besides, she wants to try a new Puerto Rican restaurant a staff member in Oakland shared with her. Something a little more spicy on this joyous weekend at home. Besides, they will end up at the Bakery near their home for her favorite chocolate dessert. Or maybe have her favorite chocolate dessert at home!

Chapter 21
A Bifurcation
March, 2035

"Both bags are in the car. We had better get going," says Omar as he hands Bella's purse and phone to her. "Dri and Tiago just pulled up."

"I'm usually the one saying that," laughs Bella. "Don't know what's with me today."

"Have you told anyone yet?" asks Omar.

"No. I'll tell Dri once we get going. And I'll see Sarah at the airport. Thought I'd drop the news on her then."

They come out as Tiago is putting their bags into the trunk.

"Think they'll be surprised?"

"Yes, and no. I think Dri has been suspecting this for a while. Sarah, on the other hand, has not been around as much. It might surprise her."

"That'll be fun. Please make sure I'm there when you tell her. I want to see her reaction."

"Of course," says Bella. "Should be fun."

As they reach the car, they give Dri and Tiago hugs, then the all climb in, Dri and Tiago in the back seat.

"Thanks for driving us," says Dri as she closes the door. "How are you both?"

"We're doing great," says Bella as she places her left hand onto Omar's shoulder.

"OK! Finally!" laughs Dri as she spies her mom's engagement ring.

"Finally what?" asks Tiago, a puzzled look on his face.

Dri unstraps her seatbelt, leans over and kisses Bella's ring in a queenly gesture.

"Oh, congratulations, Bella! That's wonderful. When did this happen?"

"Last night, at dinner," responds Bella. "Omar took me out to Italian restaurant, then proposed just before they brought dessert. It was beautifully romantic, and I'm so happy!"

"How sweet," says Dri. "I'm very happy for you, Mom. It's about damn time," laughs Dri as she reaches over and squeezes her mother's hand with both of hers.

"Yes, I know," replies Omar. "I didn't want to push too soon, and it finally felt like your mom was ready. We had talked about it a little. But I also wanted it to be a bit of a surprise."

"Happy for you both," says Tiago. "I think you'll make a lovely married couple. And welcome to the family, from an earlier affiliate to the newest one."

"Thanks, Tiago. I feel lucky to be joining such a loving clan."

"Have you discussed a date yet?" asks Dri.

"Probably late summer, before harvest begins. And most likely at Omar's winery again," exclaims Bella. "We'll need to check the schedule, but some Friday or Saturday in early August."

"That will be fabulous. Maybe in July," Tiago says with a laugh. "Only nine years after we tied the knot."

"Maybe. We'll see," replies Bella.

They talk about guests, colors, and a few other wedding details. Then the conversation evolves to the discussion they will have at the Coalition meeting. Bella exudes excitement as she shares about the restoration work the three Native American tribes are doing in California and Washington. Part of her intrigue centers around the way these tribes have incorporated their history and spiritual perspectives into this manner of healing the earth. It is more than restoration. It is a true salubrious process between humans and their environments.

As they arrive at the airport, Omar drops off the three passengers and bags, then parks and meets them at check-in. The process goes smoothly there and through security without any long waits this Saturday morning. As they approach their gate, they see Sarah and May.

"Mom has some news," relates Dri, who reaches out her arms to give Sarah a hug.

"So do I," says May, who gives Tiago a hug, then Bella and Omar.

"Oh my God, Mom," shouts Sarah, spotting her new ring, reflecting the sun shining through the terminal window. "When did he propose?"

"Last night at the restaurant. And I said, yes!" exclaims Bella, an effervescent smile appearing on her face.

"Want to guess what I was doing, maybe about the same time?" asks Sarah.

All eyes turn to see the new ring on May's left hand as she begins to raise it up for people to view. A smile forms on her mouth so big it lights up her eyes.

"Wow, Sarah, I wasn't sure that was ever going to happen," says Bella as she gives her oldest another hug. Then Bella leans back to look at a single tear forming in Sarah's right eye.

"It took me a long while," responds Sarah. "Every time I thought about it, I felt like I was betraying my love for Marsha. Fortunately, May understood and has been extremely patient."

"What changed? What made the difference now?" inquires Bella, in a near whisper.

"A dear friend, who knew and loved Marsha too, suggested maybe that's what Marsha would want for me. She loved me that much. That unconditionally. I sat with that for a while, deciding she was right. So then I found a ring I thought would be perfect and gave it to her last night. I knew she wanted to get married. She was just so patient and loving. I think it melted my heart, finally."

"I'm so glad for you," says Bella. "And I think your friend is right. Marsha loved you that much, and you her. You can be thrilled about your marriage to May and miss Marsha at the same time. And I'm proud of you honoring your own process, not doing it out of pressure or obligation. Then you won't take more baggage into the marriage. Congratulations, my dear!"

She leans in and gives Sarah another long, loving hug. Sarah finally separates and leans back.

"Congratulations to you, too, Mom. I like this guy you're going to marry. I think you two are a much better match than you and dad."

"Thanks, my dear. Ok, I want to give May a hug too. Where did she go?" inquires Bella as she looks around the group. As Omar releases his hug, Bella swoops in to hug her soon-to-be new daughter-in-law.

"I'm so glad this is finally happening," says Bella as she leans in to hug May.

"Thanks, Bella. Me, too!" May says, whispering in Bella's ear.

"OK, are we all ready to board? I think we should start lining up," suggests Omar.

People grab their carry-ons, get into line, and soon are on board finding their seats. Tiago, Dri and Omar sit together in one row, with Bella across the aisle sitting next to

Sarah and May. The engaged mother and daughter immediately begin to talk about dates and plans, possible locations, and guest lists. So much to organize. Such a short flight.

As they arrive in Las Vegas, they depart the plane and make their way to get bags, then take the tram to the hotel downtown. None of the family have been back to this city since the memorial five and a half years ago. With three Coalition Board members living here, it seemed like an appropriate place to gather, revisiting the site where many met for the first time. They will hold their annual in-person meeting here this year and revisit the memorial, the place that brought them altogether.

Upon arrival at the hotel, they check-in and find their rooms. The family then 'doing a Dri,' meaning they organize all their belongings and get them put away before doing anything else. They gather in the restaurant for a bite of lunch, then set out for the meeting room.

Today's gathering grew larger than most, with all the board members here as well as Fadima, Dri and Ariella. They greet each other, happy to see other members in person again.

The only new member is Victoria Loomis, a Native American from the Swinomish Tribe north of Seattle. She was appointed at the last board meeting, replacing Ariella, who resigned from the board when she, too, joined Dri as a paid member of the educational team. Omar and Bella, who have been working with Victoria, introduce her around, making sure all meet the newest member in person.

"Welcome, Victoria," says Fadima. "It's great to finally talk with you face to face. And I'm excited for the connection that's building between the work your tribes have been doing and what we might learn from it in several different ways."

"Thanks," responds Victoria. "It's a pleasure to join the efforts your Coalition has been developing, too."

"This your first time in Las Vegas?" Fadima asks.

"Yes, for me. Some of our tribe who have been working at our Casino have been here, of course. But my first time."

"Well, great to have you here. Looks like our Chair is getting ready to start. Come sit next to me. I can update you if you have any questions along the way."

"Thanks," responds Victoria. The two women take their drinks to the square of tables set up in the middle of the room.

Nika asks the attendees to take a seat so they can begin the meeting. The agenda contains a number of important items needing to be discussed. Nika calls the meeting to order and asks if anyone has any corrections or additions to the minutes of the last meeting in September. With no changes announced, the group approves them unanimously.

"OK," says Nika, "let's turn to the business at hand for this meeting. We approved the motion to eliminate the commitment not to bring more children into the world without a national commitment to honoring life in our September meeting. Has there been any negative feedback from the members? I know the majority voted to make this change. But still, wondering if there are any complications from this decision?"

"I think it has been an important commitment to show the seriousness of our concerns," states Imani. "We certainly have important issues to address still regarding green and economic justice. But for me personally, it has kept these issues in front of me every day, as my husband and I delayed having another child. I think it has served its purpose, and I have heard little criticism of it. A couple of people thought we should continue longer, but otherwise nothing."

"I agree with Imani," adds Dri. "It served us well and emphasized the importance of change in this country. We have not completed the changes, but I also hear mostly positive feedback."

"Any other comments?" asks Nika.

"I, too, have had people saying we should maybe have continued for another year or two, but they would agree not to keep it beyond that," adds Fadima. "I think it's more a matter of timing than anything. I would say the bulk of the feedback has been supportive. And we also need to stay with this commitment to make sure of social changes."

"OK, great," responds Nika. "Our next order of business is the expansion of Green Justice through enhanced educational efforts," states Nika. "As a nation, we have made extensive structural decisions to expand our Green revolution, with industry, greener power sources, and electric cars. But the issue before us is the expansion of green education. Fadima, would you please share the results of the membership vote on this issue?"

"As directed last September, we asked members to vote on several critical issues the board has been discussing. Overall, we had a 83.8% response rate, which includes many phone calls from the office asking for their opinions. On this question, 79% were in favor of expanding our educational efforts as a supplement to the government changes. And it was our highest rated priority."

"Thanks, Fadima. The question is now open for discussion by all those in attendance."

"As you'll recall, Omar and I made several recommendations in the report we submitted to the board last September," Bella states. "One was to work with the three Native

American tribes in California and Washington who have been doing reclamation projects for the last 25 years. We also recommended Victoria become a member of our board, which was approved in our last meeting."

"Since then," she continues, "Omar and I have again visited the sites to learn more details about what they have been doing. Dri and Tiago also have accompanied us on two of those trips, focusing on how we could include it in our educational efforts. That's why some of us thought it would be important to have Dri and Ariella attend today. We think they are developing some solid ideas that could be passed along through our website and trainings. These new educational efforts could help people understand in more detail what all of us can do to help with reclamation of the Earth all over the world. I move that we make a commitment to expand our educational efforts to include such information and trainings to all our members and people beyond our membership. In doing so, it also may expand interest in the Coalition and encourage more people to join our efforts."

"Do you have any idea of the financial commitment this would take on our part?" asks Sam.

"I don't think much," responds Omar. "It will take some time to develop additional training and seminar materials, then place them on our website. The trainings should remain break-even, like our others. And it would take some additional expenses in travel. As we have talked about it, I would estimate about $25,000 a year would be generous. We might be able to do it for less."

"I also think it would be another way to solicit funding for such a project," suggests Fadima. "We could raise funds and ask for specific donations for the project. In the end, it may pay for itself, after the first year, anyway."

"I'm fine with that. I just need to play my role as practical financial advocate," laughs Sam.

"And we appreciate that," adds Rachel.

"Now that Ariella has been hired to enhance our educational efforts, can you and Dri handle some additional responsibilities?" asks Nika.

"Yeah, I think we'll be fine," responds Ariella. "We have some ideas already, and we'll work with members of the tribes to gain more."

"I agree," says Dri. "And I think it will add an important element to our overall educational efforts that will expand the attractiveness of what we have been trying to do as well as spread the environmental efforts internationally. We also like the way they are incorporating their historical relationship to the earth that would connect with other international groups and approaches, such as with tribes across the country. There's even a sense of a spiritual connection that feels consistent with where we, as a Coalition, are headed. I think you'll see that in our new trainings."

"Great, Dri. Thanks. Any other comments?" asks Nika. There is silence from the group. "OK. All those in favor say, aye."

The vote is unanimous.

"Our next order of business is an increased focus on economic justice. One thing I asked you to do was to bring a favorite quote, if you have one on this topic, to place on our website about this issue. I think it's important to include some inspirational words from famous people who have focused on similar ideas to our own. I'll begin by sharing mine. It's from Martin Luther King, Jr.'s 1967 speech:

"The contemporary tendency in our society is to base our distribution on scarcity, which has vanished, and to compress our abundance into the overfed mouths of the middle and upper classes until they gag with superfluity. If democracy is to have breadth of meaning, it is necessary to adjust this inequity. It is not only moral, but it is also intelligent. We are wasting and degrading human life by clinging to archaic thinking."

"I love the notion of getting away from archaic thinking. Thanks, Nika," says Rachel. "The one I brought is from Gandhi's 1916 speech. He said:

"The test of orderliness in a country is not the number of millionaires it owns, but the absence of starvation among its masses. . . . Ours will only then be a truly spiritual nation when we shall show more truth than gold, greater fearlessness than pomp of power and wealth, greater charity than love of self."

"I love the emphasis away from money to helping others," says Sarah. "There is a similar focus in my quote by Ruth Bader Ginsburg, who said:

"I tell law students... if you are going to be a lawyer and just practice your profession, you have a skill—very much like a plumber. But if you want to be a true professional, you will do something outside yourself... something that makes life a little better for people less fortunate than you."

"That's a great quote," adds Tiago. "I have two short ones, also from Gandhi. He said: "Poverty is the worst form of violence."

"He also stated that, 'if we know how much passive violence we perpetrate against one another, we will understand why there is so much physical violence plaguing societies and the world.'"

"The notion of passive violence relating to physical violence reminds me of some reading Nika and I talked about fifteen years ago," adds Dri. "A very insightful therapist wrote about how trauma can come out in violent ways with Blacks, Whites, and police officers. It's important, I think, to keep in mind how insidious passive violence and trauma impacts our interactions and responses."

"I never thought about poverty as violence or that passive violence can be so significant," says Kiara. "I'd like to add a quote from Alice Walker, a favorite author. She said:"

"It's so clear that you have to cherish everyone. I think that's what I get from these older black women, that every soul is to be cherished, that every flower is to bloom."

"I love the metaphor that every person blooms. I'd like to add a similar focus with a quote from Nelson Mandela," says Sam. "He once said, 'The true character of a society is revealed in how it treats its children.' I think this is important to keep in mind as we talk about economic justice for all young ones."

"I want to add one from a different voice," says Omar, "Alexandria Ocasio-Cortez. 'Justice is about making sure that being polite is not the same thing as being quiet. In fact, oftentimes the most righteous thing you can do is shake the table.'"

Bella suddenly shakes the table where she is sitting.

"I love this quote. Because when I shake my table, don't you all feel something? Doesn't it ripple to other parts? And isn't that what we're about? Shaking the system and letting it ripple?"

"Great point, Bella," adds Nika. "I think we do need to shake a little from time to time."

"These are all wonderful sayings about justice and change," comments Victoria. "What I would like to add is a reflection on doing, a very different way of interacting from our world. This is a quote from Chief Maquinna of the of the Nuu-chah-nulth people of Nootka Sound in the Pacific Northwest. He talks of the city of Victoria in Canada."

"Once I was in Victoria, and I saw a very large house. They told me it was a bank and that the white men place their money there to be taken care of, and that by and by they got it back with interest. We are Indians and we have no such bank; but when we have plenty of money or blankets, we give them away to other chiefs and people, and by and by, they return them with interest, and our hearts feel good. Our way of giving is our bank."

"Thanks for being a part of this group, Victoria, and adding a perspective we've been missing," says Nika. "Your contributions are significant, and it is wonderful to have you with us. These all are great quotes and will add touching comments to our website as well as some diversity. Any others before we move on to how we approach this issue?"

Again silence from the group.

"OK. With these inspirational comments in mind, how do you want to expand what we do with this issue? How should we address further change as a group?"

"I think, in this case," responds Imani, "we begin by working with the idea from Chief Maquinna. There is something fundamental about sharing and giving as a place to start, not as a place to end. We usually think about structural changes first. As Gandhi also said, 'our greatest ability as humans is not to change the world, but to change ourselves.' And another quote attributed to Margaret Mead. 'Never doubt that a small group of thoughtful, committed, organized citizens can change the world; indeed, it's the only thing that ever has.' If we act like thoughtful, committed, and organized world citizens, we can continue to transform ourselves and the world. But I think we begin with the sharing, giving, the kind of helping Victoria suggested in her quote. I think we should begin there."

"I like that idea," adds Bella. "When Dri and Tiago talked about efforts to create a change in the world, I had serious doubts. Sorry to you both, but you know I did. And now, five and a half years later, how many members do we have, Fadima?"

"I think the latest number is just under 637,000 people, internationally."

"Yes, and we are just getting going," says Bella. "People get excited, sharing ideas with others. I, too, feel inspired by Victoria's quote and the contributions of loving reclamation these tribes have been developing. It's time for all of us to modify our relationship with and heal the earth. That kind of reclamation needs to be applied to healing our own interactions. For as Sam said about the Mandela quote and others, the way we treat our children and the most vulnerable among us is the greatest mark of any society. I think it's another way to keep our work spreading like wildfire, creating peace everywhere."

"That reminds me of something else Dr. King said," says Nika. "'There is no peace without true justice.' And that would include more equitable opportunities for all children."

"Agreed," concurs Ariella. "One thing I think we should encourage is more equitable allocation of educational resources. This could be a focus on the federal government to increase support to schools with fewer resources and increase educational salaries. If education is a fundamental contribution to our society, salaries must represent that priority."

"I like that idea," suggests Rachel. "I also think we should begin working on a separate service program internal to the country where young people are hired and receive similar benefits to military personnel with a focus on helping our most vulnerable citizens build and repair housing, reclamation projects with the earth, and even teaching trades to young people. It could be our civil service, a contrast to our military service. It could even have an international component, working with volunteer programs overseas doing much of the same kind of work. It would be similar to the Peace Corps, but focusing on open hearted connections as well."

"I think that's a great idea," says Tiago. "It would be a great way for young people to expand their skills and have benefits for contributing to these efforts."

"I agree with Tiago," says Sam. "And there's a third component I would like to suggest to these efforts. This would be a more structural change. And it's why I waited until now to suggest it, with the other ideas to proceed this one in any list or proposal. I think it's time for our government to levy a higher tax on companies that pay greater than ten to one ratios to executives compared to the lowest paid employees. When a ratio greater than that exists, it puts pressure on the government to support people with lower incomes and they collect less tax. If companies insist on such differences, they need to pay a greater share to help the government with its responsibilities. Although we originally agreed to a five to one ratio as a group, I think we need to start with a higher amount. Then, over time, that could be adjusted to a lower ratio."

"Wow, that's rather drastic," responds Omar. "And I love it! It's time to create such a structural change, I believe. And you're the perfect person to suggest it, knowing so much about finances and all. Thanks for the idea. I second such a suggestion."

"Any other ideas or proposals for our emphasis on economic justice?" asks Nika, pausing.

"Hearing none, I move we adopt these three initiatives for our focus on greater economic justice," remarks Rachel. "I think these are strong, and it may be better to limit it to these three."

"I agree, and I second the motion," adds Kiara.

"All those in favor say, Aye," says Nika.

The vote again is unanimous.

"Great. Thanks to you all for your ideas and support. I think we have accomplished quite a bit this afternoon. We'll now break for dinner and meet up at the memorial at 7:30. We'll have an informal gathering and remembrance of those we lost six and a half years ago, which also brought us together. Thanks to you all for essential contributions. And we will see you after dinner."

As people are gathering their belongings and talking among themselves, Fadima approaches Nika.

"Do you have specific plans for dinner? If not, I would love to talk with you about your meetings with Carl and how that's going, if you don't mind."

"I don't have plans. And I'd love to join you for dinner. I think Dri wanted to talk about it too. Mind if she joins us? Meet you at the restaurant entrance at 5:30?"

"That would be great. See you both then."

People leave for their rooms, chatting as they go. Bella waits for Victoria. She asks her to eat dinner with them. She agrees, and will meet them at the restaurant shortly. Tiago asks to join them also, as he would like to get to know Victoria better.

Fadima and Dri are following the hostess to a table as Nika suddenly appears. They sit and catch up for a few minutes on each other's lives and hearts. Fadima has become close to both of them through the Coalition work and thrives on such conversations when they happen, especially in person. Following updates, Fadima shifts to the topic that brought them together.

"Now, I would love to hear about your conversations with Carl, if you don't mind. I'm fascinated by your visits and wondering how they are going now?" Fadima asks.

"Sure. Happy to share with you two. As I mentioned some time ago, I had a strong rage reaction towards Carl after the shooting. Dri helped me get in touch with related issues that were intertwined with this event, including racial injustice and emotional reactions to my own racial identity. But when he was sentenced to 10 years on second degree attempted murder, I was surprised in a different way. That's when my curiosity about the man started to emerge."

"What were you curious about? Why did you even care about him?" asks Fadima.

"I didn't know at first," responds Nika. "But there was something about why he would try to kill me when he didn't even know me. And he didn't seem to be that strongly connected to PFF. I think it was part of a larger question about why Whites have been killing Blacks for so long when they often don't know them. And here was a guy that represented that to me. I think it was indicative of that larger question, without realizing it at the time. I just knew I needed to go talk with him. So I did."

"And you initially talked about his background?" asks Dri.

"Yes, that was our first visit," replies Nika. "But then we began to talk about our lives and how we ended up where we did. I was struck by the fact that a young Black girl would end up in a more successful position than a young White boy. It pointed out in a stark way how important resources and support can be in creating opportunities for young people. Then we talked about how the PFF began to influence his thinking, basically brainwashing him because he didn't have the tools to think critically about what they were saying. He had little experience questioning a point of view or asking about evidence for what they were claiming about us. And he didn't see any of our ads or literature. He didn't look at our website. He simply took what they said as the truth, believing how awful we were to kill babies, force women to have abortions, and hold down White people, limiting their opportunities. He essentially was believing what White racists had been telling him while growing up. That people of color were going to destroy this country."

"And he just believed it all? Never questioning what they said?" asks Fadima.

"If you don't learn to question ideas, if you grow up with a view that others are out to get you, then a boy like him has no alternative reality, no other perspective," says Nika. "It can happen with racial issues, gender issues, political values, or religion. People can be indoctrinated if they only hear one perspective that never gets challenged. In part, that's the value of diversity and education. Learning to see and understand other points of view. Learning to live in color instead of just black and white."

"Would you repeat the last thing you said again," asks Fadima. "How do we live in color?"

"Instead of seeing everything in black and white, opposing views, we begin to see multiple perspectives, many different alternatives," responds Nika. "We learn to see many different colorful views. Views across the color spectrum."

"Sounds like these conversations have become enlightening for both of you," says Dri.

"Yes, they have. I get to see Carl's world and how he came to see life from a narrow perspective. And he has helped me see the challenge we face in getting an alternative perspective out to people. It's important that we first see their view before trying to change it. At the same time, providing an alternative possibility is essential to change and growth," responds Nika.

"What will you do now? Will you continue to see him or are you finished?" asks Fadima.

"I want to continue visiting with him. He apparently likes it now, too. He seems less angry and resistant. So now we talk about different parts of our lives, what each wants, and what we'll do in the future. One thing that interests him are some of the ways we are looking at conflict resolution and resolving differences. I think he feels bad about trying to kill me, although he hasn't said that in so many words. Yet, in some odd way, we've become friends. Who would have guessed that at his sentencing?"

A faint smile appears on Nika's face with a hint of sadness in her eyes.

"Thanks for sharing this, Nika," says Fadima. "I find it fascinating. But I guess we'd better get the bill and walk towards the memorial. I see others getting ready to go."

They pay for their dinner, get their jackets, and leave the restaurant. Suddenly, Dri is back at leaving the hotel with Alex before the concert, jackets in hand, even in July. A jacket covered with her brother's blood that she later discarded. The hurt lessens. But the memory will never fully decompose.

As the three approach the memorial not far from the hotel, about a half dozen from the group already have arrived, along with a couple of other people not known to Dri. She walks over to the plaque for Alex, where Bella and Omar already were standing. Dri tenderly takes her mother's other hand in both of hers, then brings it up for a soft kiss on the back of it. She lowers her mother's arm as her mother turns to give her a sad smile.

As others gather, Ariella and Rachel walk to Joseph's plaque, Kiara and Sam in front of Diya's plaque, and Fadima in front of Husayn's plaque. Other Coalition members fill in the gaps between parents who lost a child, holding hands in a circle around the fountain. The two already there are invited to join in with the commemorative group gathering.

People stand around, mostly in silence, with a few uttering, "I miss you, Joseph," "Love you Diya," "love you, Husayn," and "you'll never be forgotten, Alex." shared by a family member and a guest. After a respectful silence, Bella speaks.

"We miss you kids, grieve for our loss, as family or friends. And may we also allow the gratitude to exist with our sorrow for bringing us all together. Connecting us in our mourning, with the blessing of this group forming to address change. Not only to prevent more loss, but to improve lives, increase justice, and allow love to flow more freely. Thank you. And we will never forget you. Our hearts will always embrace and remember who you are and the joy you brought to our lives, even if just for a few moments."

Several amens flow out of those gathered, including the two new people who lost a dear friend that day. As silence sets in again, Bella reminisces about her son, his humor, his joy for life, his ability to make light out of darkness. A lesson she still is learning from him.

Suddenly, Rachel begins to sing, *I'll Be Seeing You,* a touching song made famous by her favorite singer, Billie Holiday. After singing the first four lines, others began to join in, some humming when they get to lyrics they can't remember. But Dri and Bella sing out, a song both of them love from the rendition by Norah Jones.

It feels to Bella like a perfect way to honor these people who have passed but will never be forgotten. As they sang the last four lines "in the morning sun and when the night is new, I'll be looking at the moon, but I'll be seeing you," tears stream down faces all around the circle. Bella looks around at each one in the group. Her heart aches for Alex and feels joy for the group at the same time. Out of her grief rises hope. Out of her misery, some joy.

She's grateful in the moment to be able to feel both at the same time. It's some compensation derived from such a tragedy. Something Dri mentioned a long time ago, but has taken time and experience to sink in. She squeezes Omar's hand on one side and Dri's on the other. As the circle begins to break, Bella walks over to give Sarah a long hug too, grateful to have her two daughters here with her and the man with whom she has fallen in love.

The next morning, Bella feels lighter. It is useful to remember and mourn, feeling into the emotion until it dissolves. Then some joy can appear too, as she and Omar go downstairs for coffee and a light breakfast in the meeting room. Some already are gathering with a bit of melancholy still lingering among the group. Yet, others, too, seem a bit lighter this morning.

Nika asks people to find a seat, maybe next to someone they did not sit near yesterday. As people settle, she calls the meeting to order.

"The first item on the agenda this morning is a suggestion made by Kiara and Rachel to identify clearly that what we are about is a revolution of the heart. Would either of you like to speak to this issue to get our discussion started?" asks Nika.

Kiara looks at Rachel, who offers her hand back towards her.

"Alright, I'll start it off," says Kiara. "Rachel and I were talking after our last meeting about being more forthright in our organizational intentions. We think that one main thing we desire is to create a revolution of our hearts. An opening for more obvious love and caring for others as well as ourselves. I just think we should be more blatant about our designs and quit trying to be so subtle."

"We haven't hidden other intended changes," adds Rachel. "Why not be clearer about this one too? Why not say it plainly? Why not shake the table?"

"Now that you mention it," says Tiago, "we haven't been very direct with this intention. And it may be one of the most important ones we have. But revolution has a bit of a negative and violent connotation. I wonder if transformation would be a better term for what we want?"

A BIFURCATION   269

"I could live with that term," responds Kiara.

"Yes, that's a great term," reflects Sam. "And I like the idea of being clearer about this intention. But oftentimes, before a group can go through a transformation, there typically is a reformation in an organization, with reformational leadership that provides a new strategy. So I wonder about calling it a reformation of the heart."

"I understand what you mean by that," remarks Imani, "and it's useful to know about what other organizations do to create such change. But I think there is too much of a Christian connotation to reformation. If we want to get beyond a single religion, I would suggest we use the term transformation. I think it's both reformative and revolutionary without the negative connotations of either."

"I think for me, I prefer transformation also," responds Bella. "I think that works well."

"I would like to add one additional word," says Omar. "Dri and I have been discussing her earlier conversations with Nika about race while in college. One thing she pointed out focused not just on love, but particularly unconditional love. I wonder whether it might be clearer if we added that term and describe us as focused on an unconditional transformation of the heart?"

"Any objections to adding unconditional transformation of the heart to our mission list?" asks Nika.

Heads nod and no one responds verbally to her question.

"Hearing none, all those in favor say, aye."

All appear in agreement with this motion.

"Great," continues Nika. "In relation to this addition, there are two quotes I would like your response for adding to our website. I think they might be useful. Victoria found another one I also would like us to consider. The first is from Gandhi, who uses the term Ātman. This term refers to a Sanskrit meaning of inner self, spirit, or soul. It also is the first principle in Hindu philosophy, referring to the true self or essence of an individual beyond identification with the physical world. What he said was this:"

"Non-violence is not a garment to be put on and off at will. Its seat is in the heart, and it must be an inseparable part of our being. . . . Love is atman: it is the very property of atman. If we have faith enough, we can wield that force over the whole world. . . . Even a heart of flint will melt in the fire kindled by the power of the soul."

"The second quote I thought we might add is from a late speech by Dr. King:"

"I say to you, I have also decided to stick to love. For I know that love is ultimately the only answer to mankind's problems. And I'm going to talk about it everywhere I go. I know it isn't popular to talk about it in some circles today. I'm not talking about emotional bosh when I talk about love, I'm talking about a strong, demanding love. And I have seen too much hate. I've seen too much hate on the faces of sheriffs in the South. I've seen hate on the faces of too many Klansmen and too many White Citizens Councils in the South to want to hate myself, because every time I see it, I know that it does something to their faces and their personalities and I say to myself that hate is too great a burden to bear. I have decided to love. If you are seeking the highest good, I think you can find it through love. And the beautiful thing is that we are moving against wrong when we do it, because John was right, God is love. He who hates does not know God, but he who has love has the key that unlocks the door to the meaning of ultimate reality."

"This one relates to a quote Victoria shared with me that I also appreciate. Would you share that quote for Chief Crazy Horse, please?"

"In one of his last speeches before being murdered, he prophesied this:"

"The Red Nation shall rise again and it shall be a blessing for a sick world. A world filled with broken promises, selfishness, and separations. A world longing for light again. I see a time of Seven Generations when all the colors of mankind will gather under the Sacred Tree of Life and the whole Earth will become one circle again. In that day, there will be those among the Lakota who will carry knowledge and understanding of unity among all living things and the young white ones will come to those of my people and ask for this wisdom. I salute the light within your eyes where the whole Universe dwells. For when you are at that center within you and I am that place within me, we shall be one."

"Thanks, Victoria," responds Nika. "This touches me so much, and I think it's quite appropriate for us now. Any objections to adding these three quotes to our website as we talk about a unconditional transformation of the heart?"

Nika pauses.

"Hearing none, it shall be done. And thanks."

"Now, let's turn to the next item on our agenda. As you know from my recent emails, it looks like the Democratic Party is about to split into two separate groups: the Democratic Party and the Progressive Party. While it doesn't affect us directly, I thought it would be important to discuss here, including what, if anything, we decide to do as a group. At this point, the size of the Progressives looks similar, although we don't know exactly who will end up in either group. But I wondered if we want to take a stand with one group or just remain silent and let members decide where they feel most comfortable?"

"As you suggested," responds Fadima, "we included a question in our recent survey of US members. The majority favored supporting the Progressive Party, saying they thought that was a closer fit. But about twenty three percent still felt more comfortable with the Democratic Party."

"I'm inclined to let people make an individual choice," says Rachel, "at least for now. We can see how it all plays out, and it may become clearer later. While I lean toward the progressives myself, I think we should give it more time before doing anything as a group."

"I would agree with that," adds Imani. "We may have a better sense of needing to declare support one way or the other. But I wouldn't want to divide our membership unnecessarily."

There were several other people agreeing with Rachel and Imani through quieter conversation. Finally, Nika proposes the question.

"OK. Thanks for your responses," says Nika. "It seems like the preference is to not make any decision of support for one party or the other at this time. We'll let it play out and see where it goes over some time. Any objection to that?"

Again silence.

"Then it looks like the decision is made on this for now. Thanks for your feedback and direction. I, too, think this is the better thing to do at this point. But I thought it would be important to verify that with the board."

"Now, for our last item on the agenda," continues Nika. "As you know, I have one more year as board chair. We've not made a formal decision about this. But, as I indicated to you in the email, I think it would be useful for me to become Past Chair this last year to support a new person taking over with any assistance I might provide. Is there any objection to this change?"

People look around the room. Finally, Sam responds.

"Well, I object to you ever stepping down as chair, personally. But assuming you, in fact, insist on doing that, I think it would be important to have a year of transition for a new person to fill this role."

An ear to ear smile develops on Sam's face as he finishes, and he winks at Nika.

"Thanks, Sam. So nominations are open for a new person to become chair of our board."

"I have talked privately to several people since you sent out the email," says Imani, "and all feel grateful for being recognized as a possible replacement. But most also feel overwhelmed in their lives currently. One person did not respond with overwhelm, and

I think would be great in this position. I would like to nominate Bella as our new board chair."

"I second that nomination," says Rachel.

"I agree," responds Sam.

"Any objections?"

Once again, the group is silent.

"All in favor?"

The vote is unanimous.

"Congratulations, my second mother," responds Nika with a smile. "I'm thrilled to have you take over, and will do all I can to inform and support you in this change. Would you like to make a few comments?"

Bella takes a moment as she looks around at each person present.

"I want to thank you for your trust and support. I've not been on the board for that long a time. But I guess I have been involved in different ways since the beginning, including support with the first meeting. I had my doubts about this in the beginning, as I said previously. They are gone now. I believe in what we're doing here, and I will work my hardest to carry on what all of you have started. Thank you for your confidence. I will try my best to live up to our dreams."

"Thanks, Bella. Feels great to have you take the helm," says Nika. "OK, that completes our agenda. Our meeting is adjourned, just in time for lunch. Safe travels to all of you, and we'll see you all again soon, I hope."

As group members stand, hugs begin immediately, some with a tear at the leaving.

Nika looks around at the group between goodbyes and hugs, thrilled at the work this group has accomplished in just a few years and honored to have been a leader in the process. And now, it is time to move on to other ways she can integrate this work with her increasing influence within the House of Representatives. The integration and transition both feel right, a continuation of her heart's work.

Chapter 22
Expansion and Explorations
November, 2035

The Saturday following the Thanksgiving weekend, Nika and Naeem drive up to Napa to visit her second family. Cate, now six and a half, opens the front door, jumping up and down while her "Auntie Nika" and "Uncle Naeem," as she knows them, come up the walkway. Nika bends down to give her a mighty hug. Naeem picks her up, squeezes her, then tosses her into the air. Cate squeals as she comes back down into his arms, a smile all over her face.

"How's my favorite niece doing?" asks Naeem with a smile of his own.

"Better, now!" responds Cate. She rides in his arms as they enter Dri and Tiago's home, although it still feels like Bella's place.

"I can't get used to you two living here," chuckles Nika. "Glad Bella didn't just sell it when she moved into Omar's place after their marriage this summer."

"Me, too," Dri adds.

She reaches out to place both hands on Nika's face, then kisses both cheeks, avoiding any crush on her expanding abdomen.

"I always loved this place. And it feels natural to be here. Glad we could work it out financially."

"But where is your new one? Don't think we came just to see you three," snickers Nika.

"He's with his dad on the couch," laughs Dri. "I know your priorities, my dear."

"Well, now that we are having one of our own, I think such a priority has increased," Naeem chuckles.

Nika walks over, gently removes Alejandro from his father's arms, and cautiously sits on the couch next to Tiago.

"He's adorable. I love his black curly hair and soft skin."

Nika carefully pulls out a hand from underneath the cuddly blanket to see the baby's miniature fingernails, something that always fascinates Nika. She examines them closely.

Cate now snuggles on Naeem's lap in one of the soft blue chairs, Dri in the other one.

"How was the finish of your show in DC, Naeem?" asks Dri. "I'm so glad we got to see it in the summer. I loved so many of your works."

"It went extremely well. I sold eleven pieces by the end of the exhibit, and two more afterwards. Now I've been invited to do a second show here in Oakland next summer. More pressure to get additional pieces finished. But a deadline helps me stay with it. I'm just glad Nika will be here for a while this month."

"That's great. When do you start on your next campaign, Nika?" asks Dri.

"The day after my last election," laughs Nika. "But it starts getting serious while I'm here in December, at least for some organizing and planning. We won't get going with more activity until February. But I need to get some things in place in case we face a challenging primary."

"It will be great to have you closer for a while. And when is your baby due?" Dri asks.

"March fourth," Nika responds.

"And is it a boy or a girl? Do you know yet?" Tiago inquires.

"It's a boy," Naeem offers. "Which excites me more than my wife, I think."

"No, a boy's great. He can be a playmate for Alejandro, just a few months older," says Nika. "It will be fun to have them grow up together."

"Well, maybe not exactly together," chuckles Tiago. "Unless you quit Congress and move back here. I can't imagine you being beaten in an election. Your constituents seem to love you."

"Well, many of them anyway," laughs Nika. "There's always some who criticize what you do, anywhere. By the way, are you going to shorten Alejandro's name too?"

"We talked about it," responds Tiago. "We've shortened for everyone else. Why not him?"

"Yeah. I like Alee. For me, it feels like some connection to Alex. Without calling him by my brother's name," Dri says, with a hint of both a smile and sadness.

"I like it. And thanks for sharing your reasoning," mutters Nika. "It will help with my own connection without imposing Alex's personality or traits if he had the same name."

Nika beams at the newborn she continues to cradle in her arms.

"How are you feeling, Dri?" Nika asks. "It's only been about 11 days since the birth. You still sore? I want to know what to expect."

"I'm doing pretty well. He was a little smaller than this big girl."

Dri reaches over to give Cate a tickle, making her squeal and move out of her cosy position on Naeem's shoulder. But after a short giggle, she settles back into his arms.

"So the recovery has been a little easier."

"OK, great to know. Note to self, pay attention to his expected weight," chuckles Nika.

Naeem turns to Dri.

"How are Sarah and May doing? Still happy about their marriage? Doing well?"

"Yes, very well," responds Dri. "They were here last weekend for Thanksgiving. Well, not here, but at Mom and Omar's place. They appear happy with each other and life."

"Terrific. I'm glad for them," says Naeem.

"Thanks. And how is your family doing, Naeem? An enjoyableThanksgiving at their place?" asks Dri.

"Oh yes. As you know, Nika's family joined us as well. It was a big crowd," offers Naeem. "And a great meal. But it seems like my older brother, Dewayne, and his wife are struggling a bit. They didn't say anything, and it may not be serious. I hope not. I like her. But it's their choice, not mine."

"Wise man," suggests Tiago. "Help if they ask. Let them work it out if they don't. Especially an older brother. I know. Mine seldom takes any advice from me," he says with a grin.

"Nika, any more about the push by the PFF for a congressional investigation into our Coalition? Is it likely to go anywhere?"

"No, it doesn't seem so, yet. I had a useful discussion with Speaker Sanchez before leaving DC," responds Nika. "A few of the Republican House members keep trying to push it among conservative Democrats, in part because one heads the committee that would call for such an investigation. Speaker Sanchez is remaining with that party, who still holds the majority, at least for now. About forty percent of the party is switching to the Progressives. So far, the Committee Head keeps focusing on the lack of proof for their claims. Of course, they keep driving the investigation to gather evidence. So it's a push-pull over this issue. At some point, she may cave to them, given that I switched to the Progressive Party, too."

"That makes a big difference there, I take it?" says Tiago.

"Oh yeah. Party affiliation is everything. I'm keeping a close watch on the process. And while I'm in a different party than the Speaker, we maintain a solid relationship. She knows I support her. Still, if the committee calls for an investigation, there could be people who lie about us or twist the facts. But it also provides us the opportunity to bring forth witnesses to testify about the positive things we are doing and the support we are accumulating. It's this latter issue, I think, that is most disconcerting to the PFF. They seem to be stagnant or even losing support."

"Are you worried at all about an investigation?" Dri inquires.

"I don't see anything yet that would raise an alarm. But you never know what desperate people will do. The PFF are closely tied to what's left of the Christian Nationalist conservatives from the Trump era. They keep getting smaller, especially from a loss of members and financial decline. So they attempt to yell louder. But they continue to avoid putting forth any policies that appeal to people or stand on any consistent principles. Like Stuart Stevens wrote about in his book fifteen years ago. The Republican Party has a long history of talking points rather than substantive and consistent policies they work to accomplish. And what remains of it shows up with increasingly twisting the truth, fighting those with different views."

"Is there anything we should do on the part of the Coalition to prepare for a possible investigation?" Tiago asks.

"No, other than what we've done. I've been in communication with Sarah and Marcia, a local DC attorney I respect there. I've also been in discussion with Bella, Fadima, and Sam to keep them apprised of the situation. We have laid out some initial funding to retain Marcia, so she is prepared for what could happen. She knows the PFF and also doesn't think they will get the investigation. But Sarah's been staying in touch with a friend in San Francisco who heard the PFF may file an injunction in California federal court to prevent us from threatening women not to have a baby." Nika begins to snicker. "I can't believe they will dare do that. But that's what she heard."

"What evidence do they have?" Dri asks, her eyes wide and mouth still open.

"That's the humorous part, in some ways. Apparently, they have a witness saying that three Coalition members came to her door in black coats and ski masks, threatening her with her family's life if she had another baby."

The group looks around at each other during a long moment of silence, uncertain whether to laugh or cry.

"Yeah, that was my response too," chuckles Nika. "But we can't ignore it, either."

"This sounds like all sorts of fabrications extremists have put forward, from Obama not being born in the United States to QAnon and the conspiracy theories that President Thomas had to put up with in her election," snickers Naeem.

"Yes, it does. But you know how many court cases Trump's attorneys submitted and lost in the 2020 election. We can't get caught totally off guard either," remarks Nika.

"I'm so glad you are staying on top of this. It seems like your proposal of moving to Past Chair with the Coalition was very prescient," comments Tiago.

"It can look like that now. We don't have to tell anyone that I also was getting pressed at work and looking for a way to lighten my load," chuckles Nika. "Instead, I just took on another assignment. Glad to have handed off responsibilities to Bella when I did, though."

"How would you say she's doing as board chair?" inquires Tiago.

"She's been great," responds Nika. "Still a learning curve. And I think her real estate work has dropped off a little from the focus. But she doesn't seem too worried. Do you think so, Dri?"

"Yeah, it has slowed some," remarks Dri. "She hasn't been as active on social media or sending out mailers. It hasn't helped that I've been busy too. But she hired a new assistant, who is still getting up to speed. So it may pick up. Or she may not care. She also wants to spend more time with Omar. So there's less motivation to be a top agent."

"Sounds like she's living her dream, right now," responds Naeem. "She sure looked happy the last time I saw them together."

"Oh, yes, I'm sure she is," says Dri. "Speaking of dreams, I think I should feed Alee and put him down. Anyone ready for some lunch?"

"I am," shouts Cate. "Thought you'd never ask."

"How about if Cate and I go pick up some pizzas, while the boys make a salad," suggests Nika. "Then we can eat some lunch and find out more about Cate's life instead of this boring adult stuff. You OK with that, Cate?"

"Yes. Yes. Let me get my jacket. That OK, daddy?"

"I think that's a grand idea," responds Tiago. "Take my car, Nika. Then you won't have to change Cate's car seat. The keys are on the shelf by the front door."

Dri unhinges Alee from Nika's arms, just as he's starting to fuss. Cate goes to snatch her jacket off the hook, and turns to wait. Nika takes her hand and they walk to the car, settle in, then drive to Life Fire Pizza at Oxbow Market. Meanwhile, Naeem calls ahead to order.

Tiago and Naeem chat as they make a salad and set the table.

"You excited about becoming a father?" asks Tiago.

"I am," replies Naeem. "I always knew Nika wanted to have children, and I did too. With such busy lives and the Coalition commitment, I began to wonder if we would. But we both got excited after the national commitment from Congress and the removal of the statement by the organization. It felt like the right time, neither of us wanting to wait any longer."

"I'm so happy for you both. And I hope the two boys will know each other as they grow. I guess they'll both have a strong sister to watch out for them, too," laughs Tiago.

Upon Nika and Cate's return, the boys complete preparations. The five of them sit down to talk about Cate's school and her experiences this year. She becomes animated as attention finally turns to her after a boring morning conversation. Laughter and chatter fill the air in between tasty bites of pizza and salad. When finished, Cate pulls up her stool so she can clean off the dishes as Nika stacks them in the dishwasher and Dri clears and wipes the table. Cate leads Naeem and her dad downstairs to play a game, leaving Nika and Dri to talk about a different issue.

"You look worried or down, Dri. Is something else going on with you?" Nika asks.

"Yeah, and I was hoping we would get a chance to talk," responds Dri. "You know that Tiago, Ariella and I are working on the new parenting manual for the Coalition. And I like where it is going. But I'm not sure I'm the one to be doing this. I just don't feel comfortable yet, and I'm not really a parenting expert. I'm not sure I can do a great job with this."

"You've been doing extensive research on the topic. Your marriage and family therapy background certainly helps. Your own work with Doc and exploring that with Tiago and Cate have given you lots of practical experience, too. What else is going on? Why no trust now?"

"I'm fine working things out with Cate and Tiago. And my experience with couples and families gives me courage to problem solve with them. But talking about what parents 'should' do with children makes me very uncomfortable."

"Are Tiago and Ariella experiencing the same doubt about this?"

"Tiago is. Ariella and Rachel have raised two kids to adulthood. Daniel was 23 when he was killed in Las Vegas, and their daughter now has two children of her own. Ariella's had more experience personally and as a social worker. She keeps encouraging me to just put forward my ideas, and the group can sort out issues of how to present them. But my old judge rises up at times like these and yells, 'incompetence.'"

"Yeah, I remember that judge. She used to be much stronger in high school and even into college. I thought we had her disbarred some time ago," chuckles Nika.

"No. She keeps showing up, especially when I make space for her to render a decision."

"I see," replies Nika. "Well, I want to share some advice my dear friend, Dri, would say if the judge were rendering decisions in my life. First, let's thank this judge for her perspective. She gives you the opportunity to consider her valid but negative point of view. Cautions about what you are doing exist, and they provide a way to question how you go about this. Take it into account. But, gratefully, she is only one on a panel of three judges, even if she yells the loudest. There also is the 'Doc' trained judge, who has, I would bet, a different and more positive view. Am I right?"

Dri smiles at Nika, as she hears words coming back at her she has used with her best friend in the past.

"Yes. But his perspective relies on possibilities that have not been tried. So I don't know whether or not I can achieve this."

"OK. Then there is the third and deciding judge. This judge has the opportunity to take the best of both perspectives in making a final decision. Maybe the first, cautionary judge provides a different way of talking about insights for parents as ideas to consider rather than truths to be followed minutely. The second, more expansive judge, helps you see new possibilities that you have been developing without even being aware of it. Or you see options presented by others that compliment and expand what you've been thinking. But it's done on a foundation that this can be accomplished, with some caution based on the first judge's opinion. The third judge gets to put these together to render her decision. Maybe that decision is yes, this can be developed as possibilities rather than laws or truths, keeping in mind that parents have a myriad of ways for them to implement your suggested guidelines."

Dri reaches out to grab Nika's hand in both of hers. "Thank you, my friend, for the fabulous advice from your dear friend. I still forget that I'm not limited to a single judge in these decisions. So grateful for you and the three judge panel."

"You're welcome, my sister. That's one reason our reflections to each other have been so important over the past twenty years," responds Nika. "Stay with your style of asking questions, rather than giving directions."

"Great advice," says Dri. "We intend to talk more about possibilities than what parents should do. And questions will be a great compliment."

"Well, let me ask another question," remarks Nika. "May I experience your new skill? We've talked about it, but I've never felt it in person."

"Of course, if you want. Now?" Dri asks.

"Now's as good a time as any. I feel like my heart already is open some with our conversation. It would be interesting to experience it when it's not closed down."

Dri releases Nika's hands. She closes her eyes as she holds her two palms together in her lap. After about a minute, she opens her eyes and places her right hand on Nika's heart as her eyes focus there as well. Dri closes her eyes again while holding her hand in place as she amps up her own energy, focusing increasing amounts through her right hand. Then she squeezes her left hand behind Nika's back to connect with her heart from both sides. She holds them there for several minutes. Finally, she opens her eyes and removes her hands.

"Wow! My heart expanded, even from the opening it had. It didn't experience any force in the process. It was like a strong invitation. And my heart just followed. Responding to your energetic supplication. That's amazing, Dri. How did you learn to do that?"

"It started when Cate was in a bad mood, and I thought I might be able to encourage her in relaxing and expanding her heart opening. It just worked. Then I began to experiment on myself and Tiago. I haven't tried it with anyone else. Until now, anyway."

"Are you going to include your new skill in the child rearing manual?" Nika asks.

"I hadn't thought about that. Do you think we should? I don't know how many people can do it. Tiago seems to be improving. But I haven't encouraged anyone else."

"Maybe talk it through with Ariella. She could practice on Rachel and their daughter. If they both can learn it, maybe even me too, then I think we should. We can just say we don't know how many will be able to do it. But if they can, what a useful tool in helping children and others. Not forcing. Just inviting. Encouraging."

"OK, I'll talk it through with them. And thanks for your support and suggestions. Maybe you and Naeem can practice. See how that goes," suggests Dri.

"We will. And I'll let you know."

Tiago, Naeem, and Cate emerge from the basement, holding hands and laughing.

"It's Cate's bedtime," Tiago says as he reaches the top stairs. "Now that she's beat us at three games. I'll get her ready, in case Alee starts to fuss. Cate, how about you give everyone a kiss goodnight, if you want to. Then we'll go get you ready and read a story."

Slowly, Cate walks to the other three adults to share a kiss and hug. Then she takes her daddy's hand as they walk towards her bedroom.

Naeem gets the open wine bottle and gives small pours to finish it off. A delicious wine also nourishes the conversation among these friends.

By the end of May, the educational sub-group for the Coalition submits its draft of the new Family Discoveries Guidebook to the board members. Dri remains anxious about the reaction, although there have been some early discussions with Bella, Nika, Rachel, and Fadima about parts of their work.

"This is exactly what we've always dreamed of sharing with others," wrote Fadima.

"I think this is a great balance of ideas and expanding possibilities for parents," says Rachel to the group.

"I wish I had such a guidebook when you were growing up," Bella said to Dri, who passed it along to the other two authors. All thought the remainder of the board would be delighted to review it.

At the beginning of the guidebook, the group outlines nine basic precepts used to develop their recommendations and concepts for exploration by families. These precepts guided the development of ideas and recommendations for people to explore. They include the following, which are further explained in the Guidebook:

1.   Expand your heart prior to interactions with others. A basic notion for all explorations is to approach these ideas by first boosting one's heart opening. Notice, during the explorations, whether the heart remains available. If closing, take time to expand it before continuing.

2.   Fill hands with love (or oxytocin) before touching a child or others. Parents, siblings, and other family members express love through words and actions. A fundamental precept is the articulation of unconditional love through touch. To amplify that experience, take a moment to intend love to increase in the hands before touching. An alternative is to intend oxytocin, sometimes referred to as the love hormone and neurotransmitter. This provides a more concrete way to fill one's palm with love.

3. Stay connected with your body and heart through interactions with others. When people begin to get conceptual in their communications, their awareness of their body and heart can dissipate. To access all our wisdom, retaining cognizance of one's body and heart remains essential.

4. Balance between the physical and energetic world. Children seem to be born utilizing energetic information. As they grow older, we can get them so focused on the physical world that they quit paying attention to this source of knowledge and wisdom. If we interact energetically with children and encourage that connection, they will more easily incorporate that information into their life.

5. Support intuitive information with children and others. Pay attention to our own intuitive knowledge and encourage children to do the same. This provides them with trust for incorporating such sources of wisdom into their decision making process.

6. Help children and youth learn to work through decisions rather than primarily giving directions or answers. Adults often find it convenient to give directives for many reasons, including time and work pressures, ease, and/or convenience. What children miss in the process is learning to gather and incorporate information and diverse perspectives in making decisions. Take the time to ask questions rather than give answers and support the learning of such processes. This helps young people develop important adult abilities.

7. Pay attention to energy fields and exchanges. These sources of information provide important assets that typically become ignored. Such knowledge can assist in gaining insight into ourselves as well as other aspects of our interactions that can be informative.

8. Be open to "strange" or unusual stories. Children seem to access information or memories that may not seem possible when that has not been the experience of adults. Yet, evidence supports the idea that young people may remember or know things adults did not access or recall. Allowing for these possibilities increases the information exchange that can take place and may be accurate and useful later in life.

9. Support children's Essence as Love. Many, from diverse perspectives and evidence, have argued that at our core, our Essence or Higher Self, we are the manifestation of love. Particularly unconditional love. Parents may not experience that in themselves. Yet, as people explore such a possibility, they report experiences of accessing that information. If we treat children with that same option, they may be able to develop through life knowing this to be true about themselves. Even treating children this way may benefit their growth and development.

Dri, Tiago, and Ariella all contained some doubts about their approach and what to include in this Guidebook when they began. In the end, meager amounts of anxiety remain for each related to different elements of the product. Yet, overall, they believe in their precepts and how these guide their ideas and suggestions for family exploration.

As Nika suggested, it turns out to be a book of possibilities rather than directions. It is a way for people to expand their own experiences and investigate novel ways of interacting and connecting across generations. Now, these three creators hope the full board understands and supports their vision.

Chapter 23
Trials and Turning Points

June, 2036

O nce the board approved the Guidebook with minor changes, all involved in developing it found relief and satisfaction. Even more delight occurred for Dri when the other two judges put the original old judge on sabbatical. That decision provided her much relief.

Nika continued to practice the heart invitation energetics with herself and Naeem. After Hakeem's birth in March, she practiced inviting his tender heart to remain open as much as possible. She sensed it closed when hunger would strike or he needed to relieve himself from gas. She would try to assist some change and encourage the heart to expand. But even with a particularly odorous diaper, he seemed proud of himself and the heart felt quite open. With Nika increasingly focusing on the new court case, Naeem gets his own time to practice what his wife shared with him regarding the hand invitation to the heart.

Sarah and Nika sit in the first row behind the defense table. Dri sits on the other side of Nika and Tiago settles to Dri's right. They all drove to the courthouse to hear the discussion or possibly provide further evidence if needed against the submitted petition. With school out, Tiago desired to be there with Dri and Bella volunteered to watch the kids. These leaders also want to witness first hand what the judge decides. Sitting at the table in front of them is the Coalition's lawyer, Mr. Greg Samuels, a local attorney who specializes in such cases.

The Primordial Family Foundation has requested a prohibitory injunction by the Northern California Federal Court. The PFF argues that The Catalyst Coalition is sending "armed patrols" around at night to threaten its members not to have more children. If women do get pregnant and do not have an abortion, patrol members say they will come back to harm the mother, infant, and the family. Mr. Crenshaw, the PFF attorney, is requesting a preliminary injunction against The Coalition continuing to solicit members until they can gather more evidence regarding the scope of such threats across the US.

The judge has called this hearing to evaluate the evidence the petitioning attorney has included to justify the requested order. They have submitted sworn testimony by a woman who experienced these threats. She is willing to testify this morning, although she included in the responses her fear of Coalition repercussions if she becomes a witness against them.

The judge and two attorneys begin the initial discussions of the case and the submitted affidavit. The PFF attorney requests the judge to issue an injunction, while Mr. Samuels moves for dismissal. They talk though some of the submitted paperwork. Then the judge asks if the one witness is in the courtroom today. The PFF attorney responds that she is available to testify.

Mrs. Silvia Stevens is called to the stand and swears an oath to tell the truth. She states her full name and address in Fresno, California.

Mr. Crenshaw begins.

"Mrs. Stevens, were you visited by three strangers at your home on the night of March 18th, 2036?"

"Yes," responds Mrs. Stevens.

She goes on to tell the court what time, how they rang the bell over and over in quick succession. Then they stood on her front step as she came to the door.

"Did you recognize any of those people?" asks Mr. Crenshaw.

Mrs. Stevens reports that she could not, because they were wearing all black clothing and had on black ski masks, covering their faces and hair. She described two, probably men, who were large and muscular. The third person was shorter and sounded like a woman. She did the talking, the witness reports.

"And how did you know they were from The Catalyst Coalition?" asks Mr. Crenshaw.

Mrs. Stevens says they told her so. Also, the woman had on a black sweatshirt that included 'Catalyst Coalition' in white lettering on the front of it.

Mr. Crenshaw asks Mrs. Stevens what the woman said to her.

"She told me that they were there because I was a vital and important member of the group. But if I got pregnant, they would come back and seriously harm myself, my new baby, and even my husband and other children," says Mrs. Stevens. "She went on to say that it was important to follow all the rules. After that, one of the men said, 'that's right. You better listen.' Then they left the porch and hustled down the street to the south. I don't know where they went after that."

Mr. Crenshaw asked the witness if she took what the woman told her seriously.

She responded that she absolutely did. They sounded mean and very intense about it.

"And did you call the police after they left?" asks Mr. Crenshaw.

"No. I was too scared. The one man told me they would come back and kill me if we reported this to the authorities."

Mr. Samuels questions her next. He asks her how long she has been a member of The Coalition. She tells him she joined the group about six months ago.

"How strong a member would you consider yourself, Mrs. Stevens?"

"Oh, I would describe myself as very devoted to this group and their focus on justice and non-violence. That's why they said they came to see me."

He then asks how much of the materials on the website she has read and whether she found any of it useful. She responds that she read lots of it and found it interesting and useful. He asks what she found most interesting and what was most useful. She hesitates for a few moments, then says that the information is so extensive she does not recall any specific items that would fall in either category. Except she likes the justice part.

Mr. Samuels picks up some papers and looks at them, then looks at the witness. He asks what she thinks of the 18 basic principles of The Coalition's mission statement, and whether she had problems with any of them. Mrs. Stevens responds that she only had a problem with the rule that women couldn't bring more children into the world until all violence had disappeared. She liked the idea of no violence. But she thought it was strange that they were threatening violence if she bore another child.

The defense attorney puts down all the papers except a brochure, which he hands to her. He asks her if she recognizes this brochure. She agrees that it belongs to this organization.

"How many items do you see in the mission statement of this brochure," asks Mr. Samuels.

"There are ten. Um, ah, I guess the other eight are on the website."

"No, Mrs. Stevens," responds Mr. Samuels. "There are only ten on the brochure and ten on the website. Would you please read item number 10 to the court?"

"Consider not bringing children into the world until we truly honor life," reads the witness.

"Where do you find that it's a rule not to have children, Mrs. Stevens?"

"Ah, that must be on the website too," she replies.

"Your honor, I would like to submit this copy of the Catalyst Coalition Statement from their website as Exhibit A. As I stated earlier, it contains only ten items, worded exactly as they are on the brochure. Further, I call your attention to the copy of page 3. There, the organization spells out in more detail their intention about these statements, including that number ten is a personal commitment which members are free to make or not. They go on to say that this is optional and in no way required for membership in the organization."

Mr. Samuelson hand the paper to the judge, who then passes it on to the court clerk.

"Now, Mrs. Stevens, I'd like to refer back to an earlier part of your testimony. You stated that you could not describe anything about the three people at your door, other than possibly their gender, because they all were dressed in black and had black ski masks so you couldn't see their faces. Is that correct?"

"Yes," she replies.

"But one of them wore a sweatshirt with the words, 'Catalyst Coalition' on the front. Is that also correct?"

"Yes," Mrs. Stevens responds.

"So these three people parked away from your house so you could not see their car, they all dressed alike and went to the trouble of getting black ski masks so they could not be identified. But one went to the trouble to tell you they were from The Catalyst Coalition and included a sweatshirt with The Coalition's name on it. Why do you think these three people would hide their identity and car when they are so forward about the group they represented?"

"I don't know. I guess you'd have to ask them."

"Fair enough," responds Mr. Samuels. "Did these people say anything else about the organization's other rules that had to be followed or you would be hurt?"

"No. Just that one."

"Where on that brochure or the website, Mrs. Stevens, does it say there are certain rules that have to be followed in order to be a member?"

The woman looks over the brochure again, then her gaze returns to Mr. Samuels.

"I guess that's on the website too," Mrs. Stevens replies.

Mr. Samuels walks over to the witness and puts his hand on the brochure to press it against the witness stand. "How much money did it cost you to join this group, Mrs. Stevens?"

"We paid the lowest fee to join. As I recall, it was a couple of hundred dollars."

Mr. Samuels removes his hand. "Please turn to the back and read the part about membership fees."

Mrs. Stevens searched the back and finally read the statement. "Donations are accepted, but there is no fee to become a full member of the organization."

"So how much did you pay, Mrs. Stevens?"

"I think my husband suggested we make a donation to let them know how serious we are about participating in this group. I get membership and donations confused sometimes."

"I see. Well, thank you for your testimony, Mrs. Stevens. You've been helpful."

The judge tells her that she can step down. Then he asks if there are any other witnesses.

Both attorneys tell him no, unless he has any questions of the organizational leaders. The judge says he does not.

Mr. Crenshaw gives his oral summary of the case, pointing to the witness and her terror of testifying in person. He has heard of other cases but has not had time to investigate them. Given the national and international scope of the organization and the likelihood that many others have been intimidated and threatened, he requests that the judge issue a preliminary injunction, providing more time to gather evidence of such threats before people are harmed or killed.

Mr. Samuels points out many of the inconsistencies in the witness's testimony. He argues that someone may have come to her home, but there is no clear connection, if they did appear, with the organization or any actual harm that has been done by The Coalition. With a group now numbering over 1.6 million members and existing over the past seven years, it seems like there would be more clear evidence of such conduct, especially given that more than 300,000 members reside in California alone. Given no clear evidence or connection to the organization, he requests a dismissal of the injunction.

The judge looks over the papers for a few minutes, asks either attorney if they have any more evidence to provide, then looks over the papers again.

"Finding no clear evidence that this organization has done anything wrong, the motion to dismiss is granted. Court adjourned."

He pounds his gavel once, stands up and the audience rises, then he leaves the courtroom.

The four sitting on the front row let out small cheers of 'yes' and 'awesome.' They thank Mr. Samuels for his fine work today, then leave the room.

"Let's go get some lunch. I didn't get much breakfast, and I want to celebrate," suggests Tiago as they move into the foyer.

"That's a great idea," responds Sarah. "I thought we'd be longer, so I don't have anything until this afternoon. You have time, Nika?"

"Yes, for you three and delicious food, I do," says Nika. "I just need to call Naeem, who's home with Hakeem. He wanted to know as soon as we heard. Where do you want to go?"

"Feel like having some sushi?" asks Sarah. "There's a great place just a couple of blocks from here on Van Ness that's really fresh."

"That sounds great to me," says Dri. "OK with everyone else?"

They all agree and start walking that way, with Nika on her phone a few steps behind. They choose to walk on the sunny side of the street, enjoying the unusual warmth provided this day in the city. They find the place, get a table, and begin to discuss the menu. Nika joins them as they begin to discuss possible rolls to share. They order, then return to the main topic of the day.

"Thanks for finding Mr. Samuels, Sarah," offers Nika. "I thought he did a great job, both with the witness and their attorney."

"Yeah, I liked how he handled everything today," responds Sarah. "Witnesses like that are tricky. You don't want to charge too hard, and you need to challenge their testimony too. I thought he created a strong balance."

"I liked him, too," adds Tiago. "He wasn't too soft and was great about poking holes."

"Did you two like his summary?" asks Dri.

"Again, I thought he found a nice balance," responds Sarah. "He questioned enough, prodded some holes, but didn't attack her directly. I'm still curious if three people did show up at that woman's house and where they were from. I keep wondering if the

PFF put them up to it. Without any identifying information, they would be difficult to connect to any group."

Dri turns her focus to Nika.

"How are Naeem and Hakeem doing?"

"They're doing well. The au pair has him settled for a nap, and Naeem is about to leave for his studio. Hakeem was a little stuffy this morning, so Naeem stayed home in case they thought he needed to go to the doctor's. He's only three months, so it's challenging to figure out what to do and what's necessary. Fortunately, Naeem's an involved dad. He knows the baby well. Hell, Hakeem's probably in better hands there than with me," chuckles Nika. "If Naeem could breast feed the baby, I would be nearly useless," she says, her chuckles continuing.

"I doubt that," says Dri in a straight tone. "I've seen how involved you are. And happy that you share responsibilities with such a caring father."

"Speaking of caring, how are your visits with Carl going?" asks Sarah. "I think we're all kind of intrigued by this odd connection you two are developing."

"I'm a little surprised by it myself," responds Nika. "But I've also found his life both fascinating and sad at the same time. He's had a rough upbringing, which makes me appreciate my own. The race and gender differences also stand out, making the contrast even starker. But part of the value to me is to understand how people get so discouraged and angry, feeling like the world is against them. And I think what makes it even more demoralizing for Carl is that this is happening to a White man, a part of the group that sees others like them create so much success."

The server brings the four rolls, placed on one platter. He makes sure everyone has a plate and chopsticks. He refills water glasses, finally leaving them to their food and conversation.

"Oh, this looks delicious," continues Nika. "Anyway, in the Black community, the same thing happens. But there, the expectations already are dashed and have been for hundreds of years. It's only in the last 60-100 years that Blacks and women have been able to visualize the possibility of greater success."

"I find that contrast interesting," adds Tiago. "Hispanics have not been enslaved like Blacks, but their expectations also have been limited. It becomes built into large swaths of our community, so people don't expect too much, become too disappointed. But it also limits dreams and confines possibilities. I see it so much in my interactions with my students. I think that's why it's so important to have models in the classroom, on the fields, in community leadership, and national torchbearers to help them visualize greater capabilities. If kids can't see it, they don't go after it."

"Exactly," says Nika. "I think one of the issues that makes for a strange relationship with Carl is that it is a Black woman who is encouraging greater possibilities for a White man. And he seems to be opening up to it. I think he's become curious about what we are wanting to accomplish. He's become less resistant to racial justice as he expands the possibilities of his own future. In fact, we've been having interesting conversations about anger, conflict resolution, and understanding other perspectives when we release some of our judgments."

"OK, that surprises me," chuckles Dri. "I didn't see that coming."

She takes more pieces as others do the same.

"Love this salmon roll," she exclaims.

"I didn't see that coming, either," adds Nika.

A broad smile appears while her eyes look reflective, as if taking in a past interaction with Carl.

"But I find that if I can hold my heart open as we speak, his own seems to soften. If I don't get reactive, his responses mellow. And a little humor from time to time doesn't hurt. I just try to not pull 'An Alex,' meaning I don't say something funny just to lower the tension. Alex always made it look so natural. It took a long while to see the dynamic that was triggering his behaviors."

"He was a champion," laughs Tiago. "He could get a coach to laugh, even when he was pissed off at the whole team."

"I think he was even better with Mom," chuckles Dri. "And then she got into it for a while, especially after his death."

The smile fades from Dri's face, and she goes quiet for a moment.

"I think that's the first time I've said that word. Still chokes me up."

Tiago leans over, puts an arm around Dri's shoulders and gives them a squeeze. He just holds her as she appears to reflect for a moment.

"It's not easy to say out loud. Not for someone so close," shares Tiago. "A similar thing can happen when I talk about my Gpa dying. And that was ten years before Alex."

Tiago quits talking. The group sits in silence, giving respect to a loved brother and friend.

"And life goes on, too," says Dri, breaking the silence. "The gift from that tragedy was the work we've done. And your reaching out to Carl may be a prime example of what is possible when one opens her or his heart. I just hope we can help Cate and Alee keep their hearts expanded. Help them stay in the wonder of life."

"We all hope and want to help with that," adds Sarah. "If we can do it around Alex, Marsha, and Doc, it's an excellent practice for the Carls and PFF crowds of this world. That's the other challenging habit. How do we hold hearts open for people who try to shoot or destroy you?"

"An interesting question," responds Nika. "Fortunately, I didn't approach Carl with that in mind. I think it would have been more difficult if I had. I was simply curious. Once we began connecting, then I could practice. But by then, I already had found him interesting."

"I see you as courageous too. But isn't that part of the practice?" asks Tiago. "See what I'm hiding in myself with my judgment of another person? What am I not seeing of value in someone else when I am angry about who they are or what they're doing? It seems to me that the PFF is desperate. They've boxed themselves into dying beliefs and challenged standards, holding on for dear life. It's similar to what happened to the Republican Party, even before Trump became President. They were holding onto White power, conservative religious ideologies they wanted to remain dominant, when in fact their values were increasingly being challenged. And they couldn't include others without expanding their beliefs. So they fought harder and yelled louder."

"But what I find as an especially heinous crime against humanity is when men behind the power try to turn women against each other and the pure act of creation," says Sarah. "It's something authoritarians first try to crush. They attempt to control women's bodies and personal decisions, using other women as a front. They go after books, art, academicians, and journalists who create alternative perspectives and the hope brought about by contrasting views, new possibilities. All this challenges the authoritarian's point of view. This is the most basic destruction. And it seems to me that's what men have done with the PFF. Especially when an alternative view is seen as challenging their financial situation. Destroy challenges. Destroy the essence of creativity and hope."

"I agree, Sarah," Nika adds. "And that's well put. I think their money and influence permeate the PFF and similar groups, like the Christian Nationalists. It's all about power and money. Fighting a losing battle to hold on to their traditional male power and privilege. And it's time power is shared and privilege is deflated."

"You can see the desperation with the pathetic response that was illustrated today," responds Sarah. "With education, personal connections and open hearts, more and more young people are less committed to White supremacy, more open to gender fluidity and inclusion, and feel less bound by an external supreme authority that's been used in divisive, hateful ways. When you can't change, it's difficult to lead people who don't want to follow you."

"So do you think Carl was talked into shooting you by the PFF?" asks Dri. "Any sense they put him up to it?"

"They certainly didn't discourage people from acting violently," responds Nika. "But I also don't think that as a group, they were behind it. Carl was increasingly frustrated by his situation and decided he should stop our 'evil' efforts by taking out our leader. There seems to be some race issue, but that wasn't the most dominant drive. I simply became the symbol, as a successful Black woman, of what he wanted and didn't have. I had no redeeming qualities in his book. And some of the disinformation put out by his conservative political and religious leaders reinforced his growing rage."

"You were very lucky. He sounds like he was pretty determined," says Sarah.

"Yeah, he was. Fortunately, he didn't have much knowledge about guns and shells," adds Nika. "And he wasn't the best shot, all of which favored my survival. But what's most interesting to me is that as we continue our conversation and begin to understand each other's worlds, there is less animosity and a greater ability to connect. And I think he's as intrigued by that as I am."

"What strikes me most about your interaction with Carl is that his wounding you with a bullet or a knife shows the scar from his attack, around which people provide concern and support," shares Dri, her face completely somber. "And the body works to heal itself. But the slicing cuts of his family's verbal knife show no wounds. They cut just the same. But unless you are telling others, there is no concern or support. Unless we are working with the emotional wounds, the body does not heal in the same way. It may surround the wound and close it off, but it does not do the same healing. We have not cleaned out the infection, have not removed the inserted poison. Words can cut again, and again, and again with no apparent scars."

"What are you saying, Dri?" asks Sarah.

"What I'm saying is that we have to clean out the poison and infection of our emotional wounds before we can fully heal. I believe that is what you are doing with Carl, Nika. And that's what we all are trying to do. It's also why it is so important to be conscious of what we say, to ourselves and others. That's what Doc was doing with me. His cuts with me were clean, clearing out the poison and infections I had taken on, even said to myself.

When we clean out the infectious parts, we not only remove our worst nightmare, such as feeling unloveable, but we then can no longer deflect the truth of who we really are inside. That is when I had the incredible experience of feeling into the inner light. That is when I found the core of who I am."

Everyone looks at Dri in silence, taking in her shared view.

"Yes, Dri," responds Nika, breaking the silence. "You are absolutely right. That's brilliant."

"I'm just verbalizing what I now see as my experience with Doc," says Dri. "What he was offering me. And what I seized in the invitation."

"And what you offered us afterwards," whispers Nika. "And now trying to share with more people."

"I never saw it in that way," offers Tiago. "And I would agree with you about my experience with Gpa as well. That is what he wanted to offer people in different forms."

"And I experience that with you all. That is what you are doing," shares Sarah.

Again silence hangs over the group, having quit eating momentarily. Sarah turns to Nika.

"Are you going to continue to visit Carl?" inquires Sarah.

"Yes, for a while at least," responds Nika. "As I mentioned, he's become interested in other ways for solving conflicts that he never considered. And he's beginning to see how that would have made his life easier. He's also intrigued with how people develop an inner strength, their own inner guidance, instead of relying completely on external authority, as he has his whole life. I think he's less interested in following other people's directions of what's right in contrast to an inner guide. I've shared about the work Dri, Soph, and I began our last year of high school and how it changed my life. I think he's curious about that and how he might explore his own personal possibility, his own wonderment of the future, even rewriting his future."

"That's awesome," responds Dri. "I find this whole interaction fascinating."

"It is for me, too," adds Nika. "Just like this new report from Bella and Omar about a shift in our whole connection to the Earth from the work with the Native American tribes."

"Oh yes, I, too, find the fundamental shift in relationship appealing," says Tiago. "They have some creative ideas about how to clean up our land and waters, which are fabulous. And their recommendations seem to be catching on in other countries as much as here. Small experimental places are cropping up all over the world."

"Cropping up. That's a great way to describe new ideas of reclamation being shared now from their efforts," laughs Nika.

"OK, sometimes I'm funny without meaning to be. I did hang around Alex quite a bit," chuckles Tiago. "But I love this shift from 'controlling' the Earth to working with our world. The emphasis that we share the same elements in our bodies as we are working with in the Earth. The clay, water, air, sunshine. When we begin to shift our perspective from 'owning' the Earth to having a relationship with this physical planet, I begin to experience a very different connection. I think the intensity of our climate change has helped us reexamine how we and the Earth are in this life together, just as all people are better off with collaboration instead of competition and domination. Cooperate rather than captivate."

"I like that notion," remarks Dri, as she reaches out, placing her hand on top of his. "I don't think I've ever heard you say it quite that way. And it seems to be stimulating more people developing their own grown gardens for vegetables and fruits. Even sharing with others by giving them away. I love it."

"I've been doing a lot of internal processing since reading Bella and Omar's latest report," adds Tiago. "It's made me change my view and how I think about walking on this planet. How do I work with rather than dominate it? What is my spiritual connection to our foundation of life? In ways, I think all our discussions about race relations have impacted my view of Earth relations, maybe even all my relations. I love that saying from the Native American heritage. I think it's true. It *is* about "all my relations." I'm happy about our efforts to expand our inclusivity rather than making it about you, me, or the small 'Us.' I like the expanding composition of our group and the invitation for all to work together."

"Even when I piss you off?" laughs Dri.

"Yes, my love. When you piss me off, I get to look at what's not yet healed. And then I get to love you more. Well, once I focus more on healing and less on my pissiness," laughs Tiago.

All three women laugh with him.

"What else could a man say in this group of strong women," chuckles Sarah.

"Yes, and you're an excellent model for Naeem and Omar," suggests Nika. "And they for you. Guess we've made great choices in partners, including May."

The smile is less needed in this moment as the heart arises through all their vocal expressions.

Chapter 24
Expanding
Heartful Growth

September, 2038

A s the distance from the failed injunction increases, the Coalition staff hear less and less from the PFF. It appears as if the demoralizing loss at the hearing has became an increasingly discouraging apex in their movement. The silence might also have been a result from the decline in memberships in religious organizations, consistently replaced by community groups with a core teaching of service to others. Even the richest religious institutions could not avoid the dramatic decline in membership.

A core mission of several service organizations focus on the transition of paroled prisoners into better jobs that include helping others and the return of voting rights. This emphasis enhances their contributions back to society as well as their own sense of value.

One additional consequential change occurred with the US Supreme Court. After the passing of Justices Thomas and Alito and Justice Roberts retiring, three more liberal justices were appointed. The most recent appointment includes Chief Justice Valeria Pérez. With this transition, the remaining justices and the US Senate agreed on a fundamental and long sought change. Terms of 18 total years were established for all new justices on the Supreme Court and all federal courts. This pivotal modification, along with the decreasing impact of the extreme radicals in the choice of judges, assists in the renewed respect for all federal courts.

While the Coalition continues to grow, the necessity for additional materials simultaneously increases. Once again, Dri and Ariella collaborate to create an additional guidebook with the primary writing responsibility descending on Tiago, a responsibility he cherishes, even with the additional weight.

A slight taste of cool softens this warm Saturday morning. The scent of harvest permeates the outside atmosphere, while freshly brewed coffee lingers in the air as Tiago enters the kitchen. He pulls out two large mugs, pouring milk into one, then zapping it for 20 seconds to warm the liquid. He watches the steam as he fills both mugs with coffee. This stimulates a slight bend forward to savor a favorite aroma. He carries the mugs to the garden where Dri relaxes under the table awning. She chooses to make it. He chooses to serve it.

"I had an interesting dream early this morning," begins Tiago as he takes a seat.

"Yeah? Want to share it?" asks Dri.

"I do."

"I still love to hear you say those two words," laughs Dri. "Even after all these years."

"I still love to say them," responds Tiago. "Anyway, I was sitting at a strange metal desk with a side chair. Kind of like those green desks you might see in a classic old detective movie. I was wearing a suit, so it kind of started out as a nightmare," laughs Tiago. "But I noticed my Gpa was sitting in the side chair, as relaxed as can be."

"Interesting. Did he say anything?"

"He asked how I was doing and about the family. I told him we were doing well. Then he asked how I was intending to integrate what he taught me about exploring hurts into the conflict resolution videos we're developing."

"That's timely, given that we sent away our kids to your mom's so we could work on that today. I guess you were working it through before we woke up."

"I guess so," responds Tiago. "I told him a couple of ideas we wanted to be sure to include, like beginning with an open heart. I'm thinking I'm way ahead of him, this time." Tiago bursts out laughing. "I'm feeling strong. I've got this, I say to myself."

"And what does he say?" asks Dri.

"He looks me straight in the eyes. 'Don't forget to use conflict as a mirror.' I gasp. I haven't considered that piece. It's one he and I talked quite a bit about, and it didn't even occur to me that we might include it here. Then he got up and left. What's also interesting is that I simply feel grateful for his suggestion. There's no shame, no guilt that I didn't think of it before then. He just says it, matter of fact. Then he moves on, having shared his insight once more."

"That sounds so consistent with the way I knew him, too. Not as well, of course, and not nearly as long. But totally consistent with the way he'd talk with me. And what a great idea. I love it. That will add to the creativity and compliment the other pieces we want to propose."

"Then, after he left, I felt great sadness. I miss him so much some days," comments Tiago.

"Yeah, me too," responds Dri. "Do you think it was your Gpa appearing to you? He's done that before, hasn't he?"

"Yeah. He appeared in my dreams several times during the first couple of years after his death. Then once, I thought I saw him in my bedroom, maybe a couple of months after he died. The first time, he appeared to be an adolescent beginning his path. Later, he appeared as a young man, maybe about the time he married. He was just standing there, a slight smile that often accompanied his watching me. He didn't say anything, but I felt like he was telepathically telling me he was fine. I shouldn't worry. It's always a joy to see him, and some sadness when he leaves. Still is, even today."

Tiago takes a sip of coffee, now looking at the bright yellow roses blooming in their garden. He takes a slow deep breath, another sip of coffee, then turns back to Dri.

"It's wonderful you had such touching dreams about him or able to see him."

"Yes, it is. And he was especially helpful this time. But I also had the impression that he wouldn't be back much. Like he had other matters to attend to now." Tiago takes a leisurely sip as his fingers play on the table top. "Well, we had better eat something. Ready for some breakfast? I think it's my turn to prepare it."

"First, just wondering if you felt any discouragement afterwards, that you didn't think of using the mirror with the conflict? That you hadn't considered including such a piece?"

"Yeah, a little. I guess I'm always sensitive about not measuring up to him."

"Oh, I know that feeling. I'm all too aware of my own self-punishing behavior, especially when I think about your Gpa. But I'm also learning the importance of going inside and making that core connection when you're down. For me, that's the most important time to do it. That's when I need it most. I suggest you take a few minutes to do that before you start working today."

Tiago looks into her eyes, noticing in this moment a similar depth he saw in his grandfather when he shared a piece of wisdom.

"You're right. I will do that. Thanks."

"Now, how about a bran muffin and a small smoothie?"

"Coming right up."

Tiago picks up his morning addiction and carries it back into the kitchen as he begins preparations for a smoothie and muffins before they begin their day's work.

After discussing the basic ideas to be included, Dri took the lead in drafting the family guidebook, the initial one approved earlier this year. Tiago and Ariella made additions and did primary editing before hiring Harper, a developmental editor, to review it for consistency and any additional errors. After seeing the extra changes Harper suggested, Dri was grateful to have such a qualified reviewer help them make their guidebook a more professional product.

For this Conflict Guidebook, Tiago will take the lead while Ariella works on the initial draft of the video scripts. He wrote several pages for the overview and outlined the process during this past week. Today, he'll revise that description, then try to finish a draft of the remaining two sections while Dri edits his initial pieces and the basic steps he has described.

Tiago goes downstairs to his office. Before getting to work, he spends some time in meditation and connecting with his core. Today, he wants to write from his essence, not just his personality. He wants all the inspiration he can activate for this work. He hopes Gpa has not removed his inspiration completely.

The morning is well spent with phone ringers turned to Do Not Disturb, allowing only calls from Gabriela in case of some emergency. Tiago finishes the process revisions and gives those to Dri. Then he drafts the last two sections in his office while Dri edits at the patio table, each having undisturbed work space.

About noon time, Tiago emerges from the basement and begins putting together avocado, lettuce, and cheese sandwiches for lunch. A chef break helps his body and brain relax for a few minutes. He adds a few quinoa and black bean chips, with one dark chocolate mint cream for a tasty finish. He takes the plates out on the patio and asks Dri what she would like to drink.

"I'll just have some water, thanks. Oh, this looks lovely," she adds as he sets the plates down on the table. Dri moves her papers to make more room for her meal.

Tiago returns to the kitchen, gets two glasses of water, then goes back out and sits at the table.

"How's the editing going, my love?"

"Great timing. I just finished with the steps you outlined. I added a bit and made a few minor changes. May I read them to you? See how they sound now?" she asks.

"Yes, please."

Dri picks up her marked paper and begins to read:

Steps for Growing through Differences, Disagreements, or Conflicts (DDC):

1. Open your heart, through meditation or other expanding processes to create a more loving space for yourself to enter such discussions. Invite your heart to stay open, even if a pause is needed, throughout the conversations.

2. Use what ever issue is identified during a DDC process as a reflection for yourself first. What can you learn about yourself regarding the issue by looking at it as a mirror? What gets triggered in you about such differences you are experiencing? What can you release or transform to increase your own healing and decrease your emotional and physical reactions? Think back to your biggest lie and higher lesson. Which is taking priority in your reaction at this moment? Is that the one you want to be in charge? How can you grow personally from this disagreement? How does any change you make now impact the current DDC?

3. As you engage in a dialogue with the contrasting individual, listen deeply to yourself and the other person. What are you both wanting to share from the heart? What is underneath the words, if anything, especially for you? Is there something else that is part of what you're saying that you're not sharing? Is there a hidden personal issue you are not seeing or understanding? If so, investigate it before proceeding. Explore what else is there, other aspects involved, elements hidden that you have not been noticing or understanding.

4. What is your most loving guess about what is going on with the person holding a contrasting view or opinion? What does he or she want most? How does that relate to your reaction, hurt or anger? Spend a few moments in her or his shoes, perspective, and heart. What do you learn about the other person and yourself by taking their perspective?

5. Where might areas of agreement and connection lie with the other person? Where might there include areas of compromise or ways you might agree? Is there some alternative that neither of you are suggesting or seeing? How might you grow in finding a second or third or even more possibilities to what you first wanted or suggested? How might you work towards greater peace, in you and between you both, with your offerings or suggestions?

6. Use your open heart to create a win-win from the DDC. You may not get every-thing you want, but how do your offerings and suggestions bring peace to your heart, love and openness in your interactions with others? Is the outcome you first wanted more important to you than a peaceful open heart, for you and the other person? If so, why? What is your highest priority? What is holding you back from a peaceful, open heart in this interaction?

7. Work to find a way of growth and settlement for you both that resolves the original DDC and brings peace and love to both your lives.

"What do you think of the changes I made?"

"I like them and the way it sounds now. Great work," says Tiago.

"Thanks. I'm pretty happy with it too. You ready to give me more?"

"Yes, right after we eat. I'm not finished, but I have more for you to add your improving touches. You have a great way with words. Thanks for your suggestions."

They finish their lunch while talking about the garden and how quiet the house is without their two kids.

"Yeah, I miss them too, sometimes," laughs Dri. "And it's great to take some time just to work once in a while."

"I see you're wearing the green necklace Mom gave you at our wedding," comments Tiago.

"Yeah, it helps me write. I like to wear it often, but especially when we're working on Coalition offerings," responds Dri.

Tiago and Dri spend the remainder of the day writing and editing. Near dinner time, Gabriela shows up at their door with a basket containing three Guatemalan dishes that immediately ignite the flow of saliva from the aromas as she takes off the lids. Miguel holds Alee's hand as their nearly three-year-old boy walks into the house.

"I know you're hungry Cate. But go wash your hands while we set out the food, please."

Tiago and his dad take Alee in so all can clean hands as Cate joins them. Then they find places at the dining room table and ready themselves for this feast. Nine-year-old Cate is far ahead, helping to set the table so her grandmother's food can stave off her starvation.

"What fun have you kids been having all day?" asks Tiago.

"I got to play in the little house downstairs and ring the doorbell, til Gpa made me stop," stated Alee in a matter of fact way.

"Gma and I made cookies," responds a boisterous Cate. "You'll get some if you eat all your dinner," she chuckles.

After the kids finish, Tiago tells his parents about their day's work. They will finish their edited draft tomorrow and submit it to Ariella for further review. In exchange, Dri and Tiago will review her script drafts as soon as she forwards them.

"Sounds like it was a productive day," says Gabriela.

"Yes, it was. And my writing necklace helped," responds Dri, holding the stone between her thumb and forefinger.

"Excellent. I'm glad. Dad and Grandma would be proud, I know."

Three weeks later, Fadima calls Tiago.

"Love what you three have created with the Growing Through Differences Guidebook. Harper, who also is fluent in Spanish, is going to begin translating it. Her mom pushed her to grow up with the language, so she's a natural. I have three others who will work on the French, Italian, and German translations so they all can be placed on our website. And Harper's sister, Bailey, who is a great videographer, will begin making the videos in a month or so. I have a lead on a director, and she might know some strong, inexpensive actors. I think this is going to be a great addition to our work."

"Thanks, Fadima. Glad the board was so supportive and excited with proceeding. Dri and I are happy with the way the guidebook turned out. And I love the creative situations Ariella came up with for the videos to illustrate the processes. She gets the messages we're trying to share with this guidebook. I think they'll be great illustrations of our main points."

"I agree. And the suggestions by the two new board members from Europe and Mexico I think helped. I believe it's important that we are getting beyond the original small group and expanding the perspectives offered by our newer members."

"Are you making headway with the other translations, too," asks Tiago.

"Oh yes. I've found someone I worked with at the UN to begin the Arabic translation. She's strong, and I can check that one. I've found another UN translator who is starting to work on the Japanese versions and a third to make a Hebrew version. We're going to limit that for now. But I have my feelers out for other people, when we get more translation funds, who can work on the Chinese, Hindi, Korean, and Russian versions. It's a lot, I know. But we all agree they're important as soon as we can afford to do them. I'll be happy to have these six other languages soon. And this guidebook will be an essential contribution to our work."

"Thank you, Fadima, for your kind words. I think you're doing a great job as Coalition director. So glad you took on the task. And your UN connections sure help us reach out to more diverse people and backgrounds."

"Thanks, Tiago. I love this work and what we're trying to share. Grateful to be a part of it and facilitating our outreach. I believe it's stretching me, helping me grow personally, and touching my heart deeply. I'm grateful for what I'm learning along the way too. Well, I had better get to some other work. I wanted to bring you up to date. Oh, I also wanted to ask. Has Sarah and May's adoption gone through? Do they have their little baby yet?"

"Yes, they have. And they're thrilled. She is the cutest little girl. And they're wonderful mothers. May can hardly let her go some days. Luckily, she gets tired and lets Sarah have a turn. But it's even harder for any of us to hold that darling little snug."

"That's her name? Snug?" Fadima asks.

"Oh no. Her name's Shreya. She just squirrels into your body, almost like a sauce over ice cream. She stays that close."

"She does sound adorable! Well, please give her a hug for me next time you see them. I'll call and congratulate them. OK, talk to you soon."

With that, Fadima ends the call.

Once Tiago gets home from school and spends some time with Cate and Alee, he tells Dri about his conversation with Fadima. She has the same enthusiastic reaction Tiago expressed on the phone. She loves Fadima's leadership and the changes she's introducing.

"So my news is not as thrilling. Nika called this afternoon. The congressional committee chair finally agreed to initiate an investigation into The Coalition, as Charlene Hoover, the PFF President, kept pushing him to do. Nika believes that as she gains more prominence within the Progressive Party, the conservative Democratic chair wants to bring her down a notch. She thinks the Speaker also must be increasingly concerned with her expanding influence. As third in line in her party, others become more threatened by her."

"Are you kidding me right now?" asks Tiago, his eyes wide, his mouth hanging open.

"Nope. We have about two weeks to prepare for it. And, Fadima, Mom, and I are all asked to testify. Besides Nika, of course. I have to say, I'm nervous about being a witness for a congressional investigation. Even about something I know and believe in. I still worry about saying something wrong, sharing information that gets twisted or used against us."

"I don't blame you. I would be, too. My God, I can't believe this is happening. Is Nika nervous about it?"

"She's not happy with the investigation," responds Dri. "But she's trying to remain calm and just plan out our strategy, wanting to anticipate and be ready with what they're going to slam at us. She's sure they'll talk about issues from the court case a couple of years ago. She also heard they'll probably attack our focus on injustice being overblown and our commitment to economic equality as anti-American. A communist conspiracy or something like that. They haven't used that as much lately, and they're trying to resurrect that theme from the 2020s to attack the whole Progressive Party."

"Hasn't that kind of been burnt out? They tried it for quite a while then. Think they'll have any better chance now?"

"No, Nika doesn't think so. None of us do. But we also can't predict what's going to work and what won't. We have to prepare for several possibilities."

"What can I do?" asks Tiago.

"Nothing right now. But I'm sure you'll get an opportunity to apply your research and prep skills before the week's out."

"You know I'll do anything I can to help."

"Yes, we all know that. You've proven that over and over. Sarah and Soph have both offered their assistance too. At least I'll get to see Soph again. She'll be there, too. I believe Omar's going out with Mom. But I think I'll need you to stay here with the kids."

"Yes, of course. Or Mom and Dad might be willing to help. They could come here, or I could take the kids to Albany and fly out of SFO. Whatever you think is best. If I could help in DC, I'm happy to go with you. Or I'll hold the place down while you shine there."

"I love you, Tiago. This has been quite a ride. And I've never doubted your support for a minute. Well, maybe just that one day, before going to the hospital when Cate was born. But it only lasted a minute before I understood what you were saying. After two years of going together and twelve years of marriage, I still adore you. And I kinda like you, too," chuckles Dri. "I'm so grateful I fell into what I thought may be the unsafe. Little did I realize it was the bliss."

Tiago wraps his arms around Dri and gives her a lengthy kiss, emoting from his heart. He backs up enough to look into her eyes.

"I'm so glad we both did. 'Cuz it's bliss for me too, my love."

Chapter 25

Coalescence

August, 2039

With the new barriers installed around the San Francisco/Oakland Bay and raised platforms in the harbor, the area remains sufficiently safe at the moment from rising ocean levels. But many more changes need to continue for further reduction of climate change.

People have further decreased their demand for white and red meat, increasingly relying on organic vegetables, fruits, grains and legumes. The development and installment of a hack proof Internet with quantum particles in fiber optic network under encryption make it more available and reliable as well as preventing cyber intrusions. And the increased transition to solar collection, cold fusion power sources, and the nearly final transition to electric vehicles and trains, all assist in critical reductions.

One of the most essential modifications is the improvement in electric vehicles with better batteries that rely less on rare materials. These critical containers also become self-restoring batteries by incorporating solar cells into the body of the car so the entire shell becomes a type of solar panel. Yet, more social changes continue to be needed.

Coalition growth has picked up again after the feeble congressional investigation that raised more fears than facts, more insults than issues. Nika's allies on the committee assisted in providing an opportunity and platform to share their philosophy and expound on the type of changes in conflict resolution that reduce violence, environmental changes that continue to reduce global warming threats, and alternative solutions to reduce consumption of limited earth resources. For the leaders themselves, meeting with the congressional committee allowed them to practice holding on to their core and keeping hearts open in the face of attack and chaos. Increasingly, the leadership became clear how turmoil and confusion become the most common ways people move from their place of strength and insight to doubt and judgement. Prior to the hearing, all committed to use this time to practice holding solid to their core. In that way, the hearing became an essential practice.

On Sunday, August 28th, Nika prepares to give a major speech for her election to the US Senate at the Frank Ogawa Plaza in Oakland. She chose this location because Kamala Harris launched her presidential campaign twenty years earlier from this place. The day also commemorates the "I Have A Dream Speech" delivered by Dr. King. Nika asked former Congresswoman Jennifer Bradshaw to introduce her after Dri says a few words of endorsement.

Dri steps up to the microphone. "Good evening, all. My name is Audri Giovani. I am here today to voice my support for a sister from another mother, whom I also love. This amazing woman is running for the United States Senate from our dear state of California. I have known Tanika most of my life. We studied together, worked together, laughed together, and cried together. She is a great student, competitive tennis player, fabulous attorney, effective congresswoman, and loving wife and mother. I know her brilliant mind and her loving heart. And that combination of mind and heart calls out for my support and to encourage the same from all of you.

"She cares about this city, this state, and this country. And I mean every person within our boundary and beyond. She has worked many years for Congresswoman Bradshaw, then later served in the House of Representatives for eight years. Her diverse experience combined with an insightful mind and caring heart makes her very qualified to be a leader. I ask you all today to support her efforts. And now, I have the privilege of introducing the great Congresswoman, Jennifer Bradshaw."

Audri steps away from the mike, and the Congresswoman gives a personal introduction and her own endorsement of Nika's candidacy. It now becomes Nika's turn to make her announcement and begin to convince people she will continue to be worth supporting for this new position.

"Thank you, Audri, for your kind words and Congresswoman Bradshaw for that lovely introduction. Many of you know my dear friend and sister, Audri Giovani and her husband, Tiago Garcia. We were, along with a few others, co-founders of The Catalyst

Coalition. They also have their two children here with them, Cate and Alee. They have been constant supporters of my efforts, as I have been for their enlightening work.

"You also know my wonderful husband and friend, Naeem, and our son, Hakeem. It really is for Hakeem, Cate, Alee, and all other children that compels me to run for this office.

"I especially want to thank others who paved the way for my senatorial race. Most recently, former President Harris, who was the first African American and Asian American to represent this golden state of California in the US Senate. Of course, others paved the path for her, including Hiram Revels, the first African American elected to the senate when he represented Mississippi only five years after the Civil War. Much later, Shirley Chisholm, the first African American woman elected to congress and the first to run for president paved the way for women of color, and Kamala Harris even further as the first woman, African American, and Asian American to be elected Vice President. But it is not just former Vice President Harris's policies that inspire me. It is the hearts that she and former President Biden brought to the White House, their love of family and concern for others that touches me most.

"All of these people and many more worked to fulfill a dream that was expressed so eloquently seventy six years ago today at the Lincoln Memorial in Washington, DC. A visionary Civil Rights leader and iconic orator laid out an aspiration for us all. The still young Dr. Martin Luther King, Jr. shared with an absorbing crowd and later the world his vision of change to bring not only freedom, but a fulfillment of a promise laid out in the Constitution of these United States. His dream is the actualization of the inalienable rights for all human beings of life, liberty, and the pursuit of happiness. Today, many are close enough to taste the accomplishment of Dr. King's dream, but other children remain prevented from realizing their aspirations and potential.

"Dr. King created a vision of freedom for all. But I don't believe it is only a freedom from violence and racial injustice. It is not just loosening the bands of segregation and degradation. In his 1964 Nobel Peace Prize speech, he talked about a 'new sense of dignity' and a 'new era of progress and hope.' His dream included sitting together at a table of what I call humanhood, living in a world where people are judged 'by the content of their character.'

"There is another aspect of Dr. King's later speeches that I believe serves as a culmination of his dream. He gave two additional significant speeches that clarified how violence perpetuates violence, and darkness extends darkness. Only light changes the darkness.

He went on to say that we do not transform darkness with archaic thinking and the propagation of scarcity. He also recognized what a burden hate was on people's hearts, and he experienced a concerted look at anger and hate. But in the end, he chose to 'stick to love.' He said, 'If you are seeking the highest good, I think you can find it through love.' For 'he who has love has the key that unlocks the door to the meaning of ultimate reality.'

"For the past 20 years, leaders in diverse positions and settings have worked hard to bring about a restoration of our world, the means to take better care of it, and the reduction in its destruction. We have nearly eliminated combustion engines in cars, busses, and trains. We are increasing our renewable energy while also developing more jobs for people whose work relied on fossil fuels. There is greater economic and racial justice with expanded access to low cost education, training programs, and greater equity in home buying. Groups increasingly are emphasizing the value of diversity rather than the fear of change. Greater ease in voting access that allows higher percentages of people to participate in this democratic experiment through the expression of their views. We have created significant police reforms and decreased the killing of unarmed people, especially people of color. We have dramatically restricted incarceration rates, particularly among African Americans. And we are shifting the emphasis away from prisons to retraining programs. We are inching closer not only to fulfilling Dr. King's dream, but creating a more colorful outcome along the way.

"Yet, there is more to do. From the beginning of this nation, the United States has been a divisive country: White against Black, Native American, Hispanic, Jewish, Irish, Italian, Chinese, and Japanese. But it was not limited to their country of origin or race. Men refused to let women vote for nearly 150 years. We have had movements to change those repressions, from the Suffragettes, Civil Rights, Native American Rights, Gay Rights, contraceptive and abortion rights, and Transgender Rights. We have seen many changes with all of those challenges. And we still experience pay inequality, economic inequality, educational inequality, and age inequality. But most of all, we still have truth inequality, caring inequality, heart inequality, and love inequality.

"Previous challenges brought to the forefront our need to refocus behaviors towards these three principles: First, sustaining our world; Second, understanding how what effects one impacts us all, and third, the importance of dreams based on love rather than fear to guide us in the decisions we make. Love based on cooperation rather than domination with our earth. Care for and collaboration with others rather than attempting to control them. Share equality, liberty, and the opportunity to pursue happiness for us all equally. It is through truth, harmony, peace, and love for our world, families, neighbors, and all citizens that we are able to experience the final fulfillment of Dr. King's dream.

"Today, I promise you that I will use these three principles to guide my work for you in the US Senate. I go there not for me or my friends, but all people of this beautiful state. And I go there especially for our children. From corporate heads who provide many goods and services to laborers who provide us with food for our table. From new born babies to those ready to pass into another part of our experience on this beautiful Earth. From those with very light skin to very dark skin. For people who identify as a specific gender to those who feel more gender fluid. And I will work not just for California, but for the good of all. For we do not succeed here to the detriment of other states. We do not succeed in this country any longer to the detriment of other nations. We do not succeed in the world to the detriment of our beloved Earth.

"Thank you for coming here today. I ask for your support, your vote, to take this dream to the United States Senate. I know many of you. I want to hear from and represent all of you. I want to manifest this dream for you, for us, and especially for our children. I hold your precious dreams in my heart as I ask you to hold mine in yours. Thank you. And blessings on us all."

The crowd, spilling into the nearby streets clap, and roar with jubilant support. It feels to Nika that it's her best speech yet, and she's grateful for Harper's help in writing it. People come up to congratulate and talk with her, volunteering time in her campaign office or other needed tasks. Harper staff's a table for volunteer signups and Bailey ends up helping her with so many people wanting to get their names on the list.

"Great speech, Nika," Jennifer says. "I must leave for another appointment. But I think this may be your finest speech, so far at least. I think you have a good shot, and you're climbing in the polls. Your trip to the LA area will be key. But my friend down there, state Attorney General Gonzalez, will introduce you at your first rally and announce his formal endorsement. That will help. Anyway, I must leave. Good luck down there, and let me know if there's anything else I can do to support you."

"Thank you so much, Jennifer. I so appreciate all you've done," replies Nika.

"Just keep thinking positive and accomplish all you can. That's all anyone can do."

People again step in between to congratulate Nika, shake her hand, and get a selfie. Like Senator Elizabeth Warren in her 2020 presidential campaign, Nika is committed to doing photos with anyone who wants them, no matter how long it takes. Her commitment creates availability for her current and potential constituency.

Nika notices a woman holding back, finally reaching the front after everyone has gone. She holds out her hand. There's no smile on the woman's face or sense of celebration.

"Well, I didn't expect to see you at this rally," remarks Nika, her eyes wide and mouth half open as she shakes her hand. "What would bring you to a gathering of mine, Mrs. Stevens?"

"I really wanted to hear ya speak, and I know you won't be comin' to Fresno until late in your campaign," replies Silvia. "May I take a minute of your time?"

"Sure. What's on your mind?" asks Nika.

"I needed to talk with ya. After the injunction hearing, I had misgivings about my testimony. But after I spoke at the congressional investigation, then heard what Mrs. Hoover and others said about ya and your organization, I really got depressed. You know they paid me, right?" Silvia's eyebrows narrowed and her lower jaw extends slightly to the right.

"No, but I wondered," responds Nika, noticing a release of energy pass through her body. "In fact, I had a feeling you were financially influenced. And when the other two witnesses came forward with almost exactly the same story, it really started to sound fishy. Not just to me, but to everyone, except Charlene and the committee chair."

"I just needed to apologize to ya. My husband was out of a job, and they paid us over twenty thousan' dollars. I didn't want to do it. But my husband insisted. We really needed the money. We were desperate. And that's why they could pressure us to do it."

"I understand, Mrs. Stevens," says Nika, a slight smile appearing on her face. "I don't know what I'd have done under those circumstances. I want to think I wouldn't participate. But I honestly can't say."

"After I heard ya and others respond to our comments and share with the committee what ya are doin', I wished I really was an important member of your group. I like what ya stand for, supportin' people like us. And I love what ya said tonight. But now, I think I need to tell the cops what I've done. I can't live with myself any longer."

Silvia sounded riven with guilt.

"It is a crime to lie to a judge and to congress," responds Nika. "And as an attorney, I can't tell you not to go to the police. But with the injunction case and the congressional investigation both over with no harm from either to our group, I'm not sure what would be gained. You have told me the truth, and I really appreciate that."

Nika holds out her hand to shake Silvia's again. Nika also pays attention to her heart and listens for any intuitive information that may emerge. It feels to Nika like Silvia's telling the truth.

"Maybe you could wait and see if anything else comes up. If the PFF comes after us again, you could come forward then. I think they pretty much have backed off. People are not believing them, and their membership continues to fall. They may be done."

"Oh, I hope so," says Silvia, glancing towards the ground and shaking her head. "They're awful people with their anger and lies. They even lie to each other sometimes. And they certainly lied to us. I want nothin' more to do with them."

"I understand, and I'm grateful for your honesty," says Nika. Again, she listens and feels the nudge inside. "I want you to know, Mrs. Stevens, that I understand why you did what you did. I can't speak for the courts or congress. But you would not be the first dishonest witness. Telling me was a brave thing. And I think you and I should just let this go now. I'm willing to let it go. And I encourage you to do the same."

Silvia looks at her, not moving, her mouth gaping open, tears welling up.

"Thank ya, ma'am. Ya really are a fine woman."

"I try to be, as do you. How's your husband doing? Has he been able to find a job? Are you getting by financially these days?" asks Nika.

Silvia looks back at Nika, a bit surprised by her question.

"Well, he got a job at a tire store. And we're gettin' by. But I lost my job, so we're still livin' on the edge. Our fault, I guess, for takin' bad money."

"It's hard when some people have so much and others still are struggling," responds Nika. "Let me ask you another question. How do you feel about my candidacy? Could you be a supporter of mine for the Senate?"

Silvia's head goes back and her eyes widen as she takes another look at Nika.

"Well, yes. That's the other reason I drove nearly three hours to get here. I not only wanted to apologize. I also was excited about what ya are doing now. I loved your speech and would do anythin' to support ya. And I didn't want to wait until you get to Fresno next year to know that."

"Great. I have a temporary full-time position open in my Fresno office to do some organizing, phone calls, and other things. Would you be interested?" asks Nika.

Silvia cocks her head to one side and twists it slightly. "Are you fuckin' kiddin' me right now?"

She puts her hand over her mouth, then removes it slowly.

"Sorry. I didn't mean to say that. I'm just a little taken back by your offer. Yes, of course I'm interested."

"OK, great. It's not executive pay, and we may need you to help get a couple more volunteers, which is why someone who has lived there a while would be extremely useful. It's also just for a little over a year. But it's not easy to find help for the libs in Fresno," laughs Nika. "I'll call the office manager tomorrow and let her know. Could you begin right away?"

"How's eight o'clock in the mornin'? My oldest can watch the other two, and I could have my husband drop me off on his way to work."

"Sounds great. I'll call my manager tonight. When you get there, just ask for Tina. She's great and will be excited to have more help. And we'll see if we can't help you find something after the campaign's over."

"May I give you a hug, Congresswoman Washington?"

"Sure."

Nika reaches out her arms and hugs her new assistant.

"And call me, Nika," she says as she steps back. "Oh, and this is my husband, Naeem," she says as she reaches out her arm to pull him over, "and our son, Hakeem. Naeem, this is our new staff member, Silvia, for the Fresno office. You'll see her again early next year, if not before."

"Nice to meet you, Silvia. Welcome to the team," says Naeem as he extends his arm and shares his wide smile.

Nika looks at Naeem again. "Hey love, do you have any cash on you? I don't have my purse with me."

Naeem pulls out his wallet. "I have sixty bucks." "Great. Give it to Silvia, would you? We can't have a brand new staff member run out of gas on her way home. She might be late to the office."

Nika laughs again as Naeem passes the money to Silvia.

Silvia holds her palm up in the air, starting to push the cash back.

"Take it, Silvia," says Nika. "Call it a small advance. I want you to get home safely. And thanks for coming to talk with me tonight. It feels really good to have the truth between us."

Silvia reaches out to give Nika another hug, then turns and leaves. Nika watches her walk away, content to have sorted out another tangle in her life. Then she turns to see Dri and the family approach her.

"What did you think of the speech, Cate?" asks Nika as the ten-year-old approaches with her family.

"I thought it was wonderful. And people seemed excited by it. Great job, Auntie Nika. So happy for you," responds Cate, as she gives her aunt a hug.

"Thanks, girl. You inspire me; you, Alee, and Hakeem. You keep me awake, knowing we need to do more to create the kind of world I want to leave for you all."

"And that's why your candidacy is so easy to support," says Tiago, squeezing Nika's arm.

"You all driving back tonight or staying in town?" asks Naeem.

"No, we have to get back. We both have work tomorrow," says Dri. "Fabulous speech, Nika. Now I *know* I should have done that vigil with you in high school and had you talk to the audience."

Dri giggles as she finishes, then leans in for her own hug. She follows that with hugs for Naeem and Hakeem.

"OK, we'd better get going."

"Wait. Auntie Nika, I want to show you something. Stand right there," says Cate as she backs up about ten feet from her.

She raises both palms to face Nika to focus her energy towards her aunt. She remains still and silent for a couple of minutes.

"Wow, Cate. That's awesome. You've really learned to do what your mom does with her hands over my heart. You're becoming very powerful at that."

"OK, I want to feel it," says Naeem. He turns toward Cate, then stands still.

Cate rotates her body to face Naeem directly, holding her palms out and remains quiet.

"That's amazing, Cate. How long have you been doing that?" Naeem asks.

"Oh, about four months now. I practice with my folks. Dad's also getting good at it. And Alee, too. I'm surprised at how good he is with it already. Show them, Alee."

Alee stands with his palms out towards Hakeem, then focuses his energy towards the heart.

"Oh, that feels soft and nice," says Hakeem. "Can you teach me that, too?"

"I'm sure we can," responds Cate. "If Alee can do it, anyone can," she says with a laugh.

"OK, kids. We'd better get on the road," says Tiago. "Hug them all goodbye, and let's go."

The two families hug each other member and share their goodbyes. Then Tiago, Dri, and the two kids walk to the car and begin their journey home.

"Mom, I remember a time when I used to be able to do that," shares Alee. "But it was in a very different town, and you and Daddy weren't there. I became very good at that and other ways of helping people. It felt very good, and I was happy to be doing it."

"Oh yeah? What was that town like?" asks Dri.

"You don't remember a different town, silly. We've only lived in Napa all your life," snickers Cate.

"My darling daughter, you may not know what others know," Dri responds. "Do you remember when you told me about my dream, when you talked with me before being born?"

"I remember telling you that and the feeling I had. I kind of remember spending time before coming here. But it's getting kind of foggy."

"Well, you seemed to remember clearly then. Sometimes we get so involved with our life here that we forget early memories. But others may remember. And I'll ask you to respect that possibility, please, as I respected and appreciated your memory when it happened. OK?"

"OK, Mom. Sorry Alee," responds Cate softly.

"Please continue, Alee. Tell me more of what you remember."

"I remember living in a small house. It was a lot smaller than ours now. And made of mud or something. It was like our summer most of the time, only hotter. And it lasted longer."

"Interesting, Alee. Who else was there?" Dir asks.

"There were others there who were reading papers you unwind. They spent a lot of time doing that. I played a lot and was happy. Maybe you were there, Mommy. But you looked different. You had long dark hair, and there was lots of light around your head. Kind of like now, but with more blue rather than purple. And we wore mostly white robes with ties around our waist. And shoes with straps. And I didn't have many toys, but it was still nice there. Everyone was nice to me."

"And what did I do there?"

"You read the papers you unroll and talked with others, especially kids. And we danced while we hit sticks and drums. Then we would sit, like when you put your hand on my heart now. We would sit that way sometimes then too."

Dri looks over at Tiago, who quietly drives. He looks back at her and smiles, then turns back to watch the road.

"And was Daddy or Cate there too?"

"I don't know. Everyone looks different. Maybe. He feels like an older boy I knew then who would tell me fun stories and read from the paper sometimes. About a teacher who was coming. And everyone wanted to be prepared. Everyone was excited he was coming. Maybe soon. It's hard for me to remember everything."

"Well, that's a lot, sweetie. Anything else you remember?"

"No, I don't think so. Is it OK that I remember this, Mommy?" asks Alee.

"Of course, Alee. It's great. Maybe you remember because it relates to your life here in some way. Maybe there is something connecting your memory and what you are doing here. That seems to happen for some people. We don't just live in isolation. It's all connected."

"OK. I'll tell you if I remember anything more."

"That would be great. Your dad and I would love to hear if you think of anything else. Wouldn't we Tiago?"

"Yes, of course. Thanks for telling us about that experience. I love to hear it," adds Tiago.

He drives on in silence, and he considers what his young son just shared with him. He wonders where Alee might have lived before, given his firm belief in reincarnation after long talks about such a possibility with his Gpa. This simply confirms what they discussed many years ago.

Nika continues her campaign efforts through the weekend, then returns to Washington on Monday evening for important votes in Congress that week. She is in her office late Tuesday morning when an assistant informs her that a man wants to see her.

"What's his name?" asks Nika.

"Carl. And he says he knows you."

"Please ask him to wait five minutes while I finish these two emails." Nika takes her time to make sure what she wants to say is clear. Then she sends off the emails and goes to her door. She opens it and invites Carl to come in and sit down.

"It's nice to see you again, Carl. I heard you were released, but I haven't heard anything from you. How are you doing?"

"I'm doin' alright, thanks," he says as he sits in the chair across from her desk.

"Good, I'm glad to hear that," responds Nika as she takes her chair behind the desk.

"I wanted to thank ya personally for ya'lls letter of support. As you said the firs time I saw ya, it did help. The board done let me out on my firs review. One lady on the board sayin' she never herd of a victim writen' a letter like this un. So thank ya, ma'am."

"Of course. I'm glad it helped, because you helped me too."

"Rally? How's that?"

"It was helpful to understand how you came to the point of wanting to kill me. I'm very grateful you didn't, of course. But you helped me see more directly how people struggle and how that affects your views and values. I've seen others struggle, of course. And it hasn't always been easy for me or my family in different ways. But I appreciate seeing the world from your eyes too, your experience and perspective. So, thank you."

"Don't know how that would help ya much, but I did enjoy our conversatuns."

"What are doing now? You living locally? Have you found a job?"

"I'm stayin' with a friend, lookin' for work. But I think I gotta go back to Kentucky. Jus not many jobs there for my kinda skills right naw. But I was wonderin' if you'al had any books on the stuff ya'll been tellin' me?" Carl asks.

"We have a lot of reading materials on our website and a few you could purchase. What interests you most?"

"That thing 'bout the lie we tell ourselves. I kinda wanna know more whether I got one."

"I think most of us do. I have a copy of a book I could give you if you want to take a look at it. But let me ask, what are you doing next Friday through Sunday? Will you be in town?"

"Just lookin' far work. Why?"

"You remember me telling you about my work with two friends, one of whom studied with a man she called Doc?"

"Yeah, he sounded kinda interestin'"

"Doc's daughter and the mother of a good friend of mine is going to be in town teaching a workshop on this information starting Friday. Want to go?"

"How much is it? I don't got a lot a money."

"If you commit to attend the entire weekend, I think I can get you a scholarship, along with a small amount of extra money for food and travel. You interested?"

"Yes, ma'am. I been thinkin' a lot about our talks and how you don't even seem angry at me any more for shooting you. It's hard to get that off my mind. So I gotta find out more about all this stuff. I wanna know. Yeah, I wanna go."

"I really appreciate you talking with me, too, Carl," responds Nika. "You helped me see how you were walking the course that made the most sense to you at the time. The challenge we all have is getting to know other paths, ones that could lead us to more truth, harmony, peace, and love. That's what we're trying to do as a group."

"And I wanna know more about that."

"Great." Nika rolls her chair back, opens a cupboard behind her, and pulls out a book. She turns back to her desk and picks up a brochure. "Here's the book I mentioned. This will give you some reading that will go along with what Gabriela will present in the workshop. Here's a brochure with the address and times of the meetings."

She hands those to Carl as she walks around her desk.

"You hold on to these. I'll be right back."

Nika goes out of her office, then returns in a few minutes with an envelope.

"Here's some money to cover your transportation and meals. I'll call the registrar to arrange for the scholarship. Then I'd love to talk again after the workshop to see what you think. But I'm kind of in and out of town with a big campaign going on in California. Here's my assistant's card. Call her to make sure I'll be around when you are available to discuss this. OK?"

"What if I don't show up and jus keep the book and money?" asks Carl with a snicker.

"Then I made a bad bet," responds Nika, looking deeply into Carl's eyes. "But I don't think I have, Carl. Do you?"

"No, ma'am. You haven't. And thanks. See ya after the workshop some time," says Carl as he shakes her hand, turns and leaves her office.

***

Nika spends much of her time until the election on November 6th of the following year in California, working on her campaign. She visits every one of the 58 counties in the state. Concern with climate change continues to intensify in coastal and rural areas. Yet, much of her time is in the Bay Area and especially in Southern California where her name lacks recognition. Her opponent is a strong more conservative Democrat and well known in the South. But as the candidate of the Progressive Party that burgeons in the metropolitan areas, Nika's hope grows. Her development of a national reputation also helps increase financial support. These other factors give her the edge for a competitive race, and she still enjoys good, clean, competition.

On the evening of the election, people gather in the main ballroom at the Waterfront Hotel in downtown Oakland to cheer a win if Nika comes out on top. Nika and her family are in a room upstairs, with Beverley, Tyrell, and Denzel. Dri and her family along with Bella and Omar spend time with them watching results come in, district by district. Currently, her opponent is doing better in some of the rural voting areas, where results report sooner. But populated counties around the Bay Area and Los Angeles could help considerably.

Dustin, Nika's campaign manager, is in the ballroom, texting reports of how people are reacting. It gets quiet when districts come in for her opponent, with loud cheers as other rural districts weigh in for Nika. It's a good sign that she is holding her own in some of the more rural coastal districts. When San Diego county, her opponent's home city, comes in for him, concern spreads in the crowd and upstairs. The result is somewhat expected, yet disappointing. When Orange County follows suit, again there is not a lot of surprise. But Nika's deficit grows, as does anxiety in the crowd. Finally, three Los Angeles districts come in for Nika, none for her opponent. There is some sigh of relief, but the election is not yet over.

Late into the evening, Nika starts getting additional results from Northern California. Napa County votes go in her favor, followed by Marin and eventually Sonoma County. Solano County swings to her opponent, as does San Joaquin, Stanislaus, and Merced. But when Fresno County ends up in Nika's column, she finds new hope.

Thank you, Rachel and Silvia! I will be taking you two and your staff out to dinner, for sure!

Finally, Contra Costa, Alameda, Santa Cruz, San Mateo, and San Francisco all end up going for the next Senator of California, Tanika Washington. People begin clapping and jumping, upstairs and downstairs. After cheers and hugs all around, Nika sits down with Harper to go over her acceptance speech. Dustin announces that she will be down shortly to say a few words, and the crowd gets excited again. Once Nika is ready, all follow her out and take the elevators down to share in the joy of her victory.

Nika thanks Greg and all on her campaign who made this happen, in offices through-out the state. She recognizes the many volunteers who registered new voters, knocked on doors, made phone calls, and encouraged friends and neighbors to take a chance on this woman. Next, she expresses gratitude to her families, close friends, and all who endorsed her, encouraged her to run, and supported her efforts. She thanks her opponent, who ran a clean and strong race, and knows there will be plenty for both of them to do in working towards a brighter future. Finally, she thanks all those present and those who voted for her, making this possible. At the same time, she commits to represent, to the best of her ability, those in the state who also supported her opponent. She will work for them in the same way she knows her opponent would have worked for her supporters if he had won. And that's the way elections in this democracy need to work, for she and Senator Cortez represent all the constituents in their state as they go to Washington to address the challenges of this nation and the world.

Nika closed her remarks with two quotes by former President Obama. "He said in a 2008 campaign speech, 'Change will not come if we wait for some other person or if we wait for some other time. We are the ones we've been waiting for. We are the change that we seek.' He inspired many people, including me.

"In his farewell address, he stated that 'The long sweep of America has been defined by forward motion, a constant widening of our founding creed to embrace all and not just some.' I want to continue that vision, and I invite all of you to join me in that effort. For this is the continuation of Dr. King vision as well as so many other leaders of this great nation. This is our work. This is a vision that can be shared by all."

Chapter 26
Reaching Farther
August, 2043

A n empty seat invites Dri to sit next to Gabriela as the extended family flies towards Guatemala City. Cate, now 14, is excited about her first flight and loves looking at the sights below. Tiago keeps her company, pointing out towns and hills as they begin to pass over the stunning Sierra Nevada Mountains and later the Southwest. Dri leaves these two with their Daddy-daughter connection time. Meanwhile, Alee, nearly eight-years-old, remains in Napa to play with Bella and Omar for ten days.

"Mind a conversation while Miguel naps?" asks Dri, as she slips into the aisle seat next to her mother-in-law.

"No, that would be lovely," responds Gabriela, turning to share an inviting smile with Dri.

"I was wondering how many times you've been back to your dad's birth place?"

"Just once, when I was a little younger than Cate. Dad took me back as his father was nearing death. He wanted to say goodbye and care for his mother when he passed. Mom wanted to go. But I wasn't old enough to take care of the two young ones, and they didn't have any family nearby to help. Dad took me instead so I could meet them once, at least."

"How was that trip for you?"

"It was great and sad too," replies Gabby, her family nickname. "I loved meeting them. But it was a time of grief, also. Grandmother was pleased to meet me, happy to get to know me better. She also told me that she sensed quite a bit of Dad's loving energy in me. She never called me a Cib, though, like she did Dad. But she also was pretty focused on my grandfather at the time, who was in and out of consciousness by then. Grandfather did recognize Dad, which was lovely. And he seemed to understand that I was his oldest. He told me a couple of fun stories about my dad playing at the pond near their house and how great he was at soccer. I didn't know that until then. Dad never said much about playing, although he loved to watch games on TV once in a while."

"Were you there when your grandfather passed?" Dri asks.

"Yes, we stayed for his transition, then the funeral and burial. After that, Dad had to get back to his work, and I needed to return for school. She was pretty sad when we left, and that ended up being the last time Dad saw his mother. He went back for her funeral. By then, Mom got help with us, and she went with him. That was lovely. And I haven't been back since that first visit."

"Tiago mentioned that he's never been there to see the old home and where Doc grew up. He seems excited about that," says Dri.

"I'm glad we get to do this as a family. I'm pleased the three of you will see where my father was born and the neighborhood. I'm sorry Javier couldn't come. And Miguel has never been to Guatemala either. We might even go into the little neighborhood church where the funerals were held for my grandparents and where they are buried."

"It didn't seem like your dad was into the Catholic faith much when I knew him. Was he ever? Or did I just not pick up on that with him?" Dri asks.

"No, he only went to church for funerals or weddings," responds Gabby. "He was much more interested in the Christian Gnostics or people who would discuss spiritual ideas from the near-death research. He felt like the Christian Churches were too focused on sin, hell, money, and control. He became more focused on unconditional love and on an inner connection with the Divine rather than having to rely on an external link through men and church structures. I think he got some of that from his mother."

"Yeah, that's the sense I got. He seemed more focused on spirituality, although we never talked about it," remarks Dri. "We did talk about his intense interest in the near-death research and how the experience had such a profound impact on people's lives afterwards. I also became fascinated with the reports about us being love rather than simply sharing love as an emotion."

"Excuse me, ma'am. Would you like something to drink?" asks the flight attendant. They order water and orange juice, then open their packages of salty nuts given out to the passengers.

"In his later years, he began reading about people who reported on previous lives and the insights from that experience. Do you believe in reincarnation, Dri?" Gabby asks.

"Yeah, I do. The readings about near-death experiences pretty consistently report that it's true. And I, too, have begun reading about children who report past lives, ever since Alee shared his experience with us."

"Yes, that was pretty exciting to hear. I talked to him about it later. But he couldn't remember much more. I continue to wonder where it was and what might be important about that life. But have you read about those who report past lives at the time of Jesus and Mary Magdalene? Dad found those fascinating, especially her gospel and her greater focus on energies and unconditional love."

"No, I haven't. Are they interesting?"

"I think so. I have a few books on it at home, if you would like to read them. I'm really drawn to that period. Someday I think I'll try experiencing a regression, see what happens."

"Wow, that would be fascinating," responds Dri.

"Yes, I want to know if I had any experience with the Essenes, or Mary. Or their time in France after the crucifixion. I've been drawn to that period and fascinated by alternative explanations of what happened then. I gave a book to Nika's mom when she was here last, as she expressed an interest in it, too. It's also interesting to read about how people incarnate sometimes with others they know, possibly even several lives. Makes me wonder if you and I were ever together before this life. It certainly feels like a possibility to me. Maybe even at that time."

"You think that's possible? I certainly felt at ease with you the first time I met you. But I figured that was because I cared about your dad so much," says Dri.

"It would be fun to explore. It feels to me like you have some energetics from that era. You took to Dad's work like no one he has ever seen before. And you seem like a natural with your focus on a core connection, unconditional love, and interconnection of us all. Apparently, that was the main teaching that Mary focused on, especially after getting away from the dominant male disciples."

"Huh, I didn't know that. I'd be interested in finding out myself. This gives me a whole new area to explore. How fun."

They talk for a while longer about their connection and the ease both experience with each other and that time period.

The flight attendant comes by again, picking up glasses and asking them to put up their tables and put away their personal items. They will be landing in Dallas soon.

"Thanks for the great conversation. I think I'll check on the other two. But I would love to continue this sometime and borrow those books you mentioned."

Dri moves back to her seat and takes Tiago's hand as the plane descends for landing. They quietly discuss his time with Cate as they flew across the country. She loved looking at the manicured fields and tiny towns appearing to have toy cars and trucks moving around the miniature streets.

The travelers get an hour and a half layover in Dallas, enough time to get a late lunch. They walk to the boarding area for their next flight, then find a place nearby to relax and get some food.

The airport is noisy with people moving in many different directions, while the extended family enjoys a bit more room for a short time. They finish lunch and return to board, find their seats and ready themselves for the second leg of their journey. There is quiet discussion and some napping during their flight to a new land for most of them.

Upon arrival, they slowly work their way to the cab stand, then off to the hotel Gabby and Tiago picked out near her father's childhood home. Dri has been practicing her Spanish, and even Cate knows some basics, allowing them to feel more at home in this busy city. In the evening, they get some dinner, wander the local area, then retire.

The next day, the family visits Doc's family home and the little church just down the street. They find the grave sites of his parents and place fresh flowers while Gabby shares more about her experience with them. They discover fun shops in the neighborhood, get some lunch, then spend the afternoon at the enormous central city market. The following day is spent on a bus tour of the city, with stops to dig deeper into the Metropolitan Cathedral and the National Palace of Culture. Following Gabby's strong interest, they visit the Ixchel Native Costume Museum, which holds many Mayan textiles and other artifacts.

Friday morning, they change hotels, moving to the location of the First Enneagram Shareshop to be held in Guatemala. After settling into their rooms, Miguel and Cate take a bus to Antigua, spending the day exploring that city and area, while Dri and Tiago review the timing of their contributions with Gabby. Then these three visit the meeting room to check on the set-up and place a vase of fresh flowers, including some monja blanca, the national flower of Guatemala. As they put final touches for an inviting ambiance, Nika and Alisa enter the room.

"Welcome to Guatemala," says Gabby as she walks over to extend a welcoming hug to both women. "How was your flight?"

"It was uneventful, so good," chuckles Nika. "How was your visit to Doc's old home?"

"It was delightful, very fun to see some 60 years later," responds Gabby.

"Great to have you both here, and lovely to see you cuz," says Dri as she gives Alisa, Emma and Phil's daughter, a hug. "How did the meetings go in Mexico City?"

"They went well, thanks," remarks Nika. "Met some great people excited to expand what we're doing, had lots of questions, and they look forward to the shareshops there."

"I'm looking forward to going there in October. Just sorry Tiago won't be able to go this time. But Mom and Omar will come with me. Omar's Spanish will be crucial," laughs Dri.

The group goes to the hotel restaurant, finds some lunch, then returns to the room ready to greet the guests. They begin to show up as Dri and the others appear. They sign people in just to keep a record of who attends. A list may help to identify local teachers as interest increases.

After the 78 attendees are settled, Gabby begins her introduction. In contrast to the shareshop for the board, the group was asked to do some preparatory reading from the Spanish Enneagram books Fadima sent down beforehand.

This afternoon, Gabby reviews the first four types of the Enneagram: nine, eight, one, and three. On Saturday morning and into the afternoon, she goes over the other five types, with some questions as they go. Dri practices her Spanish as she explains Type One. Later, Tiago helps with reviews of types five, six, and seven. Having grown up bilingual, his Spanish is strong, although he needs a word from Gabby once in a while.

Following the final review of types, attendees move chairs into nine circles, according to the number of the Enneatype they believe is theirs. Dri and Alisa place card holders in the middle of the circles for people to identify which type the group represents. Then the group discusses the challenges and some of the humorous aspects of that Enneatype. If people don't feel like that type fits them as the discussion proceeds, they try a group focused on a different one. When people struggle knowing which type they might be, Tiago and Dri, with Alisa helping Dri's Spanish, assist the attendee explore what type may best fit them.

On Sunday, the nine groups form again. This time, the attendees discuss the value of learning and ways to manifest the primary lesson for that type. Gabby, Tiago, and Dri, dragging Alisa with her, spend time with different groups to suggest ideas or other ways of incorporating the primary lesson into their lives.

After lunch, each group provides a short oral report of their distortion and lie chal-lenges, followed by the advantages of living from the primary lesson. In this way, others learn more about the eight types where they have not participated in the discussion. Finally, people organize into local discussion groups to continue the dialogue and learning after the shareshop ends.

Just before the gathering is dismissed, those attending provide feedback to the fa-cilitators, sharing what they liked and what worked for them. They also shared a few important suggestions for change. One of the changes they wanted was a revision to the questions in the book that helped them identify a possible Enneatype. The suggestions are valuable, and Gabby promises they will be incorporated. Overall, people were grateful for the gathering.

After the final attendee leaves, the five leaders find a table at the restaurant to have their own debriefing discussion during dinner.

"What do you think went well?" asks Gabby after the group settles.

"I think the discussion groups went quite well," responds Tiago. "They got into useful conversations, bringing up important challenges and gifts, with some help from us."

"I liked the way that went, too," adds Dri. "I think it was a great idea, especially for more social participants. And it made them think about it more than just hearing from others."

"Yeah, I think the groups were useful as well," responds Gabby. "I also liked their suggestions for modifying the online questions and changes in how we initially present some of the types. They seemed to get a lot out of it, and I think it will help if they continue their discussions with other attendees. It may motivate people to continue working towards change."

They talked more about how they enjoyed teaching and interacting with this group and each other. The dialogue veers off into more diverse topics, including how people are doing, given they have not seen each other for some time. Others are happy to get to know Alisa, who was recently hired as Nika's half time Latin American assistant and new half-time teacher for The Coalition. Her 20 years working for the US State Department in Latin American gave her useful experience to advise Nika and fluency in Spanish, also a great contribution.

Cate and Miguel spend Saturday at *Pacaya*, a little over an hour bus ride from the city. They hire a guide and prefer a shorter hike than other mountains while still getting a memorable view of an active volcano and the surrounding area. Cate could talk about little else that night in her hotel room.

"It was fun to do with Grandpa. And the volcano was amazing! A few people were roasting marshmallows from the heat. But it didn't look that appetizing to me," laughs Cate.

On Sunday morning, Cate and Miguel leave for the airport to return home while the others complete the shareshop. The following morning, the five leaders travel to the airport to catch a flight to Panama City, their next stop on this Latin America tour.

Dri and Alisa sit next to each other so they can catch up on their lives the past few years. Gabby sits between Nika, who loves to look out the window, and Tiago, who wants the aisle seat this flight.

"How are you enjoying your work in the Senate, Nika? Must be pretty exciting," says Gabby after the plane levels off and the sound diminishes.

"Yes, it is in many ways, and challenging at the same time," responds Nika. "As a junior Senator, of course, I have less influence. But with the Progressives now controlling the Senate and White House, I'm more active than I otherwise would be. And this trip allows me to get to know some of our Latin allies and a better sense of cultural differences, which are important."

"How is Alisa working out as your assistant?"

"She's a gem. Her work with the State Department and knowledge of key players in different Latin American countries is invaluable. I was just lucky she wanted to do something different and desired experience in the legislative branch."

"How did you two connect?" Gabby asks.

"Bella was talking with her last time she was visiting her Mom and Dad, Bella's sister and her husband. When she expressed an interest in working for a congress member or senator, she suggested Alisa contact me. Bella thought I might know someone looking for an aide. Sure enough, I did know someone - me," laughs Nika.

"What great timing. Glad it worked out for you both."

"I couldn't be happier," remarks Nika with a smile. "And it's great to know her family already. Yet we're not related. So that doesn't cause any problems in hiring her."

"She seems strong, and her Spanish is excellent," responds Gabby. "She even speaks with almost no accent. She must have started early with it."

"I think she did, given the large number of Hispanics in Napa Valley. She speaks some Italian too, because of the other side of her family. But she's most fluent in Spanish now."

"And what do you think of The Coalition offering more shareshops outside the US?" inquires Gabby.

"I'm happy about it. I think it will increase people's understanding of key Coalition ideas and may increase excitement, too. Thanks for doing the shareshop in Guatemala. I'm not sure I told you this, but it was excellent. And I was happy to sit through it again and assist where I could. I still find it useful not to get caught up as much in my lie and distortions. Still not living from my heart all the time or manifesting my higher lesson. But I keep at it. Isn't that about all we can do?"

"Yes, that usually gives us plenty of personal work to do. I've been working with it for decades now, and there still are times I stumble. It's all part of learning and re-choosing our priorities every day," says Gabby with an accepting smile that shines through her eyes.

"Speaking of work, my mom said to thank you for the books you gave her a couple of years ago on people who reported working with Mary Magdalene in previous lives. It took her a while to feel comfortable with the possibility. But the more she read, in those and other books, the more it felt accurate. She especially liked the four different types of children that have been born over the last few decades. I think it was from the Power of the Magdalene book. She's been seeing greater differences the past several years in her school, and the descriptions helped. Even my dad has noticed that kids have become less competitive, which is not so great as a football coach. After he read the books, that made more sense to him, too. Mom said she'd get them back to you soon," says Nika.

"No need. Those were gifts, and I have more copies. I think Dri wants to read them when we get back. It would make for an interesting discussion some time," adds Gabby.

"Yeah, it sure would."

They continue their conversation about Nika's parents being retired and enjoying it. With Bella, Gabby, and Miguel also retired, Gabriella talks about enjoying more time with family and doing primarily what she loves. Omar is mostly retired, but Gabby doesn't notice, given that he still spends much of his time writing, now working on his fourth novel. With the other three already published, his agent anxiously awaits the next manuscript, which keeps the pressure on him. But so far, he finds great joy in his efforts to paint pictures with his words.

The plane lands in Panama City on time, and the group members find their bags, get through security, and take a taxi to the hotel. They settle in, have some lunch, then survey the rooms for the gatherings tonight and tomorrow evening.

Gabby and Dri will discuss ideas and do some role play from the Family Guidebook in one room, while Tiago and Nika will work on concepts and exercises from the Growing Through Differences Guidebook in the other. Alisa will spend this evening in the family meeting, then sit in on the other gathering tomorrow night, when the same two shareshops are presented to another group of locals.

A few items get adjusted in each room, as everyone has their own preference for arrangements. The group wanders in the neighborhood the remainder of the afternoon, in and out of interesting stores. They also find a fun restaurant for dinner before returning to the hotel for the shareshops.

The two evening gatherings go well, with about 40 people in attendance with each one.

The following day, the group goes to an environmental restoration project people have been working on for several years now near the town of Veracruz on Panama Bay. They hired a driver to take them to the site to see what the group has been doing with their desalination efforts, providing fresh water for the neighboring villages and salt to sell, helping to cover their investments. After encouraging their efforts and gratified by the work, their driver takes them to the Panama Canal, a must see when people visit for the first time.

The next two days the group spends in Lima, Peru, with a similar schedule of shareshops both evenings, seeing some sites the first afternoon and another environmental project to provide reclaimed water for crops from the nearby sewage treatment plant.

The final two days of their journey take them to Buenos Aires, Argentina, with a similar schedule. Due to a later departure and longer flight from Lima, there is little time for sightseeing Friday afternoon. But they do get to see a couple of sights the following day after looking at a local attempt to decrease rapid algae bloom in the Turbidity Front near the city.

Tiago finds a lovely place for a celebratory dinner Saturday afternoon, prior to the final shareshops. They fly home the next morning, Nika and Alisa to DC, the others to San Francisco. As they chat, Dri asks Nika how Carl is doing with his teaching.

"I understand it's going well," responds Nika. "He enjoys sharing the Growing Through Differences ideas with prisoners in the DC and Maryland area. I think Fadima was concerned in the beginning about hiring him to teach. But we're getting great feedback from the wardens, who are surprised the inmates find it interesting. Change isn't quick with that population, but many seem to be trying. I guess they find it complementary to the AA meetings they hold there. And these are not the worst offenders, which helps. But Carl seems to enjoy it. And I'm grateful he suggested the idea."

"He continues to email me with questions about his lie and Enneatype, too," Gabby adds. "I think he learned quite a bit from the workshop, although he didn't contribute much in the discussions. But he seemed to be taking it in, which is more important. And I'm happy to keep responding. He's an interesting guy."

"He's emailed me a couple times about questions from the Differences Shareshops he took with me," adds Tiago. "Great questions and open to suggestions. It would be interesting to go with him sometime and observe how it's going next time I'm in DC."

"He seems happy to have the job," says Nika. "But even more, I think he feels like he's doing something important. Something of value. That adds to his commitment. And he seems to like the DC area. More interesting than going back to his hometown."

"That's great," says Dri. "I'm impressed how you touched him and influenced his life, Nika. Not many would bother with him."

"He helped me, and I helped him," responds Nika. "It was a mutual thing. It just took a while to see what he was like underneath his defenses. How he just wanted to connect, to have someone care about him. Now he's caring about others. Isn't that what it's about?"

"Yes, it is," adds Gabby. "But most people don't look beneath the surface. Don't go deep enough to see what's hidden. You young people learned that much earlier than most, and I applaud you for that."

"Your father helped with that, for all of us," says Dri. "Doc was a caring man who had a gift for opening hearts and inviting them to be filled with what's inside all of us. And I'm grateful to have his wise daughter and loving grandson so intimately involved in my life, to keep reminding me when I let go. And dear friends to reflect back their developing wisdom when I'm in doubt. While I struggle, some days more than others, I can't tell you how wonderful it is to have a community that nudges me when I need it, pulls me back or pushes me forward when I get stuck. So grateful to you all. And thrilled to have my favorite cousin joining us on this journey."

"Happy to get to know all of you and learn so much from your work," says Alisa. "But I would like to offer one other thought. From my work in Central America, I came to greatly respect the indigenous people there. Given your work with the Native Americans in California and Washington, I wonder if it wouldn't be useful, even important to gather representatives, voices and energies from First Nations across the planet, and where possible integrate them into the work the Coalition is doing."

"I love that idea," responds Gabby. "When I visited the Tewa Pueblo in Pojoaque, New Mexico, I was deeply touched by their vision and objectives written on one wall of the Poeh Cultural Center. I wrote them down so I would remember them."

She pulls out her little notebook and rummages through the pages.

"Here it is," Gabby announces. "'Their vision is to make life beautiful by bringing harmony into their lives.' I thought that was lovely. But their objectives touched my soul."

She read the following:

1.   Acknowledging the respectful awareness of the place, people and circumstances is necessary to being in harmony. Being is the process, the manner in which anything is done.

2.   Teaching that life and creativity are inseparable. Doing is part of the life path, the creating and expressing of one's soul is essential to harmony within one's social context.

3.   Living people find meaning in relationships between themselves and others. Reciprocal love and caring are important, as each person becomes a part of the whole.

"That's beautiful," responds Dri. "I see why it would touch you so deeply."

"I'm not suggesting we adopt those word for word," adds Gabby. "But I think we could learn a lot from First Nation people from all over the world, often with similar perspectives and desires."

"Yes, that's basically what I had in mind as well," chimes in Alisa. "At least begin to research and interact with these groups and see where there may be a wonderful connection and fit with what you want to do."

"You mean what *we* want to do?" chuckles Dri.

Alisa laughs out loud. "Yes, that's what I meant to say."

"Thanks for the suggestion, Alisa and Gabby," adds Dri. "I love the idea. I think we do need to make it a more prominent part of our path and group."

"Well, Dri, don't know if we'd be doing all this if you hadn't made such an outlandish commitment to change at Alex's memorial," adds Nika. "It stimulated responses in enough others that we could develop a foundation for this work."

"Under your wonderful leadership and those of the other board members," responds Dri.

"It's been an interesting journey, that's for sure," adds Tiago. "Glad we did it and continue as we have this past week and a half. I'm thrilled with the responses we've had from Guatemala to Argentina. What a fabulous week, getting to know members in four different countries, who take to these ideas rather effortlessly in many ways. It's been great to see it spread."

"Yes, it is, sweetheart," says Dri. "Glad we all could come do this. On a different topic, Nika, how's Soph doing with her training in energy healing? She still pretty excited about it?"

"Yes, she is," replies Nika. "I think she would like to add some ideas to our website and eventually do some training herself. She's becoming very accomplished, and there's some serious demand for her work."

"Cate's pretty excited about it, too," adds Dri. "She's talked with her a few times, and now wants to go to college in the DC area so she can work with Soph on the side."

"That would be great," responds Nika. "I'd love to have her close by."

"And it could get us out there more frequently, as well," chuckles Tiago. "But coast to coast presents a serious challenge to move a student."

"And Mom thought Iowa City to Davis was a long drive," laughs Dri.

"I hate to break up this lovely conversation," says Gabby. "But we have to get back for the shareshops then get to bed. We have an early flight to catch."

They continue the conversation as they pay the bill and walk back to the hotel. The final gatherings go well, bringing on relief and a wisp of sadness at leaving. It has been an exciting trip for Dri, having never visited these cities. Yet she misses Alee and Cate, ready to return home for a more local adventure with her family.

Chapter 27
Unsettling Trends
Spring, 2048

T he vines begin to bud, the grass and weeds turn a rich green, and the Golden State of August transforms into the Jade State by February and March. Even when the hills revert to dry, golden summer tops, the metamorphosis of color in Spring can't help but impact one's mood. Dri passes through the fragrance of apple blossoms, then on to peach and honey suckle as she walks by another house on Hagen, doing her regular six mile walking route. She passes homes with fresh flower fragrance and green shrubs, followed by fence lines protecting rows of budding vineyard promise on First Avenue, some also filled with bright yellow mustard. Later, she listens to the cemetery silence competing with bird chirping.

As she rounds the corner onto East Street, Dri misses Cate. Home from Berkeley for a birthday weekend, she already has returned, taking her university studies so seriously. For Dri, college was work too, along with tennis. But she depended on Alex and friends to break up a day and integrate light-hearted pleasure into a busy life. She worries that her daughter enjoys less fun this first year away. Cate was a great walking companion too, with conversations and laughter to take Dri's mind off the miles. Today is sunny, fresh, and a light jacket walk, even tying it around her waist by mile four. Still, company helps make the trek up the First Avenue hill easier. And it's a longer six miles without her daughter, especially as Dri's fifth decade is staring her in the face.

Reaching her driveway, Dri hears Nika's ring on her phone. She chuckles at how well her dear friend knows her after all these years.

"Great timing. I just completed my walk," says Dri playfully.

"Oh good. I was trying to guess it right and had difficulty waiting," responds Nika.

"How are you? DC cold this week, or are the cherry blossoms coming early?" asks Dri.

"No, it's cold as hell, and my anxiety doesn't help warm me up," says Nika.

"What's going on? I thought life was going pretty well these days. You don't have another re-election for four years, and you got your last bill through the Senate."

"No, it's not that. I . . . . I mean we have an invitation for a meeting six weeks from now in Sacramento. You, Tiago, Omar and Bella are all invited. Lucky us!" Adds Nika, not a hint of humor in her voice, a very uncommon occurrence.

"What meeting? I haven't received any invitations?"

"No, nothing official yet. I just got off a call from the Commerce Secretary, Kati Lavigne. She and a few other guests would like to talk with us about what we're doing with The Coalition that impacts consumers."

"Are we in some kind of trouble? Is this another investigation?" Dri notices her throat tighten as she asks the questions.

"No, nothing official. It's just a conversation for now. Apparently, it has come to the attention of the Commerce and Agriculture Secretaries that there are downward trends in consumption of goods and produce that have been noticed in segments of the population where there's a large portion of Coalition members. Like the Bay Area, Seattle, and Las Vegas. I guess it's even beginning to influence Chicago and New York to some degree."

"Wow, I had no idea. Guess that's something we haven't been tracking within the organization. Who else is going to be there?"

"I guess the governor of California, who is hosting, along with the governors of Washington and Nevada. There may be others, but those are the main ones. Oh, and Fadima is going to be asked to join us as executive director of The Coalition," adds Nika.

"And when's the meeting?"

"Tuesday, April 21st at 10:00 am at the Governor's office. They're hoping we can all make it. They want the key people in the development and expansion of the organization. The Secretary wants to know if we're teaching anything that would undermine the economy."

"Interesting. I had no idea this was happening, did you?" asks Dri.

"No, not until the call a little while ago. I guess they've been tracking the decline the past couple of years, especially as it has gotten steeper. And it's the only thing that correlates with the decrease, according to their data analysis."

"That's weird. It always made me nervous when people would take us to court or begin a congressional investigation," responds Dri. "But at least then, I knew what we were doing that pissed them off, or at least what they perceived was wrong. This one, I don't get. I'm anxious about being with those officials. But I feel pretty calm about what we've been doing."

"You'll be receiving an invitation letter from Secretary Lavigne's office sometime later this week. She'll want you to let her know if you'll be there. As board chair and board treasurer, I'm hoping Bella and Omar will make it and you, too. That's why I'm calling to let you know now. I'll contact Fadima next so she can arrange her schedule. I thought it might be good to pass along a couple of local member names. They could talk with state people about their experience with our organization."

"That's a good idea and probably an important gesture on our part," responds Dri.

"I suggested it to Kati, and she was going to check with others. At least we might get a few names ready just in case. Maybe Fadima could do that from her office. I'll talk to her about names from each of the three states, in case governors want to follow up. But would you let Bella, Omar and Tiago know? Have them save the dates, anyway, please?"

Nika's voice now sounds strained to Dri. The more she talks, the tighter it becomes.

"Yes, of course. I'll call them both right now. Tiago's at school. But Mom and Omar should be available. If not, they'll call me right back. Anything else I can do to help?"

"I can't think of anything at the moment. I'll be out in Oakland later this month. I'll check my schedule. We should figure out a time to talk and put together what we think they're going to discuss. I don't like being unprepared. I want to anticipate what they might ask us," says Nika.

"Yeah, that sounds good. Maybe a weekend? Tiago has baseball practice with his boys after school, so he gets home kind of late."

"OK, we can work that out. I'll let you know as soon as we can figure out good times. Talk to you soon."

"OK, thanks. And keep breathing, my friend. You sound a little tense."

"Oh yeah, that would help," chuckles Nika. "OK, love you, my dear."

"Love you, too. Always nice to talk with you, even under these circumstances."

Dri leaves a message when Tiago doesn't answer, to call when he's available. Then she reaches her mom to give her the news. Bella tells her she will discuss it with Omar.

As board chair, Bella also gets anxious about what could happen to the organization. Dri tries to reassure her that it's an inquiry, a curiosity about what's going on with the group members, rather than an investigation or court trial. Bella takes a deep breath. Yet, her nervous energy continues to run rampant. She will save the date and, as much as she doesn't want to, she'll be there along with Omar.

For the next 40 days, the core group attending the meeting spends time in research, conversation, trying to second guess what might be sought by the federal and state leaders. Fadima makes arrangements with three members in each state to talk with these investigators if further information gathering is desired. At the same time, Bella and Fadima think about ways to present the basic tenets of the group, while Dri and Tiago prepare to talk about the guidebooks.

Nika talks with Victoria about possibly attending. But the focus doesn't seem to be on the reclamation projects. She tells Nika she'd be happy to show Governor Wang of Washington what they have been doing there, although she's pretty sure he knows about the projects in his state.

Nika and Fadima fly in from Washington and New York City the night before. They get a taxi to the Hyatt, where they have rooms, across the street from the Capitol grounds. Gabriela and Miguel drive to Sacramento the previous day, to avoid Bay Area traffic on a Tuesday morning. The Napa group, including Alee, get rooms at the same hotel, avoiding traffic and allowing for a final consult meeting the next morning at the Hotel's Vine Cafe.

On that Tuesday morning, after their final strategy breakfast, they walk over to the Capitol in search of the meeting room. Miguel and Alee depart from the group for their own tour of the Capitol, an exploration of the Crocker Art Museum, and a stroll along the river waterfront.

The meeting room is easy to find and the group gets there early. Slowly, people begin to enter and find seats. Bella, Fadima and Nika sit in the middle of the long conference table, as Secretary Lavigne takes a seat directly across from Fadima. The governors sit on each side of her. There also are four staff members sitting behind them. Omar takes a chair to the left of Bella, grabbing her hand as he settles himself. Dri and Tiago next to Nika, his hand on his wife's knee. Gabby takes a seat on the other side of Tiago, clutching his arm as she takes a deep breath.

"Thank you for taking the time to be here and talk with us about your group today," begins Secretary Lavigne. "I'm Commerce Secretary Kati Lavigne. Some of you know Governor Angelina Lopez of California, sitting on my left. I know you do, Nika, and probably most others as well. This is Governor Cameron Thomas of Nevada sitting on Angi's left, and Governor Mark Wang, on my right, from the state of Washington. And we each have a staff member simply taking notes for us. Nika, since I started the invitation with someone I know and trust, would you mind introducing your fine group of leaders?"

Nika introduces the Coalition members and identifies their role in the development of the organization and on the board. She looks at and shares a smile with each one as she talks about them. Finally, she introduces herself as a Senator from California, one of the founding members of the group, and the first board chair.

"What we would like to talk about is a trend we've noticed in three states where purchasing has been declining in the areas of home repairs and accessories, clothes, food, and other goods. As we began to investigate what is going on in these areas, we came across some incidental data that may be related. But we didn't have enough or accurate information to determine whether it was relevant.

"We contacted Nika, knowing she has been closely associated with your Coalition, who helped us get some aggregate information about the number of Coalition members in these three states. And thank you again, Fadima, for providing those data. They were helpful. When we looked deeper, we found a relationship between Coalition size and a decline in consumption around homes repair matieials and home goods, clothing, and even food. When we scoured your website, we couldn't see anything that would be related to such a change in buying patterns. Given that about seventy percent of our economy is based on population consumption, we wondered if there is something else you are teaching or encouraging your members to consume less? Is there anything you are doing to discourage consumption of home goods and food?"

"I'll start," begins Dri. "As one of the founding members, we have been concerned with people learning to live from their hearts, help teach that to their children, care for others as much as themselves, and learn to connect to the love that is at our core. We had hoped that would impact them learning to grow and learn more about themselves from differences and solve problems from their heart instead of a pistol or an AK47.

"After the death of my brother, who was killed at the Las Vegas Concert shooting nearly 20 years ago, many of us, including Bella, my mom, Tiago my husband, and Nika, my best friend, wanted to have an impact on violence. We cared about economic and social injustice. We cared at the time about not bringing more children into a violent world. We were concerned with what still was happening to the Earth and wanted to see greater financial equity between highest and lowest earners in a company. But there has never been an emphasis on reducing consumption as one of our objectives."

"I'm very sorry about your brother, Dri, and your son, Bella," responds Kati." That's always a deep tragedy; one parents and siblings should never have to experience. And I applaud your efforts to change the hearts and interactions of people. If I weren't so busy, I would look into participating myself." Kati smiles at Nika and takes a breath. "But I still don't see how that would impact the decline we are noticing in these three states that seems related to group membership size. Is there nothing you have been discussing or teaching that would discourage people from consuming goods and services? Even food seems to be affected. We're not accusing you of anything. We just want to understand what's going on and how we might modify such a change across these states."

"I may have a little insight into the issue, if I may Madam Secretary," says Fadima.

"Yes, please Fadima. What do you think is going on with these trends?"

"Since you sent us this lovely invitation, we all have been putting our heads together, trying to see if there is anything we have done to impact this trend. We've talked among ourselves, and I've also been talking with our staff in the office. We don't think there is anything we have done to intentionally change such behavior. But there may be some unintended consequences that have taken place that could be related, especially with over 42 million members worldwide."

"I appreciate your candor with this," responds Governor Lopez. "Please, continue."

"To begin, I'd like to share a little context. When I was a little girl living in Lebanon, we were going through great turmoil. There was a civil war as well as conflict with Israel and forces loyal to Iran and the Shia'i branch of Islam. With all the chaos and destruction, people ended up helping wherever they could. There were few resources to purchase and limited professionals to assist. We just did what we had to do. Even sometimes Muslims and Christians helping each other or Sunni's helping Shia'i Muslims who were badly harmed. It does something to one's heart when people see such tragedy all around them.

"As Dri mentioned, we wanted to help people open their hearts and live from un-conditional love, be more selfless, care for others and the Earth. As my staff and I have talked with members during the past few weeks, it seems like they have become much less concerned about what they wear, having the biggest and best looking homes, having the prettiest furniture or newest soft mattress. They care more about eating healthy food and helping others access by sharing food and goods or giving away used items when helpful. People have been creating gardens on their property or their window seals. And it's not just for them. For example, there is a small co-op in Brooklyn and another in Harlem that are set up in small shops where the owners cover the cost of the building and electricity.

People bring in their extra tomatoes, lettuce, any kind of produce to make available to those who are having hard financial times for free. Just take what you need, and leave what you can in terms of other items. There are extra clothes, pillows, desks, chairs, throw rugs, and shoes that people can have. If you have extra of something, trade it for something you need. The biggest problem is that these stores need more space. And this is happening in Chicago, Seattle, Oakland, San Francisco, Las Vegas, and other places on a smaller scale."

Fadima looks deeply into the eyes of each governor and the Secretary as she says these next phrases.

"We didn't ask people to do this. We didn't teach them how. We simply asked them to open their hearts, We invited them to care for others. We asked them to take care of our only Earth. We found groups on social media where members were sharing ideas with others all over the world. And people got excited."

"That's very interesting. I had no idea this was going on in the Bay Area." Governor Lopez turns her head to the staff member behind her. "Jean, make sure you get this, please."

"And you didn't encourage this or organize this in any way?" asks Kati.

"I didn't even know it was happening," responds Dri. "I don't think anyone else here did either."

Dri looks at Tiago and the others from the Coalition.

"Did any of you know about this?"

"I heard of one going on in Oakland, which I thought was great," responds Nika. "But it was spontaneous among the members, I thought. I didn't hear about it anywhere else."

"I know there is one in Napa," responds Omar. "But I didn't connect it with the Coalition. I thought it was just a group of people helping vineyard workers in particular. So we would take things down from our garden at the winery. And I didn't really talk about it with others."

"But what drives all this? What about home sales and improvements? That's a large part of our economy. Have you tried to discourage people from selling homes or making improvements?" Governor Wang asks.

"Believe me, Governor. As a real estate agent, I would never discourage people from doing either," responds Bella with a momentary chuckle that quickly disappears. "We have seen a small downturn, but nothing alarming. And I've seen notices from other areas. I thought it possibly was about people leaving the cities again. And members have not mentioned anything to me. But I haven't asked either."

"I'd like to add a few words, if I may," offers Gabby.

"Please," responds Kati.

"I have not been as involved with the Coalition until more recently, with a workshop that I've been offering," continues Gabby. "But as someone who learned early from her father about the work of opening and living from the heart, I can tell you that such a process impacts a person. They want to dive into the emotional pain rather than run from it. And examining such pain allows you to heal from it instead of covering it up and filling the hole with things.

"From what I see, consumerism is the hungry ghost of emotional pain. We fill ourselves up with bright new shiny objects, which distracts us for a while. Then, it shows up again, and we fill ourselves up with more things, newer objects, more stuff. When you stop and heal the pain, you're more likely to need less and share what you have with those who have little. You need enough to survive and have some protection from the weather. But beyond that, we need a lot less than most of us have. Once the hungry ghost no longer controls your life, you have fewer needs and more options."

"That doesn't sound good for shifting the decline in consumption, unless you quit gaining more members," responds Governor Thomas, appearing rather discouraged.

"Unfortunately, I think your concerns and our interests inherently run counter to each other," says Tiago. "It's not like we want to hurt the economy or undermine any of you. But I also believe with all my heart that without such a change, we are not going to survive. Many of us don't believe our economy actually is sustainable long term. And we've known that for a long time. Yet, few people have even tried to address the issue directly. We are what? Four percent of the world's population, yet we consume twenty five percent of the world's resources, usually at the detriment to other countries. While I do not see myself as a revolutionary, I also know we need a heart revolution in this country and our world. Someone needs to address these issues. And I don't see anyone advocating and working on consuming less. No one wants to talk about the elephant in the room, do we?"

"With that kind of approach, we may have to sue for an injunction on your coalition to minimize the damage your group seems to be doing to our economy. I don't see any other choices," offers Governor Wang.

"Now, let's not jump ahead of ourselves," responds Kati.

"OK, let's all take a deep breath," suggests Nika. "I doubt such an injunction would stand up in court. But we're not there yet. What we're saying is that our group never set out to destroy the American economy. At the same time, we are not responsible as a group to maintain the economy either. When people shift to more open hearts and caring for others, it changes their lives. Gabriela's experienced it, and in one way or another, we all have. We're all here because we firmly believe in such a change. We don't want to hurt anyone in this process. At the same time, we can't keep hurting others who have little to nothing in this country and around the world. I don't know how to solve your challenge. And I'm willing to work with you to explore options maybe we have not yet considered."

Nika looks at Kati with a soft smile and her right hand coming up to her heart. Then she turns to Tiago as he begins to talk.

"We've done a lot in the last 20 years to cut back on how we destroy our Earth," says Tiago. "And yet, consumption is a major contributor that has not been addressed. Maybe there is a way to think of this differently. Maybe we need to get outside our safe consumer box to figure out how we all might work on this in a new light."

"Thanks, Nika and Tiago," says Secretary Lavigne. "All of you, really. I understand and admire the opening of hearts to live differently. And I agree with Tiago. We do need to shift our thinking. There must be something more than tanking our economy or trying to minimize your endeavors. But at the moment, I'm not sure what that is. What I would like is for a couple from your group to work with us, to explore possible alternatives that would help both the economy and your group's efforts to prosper. Would a couple of you be willing to collaborate with us?"

"I certainly would," replies Nika. "I have multiple interests to make both aspects thrive. I'd also suggest that Omar, who is our current treasurer and has a business background, and Fadima, who knows the membership probably better than anyone, be part of the group."

"That sounds great. Fadima, Omar, are you willing to participate?"

"Yes, I'd be happy to do so," responds Omar.

"I would be, too," adds Fadima.

"Great. Mary, my assistant, will get your contact information, and we'll keep in touch," replies Kati. "I appreciate you coming today and sharing your insights. We'll keep exploring this and see what we can do and what other possibilities we might have to address these changes. Does anyone have any other questions? Any final comments before we adjourn?"

The governors add their reserved gratitude for attending, seemingly focused on how they might address these recent trends. While Nika understands their reticence, she does not feel responsible to create the kind of shift in consumption they seem to prefer.

Coalition members says their goodbyes to the officials and leave the room. They decide to return to the hotel and continue their discussion over lunch.

A great table presents itself outside, ready to facilitate easy breaths and dissipate tension from their bodies. They order some food and drinks, then turn to the topic of the recent meeting.

"That wasn't as bad as I expected," begins Fadima. "But I wasn't sure what to expect."

"I didn't think it would go poorly," adds Nika. "But with several politicians in the room, one never knows," she says with a grin, "including me, I guess. The economic decrease surprises me. I didn't know we may be having an impact, even in areas we had not considered."

"It will be interesting to see what happens at the next meeting," replies Omar. "I assume the Secretary will expand the group beyond those we discussed today, although she didn't actually say that."

"She implied an expansion last time we talked," says Nika. "But she gave no indication of who she was considering beyond those of us she invited to participate."

"I think we should call for a video meeting of the board," suggests Dri. "It would be good to bring everyone up to date and begin a discussion of what we might want to do from here. But I also think we should include the staff members, as they often interact with Coalition members in ways board members might not hear."

"I like that idea," adds Fadima, as she places her hand on Dri's arm. "I'd be happy to organize it."

"I think that would be timely and important," Nika says, looking intently as she does these days. "I hink we should include all our teachers as well. They also talk with members and maybe have heard comments or suggestions which have not been brought to the foreground yet. But first, I think it would be good to have a written summary of this meeting to share with everyone before we gather. That way board members, staff, and teachers will have a common baseline for the discussion. And I'd be happy to draft that, then have all of you who attended review it for accuracy and suggestions."

"I took pretty good notes," says Omar. "I could draft what I have as a beginning and forward it to you, Nika, to add your perspective. Then you can submit it to all of us for any further suggestions or additions."

"That would be a great help, Omar," responds Nika. "Thanks for taking the initial task off my shoulders. I appreciate the support."

They finish lunch and chat more about the completed meeting, sharing relief that it wasn't more intense. They also discuss a bit about the new board members from other parts of the world and the expansion of perspectives and experience they bring. About that time, Miguel and Alee show up, laughing and swinging arms as they walk into the outdoor area.

"Aren't you ready to go yet?" inquires Alee as he spots bits of food left on the plates. "I can't be late for my baseball game."

"Patience, Alee," replies his father with a half laugh. "We'll make it in time." Then he takes his last bite and wipes his mouth.

They begin to stand and say their goodbyes as hugs are shared. Dri thanks Nika for all her work, knowing there is much ahead still. They separate, now off to their cars or the airport shuttle, ready for their return travel.

Alee thanks Miguel for the great time, then catches up with Tiago, as his father runs towards their car, laughing at his nearly thirteen-year-old son initially lags behind.

Chapter 28
Scoping the Future
November, 2048

F adima organizes the meeting for the full board, staff, and teachers. It becomes a large group, the board having expanded from 12 members, representing North and South America, to 18 members from around the world. The number of staff and teachers also have been increasing as programs spread into new areas.

The new representatives hail from Europe, Africa, South Asia, North Asia, and Australia. With staff and teachers, 47 people receive invitations to participate in the video meeting. It took considerable time for Fadima to organize all the needed materials and to find a time all could attend, facilitated by some even joining during their evening or night hours.

Participants log onto the virtual gathering, sharing brief conversations with those they know. There are new board members and teachers several have not met before. Fadima begins by introducing Baburam from Nepal, Isis from Egypt, Jade from France, Jack from Australia, Maita from Zimbabwe, and Seohyun from South Korea. The other board members, teachers, and staff introduce themselves, younger participants often speaking quietly, looking serious and even a bit scared. Others smile and begin with a wave as they share their name, responsibility, and years with the organization.

Omar jokingly asks if the new members know what they are taking on with this opportunity, then more seriously thanks them for their willingness to contribute. Fadima also welcomes the staff and teachers attending their first meeting, grateful to expand perspectives and experiences with the newly elected representatives and teachers. Baburam responds with a Namaste.

Fadima makes sure everyone received their summary of the meeting with Secretary Kati Lavigne and the three governors. She asks if there are any questions.

Maita asks if there is any concern that the US government will try to stop what the Coalition is doing.

"There is no indication of that at this point," responds Nika. "They just seem concerned about an increasing impact and what we might do to assist them, hoping we help to prevent further economic decreases."

"Where do you think we should go from here?" asks Omar. "I certainly don't want to see an economic collapse, and probably no one else here does either."

Many of the current and new members nod in agreement.

"Yet, I also don't want to suspend our work and achievements over the last nineteen years," continues Omar.

"I agree with you on both counts," adds Alisa, a newer member of the board. "I think we just continue the path we're on. There's nothing wrong with it that I can see. At some point, we, as a nation, must face the fact that we and this world can't sustain unending growth. We have to address that with viable alternatives. No better time to complete that than now."

Tiago looks at each person on the screen as he takes a deep breath, his face showing no indication of a smile.

"I wanted to create change when we first began The Coalition," begins Tiago. "And this was not one I had included in my list. But as you say, Alisa, we need to solve this issue sometime. All of us around the world. I think there's also more we should address to increase greater economic justice. Maybe as we focus on consumer consumption and economic distribution, we could dovetail these two issues in some way, increasingly impacting an area where we want to see greater transformation. I've come to believe that it is not just in the performance or outcome, but in the coalescing and creativity, our expansion, that challenges and conflicts are more readily resolved. From the initial inability to solve differences and difficulties, often comes our growth and learning. That's especially true, I think, when we release our wounds and come together in healing."

As he looks at the people on his screen, he notices several heads shaking or people sharing a thumbs up in agreement.

"I like that idea," responds Naeem, another newer board member. "I think that could be interesting to explore."

"We're creating change in areas we said were important in the beginning," says Dri. "And both issues and solutions seem to have snowballed. I'm happy about that. We've done a lot in the nearly twenty years since our humble beginnings. While we all miss those we lost so many years ago, I think they would be proud of what we've accomplished. What their deaths sparked in us to change is as fitting an honor as any we could have imagined."

Dri images Alex smiling at her, with his hand once again reassuringly on her shoulder, as he did so many times when her life was challenging.

"I agree," says Ariella. "It doesn't compensate for the loss, but it does help me every day. I feel like some good came out of such tragedy twenty years ago. I also agree that this unintended consequence, if it is one, is fitting for the way our son, Joseph, lived his life, too."

She looks off to her left, momentarily biting her lip.

"Alex didn't care about having lots of things either. This, if it is stemming from change by our group, would make him happy," says Bella.

She raises her tissue to dry a few tears, keeping her focus off her computer camera.

"By the way, Fadima, I loved the example you gave at the meeting of sharing from your childhood in Lebanon," Gabby says. "Glad that's in the notes. It was very succinct and powerful. Thanks for talking about that. I think it helped expand the officials' point of view."

"Thanks, Gabby. It just felt like I needed to put some of the change into perspective."

"It's yet another reason you're such a great executive director," suggests Naeem.

Several people applaud, while others share verbal agreements or virtual clapping.

"I haven't been at this as long as all you have," says Isis. "But I find that if I keep my heart open when in disagreement and conflict, I don't respond like I used to do. When that happens, I find my body slows down, becomes more calm, and I feel at ease."

"Great point," responds Alisa. "I think that's so important too, and we need to keep sharing the process. In fact, I'm hoping we could do more of the heartful conflict resolution training in nations that still get into conflict. I would love to see us do more cooperative trainings there."

"I love that idea," offers Isis. "I'd be happy to participate in that, if you'd have me."

"Have you! Of course, and I would work with you and others to expand that piece of training," responds Ariella.

Ismail, a new teacher in Israel, joins in. "I think it would be very helpful, and I'd love to support such an initiative."

"I would love to assist you all with that," says Dri. "And Ariella has some great experience she could contribute. The one thing I suggest we include is the light center exercise that we've done before. That seems to be an important part of any authentic, inner growth."

"It sure was for me," says Baburam. "While the exercise is similar to one we have done in our culture, there is something about the way you go about it that seems to be more effective than I have experienced in the past. And that's true for many of our members here too, I think."

"That's great to hear," responds Dri. "I'm so glad it's been useful. And I'm sure it would please Doc to know that as well. Wish he were still here to hear that from you. At some level, maybe he can."

"Yeah, I wish he were here too," adds Tiago. "He did all he could. Now it's our responsibility to create a foundation within each of us that stimulates societies to live from open hearts. That's our challenge and the gift we give ourselves when we live from such a place."

"But what if the economy fails," inquires Sarah. "Wouldn't people turn to fear and anger rather than cooperation and support?"

"And how would people be motivated to work, especially if they are fully coming from fear and anger?" asks Jack.

"I think that's why getting in touch with one's Higher Self is so critical," responds Gabby. "A transformation to open hearted living will only take place when people are coming from an inner connection to a divine love."

"I agree with that," adds Bella. "It has taken me some time to keep my focus on such a core link. And it makes an immense difference in my life now. I didn't really understand what Dri was telling me about its importance many years ago. Now, I get it. But if that does not form the foundation of our change, it won't be the revolutionary impact I believe we want and need."

"While I'm still relatively new to this movement, I would agree," says Jade. "When Soph first talked to me about your work, it was appealing and felt exciting. But it wasn't until I had my own personal experience with the light and love that I was able to comprehend how fundamental a revolution your work would make in people's lives."

"I would agree with that from a different experience," adds Seohyun, nodding her head. "My experience seems the reverse of Jade's. About ten years ago, I was in a terrible car accident. While the doctors, who doubted I would survive, were working on my body, I left it. I floated above them and watched for a while. Then I followed a bright light up and out of the hospital to a peaceful place where I saw an old Korean woman with long silver hair dressed in a white and gold hanbok. Her eyes were enticing and her smile began in her heart. She told me without any words that I would be fine and that I should return to my body. But first, she put her hands on my chest and pulled love up from my third chakra to my head and pushed it down to my feet. She told me to access this love whenever I felt afraid or doubted myself, this love that resides inside me and remains the core of my being. She encouraged me to share it with others, expanding it from my core. But mostly, she suggested I live that way everyday for the rest of my life. That's not an easy task. Some days go better than others, as I'm sure many of you know, too. But as you also know, the challenge and constant choice is a critical experience.

"When I came across your website and teachings, I knew I was no longer alone or needed to do this work by myself," Seohyun continued. "That's why I'm here, to join in your efforts. To be a support for all of you and others, as you can be for me, keeping a focus on maintaining an open heart. That is the most important thing we can share with others. Everything else is secondary, including the economy."

The others were silent for several moments, sharing only smiles from the mouth and eyes as they digest Seohyun's words.

"Thank you, Seohyun, for sharing that deeply personal experience," responds Fadima. "I had heard some reference to it from a couple of members there, but I'm pleased to hear it directly from you. It's beautiful and touching."

"So, what do we do to create societies that live from their hearts?" Alisa asks. "We've been doing this sharing of ideas and exercises for people. But how do we encourage them to focus on love rather than anger and fear? How do we keep a steady sharing of core love if the economies continue to decline? What would encourage people to continue working and helping?"

"I've been thinking a lot about this, and I want to share an idea that comes from some early community exercises I had the opportunity to explore," says Ariella. "I've been wondering if we couldn't begin to focus purchasing power based on Assisting Hours rather than dollars? Instead of people using a monetary system to identify purchasing resources and power, people could collect hours in a system by helping others. So many hours could be traded to 'purchase' goods and services. This would allow individuals to continue accumulating resources, but on a very different foundation of helping rather than focusing on monetary accumulation. I know it's maybe a bit odd. But it also may facilitate a shift in perspective toward assisting people rather than working primarily for ourselves."

"What an interesting idea," responds Omar, looking intensely at Ariella. "I think this is worth exploring. It sounds so crazy that I like it immensely. This could further the love revolution."

"I really like it too," adds Naeem. "We could explore that within The Coalition to begin with and see how it goes."

"We could begin with teachers and volunteers in the organization, making resources available for purchase through volunteer hours," suggests Soph. "In the process, teachers can provide support or mentoring sessions, especially to new members. I really missed the organization after moving to France and felt somewhat isolated for a while. That experience helped me see the importance of the group, helping each other when we get challenged, as Seohyun mentioned in her comments. Then we can explore other means to provide a supplemental economic process and compare where they takes us."

"I think it's a great idea to explore," says Isis. "But I'd also love to devise a way for testing the openness of a person's heart? Like the feather and one's heart on a balance scale, the weighing of the heart Anubis would do in ancient Egyptian mythology."

"Well, I may have a suggestion for such a contribution," says Naeem. "Our son, Hakeem, has been exploring energetic awareness with Dre and Tiago's two kids, Cate and Alee. They have been trying to see if they can decipher how open a heart is when they put their hands on each other's chest, trusting what they feel. I think increasingly they have been able to determine with pretty good accuracy the extent of open hearts in the moment. I suspect they would be happy to teach that to all of us. I've certainly been intrigued with their explorations."

"I didn't think about that, but I've enjoyed it too," adds Nika.

"Yeah, I think they're pretty excited about sharing it with others," laughs Tiago. "And it's useful information for my own introspection when they tell me I can open my heart further."

"Well, we are close to our agreed upon completion time," Fadima says. "Some great ideas and discussion, I think. Is there anything more anyone wants to say in closing?"

"I think we've done all we can, for now," Nika says. "I agree with others. We continue to move forward with our work, paying attention to the ways it impacts our lives, in some cases more that we first realized. But I also think we should not slow down or stop now. We've come too far, with more to do."

"I agree," responds Dri. "I'm glad we have you, Omar and Fadima serving on the Secretary's committee, too. We can keep up with the trends over the next few years. It's a tricky dilemma, the balance between giving and consumption. Yet, I'm more and more convinced that we will find the best way to proceed if we live by our principles and are guided by an open heart. Anything less than that isn't worth it to me any more."

Dri suspires and sits in rich silence for a moment, sharing a warm smile with the participants.

"In the end, I think our mission statement might simply read now, live from an open heart and manifest unconditional love," says Dri. "That basically says it all for me. In the end, our job is to create a vision of living from an open unconditional heart that no one else has yet seen and a way for that to emerge that no one else has yet manifested."

"I think Dad would love that," responds Gabby. "It would be more than he could have hoped for. Dri, you, Nika, and Tiago have really fulfilled a dream he had as a young boy. Now all of us can contribute, too. He talked with people, sharing his ideas for living in that manner, beginning with his family. But now we all have laid a foundation of that dream by manifesting unconditional love from an open heart. You do it with your children and your guidebooks, which is awesome. I see Tiago doing it with his students. Now we're seeing the evidence of that with the new board members from around the world. And Nika shares it with complete strangers, even some who try to undermine our work or attempt to kill her. I can't think of better examples of Dad's dream."

"Thanks, Gabby," responds Nika. "I'm very grateful to Dri for sharing Doc's work after he passed away. I'm just sorry I didn't get to work with him directly. But Dri seems like a powerful alternative, as she has been with this organization. For me, the open heart meditation has made all this work possible. I'm so grateful for my daily practice."

"I agree," adds Dri. "The kids are getting into it also, and we sometimes will do the meditation as a family. I think it helps us stay close and open to discussion and change when something goes wrong, as it does at times. We aren't perfect. As Isis mentioned, if we can keep our hearts open when in disagreement or conflict, anything is possible on such a path."

"I appreciate you sharing this work with us all," Maita says. "It expands things we have been trying, and it adds a lovely foundation that we've been missing, too."

"Blessings and much gratitude for this opportunity to get to know you all, at least virtually," responds Jack. "I'm excited to see where this all goes while contributing as a member of the board.."

"Yes, agreed," adds a chorus of Baburam, Isis, Jade, and Seohyun.

"To those new to the board and those continuing, thanks to all of your for your time and commitment to this work," Fadima says. "To Bella, who is rotating off, deep gratitude and a special thanks for all your efforts and contributions. This is her last meeting. We will miss you and are grateful for your abounding contributions over your years of service. They are clearly noticed and noted. So appreciate all you've contributed."

"I have enjoyed an abundance of pleasure and so many blessings through my contributions, even with initial doubts about this organization amounting to anything," laughs Bella. "But I think it's now time to leave it up to others."

Fadima brings the formal discussion to a close. Participants say their final thanks and goodbyes, each in their native language. Some share in other languages they speak too, adding a sense of connection around the world. Afterwards, there are short discussions and expressions of thanks. Then the video conference ends.

Nika calls Dri on the phone to talk further. She shares her excitement for the concise mission statement Dri suggested near the end of the video conference. At the same time, Nika knows that the path will not be easy. They both take a deep breath and exhale slowly.

She and Dri often discuss that a valued path of substantial change is neither simple nor painless. But they promise to allow their hearts to remain open, whether in joy or disagreement, reminding each other of the importance with everyone they meet, and especially their children. They talk about the next time Nika will be in the Bay Area and the two families can gather for a more enjoyable and loving time together.

On a path of love and collaboration, they now are convinced that anything is possible, including a love revolution. They hope this revolution continues for themselves, their families, the world, and the earth.

The End of Book Two

About the author

Geoffrey K. Leigh, Ph.D., taught and conducted research at the University of Utah, University of Iowa, Ohio State University, and University of Nevada, Reno. His focus was child and adolescent development in a family context along with marriage and family therapy. He published numerous research articles and co-edited a book, <u>Adolescence in Families</u>. Later, he began to investigate human energy fields as they impact children and family interactions. He currently lives in Napa Valley and works at a local winery. More recently, he published a non-fiction book, <u>Rekindling Our Cosmic Spark</u> (2017), then began writing fiction. He has published a novel, <u>Dancing With Audacity</u> (2022), and <u>Prosetry Journey</u> (2023), a collection of short stories and poetry with co-author, Marianne Lyon, a recent Napa Valley Poet Laureate.

Also by

Geoffrey K. Leigh

Lyon, Marianne & Leigh, Geoffrey K., Prosetry Journey: Exploring Expression of the Heart, 2023.

Leigh, Geoffrey K., Dancing with Audacity: Sourcing Inner Strength, 2022.

Leigh, Geoffrey K., Rekindling Our Cosmic Spark: A Noussentric Approach to Living and Parenting, 2017.